ZOMBIE RULES

DAVID ACHORD

Chapter 1 - The Present

I stood on the second floor balcony of the library, overlooking the smoldering remains of books and the overturned shelves. Soot stained ceiling tiles told a tale of a fire which did not completely take. Nevertheless, the damage was done. Many books had survived, but they had sustained extensive smoke and water damage. Amazingly, the fire retardant system still had a little pressure left in it. The water was flowing out of the sprinkler heads at a trickle now. Tendrils of smoke were still emanating here and there. This had been set recently, within an hour. There were other acts of vandalism as well. Most of the windows were broken, and obscene graffiti had been painted maliciously on the walls of a facility that existed only as an educational facility.

Heathens. It is the noun I use to describe them. Somehow, many of them had survived when so many good people had died. They roamed in gangs of various numbers, leaving a trail of ruin in their wake. They had little regard for rebuilding society, bent only on their own shortsighted, destructive desires. There was nothing for me here.

Since the infection outbreak, my visits to the Nashville area were infrequent. The urban areas, densely populated back when society was normal and functional, were now populated with the infected.

My thoughts were interrupted when I heard angry yelling. It was not inhuman in origin, definitely human. My survival instincts warned me against it, but I was curious. I surreptitiously exited the library through a side door. The muffled voices were now more succinct, and I could discern the direction. I crept south along Edmondson Pike toward the sounds, scanning the area warily as I walked, hugging the abandoned cars for cover. I did not have to go far.

There were three of them. I used my rifle scope to get a good look at them. Two of them were rough looking men. The third one was a young girl with long dark hair. One of the men, a tall lanky man with rounded shoulders, was loudly berating the girl, and as I watched, he hit her with a stinging backhanded slap. She fell to the ground. The other one, a shorter, dirtier version of his friend, laughed loudly. Both of them had beards with some kind of beads braided in them. It looked stupid. The tall one then began kicking the girl. Not hard kicks that would have broken ribs, but softer kicks. Kicks intended more for debasement and humiliation.

I crouched beside an overturned car and rested my rifle on one of the flattened tires. About the time I got sighted in, the tall one picked up the girl by the scruff of her neck and gruffly yanked her pants down.

Correction, did I say girl? With the aid of my scope, I could see other things. Nope, definitely not a girl. He was skinny as a rail. It was difficult to determine his age, maybe eleven or twelve.

I made a decision. Kill the bastards. They were bullies. I had a special dark place in my heart towards bullies. They had been passing a whiskey bottle back and forth while bullying the little boy. The short one took a long pull from it and laughed gleefully when his friend yanked the kid's pants down.

I scanned the area with my scope, then took my eye off of them for a moment and did another quick check of my surroundings. Paranoia was a positive character trait in this day and age, and I did not want to be ambushed from behind. When I looked at them again, big and ugly now had his captive bent over the lowered tailgate of a truck and had his own pants down. He had no idea I was watching him as he started brutally sodomizing the boy. Disgusting.

His body was gyrating fervidly, too much for a clean head shot. So, I put the crosshairs at the center of his shoulder blades, took a slow breath, exhaled, and gently squeezed the trigger. If I had made it past the tenth grade, I could probably give you a nice graphic description of the destruction the boat-tail hollow point bullet caused, every action book I've ever read does it, but I won't bother. I think you get the idea.

After shooting the first one, bully number two stood there looking dumbfounded. His alcohol sodden brain was slow to process what had happened. I worked the action of my Winchester and fired again. The whiskey bottle fell out of his hand and shattered on the ground.

I didn't have to worry about being arrested. This was the way of the world these days. What a way to celebrate my eighteenth birthday.

Chapter 2 – Two Years Ago in Sophomore Hell

I was in love. You know the kind of love. Teenage, goo-goo eyed puppy love. It was exhilarating. It was excruciating. The emotion occupied my every waking thought and even my dreams. Hell, it occupied my mind even while I took my morning crap.

I was currently sitting in history class, casting glances at the object of my adoration, when I was broken out of my reverie by Ms. Snotgrass, my teacher. The teacher from hell I might add.

"Zachariah Gunderson, are you paying attention?"

That's me, Zachariah Gunderson. Currently stuck in sophomore hell. Imprisoned eight hours a day in a worn out public high school. The popular opinion is that it should have been burned down years ago. The teacher's name is actually Snodgrass, an old Nashville family name, but she had such a snotty attitude all the students called her Snotgrass, behind her back, of course.

I looked up at her. She was short and very stout, like a bulging beer keg. She was possibly around forty-five-years-old, but she looked at least ten years older. She was currently glaring at me over a pair of dirty bifocals.

"Oh, yes ma'am. I'm here." A couple of my friends chuckled. I grinned and looked over at Macie. She glanced at me without expression and turned her attention back to her text book.

Macie Kingsley was her name. She had long blonde hair, hazel green eyes, perfect white teeth, and nice teenage curves. She was on the varsity cheerleading team and very popular. I was on the track team. We had been dating for almost three months, and Saturday night, yeah, just two days ago, she finally let me.

You know what I mean. We made love. Engaged in intimate relations. Fucked like bunnies.

Saturday was our three month anniversary, and I wanted it to be special. Macie told me to surprise her. I opted for a romantic moonlit picnic, and it had to be perfect. I planned it out with the tenacity of General von Steuben.

I picked out a remote area overlooking a brook that bordered one side of the farm I worked at. It had a beautiful view overlooking a valley. I spent all afternoon setting up Tiki torches, laying out blankets, and preparing a fire. My Grandmother fixed veggie wraps, and Rick was kind enough to purchase a bottle of wine for us.

As the sun set, I lit the fire, opened the wine, and told her how I felt about her. If it were a movie, the audience would have been laughing at my awkwardness. Nevertheless, Macie responded by telling me she loved me as well. I lost my virginity under a harvest moon on a balmy Saturday night.

It was the happiest I had ever been.

The memories were causing me to become distracted, and aroused. That is, until Ms. Snotgrass once again interrupted my thoughts. "Well then, would you please tell the class what is the first National monument of the United States, hmmmm?"

The class was quiet now. The old fat ass was infamous for asking innocuous history questions to students whom she felt were not applying themselves. If you missed it, which everyone always did, she punished you with extra homework. Not merely, reading an extra chapter and answering those damned questions at the end. Hell, you had to write an essay paper to go along with it. She looked at me pointedly, coldly. A hint of a sneer was forming at the corner of her mouth.

"Easy, Devils Tower, and there is no apostrophe between the i and the s. And, it is not to be confused with the first National Park, which is Yellowstone," I responded nonchalantly and looked over at Macie again for an acknowledgement. No response.

Snotty was not finished with me. "Very astute, or you are just very lucky. But please continue, Mr. Gunderson. Why don't you amaze the class with your brilliant intellect? Tell us more."

"Must I? I mean, I answered your silly question."

This time, only one of my friends laughed, but it was more like a low chuckle that died quickly. All eyes were on Snotty now. She was a vindictive, petty woman. You know the type. Every school has at least one. She was one of those teachers who basked in the glow of power over her students, knowing that with her tenure, the school administration could do very little to rebuke her antics. A bully.

"Well then, perhaps you'd like to spend the rest of the week in detention, hmmm?" She made a hand gesture at me. She wanted me to stand to better shame me in front of the class. I had another idea.

I sighed and stood. "Very well." I inhaled. "The Devils Tower is an igneous outcropping of rock located in the state of Wyoming. Its elevation is about 1,200 feet high, give or take, and is believed to be either the product of eroded laccolith or the plug of an extinct volcano. The name originated as a result of the misinterpretation of a name the indigent Native Americans had given it. President Theodore Roosevelt, a staunch Republican by the way, dedicated it as the nation's first monument in 1907. The President is the only person who has the authority to establish a national monument, and it is generally done through the act of an executive order. There are currently one hundred and four protected areas with the title of national monument..."

"That will be quite enough, Gunderson. Sit down." Snotty tilted her head down so she could properly shoot daggers at me over those ridiculous bifocals, but it did not stop the class from applauding. Macie was not clapping, just looking at me oddly. The bell rang and I hurried for the door before Snotty thought of some form of vindictive revenge.

I waited for Macie in the hallway. "Hey." I said to her as she exited the class. I tried to sneak in a quick kiss, but she turned her head adeptly. My lips caught a passing glimpse of her cheek.

"Not here," she whispered curtly. People passed by me patting me on the back and congratulating me over my very small triumph.

I walked along with Macie and Felix soon joined us. He was my best friend. "Man, you rocked in there! Ole Snotty didn't know what hit her. You've got to be some kind of genius, Zach! How'd you know all that stuff?"

Macie and Felix looked at me expectantly. I shrugged. "I read a lot and have a good memory."

"Well, if you don't start applying that brain to your classwork, you'll never graduate high school. Then you can kiss any scholarship possibilities goodbye." Macie punctuated her statement with an upturned nose as she turned to walk off. I hurried to catch up with her. Felix started to follow, but I looked back at him and gestured with a shake of the head. He took the hint.

I caught up with Macie and walked along with her. "Hey, babe, what's up? You seem mad at me."

She glanced at me sidelong as she continued to walk. "It's not you. I'm about to start. I'm just feeling irritable," she saw my obvious confusion and rolled her eyes. "My period, Zach. I'm about to start my period. God, Zach, for somebody who is so smart, you sure are naïve."

I could feel my cheeks turning red. She scoffed at me, but then squeezed my hand briefly.

"So, you have track practice after school?" I nodded. Track and a good memory were my strong points. I was counting on a track scholarship after high school. My only living relative was my Grandmother. Her only source of income was Social Security. Otherwise, it was a life on the farm with Rick, or a long indebtedness of student loans.

Macie looked around furtively and then quickly kissed me on the cheek. "I've got cheerleading practice. So I guess I'll see you tomorrow."

It was not what I wanted to hear. "Practice is only for a couple of hours. Why don't I come over after? I can shower at school." Macie quickly shook her head. "Why not?"

The smile was gone and replaced by a frown. "Zach, quit being so needy."

I did not say anything, just hung my head. I couldn't help it. "Zach, Jesus. I'm going to a study group with the girls after practice, okay? We'll probably be late."

I looked up. "What's late? I mean, I can just stop by for a few minutes."

She stopped me with another shake of the head. "Well, how about you call me before you go to bed?" I grinned, "We can talk dirty to each other."

"Sure, Zach. I'll talk to you later," she said, almost as an afterthought, and walked off before I could sneak in another kiss.

Felix jogged up as Macie walked off. "So, Zach, how're you and Macie doing?" Felix was always asking about the two of us. He did not have a girlfriend. We'd grown up together and lived around the block from each other. He was the only one who saw me cry every night for a week after my parents died. It was a stupid car wreck, a direct result of my father's drunkenness. Felix never judged me or teased me, always a brotherly pat on the shoulder and kind words. He was a good dude, and a good friend. But poor Felix had never had a girlfriend. He claimed otherwise, but I'm pretty sure that he had never even kissed a girl. The poor guy was short, awkward, and had poor eyesight, which required him to wear incredibly thick glasses. The effect worsened his already homely appearance. But, he was still my friend.

"Well, buddy, I think she's the woman I'm going to marry one day."

His eyes lit up. The lenses magnified them to two large orbs. "Wow, I've never heard this one. Something big must have happened to make you feel this…" He stopped in midsentence and looked at me. I couldn't help but grin. It could be best described as a massive, shit-eating grin. "Oh, my fucking God," he exclaimed. "You did the two-backed beast with her!"

"Sshh, keep it down, bro," I kept my voice low. "I don't want the whole world knowing. Come on, we need to get to track practice. Maybe I'll tell you all about it."

He giggled as we turned around and started heading toward the locker room. I was not paying attention, and bumped into someone. His name was Jason Argos. He was standing around the corner, motionless. It was almost as if he had been listening to us. I apologized quickly. A lowly sophomore did not go around casually bumping into seniors.

"Oh, sorry, Jason! We didn't even know you were there," I said.

Jason looked at me oddly for a moment. "No problem. My bad."

He continued staring at me but turned aside for us to pass. Jason was a senior. He was a very handsome, biracial, eighteen-year-old, six feet, six inches tall, and very muscular. He was a varsity athlete with letters in baseball and football. All of which made him probably the most popular guy in school. He was very popular with the girls and never lacked for a date.

Felix always gushed over him, a true bromance. "Hey, buddy." Felix said, he tried to act as if they were the best of friends. Jason only nodded in response. He merely tolerated Felix, along with most other underclassman. As we walked out to the track, Felix continued with his love of Jason.

"Have you heard? He finished the baseball season with an ERA of 2.01. Friday night, he had three touchdown passes against Overton. Not only does he have his own personal pitching coach, he has a quarterback coach as well. That's phenomenal!" He looked around conspiratorially. "Rumor has it he's already been offered a load of money under the table to go with a certain SEC team in the eastern part of the state, if you know what I mean," he said with a wink.

"You think he'll marry you?" I asked sarcastically.

Felix laughed and actually blushed. "You crack me up, Zach."

Our conversation was interrupted by one of the assistant principals. "Mr. Gunderson, there is a rather rough looking man who is waiting for you in the parking lot. He said he is your boss and there is an emergency involving your Grandmother."

Chapter 3 - My Grandmother

I spotted Rick sitting in a truck waving at me. He had his three dogs with him, whom he had named Moe, Larry, and Curly. They were strays he had found and adopted. It was hard to tell what mixtures of breeding made up their genetic content. It was assumed they had the same mother, but it was hard to tell.

"Hey, Rick, what's up?" I asked when I jogged up. Rick was a grizzled old Vietnam veteran who worked at the farm with me. Technically, he was my boss. He was a little past sixty. A hard life, along with generous amounts of alcohol and cigarettes, had etched deep lines in his sun damaged face. It appeared he had been going on a week without shaving. Felix jogged up a short time later and said hello. Rick ignored him.

"I need to get you to the hospital. Your Grandmother's had a stroke." He looked over at Felix. "Your gay friend can come too." Felix started to protest, but I spoke first.

"What happened?" I asked.

Rick looked at me as if I was stupid. "I just told you. She had a stroke." He stared at me a few seconds more before he felt like he needed to elaborate. "The postal lady found her lying in the back yard and called 911. I don't know why they didn't call you at school, but the neighbor seemed to think you were at work and called there. I got the phone call." He looked around and took a swig out of a pint of cheap whiskey. "Look, get in and I'll give you a ride to the hospital. We'll figure it all out when we get to the hospital and talk to the doctors."

Felix opted out of going with us and agreed to drive my little Ford Ranger truck home, but made me promise to call him the minute I knew more. He nodded, gave me a pat on the back and trotted off. I walked over to the driver's side. "Slide over, I need to drive," I ordered. It was hard to gauge Rick's level of sobriety, or lack thereof.

Rick snorted. "I ain't drunk, you smart-assed kid."

"C'mon, Rick, you just got your license back. You don't need to get arrested again."

Rick snorted again, but after putting up an obligatory fuss, ceded the driver's seat to my smart, and sober ass.

We rode in silence. Rick was listening to a talk-radio station. The host was rambling on about government conspiracies. I tuned him out. Grandma was unconscious when we arrived. I was met by the doctor before I could get in the room.

"How is she, sir?" I asked tentatively. He did not answer me, at least not right away.

"Are you her only living relative?" He asked pointedly. I shrugged. "You are under eighteen, I'm guessing."

I nodded. He looked over at Rick, probably smelled the alcohol, and redirected his attention back to me. "She's had a massive stroke. She was probably lying outside for a while before being found. Her body temperature was very low when she came in. With her age and poor health, the prognosis is…"

He did not finish the sentence. He did not need to. I looked past him into the room. She was hooked up to some monitors, there were at least two IVs in her arms, and there was a tube shoved in her mouth. She looked terrible. Weak. Mortal.

On the drive over, I was strong, in control. Not now. I felt tears welling up. The doctor put his hand on my shoulder. "Are you sure there is no other family, son?"

I wiped my eyes. "My parents died in a car wreck when I was young. She took me in. My father has family somewhere in Sweden, but I've no idea how to contact them. There might be some cousins out there somewhere, but I've never met them." I did not tell him that my dad's family had disowned him years ago, before I was born. I looked at the doctor. "Our only income is my job at a farm and Social Security. We'll never be able to pay the hospital bills."

He held his hand up. "Don't worry about that. We have policies in place for indigent patients." My mouth tightened at the statement. Calling my Grandmother indigent really bothered me, but it was true. Hell, she and I probably had a hundred dollars between us. She did not even own the house we were living in. I had planned on dropping out of school in order to work full time, but she would not hear of it. She insisted that I finish school and go to college.

I was not allowed to stay the night in Grandma's room. The staff informed me in a polite but firm manner that I could only sit in the lobby all night with other patients' families. Rick overheard and interrupted. "Kid, do you really want to sit all night in a room full of strangers?" I hung my head. "If something happens, it happens. There won't be anything you can do about it. Come on back to the farm and stay with me," he said.

I reluctantly acquiesced. We each gave the doctor our cell phone numbers. Rick's brain sparked a bit and he realized by letting me drive, he could now drink without worrying about getting pulled over by a hard-nosed cop. He tossed me the keys as we walked into the parking lot and he drank from his bottle without worry.

We rode to the farm in silence. There used to be a gate at the entrance, but somebody, a certain person who goes by the name of Rick, ran over it after a night of boozing it up at the VFW. He forgot that either it was there, or did not care. The next day it took us an hour to get the gate's mangled remains out of the undercarriage of his truck. Rick was the caretaker, foreman, and jack-of-all trades at the farm. The main property owners were an older couple named Parsons. They owned five hundred acres and contracted another five hundred from neighbors. Rick ran the farm and I worked for him. He was paid a salary and lived rent-free in the old homestead.

Rick walked in and flipped on some lights. After getting the fire going, he made himself comfortable in his tattered easy chair, and I sat on the couch. We listened to the crackling wood in a somber silence. "You want a drink?" he asked. I arched my eyebrow at him. He chuckled and drank a hefty swallow. "You want to talk about it, kid?" I shook my head. "Look here, kid, you're hurting. I can see it plain as day. I'm asking if you want to talk about it and you give the obligatory no. This is the part where I'm supposed to coax it out of you. I'm not going to do it. You want to keep it all bottled up inside of you, that's your call. If you want to talk, I ain't going nowhere. We can talk all night."

Well, he had a good point. I guess I felt like I did want to talk about it. At least, a little bit. "What do I do, Rick?"

"Well, kid, you always plan for a worse-case scenario. And, you always recognize the inevitability. The inevitability is your Grandma is going to die," Rick said it in a matter-of-fact tone.

I was taken aback. "How do you know?"

"Hell, Zach, how old is she, 84? 85?" he asked. I responded to the latter. "Okay, 85. Her health is not good. She has a stroke and falls over in the back yard on a cold day. No telling how long she'd been lying out there. I'm no doctor, but I'm not giving her good odds, kid."

I nodded in silence. Rick was an old alcoholic who was very rough around the edges, but he also had wisdom borne from a life on the streets and some rough time in Vietnam. I liked him. He was easy-going, and in his own way, had a lot of worldly advice to give a teenage kid. My thoughts were interrupted by his loud snoring. The alcohol had put him down for the night. I got up, got the bottle out of his hand, and put a blanket on him.

I tried to call Macie several times, but her phone was apparently turned off. I left more than one voice mail. I then called the hospital. They advised me there was no change in Grandma's condition. I tried calling Macie once more, and drifted off to sleep with my phone grasped tightly in my hand.

Chapter 4 - The Worst Day of My Life

It was the crack of dawn when I woke up. I immediately checked my phone. No call from either the hospital or Macie. I called the hospital first. They were very vague, but said her condition had not changed. I then tried calling Macie. Her phone was still off. So I called Felix. He answered after the first ring, but he was still groggy from sleep.

"How's your grandmother?" he asked.

"She's not good. I'm not going to school today. I'm going to be at the hospital."

"No problem, bro. I'll let the principal know where you are. Is there anything else I can do?"

"Yeah, if you see Macie, have her call me as soon as possible. I tried calling all night and this morning, but her battery must be dead or something."

Felix agreed and we hung up. Rick woke up while I was on the phone. He was grunting and farting like, well, like an old hung over man. "Hey, you mind driving me home? I need to clean up and get to the hospital." He did not respond verbally. He went into the restroom. A moment later, I heard the sound of him urinating, followed by the sound of the toilet flushing and the faucet running. He came out a moment later and halfheartedly grabbed the keys off of the kitchen counter. His brain wasn't ready for verbal communication. He pointed toward the door and walked out.

I sat with my grandmother all day. She looked even worse. Old, tired, and feeble. I held her hand and tried talking to her, but she did not move. Not once.

I wished she could hear me. I would have told her what a good person she was. I was just two when my parents died. She was already old. She could have let the state put me in a foster home, but she took me home and cared for me. She never yelled at me, always made sure there was food on the table, and never failed to tell me how much she loved me. On my fifteenth birthday, she took me to get a hardship driver's license and then surprised me with a blue

Ford Ranger truck. It was well used and had a few miles on it, but overall, was in decent shape. She refused to tell me how much it cost. It was the best present I had ever received.

The charge nurse, a matronly looking, dark-skinned woman with breasts like watermelons tolerated me for a few hours, but finally shooed me out. I must have looked bad, because she ordered me to get some rest and promised to call me if anything changed. I was just about to walk out the door when the alarms on the machines started sounding. The nurse pushed me out just as several other personnel rushed in.

A code blue. Cardiac arrest. I watched quietly. Helplessly. They tried, they really did, but it was Grandma's time.

I spent the next hour with the hospital administration and a chaplain who was preoccupied in an ongoing cell phone text conversation. They were polite, but business was business. They needed to know what to do with Grandma's body. It got worked out somehow. I was mostly in a daze. Tired, stressed, and miserable. All I wanted to do was go see my girl and hold her in my arms. I tried calling her. No answer. At least her phone was back on, so I sent a text message. I then called Felix and filled him in.

"Oh, I'm so sorry, bro. Is there anything I can do?" he asked.

"Yeah, find Macie and tell her to please answer her damn phone. I've still not gotten in touch with her. There must be something wrong. Have you spoken to her at all?" Felix was silent. "Are you there?"

Felix answered. His voice had a different tone. "Yeah, I talked to her. Listen, don't worry about her right now. Go on home and I'll meet you there, okay?"

"What's wrong, Felix?"

After a bit of arguing, he told me. He told me everything. It seemed as though it was all over school, but I knew nothing about it. Macie was now Jason's girlfriend. Jason Argos, that guy. The massively popular jock. With my girl. Apparently, they had hooked up recently at a party, which coincidentally, I was not invited to, and now they were officially dating. I hung up the phone and sped towards Macie's.

That was my first mistake. I tried to play the sympathy card and told the cop about my grandmother. It did not work. He chided me about driving like a maniac, and smirked when he handed me the speeding ticket. I kept my speed down, and after what seemed like an eternity, finally made it to her home. She was there. So was Jason. So were a few other people. All of them were seniors, none of them were my friends. They were all loitering around the front yard laughing and having a good time. A couple of them were holding forty ounce beers wrapped in brown bags.

Macie saw me and quickly walked up the front steps to her house. I made a beeline toward her. Jason stepped in between us before I got more than a few feet. "Out of the way fucker. I need to speak to Macie."

I tried to step around him, but as I said earlier, Jason is tall and muscular. Taller than me, definitely more muscle. He deftly stepped in front of me again and held up a hand.

"Just stop and listen to me, dude. Macie and I are dating now. It's nothing against you, it just happened. These things happen. You need to go."

I stared at him. He seemed sincere, perhaps even sympathetic. I inhaled and tried to keep my emotions in check. "So, how long has this been going on?" I asked quietly. My voice was cracking and I was literally shaking. I could see two of his boys standing behind him grinning and pointing at me as if I was some sort of carnival act. Some girl I've never seen before was holding her cell phone up at me.

Jason sighed. "It's been going on a couple of weeks now. Listen, Zach, this is not Macie's fault. She was just confused. She likes you, but just as a friend, okay? The best thing you can do is leave. I'll have Macie call and explain everything to you later."

My body was numb. I could feel nothing except for a tightening in my chest. Macie refused to look at me. Jason was holding his hands up passively. I was about to turn around and walk away. And then, he smirked.

Aside from the cop, I had seen that smirk once before. Felix, Macie, and I had gone to one of the school's baseball games a couple of months ago. Jason pitched a terrific game. Only one of the opposing players was able to get a hit in, which was a home run. A couple of innings later, Jason hit him in the head with a wild pitch. After the game, a group of us gathered and we watched as a local newspaper reporter interviewed him. He asked him about the wild pitch. Jason was very apologetic. He said he was trying to throw a slider and it got away from him. He went on to say he was very sorry for injuring the other player, and he would pray for him. The reporter thanked Jason and turned away. When the reporter was not looking, Jason smirked. Just like he was now smirking at me.

I took a swing at him, a roundhouse right I was certain would knock him out. He easily blocked it and replied with a one-two combination. I hit the ground, dazed and humiliated. That would have been enough. I was done for. Once the stars circling in front of my eyes went away, I was going to get up and walk to my truck with as much dignity as I could muster.

It was not to be. While I was lying there, his two boys decided to join in. They ran up and started viciously kicking me. The last thing I saw before losing consciousness was Macie looking at me.

It was the day before Thanksgiving and my sixteenth birthday. And yes, it was the worst day of my life.

Chapter 5 - The Beginning

I regained consciousness in an ambulance. My mind was in a fog. I could not yet fully fathom what had just happened to me. The only thing I could really grasp, was that this ambulance ride to the local ER was going to be yet another bill I would not be able to pay for. The paramedic, an attractive blonde who reminded me of Macie, was asking me simple questions, what was my name, what day was it, did I have any communicable diseases. When she was finished, she smiled and squeezed my hand. I guess I answered to her satisfaction.

The ER personnel were nice, but hurried. The place was full of patients. Even the police officer, the same one who gave me a speeding ticket, was very polite as he took a report of my assault. He was even kind enough to turn his head every time he coughed.

I had multiple contusions, a black eye that had swollen shut, a mild concussion, a rib or two were broken, and my testicles felt like someone had taken a jackhammer to them. The doctor said I would live, but would be in pain for a while. If only he knew how right he was. He gave me a prescription for some pain medication and kicked me loose, no pun intended. I had no insurance, I wondered if it made a difference in my treatment.

Felix and his father were waiting for me as the orderly pushed me out in a wheelchair.

Felix. What a friend. He heard what happened within minutes. Word gets around fast in High School. He called Macie, who was gracious enough to fill him in. He and his father drove over to get my truck and then hustled over to the ER.

The two of them stared at me with pitiful expressions. Mr. Stewart was an older clone of his son. He actually looked like Mr. Magoo. They both wore the same thick eyeglasses, they had the same build, and even their haircuts were exactly the same. They gingerly helped me to my little Ford Ranger and Felix drove me home in silence. I kept my eyes closed to try to alleviate the pain and prevent needless conversation.

"Okay, buddy, we're home - oh shit," Felix gasped. I opened my eyes and looked. Someone had decided they needed to rub it in a little. They had spray painted some choice graffiti on the front of my house. Let's just say there were some disparaging references to my gender, my sexual orientation, and my penis. Very nice. I guess losing one's grandmother garnered little sympathy these days.

Mr. Stewart parked on the other side of the street and waited. He seemed not to notice the graffiti. Felix stared at the vandalism. "Bro, that is so fucked up. Why would they do that to you?" he shook his head in disgust. I would have too if my head did not hurt so badly.

"You want me to stay the night? Pops won't mind and I can try to clean this stuff up," he was looking at me with those big pathetic eyes as if he was the one who had just taken a beating.

I shook my head, making the pain worse. "I appreciate it, Felix. I really do. But I just want to be alone for a while." A tapping on the truck's window interrupted and startled me. I guess I was still shell shocked. I turned my head quickly, which caused a bolt of pain to shoot through my body.

It was Felix's dad. When I rolled down the window, with great difficulty, he patted me on the shoulder and suggested I grab some clothes and stay the weekend with them. After all, it was Thanksgiving tomorrow. I shook my head. "I really appreciate it, Mr. Stewart, but I just want to go to bed. I'll give Felix a call in the morning, how's that?" He started to argue with me but opted not to. Instead, he nodded somberly and walked back to his car. Felix made me promise him I would call if there was any problem, and gave me one of his usual pats on the shoulder, which sent yet another spasm of pain down my side.

I made it inside and to my bed without too much pain. I was lying there watching TV when my phone rang. I looked at the caller I.D. It was Macie. My brain told me not to answer, but my heart won out.

"Are you okay?" she asked.

"Wow, what a stupid question. What do you think, Macie? Let's see, my grandmother just died, you tear my heart out, I got my ass kicked, and when I come home from the ER, I discover my house has been vandalized by some immature idiot with a can of spray paint. What do you think? Do you think I'm okay?"

She did not respond. Something told me she was already aware of the graffiti. I let the silence build a moment. "So, are you going to tell me why this all happened? Or should I just go to my grave thinking what an evil bitch you are?"

"That's not fair, Zach," she responded in a scolding tone, as if she really thought all of this was in fact my fault.

"So enlighten me, please." I should not have asked. If I remember correctly, she said I was poor, immature, an underachiever, and not going anywhere in life. I was deluding myself into thinking I'd get a full scholarship in a silly little sport like track. She said a few other things that succeeded in tearing down my self-esteem even lower, but I don't remember all of the insults. My brain kind of went into vapor lock at some point during the one-sided conversation.

I listened in silence. When she was finished, I hung up without saying a word. She sent me a text a few minutes later.

It's for the best. Please don't hate me.

I did not hate her. I loved her, which made it worse. I cried some, and then fell asleep in the middle of a news alert about a bad outbreak of flu in the Middle East. I vaguely remembered the commentator reminding people to get their flu shot.

I had bad dreams. I had dreams of people chasing me and beating me. Dreams of finding Macie and Jason having sex. They would be engrossed in carnal ecstasy. I would shout at Macie, only to have Jason look at me and smirk. I'd jerk awake, which tortured me with spasms of pain.

I finally made it to morning. I struggled out of bed and saw my phone had text messages waiting. My heart skipped a beat. For some stupid reason, I thought it may have been Macie begging for me to take her back. Like I said, stupid, very stupid.

The caller ID showed the calls were blocked. The first text was a link to a You Tube video. The subsequent texts were just a series of *lol lol lol!*

I clicked the link. There I was getting my ass kicked all over again. I watched as I tried to hit Jason. I saw the anger on his face as he blocked my punch and decked me. Then his friends ran up and started kicking me. Much to my surprise, Jason pushed them away and made them stop. There was an expression on his face. Concern maybe? I guess I should have been grateful. If those two had not been stopped, I would have been in much worse shape. Macie just sat there on her stoop, smoking a cigarette, and watching with an air of indifference.

Yeah, I cried some more. My self-esteem was now officially lower than whale shit at the bottom of the ocean.

After a while, I struggled out of bed, didn't bother with a shower, and spent a futile half hour trying to clean the graffiti off the house. I had a scrub brush with a bucket of hot water and Pine Sol, but I just could not scrub for more than a few seconds before the pain would make me stop. I finally gave up. In my current condition, I did not have the strength or energy. I went back inside and lay down.

The doorbell rang approximately ten minutes later, right about the time I was nodding off. Of course, my heart leapt. I thought it might be Macie. I struggled out of bed. No again. It was Felix. He had a big basket of food, beverages, and his Xbox. He made a jerk with his head, indicating to me to get out of the way, and walked to the kitchen.

"I told my parents there was no way you'd come over, so my mom fixed us up with some food. And you're not going to believe this, but dad even snuck us some beer! Have you eaten yet?" Felix asked. I shook my head. He nodded and made a couple of peanut butter sandwiches. I normally would have smiled, but I did not have it in me.

"Alright, you go sit down, enjoy the sandwiches, and take it easy. I'll clean off the paint. Don't you worry about a thing, your old buddy Felix is here."

Felix labored over the paint for a couple of hours. He succeeded in getting it all removed, but now there were these off-colored spots on the siding that were lighter in color. If one looked closely, the words could still be seen. At one point, I logged on to my Facebook page. I was not surprised when I saw some derogatory comments posted. Oh, and Macie was no longer on my friend's list. No surprise there. I read the comments, some were supportive, but others were very cruel. Felix walked in as I was looking at it. He looked over my shoulder at the screen and sighed. "I'm sorry, bro. People can be really shitty sometimes."

"Not your fault, Felix. Not your fault." I held the tears in, deleted my account, and turned the laptop off.

We spent the rest of the afternoon eating and watching TV. At one point, Felix grabbed the remote control and turned the volume up. "Hey, check this out." It was a special news report. The news person, a young auburn haired woman with a nice chest, large mouth, and very white teeth, was commentating about the flu bug.

"News reports out of the Mideast indicate that a deadly strain of flu is reaching pandemic proportions. Hospitals and clinics are reporting being overrun with patients. We're now going live in Cairo with CNN foreign correspondent, Jim Denzing. Jim?"

The screen shot changed to a handsome but haggard looking man standing in front of what appeared to be a chaotic hospital emergency room. His shirt was soiled with sweat and his tie was pulled down. He had not shaved in a couple of days, but the look worked for him. There was the sound of sirens, and men in uniforms were in the background. They were all carrying assault rifles and running around in every direction. It looked like a huge cluster fuck.

There was a momentary pause as the satellite relayed the message for Jim to start talking. "Lacy, the best way to describe what I am seeing is total pandemonium. A nonstop stream of patients has been showing up throughout the evening and there is no end in sight. We've had unconfirmed reports some of the patients are very violent and the soldiers may have even shot some of them. Little is known about the cause of the outbreak or why it is escalating so quickly." Jim paused for a moment and held his earpiece.

"Okay, I'm being asked if there are any fatalities as a result of this apparent flu bug. We have asked medical personnel and they refer us to the military, who refuse to comment. The answer is elusive, but it is believed that the fatalities are somewhat high," there was a sudden sound of gunfire out of the view of the camera and Jim instinctively ducked down.

"I'm terribly sorry about that, Lacy. What you and our viewers cannot see is what appears to be a violent confrontation between soldiers and some civilians. We're going to pan the camera around so you can get a view. I must caution the viewing audience that this is a live feed and there may be disturbing images." The camera turned approximately 180 degrees. There, in living color, were soldiers being attacked. They were shooting back, but even though the people attacking them were unarmed, the soldiers appeared to be losing the battle. The live feed lasted approximately five seconds before the it went blank. The last scene appeared to be barricades being overrun by a swarm of people.

"Crazy shit, man," Felix said and turned the channel. We spent the rest of the night watching Ironman movies, or playing on the Xbox.

My grandmother was buried on the Monday after Thanksgiving weekend. Her pastor officiated. The congregation of the church she infrequently attended had contributed toward a simple service and cremation afterward. There were only a few people in attendance. Felix and his parents were there, of course, and some of the old farts who had known Grandma for a few years attended. I did not know any of them personally. I would say hello to them and thank them for coming. I tried to be polite, but I swear, every one of them were coughing and wheezing. Nothing is more disgusting than an old person with phlegm filled coughs. I kept my distance from them.

I struggled through it all reasonably well, I think. I had hoped Macie would make an appearance. She would see how much I was hurting and comfort me, and beg me for forgiveness, and all that stupid shit. She never showed.

When I could not take it anymore, I snuck into an empty office, locked the door, and cried in private, but only for an hour or so.

Chapter 6 – Exodus

Rick was waiting on me when I arrived at my little home. He was parked on the side of the road in his nice shiny Dodge Ram dually. His truck was a direct contradiction to his personal grooming. It was always clean and had a perpetual coat of fresh wax on it. This evening, he had a box trailer hooked up to it. When he exited his truck, he looked around as if we were being spied upon, and then quickly limped up to me. His limp was due to a bum leg, courtesy of Vietnam.

"I don't go to funerals. Hate 'em. People act really stupid and say stupid shit. So, here is the obligatory, I'm sorry for your loss and all that bullshit. Now, let's go inside and talk. It's getting cold out."

I fixed coffee and we sat in the kitchen at a faux walnut dining table. It was clean, but had its share of dents and nicks. When I turned the lights on, Rick started looking at me with a frown. "What the hell happened to you? Your face looks like a football. You get in a fight or something?"

I filled him in, and even showed him the video. He shook his head. "That's jacked up, brother. The world is a jacked up place and it's getting worse by the minute," he took a long sip of coffee and stared at me intently. "Are you going to get some payback?"

I shrugged. "I don't know how, but I'd like to someday."

Rick nodded. "When you're ready, you let me know. I'll have your back. I may be an old drunk with a bum leg, but I'm a sneaky bastard and I can still shoot."

I nodded solemnly, but I did not really know what to say. Sure, I wanted revenge on all of them, including the girl who videotaped it. But, I never even considered anything having to do with guns. Hell, I was thinking of stuff like slashing their tires or egging their house. Sneaky shit without any confrontation.

He refilled his cup, retrieved a half pint of cheap whiskey from his jacket pocket, and laced the coffee with a generous dollop. I shook my head. He shrugged and then fixed me again with a serious stare. "Alright, it's time to talk about some serious stuff." Hence, the serious stare. "I'm going to lay it all out for you and then you'll need to make some serious decisions. Since you're just sixteen, some fat ugly heifer with the Department of Children's Services will be coming around here pretty soon. No matter what you say or do, they're going to put you in a foster home until you're eighteen." He paused and took a drink, presumably to let the statement sink in.

"Now, the way I see it, you can go talk to your friend's parents and I think they'd take you in. You're a damn good kid and you're that nerdy gay kid's best friend. It'd be a good home for you. But I think I got a better idea." He motioned at me with his mug. Some of its contents sloshed over the rim. "Let's pack your shit right now and you come live with me. I've already cleared it with the Parsons."

I started to reply but he held up a hand. "I don't know if you've been watching the news these past few days, but there's something really weird happening. Something really bad. People all over the world are getting sick. A lot of them are dying, but there's something else going on. A lot of them are going fucking crazy, like zombie crazy, do you know what I mean?"

I shook my head. I might have even laughed if I did not feel so miserable. "What are you talking about? Are you saying that the end of the world is coming or something?" Rick nodded his head somberly. I managed a halfhearted snort. "You need to lay off the sauce."

Rick arched a bushy eyebrow. "Could be, could be I'm completely loco, right? I'm sure a lot of people would agree with you. I admit I've got a few screws loose, but, what if I'm right? Hmm? What if this crazy old man is right. What then?" he held a hand up. "Don't say anything just yet, because I'll tell you what will be happening if I'm right. Total societal collapse. I see the way you're looking at me. Just because I'm crazy don't mean I've lost my mind," he emphasized each word, took a drink, and leaned forward. "It's already started, Zach," he reached over and slid the remote control across the table. "Turn the TV on if you don't believe me. Put it on Fox or CNN."

I did as he suggested. There was a little bit of sports news, and then they started talking about the flu outbreak. The newswoman, the same perky woman Felix and I had ogled on Thanksgiving, was

25

talking about news blackouts in various countries in the Mideast. I changed the channel to CNN. They were interviewing somebody from the CDC. The caption identified him as a doctor and an assistant director of the center. He was staring at a fixed point on the ground and saying everyone should remain calm and get their flu vaccination. The local news was talking about the full emergency rooms throughout the mid-state area. I flipped to a couple of other channels. Same thing. I looked over at Rick. He pointed at the TV.

"You see, there's something bad going on. Now, you're the smart one. What do you think about all of this?"

I thought for a minute or two while I watched another news segment. I then muted the sound. "Le Grippe," I stated.

He frowned and narrowed his eyes at me as if to say, what did you just call me? "That's what they called it in 1918. Le Grippe, or more commonly known as the Spanish Influenza. It was a worldwide epidemic. They're not sure exactly how many people died, but the estimation is as high as fifty million. Years later, the CDC did some testing with some old preserved tissue samples and determined that it was a strain of avian flu. Before that, let's see, roughly 541 BC, there was the plague of Justinian. That was in the Byzantine Empire. It was believed to have killed as many as 10,000 people a day at its peak, and in the fourteenth century, there was the infamous Black Death. Those two were Bubonic plague. There have been others." I remembered the news report from Cairo that Felix and I had watched. It now triggered a memory in me of an old book that I had read about the Justinian plague. There had been some speculation the plague originated from infected rats on grain boats arriving from Egypt.

Rick slapped the table. "Well, there you have it. You just used a lot of words to say a few years back somebody stepped in some chicken shit, or got bit on the ass by a flea and the next thing you know, fifty million people are dead. So, Zach, it may be just a few hundred people die, or it may be damn near the whole world. And those who don't die, well, they're going to be in a world of lawlessness and starvation. Anarchy. Total fucking anarchy. You may not know this, but I'm in a social network of what people call Preppers. We've been planning for something like this. We met just a couple of hours ago at the VFW. We all agreed it's time to bug out and hunker down," Rick finished up his coffee and rubbed his beard. He gave a curt nod to himself, as if to confirm a decision he had already made.

"Well, what say the two of us hunker down at the farm and ride it out? I've planned ahead, Zach. I've got a shit load of food stored. I got guns and ammo. I got reloading equipment, farming equipment, cattle, chickens, generators, two-way radios, solar panels, fresh water from a well. You name it, I got it. What I don't have is a partner. Having a partner will help tremendously. You got something I don't, Zach," he declared. I looked at him quizzically. "You got your youth and you got brains. You got a good memory. My gray matter isn't the best, but I've been around. If you think about it, we'd make a good team. You know, like them Asians twins, Yin and Yang. So, what do you say, brother?"

I rubbed my face. His logic, although a bit paranoid, kind of made sense. My grandmother did not own this house. She rented it from some property management company. Chances were pretty good that I'd be evicted before the New Year. I was going to need a place to live anyway, so what the hell. I needed to get away. Get away from school, and get away from this house. Get away from everyone. I looked at Rick. He must have read my thoughts because he was grinning. He was even wearing his false teeth, which he only did for meals and special events. I gave him a silent nod and he slapped his hands together in victory. He knew I would say yes. Hell, what else was I going to do?

Felix and his father came over and helped load up the trailer. I could not lift very much, so I limited my activity to packing my clothes. We finished in about an hour. As I said, there wasn't much. A lot of the furniture was old and worn out. Most of it was going to either Goodwill, or to a trash drop off.

I had been standing on the porch watching them load up. Felix walked over to me. He had one of those sad, hangdog expressions.

"I'm not going to be seeing much of you after this, I'm thinking," Felix said sadly.

I resisted the impulse to pat him on the shoulder. "Why do you say that? You know where the farm is. It's not too far. You're welcome to come out and stay anytime you want. And don't think I won't be coming to visit my best friend."

"You didn't say anything about school. You're not going back, are you?"

I looked at him a moment and then shook my head sadly. His jaw dropped. "Why, Zach? You've got good grades and you know you're going to get a scholarship. It's because of Macie, right?"

I did not respond. I just stared at the ground. There was no need to deny it. He was right.

"Dude, don't let her mess your life up. There are other girls out there. Before you know it, you'll be dating someone else and Jason will have dumped Macie. Who will be the sorry one then? Her, that's who!"

I smiled at Felix. He looked like he was about to cry and I did not want him to. "You're the best friend a guy could have, Felix. But I need some time away to sort things out. Who knows, maybe in a week, I'll be ready to come back."

Felix reached under his glasses and wiped his eyes. He smiled hopefully, resisted an urge to give me a hug, and shook my hand.

"Anything I can do to help, buddy, you just call," he looked over at his father. "Pops is getting antsy. Mom is sick and he wants to get going. Give me a shout tomorrow, okay?" he asked. I agreed. "Promise?" he asked again with more feeling. I agreed again more earnestly. He shook my hand again and left with his father.

I did one final walk through of the old, small house that had been the only home that I ever knew. It could stand a good cleaning. I spent a couple of more minutes lost in memories and then turned the lights out.

Rick was waiting for me outside. It was dark out now and the temperature was already down in the low forties. "Look here, kid, I'm going to head on to the Ponderosa. Here," he slapped a wad of money and a piece of paper with scribbles on it. "Buy everything on the list that you can find. Fill your truck up with gas and when you're done, meet me at your new home. I threw some bungee cords, rope, and a tarp in the back of your truck so you can strap everything down. You got any problems, give me a call. Got it?" I nodded my head and began scanning the list. "Oh, one more thing." He handed me a knife. "It's a Benchmark lock blade with a razor sharp edge. Just flip it open, hold tight, and stab repeatedly."

I looked at it questioningly. "Okay, I think? Do you expect me to run into trouble or something?"

"You never know, kid," he said. "It might just be me and the fact that I live out in the country, but I sure am hearing a lot of sirens."

I had not noticed until he said something, but it seemed like I was hearing them as well. "How're your ribs?" he asked. I shrugged. They were sore and hurt if I made any sudden movements. At least my balls were feeling better.

"Alright, don't be too prideful and refuse to ask for help loading from the store employees."

I nodded. He grinned at me and left without another word.

Chapter 7 - The Death of a Thug

Rick's list was a little odd. Some of the items made perfect sense. Toothbrushes and toothpaste, dental floss, razor blades, toilet paper, powdered milk. Other items on the list stood out though, like tampons and Vaseline. Nevertheless, I was able to locate almost everything at the Sam's Wholesale Store. I finished up with a few more items at a local Kroger store, and went through the self-service checkout. I refused to buy the tampons, convinced that Rick was playing a joke on me. It was only a couple of sacks that I could manage, even with busted ribs. I had just gotten to my truck, lost in my own thoughts, when suddenly there was someone behind me.

"Well, hello, white boy."

I turned suddenly, which was painful. My grimace got a sadistic chuckle. "You still hurtin', boy?" I got a good look at him then and made the recognition. It was one of Jason's friends. Specifically, he was the center for the football team and one of the assholes who put the boots to me. It was not until I saw him in person that I made the connection. He was at least four inches shorter than I was, but weighed at least a hundred pounds more. Most of it was fat, but there was muscle there as well. He looked like a retarded Troglodyte wearing a ball cap sideways. Like all retarded Troglodytes wear them.

"I said hello. You gonna disrespect me by not answering me, white boy?" he stepped closer.

"What the hell do you want?" I demanded. There was a note of uncertainty in my voice and I had no doubt that he heard it.

"I hear you been talking to the police." He pronounced police 'Po-Leese'. English grammar was not one of his strong points.

"They came to the hospital and took a report. You should have thought of that before you attacked me," I said as I stepped back. I believed that I could have easily outrun him, even with hurt ribs, but I was hesitant to leave my truck behind. Gunfire sounded in the distance. I wondered who was shooting who, and looked toward the sound. It was a bad move.

He may have been fat, but he could move a short distance quickly. Before I could act, he stepped forward and punched me in the gut. I gasped and doubled over in pain.

"You stupid bitch. You shouldn't have told them po-leeses nothing. Now you gonna have to pay. Where's that money wad I seen you with earlier, huh?" He stood over me and grabbed my wallet out of my back pocket. "Yeah, there it is. That's some good money." He grabbed the remaining money, a couple of hundred dollars, and threw my wallet on the ground. I was on my hands and knees now. I could hear him chuckling at me. I could also hear sirens in the distance, but I instinctively knew they were not coming to rescue me.

"Yeah, my boy is doing that little blonde headed white girl right at this very minute I bet. You thought she was yours, didn't you. That bitch belong to my boy, not you. You know what, white boy, I think I'm gonna make you my bitch. You owe me."

I was crying again, which angered me. Talking about Macie angered me. Robbing me of Rick's money angered me. Calling me his bitch, now that was downright disturbing. I looked up at him. He was rubbing his crotch and leering at me. "Yeah, bitch, you gonna take care of me right now."

Something inside me snapped. My hand found the knife in my pocket. I locked the blade open, and lunged upward with a guttural yell.

I don't know how many times I stabbed him. It was all a blur. When it was over, he was lying on the ground dead. We had ended up in between my truck and another car. I was breathing hard and my ribs hurt like hell. I had blood all over me. I sat there on the cold asphalt beside my tormentor gasping for air. He wasn't breathing. Thankfully, my truck and the other car parked beside me kept us mostly hidden from view. I don't know how long I sat there catching my breath. My mind was in a fog, the thinking processes going in slow motion. I did not know what to do.

Rick. I needed to call Rick.

The conversation went something like this: "Rick, I just stabbed a guy. I think he's dead."

"No shit?"

"No shit! I'm serious, Rick. I wouldn't joke about something like this." I quickly told him what had happened. "What do I do?"

He drew in a deep breath and spoke sternly. "Listen to me carefully. Only answer me yes or no. Take a look around, but don't make it obvious. Is there anyone watching you?"

I peeked up over my truck and casually looked around. There was nobody within close proximity, only an older couple at the opposite end of the parking lot. They had their heads down and were hurriedly walking toward their car. I relayed this information.

"Okay, good. Now, get those groceries and money back, and then you need to get out of there as soon as possible."

I started to ask about the police but he shut me up. "No! Listen to me. You've got to get out of there pronto! Now do what I said and get yourself in your truck. Don't hang up, I'll wait."

I grabbed the money out of his dead hand, grabbed the sacks of groceries, and got in my truck. After a moment, I got back out of my truck and retrieved my wallet off the cold asphalt. I looked around again, trying to make it look casual, and then got back in my truck and locked the doors. It seemed like the proper thing to do. I relayed this to Rick.

"Alright, you're doing good, kid. Now, slowly drive away, just like you would if nothing at all happened. But, I want you to kind of keep one of your hands over your face and look up at the light poles with your eyes only. Don't tilt your head up. Do you see any security cameras?"

I looked up through my windshield. I spotted one at the far end of the parking lot near the main entrance. Rick directed me to drive away from it and choose an alternate exit. He stayed on the phone with me the entire time until I got back to the farm, talking to me and calming me. It did not help very much. I was certain at any moment there would be blue lights flashing in my rear view mirror and I would be arrested.

But it never happened.

Several minutes later, I drove over our gateless bridge to the farm. I saw Rick waiting by the barn with the mutts. They wagged their tails appreciatively as I drove up. When I got out of the truck, Rick looked me up and down.

"Lord Almighty. Strip all of those clothes off right here, then go get in the shower and scrub yourself down good."

I looked down and remembered that I was covered in blood. Curly kept trying to lick me and I had to push him away. I did as Rick told me without complaint.

The shower was hot and soothing, but I could not stop shaking. My brain told me it was a natural response to the adrenalin dump, but knowing why did not alleviate any of the symptoms, nor did it calm my nerves.

Thirty minutes later, I was showered and wearing clean clothes. Rick had a fire going. He had thrown my clothes in the fireplace, including my shoes. As they burned, they filled the house with the smell of burning rubber. He looked up at me and handed me his ever present pint of whiskey. I tentatively took a swallow and nearly choked. He grunted and took it back.

"I've got to get your truck unloaded. You feel up to a little work?" he asked. I nodded. The truth was, I hurt like hell, but I needed to do something. Rick nodded. "Under the kitchen sink there is a pair of those rubber dishwashing gloves and a big sponge. Get them and a bucket of hot water, put a little bit of bleach in it, about two cups, and wipe down every square inch of your truck, inside and out. Then we're going to run it around in the dirt and mud and get it all dirty again."

"Why am I doing that?" I asked.

"Hell, hoss, you know why. We don't want any of that boy's blood and DNA on your truck. Now, don't get any false hopes. We're not out of the woods yet. There may be witnesses and a security camera may have recorded the whole thing. But, and it is a big but, we may get by. If the police come and visit, you're going to admit you were at Kroger and yes, that boy was probably one of the boys who attacked you, but you did not see him and you did not have any kind of confrontation. Got it? If they get to asking any more questions that sounds like they know you did it, you lawyer up and dummy up, okay?"

I nodded. It seemed to make sense. He looked at me, not unkindly. "You're thinking about what you did. You're thinking you just murdered someone, aren't you?" he asked. I nodded again. The shakes made a sudden reappearance. "Okay, kid, let me tell you something. If you want to turn yourself in, good luck to you. I'll write you, if this flu thing is just a passing bug that is. But, think of it like this. That boy deserved what he got. If you hadn't of stabbed him, there's no telling what he would have done to you. You did what you had to do. I don't want to hear any whining about it. Right, boys?" he looked at the dogs. They kind of just sat there with blank dog-like expressions. "See, the boys agree."

I silently assented and spent the next hour wiping down my truck. After I finished, I drove it around the farm getting it good and dirty. I was relying on Rick's advice. I certainly did not want to go to prison. I'm skinny, blonde headed with Nordic features, blue-eyed, and a big toothy smile. I'm fairly certain my prison buddies would change my name to Suzie and have me wearing lipstick and a short dress for my duration. Not a pleasant thought.

On Rick's advice, I had a couple more shots of his rotgut whiskey and went to bed a short time later. I thought I would never fall asleep, but sleep did come. I awakened more than once due to nightmares. Rick and the mutts never noticed.

Chapter 8 – Wildfire

The police never came. Rick was right. They apparently had their hands full with another crisis. We watched the news on TV. Video footage from around the world was shown of people going crazy and attacking other people. The graphic stuff was blurred out at first, but it soon gave way to raw, uncensored footage. We watched, as sick, maniacal people would launch themselves upon hapless victims, tearing at them and sinking their teeth into flesh, gnashing and gnawing. We watched as police and soldiers stood side by side shooting over and over at approaching hordes, only to be overrun by the sheer numbers. Gunshots, other than headshots, did not seem to affect them.

We monitored blog sites, Facebook, Twitter, Jabber, Steambox, and a couple of other social network sights that I had never heard of before. Rick had his Ham radio going, talking to his fellow Preppers. He was in some sort of club comprised of Ham radio operators from around the world and they spoke to each other in that peculiar Ham radio operator lingo.

Some of the items he had me buy were large maps and a box of thumbtacks with multiple colors. We hung the world map on the wall and inserted thumbtacks on the cities where outbreaks were being reported. The color coding represented the number of reports. The red thumbtack represented the highest number of reports. At the end of two days, the entire Middle East region was festooned with red. Southern Europe and most of Africa had a number of yellow. The good ole' USA was starting to gather a number of blue tacks. I wanted to use green like the colors on a traffic light, but Rick out voted me. He thought green would be misleading. I reminded him it was only the two of us viewing the map and I doubted there would be any confusion, but I just got a withering stare. So, blue it was. Blue of course, represented minor reports.

On the third day of this endeavor, we had all of Africa red. Most of Asia was yellow, but the reds were creeping in. Europe was completely yellow, with the red starting to creep north. Most of the cities in North and South America had blue tacks, with the exception of the major cities like Rio, New York City, and Los Angeles, which had yellow tacks. I pointed out one blue tack to Rick. "What is this one all about?" I asked. It was stuck on a spot in Antarctica.

Rick turned away from the computer monitor and looked at it. "There is a research base down there. Fox news reported that a scientist was very sick and there was trouble with bad weather keeping a rescue plane from flying down there. Since then, they've lost radio contact with them. Probably should replace it with a red tack." His cell phone rang. He looked at it in surprise, as if he honestly thought the world had already ended and we were the last people on Earth. After a couple of rings, he answered and spoke tersely to whoever was on the other end before hanging up.

"I ordered a resupply of propane four days ago. They just now decided to come out. The driver is bitching about the road being blocked."

Since we no longer had a gate, we blocked the bridge with a John Deere tractor, complete with a backhoe attachment. "I'm going to move the backhoe and let him in. You keep monitoring the news, okay?" I agreed. The bridge was the only entrance to the farm. If you wanted access to the farm, you either had to fly in, swim across the fast moving creek, or drive several miles around to the back of the farm with an ATV and use wire cutters to get through the cattle fencing surrounding the farm. We had earlier agreed that the blocked roadway would at least give us time to prepare if the police showed up.

The old homestead we were currently living in was heated by propane and the fireplace. There was a tank behind the house that needed to be filled every fall. I was wondering what exactly we were going to do next fall. It was definitely something to add on the to-do list. We had a well for water, but the pump was electrically powered. We had a generator, but it was dependent on fuel. We had a large fuel tank near the barn for all of the farm equipment, but it would not last forever. Still, all in all, Rick had gotten the farm equipped pretty decently. He had a root cellar stocked with canned goods, a barn full of tools, ammo reloading gear, and various other types of equipment. We had a smoke house, a deep creek that had fish, a chicken coop with brooding hens, and Rick had harvested from the garden just last month.

I stood at the back door and watched the man transfer propane from his tanker into the large cylindrical tank. The name tag sewn onto his work shirt read Junior. I certainly hoped it was a nickname and not his Christian name. He was grossly overweight, which made every little movement a major effort for him, filled with panting and grunting. He had to wear suspenders because I don't think they made a belt big enough for him. I noticed Rick was keeping a fair amount of distance from him. He was also wearing a handgun in a holster attached to his belt. Junior either did not notice or did not care. We all paused in our thoughts and actions to look skyward, as a sortie of military aircraft flew overhead.

Junior pointed at them. "My brother-in-law is in one of them planes. He's a staff sergeant in the National Guard. They got called up this morning. He wasn't supposed to, but he sneaked a call to my sister." He looked over at me. "You see, we're not related by blood. He's married to my sister. That's what makes him my brother-in-law."

Well no shit, Junior. Thank you for the edification.

Satisfied he had successfully bestowed some wisdom upon me, a mere child, he spit a gob of tobacco juice, some of which did not make it clear of his ample gut. He casually wiped at it with his meaty hand and looked at Rick. "He told her there was some serious shit going down. After I get off work today, we're going to the grocery store and stock up." He looked somberly at Rick and lowered his voice. "You two should do the same."

Rick gave him a serious nod of acknowledgement. "Very good advice, Junior. What else did your brother-in-law have to say? Did he tell you where they're going?"

Junior shook his head. "No, no he didn't."

This time, he had the clever idea of bending forward this time. He also increased the amount of pressure between his lips, which gave a higher trajectory of the spittle. He was rewarded with a clean shot. He nodded in satisfaction. I'm sure Missus Junior would have been proud.

"But he said they had them loaded up on the planes quicker than they ever had before, and they got issued live ammunition. He said they haven't done that since their unit got deployed to Iraq."

He wiped his mouth of leakage. "He's a genuine war hero. Probably the only one in this whole danged county."

Rick was not amused. He thanked Junior and bluntly told him it was time for him to leave. Junior shrugged and waddled back to his tanker truck. Rick followed him to the road.

I had been sitting in front of the TV for over an hour and was about to turn it off when a headline flashed declaring breaking news. I grabbed the remote and turned the volume up. Rick walked in a short time later. "The propane tank is now full. Junior is long gone. I got the backhoe across the bridge again, and we are officially on lockdown. I strung some concertina wire at the front of the bridge too. It'll be downright difficult for anyone just to walk through. What are you watching?"

I turned to him briefly and pointed to the TV. "They said O'Hare airport in Chicago has suspended all incoming and outgoing flights. No official reason has been given but the news woman is speculating the flu outbreak has caused a shortage of employees."

Rick scoffed. "Yeah, right. They didn't say anything about zombies, but what do you bet, they've had some attacks. Alright, Einstein, what's so important about O'Hare?"

"Well, it's an International airport. They have flights incoming from all over the world. About seventy to seventy-five million passengers a year go through the airport, along with over a million tons of freight. If they've suspended all flights, it must be quite serious," I declared. Rick nodded thoughtfully. He walked over to the map and replaced the blue thumbtack over Chicago with a red one.

"I don't know how you know all these little facts about everything. But it's damn helpful." He scratched at his beard. "When something major like this happens, it can only mean one thing, Zach. It means it can't be contained."

My skepticism about Rick's theory was long gone. All I could do was nod in agreement. He sat down in front of his Ham radio and grabbed the microphone. "WA4OEQ, QTH middle Tennessee, calling any listening station. Chicago is now in condition red. Chicago is now in condition red, over."

After a moment, there was a response. "WD5KZZ to WA4OEQ, my QTH is Tulsa, Oklahoma. QSM please, sir, over."

Rick looked over at me. "QTH means the location you're at and QSM means to repeat your last message. I need you to learn all this." He looked at me seriously. "You need to know what a brother-in-law is too."

Rick turned his attention back to the radio before I could retort and repeated the information, going into more detail. After a few minutes of conversation, Rick bid the man sevens and threes, radio lingo for good luck, and signed off. "Okay, you heard what Tulsa said. Put a yellow tack on Tulsa, Norman, Oklahoma City, and Kansas City."

I did as told and we looked at the map together in silence for several seconds. Rick began pointing at the various tacks and making lines from each one. All of the major cities on the map were now covered in thumbtacks.

"In just two days, we have some reds and a whole shit load of yellows across the US alone," he said it quietly, as though he did not believe it, even though he is the one so certain it was going to happen. "It's spreading like wildfire."

I looked over at Rick's dogs. They were looking at the map also.

In the ensuing hours, all of the airports and seaports closed. The Interstate system became a massive traffic jam with people frantically going to some place they believed to be safer than where they were. Grocery stores were emptied of their wares. Convenience stores, popular for the ease of purchasing gasoline and minor food products, were overrun with impatient customers. It inevitably lead to short tempers and fights. Spontaneous riots were breaking out, as people could not seem to grasp what was happening. It was the government, they'd shout. Somehow, it was always the government's fault.

The President gave a live speech promptly at six o'clock. I turned the volume up on the TV. "My fellow Americans," he began.

"Oh shit, here it comes. Get ready to bend over, fellow Americans. BOHICA!" Rick yelled.

"I am speaking to you this evening from the confines of Air Force One. As you may now know, the world has been beset upon by a deadly illness of pandemic proportions…"

"Well no shit, Sherlock."

"...I have activated all military units, personnel with FEMA, and the CDC..."

"You should have done that weeks ago, numb nuts."

"...This morning, I called upon Congress to join with me in enacting martial law..." Rick looked at me. I nodded in understanding.

"...We must have faith, perseverance, and work together if we are to survive..."

"Oh, I believe you, pal. You've helped out so much already." Rick's running commentary prevented me from hearing the majority of the speech. It was irritating, but I guess it did not really matter.

"...may God bless you, and may he have mercy upon us."

The map was completely covered in red by the end of the week.

Chapter 9 - Our First Zombie

Rick folded his arms, sighed loudly, and climaxed with a loud belch. We had just finished a breakfast of eggs, sausage, and lard biscuits. I asked Rick once why, in all of his planning, he never bothered getting any dairy cows. I never got an answer, just a surly stare. We were absorbed in our thoughts as we finished off the last of the fresh orange juice. "I have made a grievous tactical error," Rick said. I looked at him. He looked at me. The dogs looked at both of us. "If everyone is going to die off, we should have gotten us a couple of ladies to shack up with us." He scratched his whiskers. "It's going to be hell without getting some pussy every once in a while."

"But you hate women. You said so yourself," I said.

He glared at me indignantly. "Not true! I like women. I like the way they look, the way they move, the way they feel, and I like the way they smell. Hell, I like the way they taste, if you know what I mean. But, I can't stand to be around them for any length of time. It doesn't matter anymore, I guess. They're all dead." He was looking at the map as he spoke.

All television, radio stations, and the Internet had gone down some time ago. It was the same with the phones, both cell phones and the landline. All of them were dead. I tried them often, but the result was always the same.

I had tried calling Felix before the phones went out, but never got through to him. I hoped he was okay. I was sorely tempted to call Macie, and was about to do so until Rick told me to quit being stupid.

I had managed to oppress any thoughts of Macie, well mostly, but when Rick started talking about women, I would instantly start thinking of her. Was she alive? Was she still with Jason? It frustrated me. I wanted to see her. At least, I thought I did. I definitely wanted to see Felix. I missed him terribly.

"Everyone isn't dead," I exclaimed as I put my shoes on. My ribs had healed to the point where they only bothered me occasionally, so I could now bend over and put my shoes on without too much discomfort. "You want me to feed the cows and chickens today?" I asked. It was cold out now, the grass was dormant and the livestock needed additional food in order to survive the winter.

I was walking toward the door when Rick snapped his fingers several times at me to get my attention. "What do you mean everyone isn't dead? How the hell do you think you know that? Neither of us has left this farm in almost a month, and this damn radio has been awfully quiet."

I finished tying my shoes. I was going to go for a jog after the morning chores were done. "Simple math," I said. Rick made a circular motion with his hand. I guess he meant I should continue. "Alright, think of it this way. The two of us basically quarantined ourselves out here, merely over a gut feeling you had and not much else. We don't know anything about this disease other than what we've been reading on the Internet and listening to on TV. It infects the host and either kills them, or converts them into a violent, maniacal murdering animal."

"Zombies," Rick opined.

"Yeah, if that's what you want to call them. So, how does a person become infected? We don't know. We've heard many different theories, but we're in the dark in this area. We didn't catch it though, which is good. So, two living souls. We can use that number as a base. There are approximately two million people who live in the mid-state area. If you assume we are the only two survivors in this immediate area, one only has to do the math." I grabbed a notepad with my ever expanding to-do list, got a fresh piece of paper, and wrote it out.

"The assumed rate of survival will be .000001%. Now, consider that there are approximately 6 billion people on the planet. That is a six with nine zeros after it." I wrote it out. "So, using our base survival percentage, at the minimum, there are approximately six thousand people left alive in the world. However, to assume that the base value is only two is not logical. I believe there are many other pockets of survivors in this area alone. I've no doubt there are people who quarantined themselves just like us, and there are probably people who are immune, just like when the bubonic plague hit Europe and the Spanish flu hit the world."

Rick watched as I wrote out the equations. "How many do you think would be immune?"

I shrugged. "I have no idea really. If I was to guess, 20% of the population, but that's a rather liberal guess," I looked at Rick. He was staring at the ceiling trying to add it up in his head. It was going to give him a migraine. Little wisps of smoke were starting to come out of his ears. I helped him out.

"Somewhere around 1.2 billion; that's worldwide, but think of this. After this infection burns out, there is going to be a massive die off due to starvation, disease, lack of proper medical care, violence, well you know the rest. You also have other variables."

"What kind of variables?" Rick asked.

"Variables like Cheyenne Mountain and Raven Rock. They have contingency plans in place for mass catastrophe events such as this. They have also thought of this possibility and created what is called a Continuity of Government plan. I'd be willing to bet all of the NATO countries have a similar contingency plan, as well as Russia and China."

I started to think about it. Did they survive? How were they going to restore order? I started a new page with the acronym COG written on top and started scribbling notes.

Rick's attention had wandered, now he focused on the other maps. Each wall had maps of the state and individual cities. He had framed pictures hanging on the walls at one time, nice nature scenes, but a couple of nights ago, he got drunk, smashed them all up, and burned them in the fire. I swept up pieces of glass for the rest of the day. I'm glad we didn't cut our feet and get some kind of infection. At least now, we had empty wall space for our maps.

He waved his hand toward them and looked at me. "Let's say you and me go on a little recon mission this afternoon? We can start with Franklin."

"What happened with our plan of hunkering down here until spring?" I asked.

Rick looked at me as if I had said something involving bestiality and dog feces. "Do you really want to live the rest of your life without a woman?" he asked sarcastically.

Now it was my turn to give him a look. "I'm going to feed the livestock, and then I'm going for a run. Anything else you can think of that needs to be done?"

"Yeah, start the generator. I'm going to take a hot shower. Then I'm going to get on the Ham radio and see if I can raise any of those 1.2 billion people. And while you're on your run, put your brain to work on planning out a recon and scavenging mission. We got plenty of food and water, but we can always use some more dog food. And fuel. And most importantly, whiskey. And don't forget about females."

I shook my head and chuckled at the old man as I strapped on a Glock handgun and a knife. I did not expect any trouble. Hell, we had not seen anyone since Junior left, but I was not going to get my ass kicked again. The days of Zach Gunderson being a meek little lamb were over. I did a press check to insure there was a bullet in the chamber, stretched, and then started out.

There was a trail around the perimeter of the farm. We used it regularly to check the fence lines. My first mile was a little rough. I had not gone running since my little encounter due to the ribs. The cold air burned my throat and lungs, but it felt good. The burning sensation was having a healing effect on my soul.

As I ran, I thought about what Rick said and what he wanted to do. In just a couple of weeks' time, the disease had spread across the planet and overwhelmed the entire human population. Neither of us were knowledgeable enough to know if it had run its course and burned out, or if we would always be at risk for infection. I thought about the sick scientist in Antarctica. How in the world did he become infected? Their remote location practically ensured a state of quarantine of sorts. Yet, one of them had become infected. It was a mystery.

I hit the second mile with an increase in my stride. I was feeling good. The third mile was upon me before I knew it. I felt wonderful. In spite of being cooped up with Rick every night, the country living was good for me. I began stretching out my stride when I caught movement out of the corner of my eye. There was a woman walking across a field adjacent to our farm. It was owned by a middle-aged couple, Mr. and Mrs. Riggins. As I watched, she walked slowly along, seemingly going nowhere. I stopped and waved at her. She did not respond. Something was wrong. I ran back to the house and told Rick. A minute later, we were on an ATV and rode back. She was still there, staring absently at the fence.

"There she is. See her?" I asked. Rick nodded. "Watch this. Hey!" I yelled out to her and waved. She was about a hundred yards off. And naked. When she saw us, she started a weird loping walk, not quite a trot, toward us.

Rick picked up his rifle. "There's something wrong with that one, kid. Look at her face. It's been torn all to hell or something."

He was right. There were several deep gouges in her face and the wounds were filled with pus. Only her eyes seemed to have any life. They were darting back and forth, first on me, then on Rick.

I looked at him in mock surprise. "But, you said you wanted a woman!" I pointed out earnestly. "Well, there you go."

She was about fifty yards away from us now. It was obvious she was diseased. Rick tried yelling at her, but she just moaned, screamed, or something. She hit the fence and bounced off of it, as if she did not even know it was there.

We watched her for a few minutes as she tried to walk through the wire. "She doesn't know how to climb, does she?" Rick shook his head.

"Try talking to her," I said.

Rick gave me a cock-eyed look. "Are you serious?"

I tried to look serious. "I need to observe her. You talk, I'll observe."

Rick shrugged and walked closer to the fence. He wrinkled his nose. "Woo, she stinks to high heaven. Her skin is all rotted. Hey, baby, aren't you cold? Where are your clothes? Those sure are some saggy looking titties you got." He glanced over at me and grinned.

She suddenly reached through one of the square openings of the fence and tried to grab Rick, emitting a blood curdling moan as she did so. Rick jumped back, lifted his rifle and fired. He hit her in the gut. He stared at her in morbid fascination. "Are you seeing this? She's not dying. Hell, I don't even think she felt a thing."

The woman kept trying to reach for Rick. The gunshot halted her moaning only momentarily.

He suddenly pointed. "Holy shit, I see it! Look, she's been bitten!"

I saw it then. There were two distinct, deep bite marks on her right arm and shoulder. I stepped forward and tried to get a good look at her then. She had pallid, scaly skin coloration, and cloudy, bloodshot eyes. There were chunks of hair missing from her scalp, as if she were beginning to decompose. There were scratches all over her, but none of them appeared to be bleeding. She actually was breathing, sort of. A painful sounding rasp.

"Shoot her in the head, Rick," I urged. He glanced over at me, grinned, and put a 30-06 round between her eyes. The kinetic energy of the bullet, coupled with the close range, caused the back of her head to explode outward. She dropped instantly. Rick stuck his rifle through the fence and poked her several times with it. "I'd say the blogs were right, only a headshot will stop them."

Rick suddenly stopped and stared quietly. After a minute, he spoke softly. "That's the neighbor's wife."

I frowned. "Who?" I asked.

"That's Susan Riggins. Henry's wife," Rick said. I stared at the woman. With most of her face missing, I could not recognize her. Rick realized my consternation. "One afternoon back in June, she stopped in. Henry had gone to Dalton, Georgia for something or another. We had a few drinks and ended up in the sack together. That's how I know it's her. See the three moles down there by her cooter? It's her alright."

I looked. Yep, three moles, each about the size of a dime, together in a cloverleaf shape. They looked swollen and cancerous, but I guess it did not matter now. She looked awful. The old phrase: death warmed over, was an apt description for her.

I had only met her once. I recalled she did not look much better in real life. I patted him on the shoulder. "I sincerely doubt it's as good as it was back then, but if you need some time alone with her, I understand." Rick reached out and goosed me in my sore ribs. "Did she smell that bad when you banged her?" He tried to goose me again but I was too quick.

We loaded the body onto the back of the ATV, carried it to a nearby sinkhole, and set it on fire.

Chapter 10 - A Trek In To Franklin

After much haggling, Rick convinced me to go along. I think he was more worried about running out of whiskey than he was about picking up women, but we certainly could use some more dog food. Those little bastards sure could eat. "If you knew this was coming, why didn't you build a still?" I asked.

"I did," he responded sheepishly. "It blew up. Damn near killed me. I was going to build another one, but never got around to it." I laughed. He glared at me. "Shut up," he quipped.

We worked the rest of the afternoon preparing the farm truck. We took some spare wood and made frames around the windows. We then stapled hardware cloth to the wooden frames. Much like we had done to the windows of the house weeks before. The idea was to keep anyone or anything from breaking out the windows and getting to us. It was not bulletproof of course, but we did not have anything for that issue. We cut out holes in the middle of each door window so we could stick our guns out. Murder holes.

"Why don't we just go up to Fort Campbell and steal a tank?" Rick pondered while we were working.

"Might be a good possibility in the future. Do you know how to drive one and work on it? Did you mess with tanks when you were in the Army?"

Rick grunted. "No, I was infantry, an Airborne Ranger. Well, it was a thought. We'll try to find some tank manuals for you to read up on. So, you got a route planned out?"

"I do. Let's say we ride over to the Riggins' house first. If there are any more zombies, we'll need to kill them off," I said. Rick glanced up at me. "Well, somebody sure bit her," I added.

Rick chuckled. "No, I agree with you. It's just, listening to you talk. It's not the same as it was just a short month ago. You've changed, kid. You're all hard core now. You've put on some muscle in the shoulders too. Maybe when we get into town, we shop for some clothes as well."

I smiled tightly as I finished stapling the last of the hardware cloth. "Well, you've certainly helped me along."

We admired our work for a minute and complimented each other with effluent gushiness. We then took an inventory of items we were going to carry with us. We each armed ourselves with a handgun, rifle, and knife. Extra ammo, water, and a cooler full of food were stored in the cab. We had pry bars, two spare tires, a gas operated Sawzall to cut open stubborn doors, rope, and chain with hooks on each end.

"Why don't we take the taillights off?" I suggested. "There's not going to be any cops writing tickets, and if we need to run away from someone, we don't need to make it easy for them to follow us."

Rick shrugged, took a hammer and busted them out. I frowned at him. "I was thinking more like using a screwdriver and removing them carefully, but whatever." I took the license plate off as well and removed the registration from the glove box.

"Why'd you do that?" Rick asked.

"If we have to abandon the truck, we don't want anyone to figure out where we live by checking the registration," I explained. Rick nodded and slapped me on the back.

"Nice thinking. Alright, my man, we've got a lot done. Let's go eat dinner and get to bed early."

We got up early the next morning, fixed ourselves some breakfast, fed the dogs, and the other usual stuff before heading out. The sun was peeking out as we crossed the creek. It was promising to be a sunny day. The start of our reconnaissance mission did not go as planned. The John Deere's battery was dead. A quick trip back for jumper cables fixed the issue. We moved it out of our way and moved it back once we crossed the bridge.

"You know, a functioning gate sure would be nice," I said glibly. Rick gave me a withering stare out of the corner of his eye.

The Riggins house was empty. No people, no zombies. What little food remained had rotted. There was a case of dog food left, and a dog's carcass tied up to a chain in the backyard.

"It's sad," Rick said as he tossed the cans into the back of the truck.

"Yeah," I said, "you're talking about the dog, right?"

"Yeah. Did you know how I got Moe, Larry, and Curly?" he asked. I shook my head. "Somebody had dumped them on the side of the road. I found Moe first. About a week later, I found Larry and Curly. They were on the brink of starvation. People can be real assholes. It makes you wonder if God finally had enough of mankind's shit and unleashed this plague upon us." He stared straight ahead as he drove. Sometimes, Rick was very talkative. Sometimes, he lapsed into a broody silence, which could last for hours, or even days. I always let him have his space. I figured his PTSD demons were awake and he just needed to work it out of his system. Today, he was talkative, so I listened.

He continued. "You know, I wonder how many pets have died just like that dog back there. And the zoos, how many of those animals died? Sad, man. Very sad." He lit a cigarette, the last pack he had. "Which reminds me. We can expect a lot of stuff decomposing and rotting. Food, trash, unprocessed sewer, dead dogs, dead bodies. The smell is going to be awful. You think you can handle it, kid?"

I chuckled. "I'll try not to barf on you. I bet the rats are not only alive, they're probably thriving."

Rick chuckled in agreement.

He was right. The closer we got into town, the more noxious the smells and odors became. We reminded each other to bring gas masks next time. Today, we had to settle for bandannas wrapped around our face.

"So what exactly are we going to do if we encounter anyone?" Rick was looking around everywhere as he slowly drove down the street. There were abandoned vehicles and corpses everywhere, but we had not encountered any impassable roadblocks just yet. Multiple tendrils of smoke could be seen in the distance. Dark black smoke, indicative of more than just wood burning.

"First, we pull our bandanna's down so we don't look like bandits, and then we wave. Most people with evil intentions won't wave back. If they don't wave, we keep going. If they do, we stop and talk to them."

"But keep our distance from them," he said.

"Yeah, absolutely. If we do run into anyone, I'd dare say they won't want to get too close to us either. In fact, anyone trying to get close to us would make me suspicious."

Rick nodded. "I agree. Zombies on the other hand, we kill on sight."

I shook my head. "We don't want to be making a lot of noise, do we?"

"You make a good point, my friend. But I have to warn you, I may have to kill a few just on principal. So, where to first?"

I looked at the street sign and down at the map. "Hang a left at the next street. There should be a liquor store on the corner."

"Now you're talking!" Rick said gleefully. His elation was short lived. When we drove into the parking lot, it was readily apparent the liquor store had been ransacked. The plate glass windows were broken out, and the shelves had been emptied. We went inside anyway. The only thing left was a half empty bottle of pure grain alcohol.

"Better than nothing," Rick mumbled as he picked up the bottle.

The next stop was a car dealership. It was also obvious that it had been broken into, as was most businesses, but it seemed like the only thing that interested people were the cars. We made our way back into the shop and broke into the supply room. We found several spare parts for our trucks. "I like your thinking, kid. Long term, always think long term. I would not have even thought of spare parts and fan cables. Let's get some synthetic oil while we're here."

We stocked up and made our way to a vet clinic for dog supplies. It too had been ransacked, but it looked like whoever broke in was looking for drugs. We found an ample supply of heart worm pills, flea shampoo, and other antibiotics intended for house pets. We also found the kennel in back. We suspected what we'd find, but we looked anyway. The cages contained the carcasses of several pets. Rick swore silently and took a swig of alcohol.

There were dead and decaying bodies scattered around. On one street, there would be none, or just a solitary corpse. Turning the corner, there were dozens of decomposing bodies stacked like cordwood. Several houses and buildings had burned to the ground. We were getting accustomed to the chaos and carnage. One house had a fire truck parked in front of it. There were some firemen lying supine. It looked like they had been ravaged. "Stop here!" I shouted excitedly. Rick hit the brakes. "We can use the fire hose, and the truck probably has some good tools on it too," I explained.

Rick looked around. "I don't see anyone lurking about, but let's make it quick."

I agreed. We gathered up a couple of fire hoses and the tools that firemen always carried. Rick pointed at one of the dead firemen. They had oxygen gear, but the oxygen was depleted. As he approached, one of the firemen started moving. "Holy shit, they're zombies!" I walked up and buried my newly acquired fire axe into his head before he could stand up and bite one of us. "Bada boom!" Rick shouted gleefully. I held my finger over my lips. Rick smiled mischievously and pointed at another fireman that was struggling to stand, even though he had a missing leg. I walked over and dispatched him as well. Rick grinned.

We gathered up anything we thought we could use, including the empty oxygen tanks. I pointed at the dead firemen. "This turnout gear could come in handy."

Getting the protective helmets off of their heads was pretty easy, but we had to wrestle the corpses to get the jackets and pants off. Both of us dry heaved a couple of times. "I don't know, kid. If we can't get the smell out of the gear, there's no way in hell I'll wear any of it." I agreed. We threw all of it in the bed of the truck anyway and drove on.

Rick started as we drove into the parking lot of a Lowes. "Heads up," he said as he stopped at the entrance. He nodded toward the front of the store. There were two men standing there looking at us. We had about one hundred feet between us. They did not look very old, maybe early twenties, and they were armed with handguns. They had them stuck in their waistbands like they were street gangsters. We pulled our bandannas down. I stepped out of the truck and waved. They did not wave back. I got back in the truck. "So what do you want to do?" Rick asked.

"Drive on. We don't need any confrontations. We need to survive. We can revisit this store later." I looked at him seriously. "After all, who is going to take care of all the pussy out there if we're dead?"

He grunted in agreement and made a U-turn out of the parking lot. I looked behind us as we left. The two men ran to a parked car. "They're going to follow us. I guess we should head back."

Rick glanced over. "Not quite, Zach. We're going back to the liquor store. The big car wreck and all those abandoned cars around it form a perfect bottleneck. A perfect kill zone. We're going to be waiting for them on the other side. They ain't gonna like what happens next." Rick punched the gas.

You had to slow down to a near crawl to get through the mass of wrecked cars and make a sharp left into the parking lot. We left the truck parked in front of the liquor store with the doors left open. It worked exactly as Rick had planned. They were in a baby blue BMW. Not the kind of car I'd be riding around in post apocalypse, but whatever. They entered the bottleneck and slowed to a crawl. Once they made the left turn, they spotted our truck and stopped suddenly. They sat there looking at our truck, wondering where we were. I could see them through the windshield talking to each other. After a minute, the passenger got out. He slowly approached our truck and peeked inside. He looked toward the liquor store, looked back at his friend, and pointed toward the store. His friend got out of the car and walked up. The tall one looked in our truck again. I heard him say, 'no keys' in a hushed voice. Apparently, it meant something of significance. Maybe they intended to steal it.

I was crouched down behind a car. Rick was in the back of a minivan on the opposite side of the wreck. If they just looked around, they would have probably seen me. They both focused their attention on the interior of the liquor store. The shorter of the two was pointing his handgun toward the entrance. The other one finally yelled out, "Hello!"

Rick must have grown impatient with them. He answered. "Why, hello bitches. Now drop those guns if you want to live," he growled out the last as he stuck the barrel of his Winchester out a broken window. I must admit, he even frightened me a little bit.

The two men turned toward Rick, but did not drop their weapons. The short one spoke. "You don't understand, we're friendly. We just wanted to talk."

There was no friendliness in his eyes.

"If you still have a gun in your hand by the time I close my mouth, you'll be talking to God. Now drop those weapons!"

The taller one dropped his gun immediately. The other one just stood there and stared at Rick. He started to say something, and then tried to bring his gun up. He did not get a chance. Rick shot him square in the chest. The other man dropped down in a crouch beside our truck and looked at his weapon lying a mere foot away from him. He was temporarily hidden from Rick. He knew it and started to reach for it. I stood up then. He jumped when he saw me, and immediately raised his hands. I ordered him to stand up as Rick walked around and faced him.

"Who the hell are you and why did you come after us?" Rick demanded.

"I'm Chad. Chad Smith. Why'd you kill Frodo for Christ's sake? We just wanted to talk to you guys!" he lamented. His whole body was now shaking and he was having trouble talking without stammering.

Rick poked him in the chest with his rifle. "You are a goddamned liar is what you are, Chad Smith. You two came after us with weapons. You jumped out of your car with guns in your hands, and then your stupid friend chose to point a gun at me. By the way, Frodo was a character in The Lord of the Rings. He was an honorable and heroic man, one of my favorite characters of all time." Rick nodded toward Frodo's lifeless body. "Your friend was neither honorable nor heroic."

Chad looked at his recently deceased acquaintance. "His real name was Francis," he said. Rick snorted in contempt and spat. He reached over and pulled a pack of cigarettes out of Chad's shirt pocket. He lit one and blew the smoke in Chad's face.

"Are you going to kill me?" he asked weakly.

"Any reason why we shouldn't?" I asked. "You were going to kill us."

"No sir!" I think he directed it toward me, although it was obvious he was a couple of years older. "I swear to God we weren't. We…we're just hungry. We haven't had anything decent to eat in a while. Just scraps of food that's past its expiration date," tears started rolling down his face.

"What's your story?" I asked. He looked at me blankly. "How did you guys survive? Where did you come from? All that stuff. Tell me everything. Be truthful," I pointed at Rick, "because he doesn't like being lied to."

Chad hastened a glance at Rick. Rick stared at him without emotion. His long hair was tied back in a ponytail and about a month's growth of beard covered his face. Crow's feet were permanently etched around his eyes. He looked like a cold-blooded killer. He must have been a mean mother back in his 'Nam days.

"Uh, well, we both are college students at Vanderbilt. Or we were. When everyone got sick, we went to his parents' house. They were vacationing in Aruba at the time." He looked at Rick cautiously. "Frodo's parents are very rich. Or, they were. I guess they're dead now."

He glanced down, lost in thought. Rick poked him again. "Oh, yeah. Well, we just holed up in his parents' house until the food ran out. We broke into a couple of the neighbor's houses, ran into some zombies. You know."

"Have you run into anybody else that wasn't infected?" The question seemed to make him nervous. It seemed odd, but then it dawned on me. "You two fuckers have been killing people, haven't you?" I phrased it as a question, but I already knew the answer. Rick poked him in the chest hard. "Answer me," I demanded.

He started sobbing now, but it did not seem real, contrived more likely. "I didn't want to. We came across an older couple yesterday. They wouldn't share their food with us, so Frodo shot them. I tried to tell him not to do it, but he did it anyway."

"And you cried for them the whole time you ate their food, I bet. Did you give them a Christian burial, or did you leave them lying where they fell?" Chad continued sobbing. He could not answer. He didn't need to. Rick and I knew the answer.

I could see the look on Rick's face. He was ready to execute Chad. Chad looked downright pitiful at that moment. His clothes were dirty, his face unshaven and oily. His hair was downright greasy from too many days without soap and water, and he was very skinny. We must have looked like aliens to him. We had showered and put on clean clothes this morning. I shaved off the little scruff of whiskers that I had, and even though Rick had a full beard, it was neatly trimmed. It was scraggly as hell until last night when I made a passing comment that he'd never get a woman looking the way he did. The next thing I know, he was in the bathroom with a lantern and some scissors, trimming away.

Rick looked over at me. I shrugged my shoulder as if to say, I don't give a shit if you kill him. Rick nodded and raised his rifle. At the moment he was about to pull the trigger, a couple of zombies came around the side of the building. When they spotted us, they started moaning in ecstasy and made a beeline toward us. The two of us shot quickly. Rick scored a direct hit between the eyes. My aim was off just a bit, my bullet grazed off of the cheekbone of my target. It continued a loping charge at me. I took aim and shot again. Bull's-eye. It dropped in a heap. Rick walked over to them, looked them over to make sure they were dead, and started laughing. He pointed.

"You just killed a cop!"

I looked at the zombie. His tattered rags were the remains of a police officer's uniform. His badge was gone, but he was still wearing a duty belt, although his gun was missing. I chuckled just a bit. Chad spoke up. "It's the noise. Those things are attracted to noise." He looked around. "There will be more of them coming soon, a lot more. We should get out of here."

I made a decision then. Killing in self-defense was one thing. Killing a zombie was about the same. Killing a man in cold blood was still murder. I was not at that point in my life. At least, I didn't think I was. I walked over to Chad's gun. It was a twenty-two caliber Ruger revolver. I unloaded the bullets and handed him the gun. I got a couple of cans of beans n' weenies and a can of peaches out of the truck, and handed them to him.

"Chad, my name is Zach, and my friend here is Rick. I want you to get in your car and drive off. If you ever come at us with a gun again, somebody is going to die. Got it?" I declared. He nodded quickly. "You should leave before Rick decides to kill you anyway."

Chad walked quickly toward his car. He paused momentarily as he walked by Frodo's body. He looked up at Rick as he got in his car, thinking that maybe we were just playing a game with him and Rick was going to shoot him anyway. Or maybe he was memorizing Rick's face for the future. In any event, Rick started caressing his rifle, which sent a message to Chad. The message was to get the fuck away from us. He got in the Beemer and hastily drove away.

I got a can of spray paint out of the truck and marked the liquor store with the standardized FEMA symbol, which was a big X, a date, any special information, and showed the building had been searched. I then spray painted something else on the wall.

ZOMBIE RULE #1: YOU HAVE TO GET THEM IN THE HEAD. I thought for a minute and then added RULE #2: THEY'RE ATTRACTED TO NOISE.

Rick looked at it and chuckled. He grabbed the can and added a big Z at the bottom. "Always sign your work," he grinned. "Okay, Zach, where to next?"

"Well, hell, let's get out of here before the zombies come. How about we head back to the Lowes Store?"

Rick's expression saddened suddenly. "No more liquor stores?"

We spent the rest of the day driving around looking for anything we could use, and generally just checking everything out. The city of Franklin was total mayhem. There were remnants of traffic accidents everywhere, which caused traffic jams, which caused abandoned vehicles. There was plenty of evidence of zombie attacks, and there were zombies aimlessly wandering everywhere. Our protected windows kept them from getting to us, although they tried. It was morbidly amazing. They would try to claw their way through the thick hardware cloth. The skin and nails of their fingers would be ripped and torn, but they seemed oblivious to any pain.

Rick would drive slowly checking each one out. Sometimes, he would drive over them, giggling gleefully when he heard the sound of a skull being squished, but he also used the opportunity to test fire a Kimber 45 caliber handgun he had taken off of Frodo. He would drive up to a Zombie and shoot them. Then he would exclaim, "Man, this is a sweet gun!"

After the fourth or fifth time he did that, I begged him to quit. Firing that large caliber handgun within the confines of the truck made it very loud. I managed to stick my fingers in my ears a few times before he shot, but they were still ringing.

"Did you see that last one I shot?" Rick asked. He had earlier found a bottle of Jack Daniels under a back seat of the fire truck and had eschewed the pure grain alcohol in favor of the sour mash whiskey. "If she weren't a Zombie, she would have been a good looking piece of tail."

I chuckled. "She was certainly admiring your beard." I checked my watch. It was a little after three. "We should head back. We want to give ourselves plenty of time to get home before dark, which reminds me, we need to find some night vision equipment for any low light work."

Rick belched and scratched his beard. I hoped he didn't have lice. "I already have night vision equipment. Give me something to eat."

I got one of his infamous lard biscuits out of the cooler and looked at him. "Why didn't you say so? What else are you holding out on?" Rick glanced over and chuckled mischievously while scarfing it down.

Rick was starting to get into his cups, so at my insistence, we swapped seating positions. About three miles into our journey back I started picking up glimpses of a vehicle following us in the rearview mirror.

"I have to make an admission." Rick had taken the jug of tea I had made and poured the contents of the pure grain alcohol into it. I tried it. It tasted awful and handed it back to him. He took a sloppy swallow and looked at me questioningly. "It would seem as though there are more survivors than I had previously estimated. In addition to Chad and the recently deceased Frodo." Rick frowned at me. "I mean, Francis. It seems as though we now have somebody else following us."

"No shit?" Rick exclaimed while looking back. "Well, I believe you're right. I wonder what they have in mind."

His brain activity was in slow motion now, due to drunkenness, but I learned never to underestimate the old man. He pointed at a boat on a trailer on the side of the road.

I looked at it incredulously. I could not help but think, why in the hell would someone be hauling their boat when they were fleeing for their lives? They must have apparently realized the absurdity of it at some point, and opted to park it on the side of the road. They had covered it with a tarp, as if they were going to come back for it later.

"Pull over about twenty feet in front of that boat," Rick said. "See if you got enough room to hide inside it with your rifle."

I parked and quickly ran back to the boat. I climbed up, checked for any sailor zombies, and climbed inside it shortly before our tail came into view. Rick got out and raised the hood of the truck. He hid the Kimber in his waist under his jacket and put his rifle under the truck. Now, it was just a matter of time.

They came into view within a few seconds. Rick gave me a running commentary while I lay hidden under the tarp.

"The dumb shits just drove up. They're about two hundred yards away. When they spotted the truck, they parked on the side of the road. I guess they think they're invisible or something. Well, we'll see who has the most patience. We can't let them follow us back to the farm, Zach," he stated. I agreed silently.

"Well, it didn't take long," Rick spoke quietly. I heard their car creeping along the asphalt. "Oh shit, Zach, there's a couple of women in the car. A man too. Along with a little kid. Damn."

I heard the car stop, probably close to Rick.

"Howdy," Rick said with an exaggerated slur in his speech. There was a muffled voice reply and then a car door opening. "Well, I'll be. I haven't seen any live people since I don't know when. Where the hell have you folks come from?" I slowly raised my head just enough to see through a gap between the tarp and the boat. An older man had exited the car, a dirty gray minivan. Chrysler I believe.

"Well, sir, we're from Fayetteville. Tennessee that is, not Fayetteville, North Carolina. We were told there is a FEMA camp in Nashville. It's supposed to be set up in the Titan's football stadium. Do you happen to know anything about it?"

I could see Rick scratching his beard. "A refugee camp, huh? That's the first I've heard of it, but like I said, I haven't seen any real people in quite a while. Have you people seen any zombies?" I could see the old man look back at the people still sitting in the car.

"We have, sir. They're everywhere. Fayetteville is full of them. We barely got out with our lives. We were making our way along I-65 when we saw you in your truck. We thought we'd take a chance." The old man looked around. "I could have sworn there were two of you."

Rick chuckled. "Might have been two of us. I tend to see people who may or may not be there when I get to drinkin'." Rick leaned toward him. I'm sure he did it so the old man could smell the liquor on his breath. "Say, do you guys have any fresh gas or food? I think I got some bad stuff in my truck. She's not running worth a shit."

The old man quickly shook his head. And I keep saying old man. He was actually close to Rick's age, maybe a couple of years older. He was about an inch shorter than I am, with dark black hair, but the roots were almost white. The moustache had the same color scheme. He had run out of that Grecian Formula 44 about a week ago, I'd guess. "I'm sorry, sir, we don't have much gas left and as you can see, I've got several mouths to feed."

Rick changed the subject quickly. He was no longer exaggerating with the slurring. "You have a military bearing to you. What unit were you in?"

The man dropped his jaw open momentarily, but recovered quickly. "The 2nd of the 502nd, Charlie Company. What about you?"

"2nd of the 75th, Bravo Company. I thought you had the look about you." Rick turned to me. "Zach! Come on out."

I heard most of the conversation. If he passed Rick's inspection, it was good enough for me, I supposed. I jumped out of the boat and walked up warily. I was holding my rifle casually, but kept it pointed in the direction of the occupants of the car.

The stranger held a hand up. "There's no need for that, son." He looked over at his family, who were still sitting in the car. "It's okay, come on out."

There were two women. One was in her late thirties, one girl was a teenager about my age, and there was a boy about ten-years-old. "This is my daughter and her two kids." His face clouded momentarily. "The rest of the family did not make it. This is what is left of the Frierson family. I'm Don."

He shook hands with Rick and me. "This is Janet, her daughter Julie, and her son Tommy."

They were a sorry looking lot. They looked, and smelled as if they'd been riding in their car for a few days without bathing. Rick and I introduced ourselves. Rick took a particularly long time shaking Janet's hand. I did a pretty good job of hiding my grin, until Rick looked at me and winked.

"Are y'all hungry? We've got some food with us," I said. They all nodded and I thought that they were actually going to start salivating at the mention of food. I retrieved the cooler out of the truck and set it on the road in front of them.

"We've got an assortment of snack foods and Rick made up a big batch of biscuits. We had to use powered milk, so they may taste a little funny. In all, not very high in nutrition, but it'll fill you up." There was a collective gasp when I opened the cooler and they gazed at the food in stark wonder. I guess they had not eaten much in a while. Don went around to the back of the minivan and came back with a case of twelve ounce cans of Coca Cola.

"I found these in an abandoned car this morning. I'm afraid we've had the heater going, so they may be a bit warm."

He grabbed one and popped it open. It spewed on him. Rick burst out laughing, which caused me to start laughing. Don looked at us, as did the rest of them. I don't think they had laughed or heard laughter in quite a while. But the laughter was contagious, and soon everyone was chuckling.

We sat in the middle of the road, eating and drinking, and asking questions of each other. "Rick, is Zach your son?"

Rick shook his head, and reluctantly offered his jug of laced tea to Don. Don took it, wiped the mouth of the jug and took a swig before handing it back.

"This here is the famous Zach, killer of zombies hither and yon." Rick looked wistfully off into the distance. Oh no, I've seen the look before. I always called it the 'here comes the bullshit' look.

"One day, I was minding my own business, when suddenly I was beset upon by a whole slew of zombies. Must have been at least fifty of them." He gave Janet and Julie a wide-eyed stare. "I tell ya', ladies, I was a goner for sure. Then Zach came along, armed with the same rifle he now has. He killed every one of them with extreme prejudice."

Rick looked at Julie, who was casting glances at me. I was feeling a little embarrassed at the sudden attention and wanted him to change the subject. "He saved my life. We've been partners ever since." He started to take another swig, but suddenly remembered that Janet, a real live female with an impressive rack, was sitting nearby. He offered her the jug. She hesitated a moment and then took it. She took a tentative swallow and handed it back to Rick with a quiet thank you. He beamed. Even I could see a shit eating grin through his thick beard.

Don chuckled. "No offense to you, Zach, but I find it hard to believe a teenage boy saved the life of an Airborne Ranger. Rick, we might have bumped into each other a time or two back in 'Nam. When were you there?"

Rick started to belch, but held it down. "Just a few months in the summer of '68. Caught some shrapnel in my leg. Messed it up pretty good, so they sent me home. If I had to do it over again, I'd of joined the Peace Corps."

"Was it a booby trap?" Don asked. Rick nodded once. Don looked thoughtful. "Those things killed a lot of good men," he said quietly. You could tell the two men had triggered some past memories.

I glanced over at Julie. I caught her staring at me and she quickly looked away. In spite of her dirty hair and face, she was quite pretty. She had deep chestnut brown hair with streaks of either highlights or dirt, and pretty blue eyes. She was a younger version of her mother, without the big breasts. I suspected the mother had a boob job, but Rick sure didn't mind. He could hardly keep his eyes off of them, even though she was wearing a jacket. I broke Don out of his reverie. "Mr. Fierson, can you tell us about Fayetteville and the trip up here?"

He looked up and then realized I was talking to him. "Oh, sure. When the flu outbreak first started, we, as in the city officials, had created refugee centers at the schools. It was working out fairly well at first. There were a few scuffles here and there, and it was pretty crowded, but overall, it wasn't too bad. But within a few days, things got ugly. The sick, and there were a lot of sick, started turning into these, these things."

"Zombies," Rick piped in.

"Yeah, whatever you want to call them. They started attacking people. The police were forced to start shooting, but it didn't seem to stop them."

"Zach's zombie rule number one: you got to go for the head," Rick said smugly, and took a big swig. I saw Julie looking at me again. So, yeah, I'm a teenager and have raging hormones. I haven't even been near a female since before Thanksgiving. Her attention, no matter how innocent it was, was having an effect. I hunched forward and crossed my arms in front of my lap, lest someone would spot the particular effect it was having.

"What's that?" Don asked of Rick. Rick smiled and pointed over to me. "Are there some kind of rules or something?" he asked me.

I hunched over a bit further. "Well, not really," I replied. "I'm kind of making them up as I go along. I've been trying to analyze them with the scant amount of information we've got. For instance, we don't know how it started, its genesis. From what we've seen on the news reports and the Internet before they went down, it started out as some type of flu bug. It quickly grew to pandemic proportions, apparently faster than any other flu outbreak in modern history." I looked around and continued.

"It appeared to have originated in the Middle East, maybe Egypt. Rick and I tracked it as it spread across Africa, Europe, Asia, and the Americas. It had no predictable pattern, which is probably due to the modern age of travel. You know, a person can hop on a plane and travel from Cairo to France to New York in twenty-four hours or less. If they're infected, they can spread it everywhere they go, and then of course, it spreads exponentially." I stopped a moment but everyone was giving me their undivided attention, so I continued.

"The virus and that seems to be what it is, seems to gestate quickly and mutates the host. It seems as though a deadly side effect of the infection is the host becomes very violent. They lose their higher reasoning and thinking processes. They can't figure out things like how to climb over a fence or maybe open a door, but their gross motor skills are probably enhanced. They feel no pain. It's possible their central nervous system is just gone, but at least parts of their brain still works. So, only if you go for the head will they truly die. Oh, we know for a fact they can hear and see, so they can probably smell as well. You might want to consider those facts in the future if you light a fire and cook outside. Or wear perfume." I had noticed the females were wearing perfume, which even though the body odor was still noticeable, smelled good nonetheless. "How long did you guys stay in Fayetteville before you decided to come north?"

The four of them continued to stare at me a moment. Don looked over at Rick. Rick winked. "He's a smart one. He would have been a doctor or rocket scientist one day."

Don chuckled and reached for the jug. Janet spoke up. "A group of us managed to secure the gym of the high school from the zombies. We had plenty of water, but the food quickly ran out. My husband and a few other men tried to go out and scavenge for food. We watched helplessly as they were attacked." She looked over at me. "They shot at them, but apparently nothing to the head. The zombies kept coming and…there were just too many of them." She stifled a sob, grabbed the jug, and took a long swallow.

"This stuff grows on you," she said.

"They were all eaten alive," Julie said quietly. Tommy began sobbing.

"Now hush, Julie. You know it still upsets him," Janet said. She grimaced as if she was holding back her own tears, but it seemed contrived.

I slowly nodded my head. "We read of similar stories on the Internet. I kind of thought it was BS, or imaginations run wild, but apparently it's true." I looked at them. "Did you see any of the zombies attack animals, like the family dog or cat, or did they only go for humans?"

"Oh, yeah, any living animal they could get their teeth on," Don replied.

"Did anyone become infected after the people were secured in the schools? I mean, you lock down the school with people who appear healthy, and one day someone turns. Did anything like that happen?"

Janet nodded. "A little girl about Tommy's age. She seemed as healthy as anyone did, but one evening she got sick. Then, she attacked her mother. It snowballed from there."

"Were you there?" I asked. She nodded again. "Tell me how it happened. What were the first symptoms?"

Janet shook her head. "The little girl's mother probably saw the first symptoms, but hid them from everyone else. The first time anyone noticed, the girl was sweating, incoherent, and her body was having spasms. It's hard to describe, but it wasn't really a seizure. They were odd muscle tics. Her skin became pale and splotchy. Oh, and she had a lot of phlegm. About an hour after we first became aware the girl was sick, she opened her eyes and latched onto her mother's neck. She had bitten a hunk out before anyone could act. It was horrible." Janet snatched the bottle out of Rick's grasp again and took another long swig. I'm fairly certain the grin on Rick's face indicated he was elated because he had a new drinking buddy with big tits. I could already tell he was planning on more trips into town to find liquor stores.

"What happened next?" I prodded. "How long was it before the mother turned?"

"It was less than an hour. She began having spasms and when a couple of women tried to comfort her, she went on a biting rampage. She was ultimately shot." She looked at me. "It was a head shot, but we still didn't know that was required at the time. He did it as an act of humanity. In any event, the damage was done."

It was a lot of information to digest. I desperately wanted to get back to the farm and review my notes. I checked my watch and confirmed the time with the sun setting. "Ms. Frierson," I paused. I did not know what her married name was.

"Call me Janet, please," she smiled at me coyly, which made me nervous.

"Janet, would y'all excuse Rick and me for a moment?"

Don nodded. "Of course, Zach." Janet looked questioningly at Don but said nothing.

Rick and I walked down the road several feet where our conversation would be private. "Well, what do you think, kid? It'd be nice to have some female company."

"You realize you're about the same age as her father. She most likely would not be the least bit interested."

"Hey, don't underestimate a woman who hasn't been laid in a while. All I can say is if they leave, the chances of me getting laid, *and* you getting laid for that matter, will be absolutely zero. I know enough about math to know that is a damned fact."

I rubbed my face. "You realize we're only thinking of our carnal desires?" I asked. He frowned at me. "We're thinking with the wrong heads," I explained. Enlightenment dawned on his face. "We're not thinking of the risks of bringing total strangers into our home. I'm suspicious, Rick. I mean, some of their story doesn't seem to make sense."

Rick looked over at Janet longingly and sighed. "Okay, kid, you're the brains of this partnership. What do you want to do?" he asked. We talked it over for a few minutes. After weighing most of the pros and cons, we reached a decision. We walked back to a bunch of expectant, hopeful expressions. They knew what we were discussing.

Rick spoke up. "Don, Janet, we'd like to make an invitation to you all. Zach and I were wondering if y'all would like to come back to our house, spend a couple of days getting some rest and food in your bellies. Our resources are limited of course, but you're invited.

Fair warning though, for the past couple of months it has been the two of us and three mangy dogs living in an old house. It's not the cleanest in the world. And it's not a luxury spa. We'll definitely expect help with chores. I want you all to know as well that if Zach or I spot any symptoms of this Zombie plague from any of you, our solution will be simple, headshots. So what do you say?"

Don stood and wiped his hands together. "Gentlemen, we'd be honored." He held out his hand and we both shook it. "And just so you know, I'm a true southerner. I'm a believer of the old saying, houseguests and fish both start to stink after a couple of days."

Janet interrupted when she ran up and kissed Rick on the cheek. Rick actually blushed. She then ran over to me and gave me a kiss on the cheek as well. Julie and Tommy were both grinning. It made me want to believe we were making the right decision.

"Okay, it's settled then, just follow us. We're about thirty minutes away. We'll get home and I'll get the generator going. Tonight, there'll be hot showers for everyone."

Janet and Julie gasped. It confirmed my suspicion that they had not bathed in a while. Don grinned broadly. "It sounds absolutely wonderful."

"Look!" Tommy pointed down the road. I looked in his direction. There were four zombies about two hundred yards away, ambling down the road. I wondered where they came from. Were they able to hear us from that far away, or had they been following the sound of the automobiles? It was food for thought.

This time, I got my ears plugged with my fingers before we started shooting. Rick insisted on having the honor. I think he wanted to show off a little bit. He retrieved his Winchester from under the truck, took aim, and made four headshots in under six seconds, excellent shooting with a bolt action rifle. Don looked at him in admiration, and maybe just a touch of concern.

Chapter 11 – Houseguests

Our house, in a manner of speaking, was a pig sty. I'm usually a clean person, but between Rick, the dogs, and me, the house was filthy. Cleanliness had not been much of a priority and was now proving to be an embarrassment.

The women did not seem to notice. They walked in the door and called first dibs for the bathroom. They spent a lot of time in there, which was to be expected I guess. Rick and I hurried around trying to tidy up. Don volunteered to cook dinner. Tommy played with the dogs while awaiting his turn. He'd really need a bath after rolling around with those mutts.

Two hours later, our guests were clean and we were seated at the dinner table. Rick had turned the generator off, so we ate by candlelight and a couple of Coleman lanterns. We had a good fire going which provided the house with ample heat. Julie and her mother had put on some simple sweatpants and tee shirts. They had also taken the time to comb out their wet hair. The effects of the soft candlelight made them both look like goddesses. My thoughts drifted to Macie. I wondered if she were even still alive. Maybe she was a zombie by now. Felix too. Were he and his parents still alive? I suddenly recalled our last conversation. His mother was sick, he had said. I forced myself to think of more pressing matters.

"Mr. Frierson?" I asked.

Don stopped with a fork full of green beans halfway to his mouth and glanced at Janet. "What's on your mind, Zach? And please, call me Don."

"Of course. Don, Rick and I never seem to have enough time to get everything done. One of our items on the list is to check all of the houses in the area. You know, check for survivors, search for food, those things. We've checked a few, but there are literally hundreds left to go. With your help, we could make some significant headway. Perhaps," I made a conscious effort not to look at Julie "you guys might find a home which will be suitable for you all to live in. That is, if the FEMA camp does not work out. We can help set it up and fortify it much like we've done here. I think I can speak for Rick, we'd love to have some good neighbors."

Don nodded thoughtfully. "I would love to take you up on the offer, Zach, and as hospitable as the two of you have been, I would like to ask for one additional favor." He looked at Rick. "Would it be possible to drive to Nashville in the morning to see if this camp actually exists? The reason I ask is that although you two have a pretty good set up, an operation such as a FEMA camp may be able to offer things the two of you cannot, such as health care. Perhaps they have even come up with a vaccine by now and we've not heard of it." He put his fork down and held his hands together. "If that is an inconvenience, I can check on it myself if one of you would be kind enough to draw me a map."

Rick started to speak, but suddenly remembered some long ago forgotten manners. He found his napkin and daintily dabbed at his mouth. "We're only twenty miles from downtown. Normally, it'd be a twenty or thirty minute drive, depending on traffic." He held his hands out. "Now, it could be an all-day affair. It just depends on any road blockages." Rick shrugged and chewed his food thoughtfully. "Yeah, we can do it. Zach has an ever expanding list of stuff we need, so maybe we can do some scrounging around while we're at it. What do you think, Zach? Good idea?"

I nodded. "It has potential, but it'll come with risks, of course. Mr. Frierson, Don, we've been monitoring the Ham radio and we've not gotten anything from Nashville. It's very possible the whole city has been overrun or everyone is dead." I looked at Rick. "Now is as good a time as any to recon Nashville. I'd be leery of going in any of the buildings though. Perhaps drive to the stadium just for a visual confirmation of any camp." I walked over to the desk where the radio and computer sat. I went through my stack of legal pads and retrieved one of them.

"What are all of those?" Julie asked. I think it was the first time she spoke since she got to the house.

"What? Oh, these are my notepads. I have a bit of an obsessive compulsive personality. I write everything down."

Rick laughed. "I have no idea why he does it. He practically has a photographic memory."

There were a few chuckles, and even Julie smiled.

I smiled as well and flipped through my notes. "We definitely need more fuel. That's a number one priority, Rick. Our generator consumes about a half-gallon an hour when it is under a full load. This evening alone, we've used three times more than we normally would in a twenty-four hour period. At this rate, we'll run out within a month. We'll put all of our five gallon cans in the truck and a hand crank. And then there are all the other secondary items. But don't worry, I have a list," I said in mock seriousness. It brought some more laughter. Everybody seemed relaxed, which was a good thing.

The sleeping arrangement went like this: Janet had Rick's bed, Julie and Tommy used my bed, and the rest of us were in the den. Rick had his chair, which was fine with him. He had passed out in it on more than one occasion. Don was on the couch and yours truly on the floor. It was a shame we only had two beds in the house, and they were small. I tossed and turned for most of the night. Curly must have heard me. He came in and lay down beside me. He was my favorite, even though he was genuinely stupid. I eventually dozed off but awoke well before sunrise. I held off on starting the generator, because it would have awakened everyone in the house. I got my canteen of water and quietly stepped outside to brush my teeth. Curly joined me and jaunted off into the yard to do his business.

It was getting colder. There was also a heavy feeling of moisture in the air that gently told you a big snowfall was imminent. I pulled my coat closer and sat in one of the rocking chairs we had on the porch. Waking up before sunrise was quickly becoming my second nature, but I liked to get up early in the morning, and think about what needed to be done in order to survive another day. I was in the middle of mentally calculating how much food was going to be consumed by four extra hungry people when I heard the door open. It was Janet. She had put a pair of my boots on, which were too big for her, and she was wrapped in some blankets. I had no idea if she was wearing anything underneath.

She sat down in the rocker next to me. "You've got big feet," she said. I smiled and shrugged. "Are you always an early riser, or could you not sleep either?"

"Both. But sleeping on the hardwood floor is seldom conducive to a good night's sleep."

She nodded. "Entirely our fault. We'll have to do something about that. And by the way, I want to thank the two of you again for taking us in. We'd been in that damn car just a little too long and our food supplies were mostly gone. Oh, and the hot water! It felt so good. I'm afraid Julie and I may have ruined a couple of your razors," she said. I looked at her. She laughed. "We just had to shave our legs and armpits."

I nodded in sudden understanding. I had never discussed the feminine aspects of shaving with my grandmother or with Macie. Macie was clean shaven. I found out when I clumsily attempted cunnilingus on her. The night when I thought she was mine forever. I caught myself wondering if Julie and Janet shaved. My reverie was interrupted.

"Is it always this quiet out here?"

"What? Oh, yeah." I nodded and forced myself to stop thinking about the silky smoothness of a woman's freshly shaved legs, and well, you know. "Ever since the world went to hell, it has been. We used to have an owl living out here somewhere. He would give a few hoots every so often, but I think he's gone now. He was probably lonely."

"Maybe it was a she," Janet said.

I chuckled. "Hmm, maybe." The contours of the trees were becoming clearer as the sun rose. If you could just forget for a moment of the current state of the world, watching the sunrise was a wonderful moment.

"Are you lonely, Zach?" Janet asked.

I shrugged. "Yeah, some. Rick's a good man. He's been like a father to me. I don't know how I would have survived without him. And of course, there are the mutts, man's best friend and all that, but yeah, I miss my friends. I miss my grandmother."

"What about your parents?" She asked.

"They died when I was very young." I was about to add some more details, but decided against it.

"Oh." She was quiet for a few minutes. We watched as the darkness turned into a dull gray and pink. I could feel the bite in the air, there was definitely snow heading our way. "I'm lonely too. Sounds weird I know. I've got my kids and…and my father, but I'm still lonely." I understood, I think. I believe she may have been talking about male companionship. "Zach, I have a favor to ask you."

I cleared my throat. "Sure, if I can."

"I want to go into Nashville with Rick and my father. I want you to stay here and protect my kids, just in case," she said. I looked over at her. "My father, he's," she stopped and drew in a deep breath. "He's not been himself lately. Just yesterday, we were on the road and there were those creatures walking right down the middle of the road. Dad just stopped the car and froze. I don't want Rick freaking out if he does it again. Would it be too much to ask?"

"Oh no, of course not. You'll be in good hands with Rick. He can take care of business and he'll protect the both of you." I looked back at the window to see if anyone was listening. I lowered my voice and leaned closer to her. "Um, just try to keep him from drinking, at least until you start heading back. And, um, well, don't take this the wrong way, but keep in mind we've not seen any living women in a couple of months now."

Janet laughed derisively. "Don't worry, Zach, I've been around men like him my whole life. I know how to handle them. You know, you're cute. Julie thinks so too," she said and tousled my hair.

Chapter 12 - Righteous Rick

Rick was dreaming about Vietnam. They called him Righteous Rick back in those days. It was a testament to his character. He always told the truth, and he always took care of his men.

Righteous Rick, even the brothers called him that, and they did not care for most of their white brethren.

It was a mission, just like any other. The Company received orders to perform a reconnaissance mission of a Vietnamese village located near the firebase. Intel had information of VC activity in the area. The Company commander, a captain who drank too much and thought too little, ordered a solitary squad to conduct the mission while the rest of the company was held back in reserve. Rick always thought the term was strange. Reserve was supposed to mean they would all come running to help if you got in trouble, but it never worked. By the time they actually did come running, the shit was already too deep.

The platoon sergeant ordered the cherry, the new guy, to take point. It was a standard practice, although Rick also felt it was a terrible thing to do to someone who was fresh in-country. So, Righteous Rick would always give the cherry his pep talk before going on a mission.

"I'll be right behind you. If you hear me make the old 'psst' noise, you freeze. Do not take another fucking step. I will come up to you and tell you what to do next. This will keep you alive, hoss, trust me. Now, if you hear me yell, it means no more noise discipline because the shit has hit the fan. Do whatever I'm yelling at you to do, and do it quickly. Got it?" he'd ask. Every one of them always gave a nervous nod. "Good."

In the dream, they were slowly making their way along an old but well used trail. He spotted a scrap of rag tied to an overhanging limb. The point man was about to walk right under it. There was a booby trap in the ground under that rag. Rick knew it. It was a common signal for the locals. "Psst!" The point man, a cherry who had been in-country for only two days, stopped and looked at

Righteous Rick. Rick held his hand up and slowly started approaching. There. He saw it. A trip wire. Rick pointed at it as he walked up. Then something really, really odd happened. The new guy, whose name Rick could never remember, smiled at him, turned, and started walking forward again.

Boom! Rick felt the pain at the very exact moment that he heard the explosion. Cherry took the brunt of the blast, but Rick caught several pieces of shrapnel in his leg. It hurt. Man did it hurt.

Rick woke suddenly with sharp pains shooting up his leg. He threw the blanket off - how did that get there - and rubbed his leg. As his senses became clear, he heard low voices coming from outside.

"Rick's a good man. He's been like a father to me," he heard Zach saying. He peered around the blackout curtains and stealthily looked out of the window. Zach was talking to someone. It was Janet. Bless that boy, Rick thought. He's talking me up and making me look good for her. Righteous! Rick listened for another moment before his bladder begged in protest, demanding a visit to the bathroom.

He stood over the toilet trying in vain to press down and increase the flow of his urine stream. Damn prostate was too enlarged to have a full flow anymore. He used the opportunity to clear his head and apply some thinking. How nice it would be if Janet took a liking to him. Under normal circumstance, he'd be much too old of course. But normal circumstances went to hell not too long ago, and he did not see them coming back anytime soon.

He finished up, tried the faucet and saw there was just enough pressure left to rinse his face and wet down his hair enough so he could brush it out a little bit. He'd take a shower when they got back from Nashville. He knew Zach worried like an old woman about their fuel allotment for the generator. He would make an extra effort to find fuel so he would not complain. He finished up by rubbing some deodorant under his armpits and shuffled into the den to start the day. He was about to walk out when he saw his dentures soaking in a glass by the sink. He vaguely remembered dropping them on the floor next to the chair before he went to sleep. Zach must have been looking out for him-again. He rinsed them off and stuck them in his mouth.

Zach told Rick about Janet wanting to ride with him and that he would stay behind. Rick smiled in agreement. He opted to drive his truck rather than the old farm truck. He wanted to impress Janet. They had rigged it up in much the same fashion and the extended cab allowed more than two people to ride. They were all armed. Rick assumed Don knew how to shoot and Janet confirmed she did as well. Don's weapon of choice was a twelve-gauge pump action shotgun loaded with double-ought buckshot. Rick loved his Winchester, but opted for Zach's Colt AR-15 with his Kimber for back up. Janet had a handgun. They ate a quick breakfast.

Zach stood beside Rick beside the truck. "Have you checked their weapons?" He asked.

Rick nodded. "Yep, did you check out the truck?"

"I certainly did. You have just over a half of a tank, which gives you a range of 150 miles. I didn't fill it up all the way because now you have a place to put twenty more gallons if you run across any fuel."

"I see, good thinking," Rick looked at his watch. "Coming up on seven o'clock. We should be going. My plan is to stay on the back roads. You know how we go to Nashville when the Interstate is jammed?" he asked. I nodded. "That'll be my route. The plan is to be home before sundown."

I nodded again. "Sounds good. If you're not back in twenty-four hours, I'll come looking for you."

Rick nodded and looked at me. We'd been together 24/7 for a month now. It was an awkward feeling knowing we were going to be apart for the better part of the day.

*****

Rick stopped on a bridge that crossed over I-65, and scanned along the ribbon of roadway with his binoculars. "How bad is it, Rick?" Janet asked. He handed the binoculars to her. "It's pretty congested. We could get through it, but it would be slow going." He pointed toward the Interstate. "There are a lot of choke points. If there are thugs out there, it'd be easy to set up an ambush at any one of them."

Don had used the binoculars and nodded. "We'll stick to the back roads. Once we get to Franklin Pike, it'll go straight into downtown Nashville. We'll be able to see the stadium before committing ourselves to crossing the Cumberland River. If there is a FEMA camp set up, we should be able to see it."

It sounded simple enough. And it would have been, if not for the zombies.

They got as far as Broadway and 8th Avenue, about where the Federal courthouse is/was located. As Rick approached the intersection, Don gasped and Rick let out a concerned, "Oh shit."

"What?" Janet was in the back seat and at Rick's direction, had been spending most of her time gazing out of the back window. She turned and looked out the front. "Oh shit!"

Rick was both amazed and frightened. "There must be thousands of them!" he shouted. They were a variety of age, race, and gender, and they seemed to come out of nowhere. They must have been very hungry. The leading edge of the horde swarmed the truck. Rick punched the gas, running over several. One got hung up under the truck, but Rick did not slow down. He accelerated and turned down a side street.

"Rick!" Don yelled. "There are cars blocking the street!"

Rick slowed only a bit, hopped a sidewalk, and performed a high speed U-turn that would have made any stunt driver proud. He hopped another curb and raced diagonally through a parking lot, which was surprisingly empty of cars due to the entrances being blocked off by chain and padlock. Rick grunted, and bypassed the chained entrances by jumping the curb on the far side of the parking lot. He narrowly avoided wrecking into several abandoned cars and eventually made it back onto Eighth Avenue. Rick put distance between them and the horde.

"Holy shit, that was close!" Rick shouted. "There is no way we could have killed all of those motherfuckers before they ripped us apart."

He glanced over at Don and Janet as he drove. They nodded in agreement.

"Nice driving, big guy," Janet said. She leaned forward and tousled Rick's hair, much like she did with Zach earlier in the morning. Rick stole a couple of additional glances at his passengers. Both had broken out in a nervous sweat, which was understandable. Janet was fine, just working off the jitters. Don though, was a deathly shade of pale and staring straight ahead. Rick looked back at Janet and inclined his head toward Don. Janet's smile faltered.

"Don, are you okay?" She asked.

Don did not answer immediately. In fact, Janet finally had to shake his shoulder to bring him back to reality. He slowly looked over at Rick. "There is no FEMA camp, is there, Rick?"

Rick slowly shook his head. "If there was, it's long gone now. We can ask Zach, but I'm thinking the reason there were so many zombies packed together is because the camp people became infected. I think the Titan's stadium can hold something like 70,000 people. If there were a FEMA camp set up there and they all got infected…" Rick left the sentence unfinished. He hoped he sounded as smart as Zach did.

Don looked defeated. "What do we do now, Rick? We left our home. We thought we were going someplace safe. Now we have nothing."

Rick slowed down to a tolerable speed and glanced over at Don. "It's not a problem, Don. You got your family out alive. That's the most important thing. Zach and I can get you guys set up in a new home. Hell, our nearest neighbors, the Riggins, their house is empty. It's a pretty nice one too. Five bedrooms, three full baths. I know for a fact they have clean well water. We can set up a generator to power the place. I helped Henry install two wood stoves, so Zach and I can help y'all with the wood for the winter," as he spoke, he looked on his windshield. The snowflakes were much thicker now.

Rick took a few slow, deep breaths to calm his nerves, stopped the truck, and made a full circular scan. Seeing no zombies, he took the opportunity to get out and check the undercarriage. The carcass of the zombie was lodged in the wheel well. Fortunately, most of the body had been ground down from being drug along the asphalt. Rick had Don turn the wheel in one direction and he was able to work the upper half of the Torso loose. As he pulled it out, the zombie's head turned toward Rick and attempted to bite him. Rick quickly dropped the torso and kicked it away from him.

"Holy shit, did you guys see that? The fucking thing is still alive! There's nothing left from the waist down, but it's still alive!" fucking amazing, Rick thought. He got back in the truck and locked the door.

"Alright, you two, downtown Nashville is definitely a no-go. The snow is getting heavier and will probably drop a couple of inches before the day is over. We need to start heading back, but there's no reason why we can't make this work for us."

"What do you have in mind, Rick?" Janet asked worriedly.

"We scrounge around to try to find stuff. We've been on the road two hours now and have nothing to show for it. Let's at least attempt to round up some supplies," he said.

Janet looked at Don and nodded. Don still looked pale, but he did not argue. Rick tried to recall everything on Zach's list. The boy could sure write a lot of lists. He tried to get Rick to take it with him, but he refused out of nothing more than pure stubbornness. The easy items to remember were gas and food, but there were a lot of other things the two of them thought up and dutifully listed. He scratched his beard as he drove and looked around. He stopped in the middle of the Wedgewood intersection. There were two convenience stores on opposite corners. The windows were broken out and they had obviously been looted. Rick used the binoculars to confirm the shelves were bare. He drove slowly south down Eighth Avenue and made their way into the community called Melrose. There were some fast food restaurants they checked out, but the freezers contained only spoiled, foul smelling food.

"We're not having much luck today," Janet said.

Rick started to agree, but then he stopped suddenly. Don and Janet looked at him questioningly. "There," he pointed to a full service gas station on the corner a block away. It was old and poorly maintained, but it appeared to be still functional and up until recently had still been in business.

Rick and Zach had agreed one of the many items they had a need for were tools. They had quite a few back at the farm, but as any real man knew, one can never have enough tools. He scanned the area with his binoculars once more. Satisfied there were no major threats, he put the truck in drive and headed toward the building. Rick circled the building and then parked among some abandoned cars.

"Okay, let's keep it simple. We'll clear the building and then you two stand guard while I go to work. Who knows what kind of goodies may be in the service bays. And, we must be quiet. Zach and I saw firsthand that these things are attracted to sound, and to a lesser degree, movement. If you guys spot any, don't yell or do a lot of frantic moving around. Whisper just loud enough to get my attention. Got it?" he got a nod out of Janet, Don was still silent. Rick stifled a sigh. He hoped they did not do something stupid and get them killed.

The three of them exited the truck and shut the doors quietly. Rick left his rifle in the truck, opting to keep his hands free and using his Kimber, but only if he had to. He got a pry bar and went to the front door, which was a standard glass with a steel frame. He tapped on the glass softly. "What are you doing?" Janet whispered.

"Remember what I said? They're attracted to sound. If there are any of them in there, they'll come see what the noise is. If there is anyone living in there and if they are halfway smart, they'll know zombies don't knock on the door before breaking in."

Janet looked at the door, looked at Rick and smiled. She grabbed the handle and pulled the door open. Unlocked.

Rick stroked his beard gruffly. "Smartass," he whispered. They cleared the building slowly and clumsily. Several times, he caught Janet waving her gun back and forth and cringed inwardly. He was somewhat worried she would accidentally fire off a round and he would get hit. They did not work very well as a team. Rick missed Zach already. The two of them had practiced over and over the fine art of both surreptitious and dynamic room clearing. Zach was a natural. Janet and Don were clumsy oafs.

Once Rick was satisfied that the building was clear, he quickstepped over to the service bay. He looked at the two and grinned. "God may be smiling upon us. Look," he pointed at a utility truck. It was a Chevy Silverado 2500. It had the utility package with tool boxes mounted on the sides. The ensemble was completed with a welder and a generator strapped down in the bed. The keys were still in it. "Let's hope the mechanic finished working on it."

Don wasted no time. He went over to a mechanics tool chest, a large Snap-On brand. "Lots of good tools in here. We should take these."

Rick agreed with a nod.

They spent the next forty-five minutes unloading the chest, and then manhandling it onto the back of the truck before reloading it. Rick went outside and got the hand pump out of the truck. Janet saw what he was doing and began unloading their five gallon gas cans. Good, he thought. She's finally starting to understand what needs to be done. He decided there was hope for her yet. He caught himself staring at her breasts longingly. So did Janet.

"You want to get your mind back on the task at hand?" She said without warmth. Rick snorted and started pumping gas out of the underground storage tank. It took almost an hour, but they eventually got everything they could. He even filled up both trucks, which he almost forgot about.

Rick stretched and looked at the sky. The snow was coming down very hard now, limiting how far he could see to just a few yards. It's going to drop three inches or maybe more, Rick thought. It was getting colder as well. Time to go.

"This is a decent haul. Let's call it and get out of here. I sure hope that truck starts. Alright, here's how this is going to work. Don, get in that work truck and start it. Janet man the service bay door. Once the truck starts, get the door up and open as quickly as you can. Every garage door I've ever fooled with makes a lot of noise, so don't worry trying to be quiet, just get it open. I'm going to be in my truck. If that work truck doesn't start, we'll grab as many of the tools that we can and then get out of here. I don't like staying in one place for too long and I think we've been here a bit too long already. If at any time zombies start showing up, we're going to stop whatever it is we're doing and haul ass. Don't worry about leaving anything behind, we've gotten ourselves a decent supply of gas and we can always come back later."

They nodded at Rick. He hoped it would work out.

It did. Well, sort of.

The work truck started right up. Janet got the service bay door open about three feet and then it stuck. Rick hopped out of the truck and ran over. He grabbed the bottom of the door and began trying to lift it like a weightlifter. It did not budge more than a couple of inches.

He stopped and inspected closer. "Ah, dang it. There's a chain looped through some holes here. It's padlocked."

Janet watched as Rick ran back to the truck and retrieved some bolt cutters as quickly as his bad leg would allow him. As he trotted back to the door, he saw them. About a dozen zombies had apparently heard the racket and were shambling toward them from a burned out building down the street. Rick slid the bolt cutters under the door and drew his Kimber. He began carefully aiming and shooting, taking down one after another.

"I can't cut it! I don't have the strength," Janet gasped.

Rick hastened a quick look under the door. Don was still sitting in the truck looking at them through the mirror.

"Don, dang it, give her a hand!" Don refused to move. "Motherfucker." Rick growled under his breath. He shot until he was out of ammo. He reloaded as he ran back to his truck. He could shoot quicker with the AR-15. More zombies appeared, at least ten more. Rick shot them all and then crawled under the partially open door. Janet was desperately trying to cut through the padlock. Rick joined in and with a mighty unified squeeze on the handles of the bolt cutter, they snapped the chain in half. Janet pulled the chain out and finished lifting the door. As soon as she did so, Don put the newly acquired truck into reverse and floored the gas. He sideswiped Rick's truck in the process. Rick looked at him like he had lost his mind.

"Get in the truck!" he yelled. Janet did not hesitate. She got in the driver's side while Rick started shooting again. He saw Janet put the truck in drive. He was suddenly alarmed. Was she going to leave him? His leg was sending electric bolts of pain up his hip and back, but he ran as fast as he could and jumped in the bed of the truck just as she sped off. Zombies were mere inches from him as she maneuvered back to Franklin Pike.

Chapter 13 - Houseguests and Fish

Zach had watched the three of them leave with no small amount of trepidation. He had full confidence in Rick, but he was still worried. In the meantime, there was work to be done. He stoked the fire and hung an old but sturdy cast iron tea kettle on a hook over the flames. Julie sat on the couch and watched.

"What's that for?" she asked.

"I'm heating up some water to wash the dishes," I said. I kind of hoped she would volunteer to help out. I was mistaken.

"What is there to do around here?" She asked.

I chuckled. "Chores. Lots of chores."

"Fuck that," Julie replied.

"I wish they were that easy to blow off," I replied. "Chores can mean the difference between survival and starving."

Julie laughed derisively. "Yeah, right."

I was getting irritated. Where had she been the last month, on Mars? I tried to put on a patient smile. "I guess you may be right. Let me ask you something. What did we have for dinner last night?"

Julie rolled her eyes and refused to answer.

"I'll help you out. Fried chicken, mashed potatoes, green beans, and biscuits. Did you think all of that food magically appeared, or perhaps I ran down to the local grocery store? Rick killed the chicken yesterday and spent a couple of hours preparing it for dinner. The green beans came from our garden. The biscuits, well, you should get the idea by now, unless you're just plain stupid."

I got a sullen, angry glare in response.

"I don't know if you have just repressed the memories of the past few weeks, but when Rick and I met you guys, you were a pitiful looking bunch; hungry and dirty. You certainly didn't turn that meal down, now did you."

Julie tried to maintain her angry sneer at me, but could not accomplish the feat. She stared at the fire instead and crossed her arms.

"One would think, after nearly starving and going without a hot bath for as long as you did, you'd be more appreciative. Anyway, I'm through with the sermon. I've got a lot of work to do. I could use your help if you would be willing to give it."

Julie glared at me. "You're not my dad and I'm not your slave. You're acting like you're all badass and better than me. You're not. In case you've forgotten, we're the same age, so quit thinking you're so special. And besides, all of this shit going on right now is just temporary."

I shrugged my shoulders "Hey, you may be right. For all we know, the government may be getting everything up and running, and it will be back to normal in no time. In the meantime, we've got to help ourselves, and the time is long over to be acting like a petulant brat. Are you going to help out or not?"

The only response I got was a dramatic display of her middle finger.

"I'll help! What are we going to do, Zach?" Tommy had come in during our little conversation and had been listening quietly.

"I'll be glad to have you help me, Tommy. We've got to feed the chickens and the cows. And then we need to check the farm for any new calves."

"Neat! Can we ride on the ATV?"

"Sure. I'll even teach you to drive," I said.

We got our jackets and made a hasty exit. What is it with girls? I did not get it. Did she think that she was so special that she could just hang out, doing absolutely nothing, and we'd wait on her hand and foot? Bullshit, absolute bullshit.

"C'mon, Tommy. Let's get the chickens fed," I said. The snow was just starting, just a light dusting at first, but I had no doubt it was going to get thicker as the day wore on. I wanted to get as much done as possible while still able.

Tommy was more of a burden than a help, but even so, I fed the chickens, gathered some eggs, and checked the hay. There was still plenty lying out in the pasture. I got Tommy on the ATV and we made a slow trek around the farm.

"What are we doing now, Zach?" Tommy asked.

"We're checking on the cattle. We have a few cows that are pregnant. You see, Tommy, when the barometric pressure drops, it can cause a pregnant cow to give birth. We need to find all of the newborn calves and get them into the barn."

"Why?"

"So they won't freeze to death. It's going to get a lot colder in the next few days I'm thinking."

"Oh," he replied plainly. I chuckled. The whole explanation was probably entirely over his head, but it was nice to have a pleasant conversation without getting a shitty look or flipped off.

We found three newborn calves in total. When we found one, I'd pick it up, and carry it on the ATV while Tommy slowly drove back to the barn. The mother cow usually followed. We did this each time and it was very time consuming. After a couple of quick lessons, I had Tommy driving while I held onto the calves, lest they fall off and injure themselves. We toured the rest of the farm, presumably to let Tommy enjoy himself, but I really wanted to make sure there were no zombies lurking around. We then drove to the Riggins house. I should have thought of it earlier. Freezing weather was going to wreak havoc on all of the plumbing unless something was done. First, we carefully drove around the house to make sure there were not any new occupants. Satisfied, Tommy and I went inside. It was a beautiful home. It was all brick, built solidly, and had a large basement. Mr. Riggins had converted into an awesome man cave with two large, flat panel televisions, surround sound, a pool table, and a poker table. He also had a wet bar and a big Jacuzzi. All of which were now basically worthless, but it was nice nonetheless.

"What are we doing now, Zach?" Tommy asked.

"We're going to make sure the pipes don't freeze," I was hopeful we were not too late. The temperature had been in the thirties and forties for the past couple of weeks. If I was too late, most of the pipes would have split as a result of freezing. We would have to fix the plumbing before anyone could live here. Tommy and I went to each faucet and turned them on. Although there was no longer any water pressure to speak of, water seeped out of each tap. The pressure tank for the well was located in the garage, as was the hot water heater. Both were equipped with a drain valve. I hooked up a garden hose to each drain so all of the water would drain outside instead of onto the garage floor.

As a final measure, I located a gallon jug of antifreeze and poured a little bit into all of the drains so they would not freeze. The house was spotlessly clean. It had five bedrooms with a gas fireplace in each, which reminded me. I went outside and turned off the gas main. I had no idea if there was still pressure in the lines, but I did not want this nice house going up in flames. I wanted to either move into it myself one day, or get a good family to occupy it and start working the farm. Rick and I had talked it out and were convinced it would be very beneficial for two or more families working the farmland as a collective community.

I thought of the possibility of the Friersons moving in this house, and I caught myself specifically thinking of Julie. Damn, she could be a bitch! In spite of her attitude, I found myself thinking of the two of us being together. She was really nice looking. Unlike Macie with her blonde hair and curves, Julie was slender, lanky, more of a tomboy, but still feminine. I sighed. Who was I fooling? I was lonely, and loneliness created fantasy. I knew she and I would never be a romantic couple.

We got back a little after three. I still had enough time to clean the kitchen and get dinner going. I was hoping maybe Julie would have gotten off of her ass and had done something, but I doubted it. Tommy and I parked the ATV in the barn. I turned the ATV off, secured it, and it was then I heard a motorized sound. As I exited the barn, I realized what it was. The generator was running!

I ran inside. I hopefully expected Julie to be running the vacuum cleaner or something, anything productive. Please let it be anything that would rationalize the burning of precious fuel.

I was wrong. She had the TV on and was playing on the Xbox. She ignored me as Tommy and I stepped inside. Fair enough. I walked back outside and over to the generator. Once it was off, I went into the barn. The firemen's turnout gear was stinking with putrescence. I made a mental note to hang the fireproof jackets and pants on the fence outside to air them out. They would need a good scrubbing eventually. I grabbed one of the axes.

As soon as I got inside, I was verbally assailed. "Why did you turn the generator off, asshole?

I did not bother answering. If she thought I was an asshole, I wondered what she was going to think in a few seconds. I buried the axe into the Xbox and then looked at her awaiting a response. She busted out laughing. "Who's stupid now? You just ruined your own Xbox."

"Very astute of you to notice, Julie. In fact, everything in this house belongs to either Rick or me. The food you've eaten, the gas you wasted, even the toilet you pissed in. Absolutely none of it belongs to you, none of it belongs to your mother, brother or your grandfather. I hope you enjoyed it."

Her laughing stopped. She crossed her arms in defiance. "What's that supposed to mean?"

"It means, just as soon as they get back, you're out. All of you."

I had not even gotten my mouth closed when I heard the sound of an approaching automobile. "Ah, perfect timing," I said with a glare directed at her. Julie's eyes burned into the back of my head as I walked outside and watched them approach. There were two trucks driving up. Don was driving the second one. Both trucks had fresh body damage, and Rick's truck had dried black stuff all along the driver's side. Blood? That was interesting. I'd ask Rick about it after he heard me out.

Rick jumped out before he had it in park. Uh-oh, I could tell he was mad about something. He pointed at me and then jabbed his finger at the barn. Without waiting for an acknowledgement, he started brusquely limping toward it. Janet started to follow, but Rick stopped momentarily and stared her down. She thought better of it and walked toward the house. The dogs ran to Rick and followed him.

"He's a little upset. Try to calm him down," she said in a low voice as she walked by me. Try to calm him down? I was ready to throttle that spoiled little brat of a daughter she had. Maybe someone should try to calm me down.

He started as soon as I walked through the doorway. "I tell you, Zach, I don't like it. I don't like it at all," he said as he punched the side of the barn with enough force I thought he might have broken his hand.

He was not just a little upset. Rick Sanders was pissed. Pissed, as in, he could have chewed up broken glass and shit it out without a second thought. I did not have to ask why, because he started right in.

"The son of a bitch froze up!" he pointed with his thumb toward the driveway. "We had found that damn truck. It runs good. And, it has a generator and a welder on it. It was parked in the garage of a full service gas station. I tell you, Zach, it was a sweet find. We got a shit load of tools and got all the gas cans filled up. We were about to get the truck out of the garage and head back home, but the garage door was chained. There was Janet trying in vain to use the bolt cutters on it, and here comes the zombies." He pointed with his thumb again. "I'm in my truck. Janet needs help getting the chain cut, and he wouldn't even get out of the truck to help!"

"You saw zombies? Were there a lot?" I asked.

Rick's eyes widened and he started gesticulating with his hands, which he did whenever he got excited. "Oh, hell yeah." He slapped his forehead. "I'll start from the beginning. Downtown Nashville is covered up with them, Zach. We drove right into a massive horde. There must have been thousands of them. We just got away by the hair off my ass. We can't go into downtown anytime soon, not without an army and some air support. Oh, by the way. One of those things got caught up under the truck when we were escaping. I drove two or three miles with it stuck under there. The entire lower part of the torso had been torn off, but when I pulled the upper half out of the wheel well, the son of a bitch was still alive! It came damn close to biting the shit out of me!"

Rick paused to scratch his presumably hairy ass. Larry ran over and sniffed. Rick was not amused and swatted him on the snout. "Anyway, there is no dang FEMA camp. At least, not anymore. It was all bullshit. So here's the real kicker, we're heading back and we're in the Melrose area. I don't see anyone or anything around, so I tell them we need at least to do a little scavenging while we had the chance. We find this garage right there on 8th just a couple of blocks from Wedgewood. But sure enough, we make all kinds of racket trying to get the dang door open and here they come. I shot a few, helped Janet bust the lock, and shot a few more so she could escape. You know what she did? She jumped in the driver's seat of my truck. My damn truck!" Spittle flew as he yelled.

I looked around to see if anyone had walked in the barn. Rick noted my concern, took a deep breath and lowered his voice. "Zach, I think she was going to drive off without me!"

Oh, man. Warning alarms were sounding in my head. I had him repeat the details. He told me about having to jump in the back as she was driving off. He was not suspicious at the time. He thought they would stop once they got to a spot without zombies, he'd jump into the cab of the truck, and off they would go. When it did not happen, he actually had to threaten to shoot her. "Zach, I would have too. I don't care if she was the last woman on the planet. I would have shot the bitch dead if she hadn't stopped right then and there."

"What did you do then?" I asked.

"I was going to make her get in the truck with Don, but he parked about a hundred yards down the road and refused to drive back to us. So I gave in and made her move over to the passenger side, but not before I took her gun away from her."

"Did she say anything, you know, try to rationalize her actions?" I asked.

He snorted. "She just said shit like, close call and, you really saved our bacon. You know, disingenuous shit like that," he snorted again, which Larry decided was a cue for him to snort at well.

I was amazed, amazed he knew what disingenuous meant. Rick looked forlorn at Larry. He must have felt bad about swatting him, so he bent down and scratched him behind the ear. Larry returned the favor by licking his hand.

"She never mentioned the fact I had to point my gun at her. You know, like, if I don't mention it, it never happened. Goddamn it all, Zach, this is fucked up." Rick was not a deeply religious man, but he never used the Lord's name in vain unless he was really agitated.

I waited a minute for him to calm down a bit. Then, I inhaled and filled him in on Julie's antics. He worked his leg while I talked. I could see it was hurting. The pain and his current disposition meant the whiskey was going to flow tonight. When I finished, he and Larry did a double snort. "Spoiled little brat," he said.

"Alright, I think we agree. This group has got to go," I said.

He nodded his head vigorously. "You got that right. There ain't no woman this side of hell worth this kind of shit."

Rick looked out of the open barn door. He smacked his forehead and gasped. "They got guns inside. You don't think..."

I did think. From the barn door, we could see the kitchen window. There was light coming out. Someone had lit one or more of the lanterns. Good. They were not savvy to tactics. If they left the interior of the house dark, they would have a good tactical advantage over anyone walking through the door.

I watched the windows while we devised a plan. I walked inside a few minutes later. My feet left tracks in the snow. It was coming down hard now and the dirty gray sky was quickly turning dark. The interior of the house became brighter. Someone had just lit another lantern. Outside it was dark. They would not be able to see Rick and what he was doing. I repressed a smug grin.

They were all sitting on the couch waiting. Don had his shotgun sitting across his lap with his hand near the trigger and pointed toward the door as I walked in. I left the door open behind me. He stared at me flatly. "I suspected you would be armed when I walked inside, Don," I commented. Don's eyes shifted nervously. It just confirmed Rick's suspicions.

"Where's Rick?" Janet asked. There was a hard edge to her voice. No more friendliness, no flirtatious smile. I glanced at Julie. She seemed very nervous. They were planning something alright.

I sidestepped away from the open door. "He's outside with a rifle pointed at you. You've seen how good of a shot he is. I wouldn't make any sudden moves if I were you. Oh, and you have about five seconds left to toss the shotgun on the floor at my feet."

Don looked out the door in sudden alarm. Rick was crouched behind one of the trucks with the rifle leveled across the hood. Realization dawned on him. If he made a wrong move, he was a dead man. I could see it in his face. "Two seconds. He said he was going to shoot you first, Don, and then Janet, so you'd better do something quick."

Janet hurriedly reached out and swiped the shotgun onto the floor. I held up five fingers. "Don, ladies, I just gave Rick the signal for five more seconds. Place your hands on your knees and do not move," I ordered. They did not like it, but they complied. Julie kept looking at her mother with condemnation. Or maybe it was how she always looked at her mother, hell if I know.

I then motioned for Rick to come inside. He shut the door with his foot and kept his rifle ready to use. I had kept my handgun in my holster. I put my hand on it now. "Would all of you please slowly stand up?" I asked. Nobody moved. Little Tommy was looking to his mother for direction.

"Get up!" Rick growled. They quickly stood in unison. Julie now looked like she was ready to piss on herself. There was a handgun hidden under her thigh. I walked over and grabbed it. "They were going to kill us, Zach. They were going to kill us and take everything we worked so hard for." Rick's tone was murderous.

I agreed. "Sure looks that way."

Don was pale. Janet pleaded. "No, you got it wrong! We thought that you were going to kill us!"

Rick started to raise his rifle. I held up a hand and stopped him. "Let me see if Rick and I understand your logic correctly, Janet. We find the four of you, lost, dirty, and hungry. Instead of turning you all away, we show some true southern hospitality. We let you into our home. We fed you. We went out of our way to accommodate you bunch of ingrates. And you thought we were going to turn on you for no reason and kill you? Bullshit. You are a goddamn liar."

I looked at Julie. "Suddenly, your behavior makes a lot of sense. You're just like your mother." She tried to maintain eye contact with me, you know, one of those evil stare downs idiotic teenage girls liked to do, but she could not pull it off. She dropped her head and started silently crying. Tough shit. I had no sympathy.

I was mad. Rick was beyond mad. Nevertheless, we weren't cold blooded murderers. I looked at Rick. He looked at me and shrugged, as if to say, whatever you want to do with them is fine with me.

"Alright then. Don, go into the bedrooms and get your family's belongings. Bring it all in here. If you happen to latch onto anything that doesn't belong to you, I'm going to have Rick cut your hands off with that axe over there," I said and nodded toward the fireman's axe, which was currently embedded in the Xbox.

His jaw dropped. "Well, how do I know what belongs to us and what belongs to you two?"

"If it looks like it belongs to a woman or a ten-year-old kid, it wouldn't be anything that we would own, now would it? You should hurry. Rick is an impatient man and you guys want to be on the road before it gets too dark out."

"You're really making us leave?" Julie finally asked. Her voice was small sounding now. All of the earlier defiance was gone. I stared at her contemptuously. She did not get it. They were close to being shot. All of them. I did not bother answering.

Janet spoke next. "Would it be possible to get some food before we have to leave?" I nodded reluctantly. "How much?"

"We're not in a negotiating mood, Janet. You'll get whatever Rick and I decide to give you. I don't expect you to thank us because I just don't think y'all are the grateful types. You're all nothing more than selfish ingrates. We could give you everything we had and I still don't believe you would be appreciative. Don't even think of asking for gas. Your daughter ruined that for all of you."

Janet frowned, not understanding. I pointed at the Xbox again. "She doesn't seem to think things through. She burned precious fuel running the generator while sitting on her lazy ass playing a video game all day." Julie gasped. I don't know why, it was true. I scoffed. "Pathetic. All of you are pathetic."

Janet continued scowling at me, but then I saw something I had never seen before. Her expression suddenly changed from a vitriolic scowl to a pitiful, pleading look. It stunned me for a moment, actually to see the sudden metaphysical change of emotions, like suddenly shifting a car into reverse while driving down the road at fifty miles an hour. It unsettled me a little bit.

"You've misjudged us. We're good people," she said quietly. Rick had told me about women like this during one of his drunken diatribes. He tried to explain it to me. I did not understand it at the time, but it made perfect sense now. I cleared my throat. "I disagree. It is you all who have misjudged Rick and me. We had suspicions about you all from the very beginning, but in spite of our suspicions, we offered our help. We were going to fix you guys up in your own house and help you survive through the winter. Now, you're on your own. Since you feel like you have to arm yourself against us in our own house, consider this a tremendous favor we're doing for you."

"You're handing us a death sentence," Janet said sadly. I almost fell for it. Rick brought me back to reality.

"That's your fucking fault!" Rick screamed. "Don't even try to twist it around," he growled. Everyone was quiet then. The only sound was Don's shuffling around in the bedroom. After a minute, he slowly walked back into the den carrying two suitcases. He sat them down, bent over stiffly, and opened them. Rick looked over the contents and gave me a nod. "Keep an eye on them please, Rick." I grabbed one of the suitcases and walked down into the root cellar. I went through the shelves of mason jars and selected various items for them. Rick and I had done a shit-ton of canning this past fall. Hell, we had enough to last just the two of us for a few years. Our only problem was going to be dog food. Those little bastards sure did eat a lot.

Rick then directed them to their minivan. I got a five gallon gas can out of the truck and carefully poured it into their tank. Rick glared at me, but did not object. "It's not enough to fill your tank, but it's enough for y'all to get far away from here. Zach is being nice. As far as I'm concerned, if I see any of you heathens again, I'll pretend you're zombies and put a bullet in your head."

They said nothing, quietly got in the car and started it. Rick stood off to the side and kept his rifle handy. I unloaded the shotgun and pistol. I knew that if they had any chance at all of survival, they would need the weapons. I put them in the back of their car.

"Tommy, do me a favor and hang onto these for a while," I said and handed him the ammunition.

"Okay, Zach. Bye," he said wistfully.

"Bye, Tommy." I suddenly realized I was going to miss him. We had a lot of fun riding around on the ATV. I walked over to the passenger window and looked in. Janet and Don looked at me tentatively. Julie lay down in the back seat and pulled her jacket up around her face.

"If we kept your weapons, I don't think you would stand a chance. But, you'd be wise not to touch them until you're well away from here. When you leave here, turn left on the state highway, go for a few miles until you see a large intersection, and then turn right. Drive about five miles. If you don't see the Interstate, you've gone the wrong way. Whether you get lost or not, don't come back," I said threateningly, nodded to Don and pointed toward the road. Don looked old and tired sitting there. I almost felt sorry for them. Almost. They left without any further ado.

Chapter 14 - The Death of Righteousness

Rick got the backhoe repositioned. I got the dogs fed, and then got Rick fed. He was in a drinking mood rather than an eating mood, but I chided him into finishing his plate. The five of us were now sprawled out in front of the fire. I had changed out of my clothes and donned a pair of sweatpants and a tee shirt. Rick had not bothered changing. He just took his boots off and let them drop in front of the old wingback chair he was sitting in. He propped his feet on the stool and produced a fresh bottle of whiskey. He saw me looking at it.

"Found it under the counter at the gas station," he looked at the label adoringly. "Jim Beam."

He unscrewed the top, took a test swallow and grimaced appreciatively. "Damn, Zach, how could we have been so wrong about them? They seemed righteous enough."

I grunted as he chugged another deep swallow. "That was my nickname, you know."

"What was?"

"Righteous Rick. It's what they called me back in 'Nam."

I looked over at him in surprise. I had known Rick for quite a while now and thought I knew him pretty good. "I never knew that."

"I never told anyone. You should have seen me back then. Young, fit, handsome, full of piss and vinegar." He took a large swallow and handed it to me. I shrugged and took a very small swallow. It was strong and burned the throat going down. Just what both of us needed.

"Why not?" I asked.

"I didn't want anyone calling me that again on account of I got some poor kid killed," he shook his head in frustration. "I've tried for years, but I just can't seem to remember his name. You see, I couldn't get to him in time and he stepped on a booby trap. It took him a few minutes to bleed out. He died in agony, screaming for his mother and wanting to go home, and there was nothing I could do."

He looked over. "That's how I got hit in my leg. When the booby trap exploded, I caught some shrapnel. It might have been okay, but infection set in and caused a lot of nerve damage. I got a purple heart and sent home because of it." He took a long swallow. "You see, according to the therapist over at the VA, I have a lot of what you call survivor's guilt in addition to PTSD. So, when I got back home, I didn't tell anyone my nickname. If everyone went around calling me Righteous Rick, all I'd ever be doing was thinking about 'Nam and the kid whose name I can't remember, dying in my arms. I'm fucked up enough as it is."

"Well, I don't think you're fucked up. You knew this zombie shit was going to happen and you planned for it. You got us to where we are today. We're going to survive this because of your foresight."

"Yeah, but without any pussy."

It was a crass statement but I started laughing anyway. Soon, both of us were in stitches. It was a good stress reliever. The dogs looked at us as if we were crazy.

Instead of going to my bed, I climbed up on the couch and pulled a quilt over me. I wanted to be near Rick and talk with him. Curly jumped up beside me and made himself comfortable. "Don't forget to soak your dentures."

"Right," Rick unsteadily stood up, "I'll do it right now."

He came back a minute later and turned the lantern out. The fire was now our only light source.

"Where do you think they're going to go?" I asked.

Rick grunted. "Don't know and don't care."

"If they're smart, they'll park under an overpass or find a secure building for the night. The snow is really coming down hard. The streets will be pretty slick."

"You're worried about them," Rick said.

"Yeah, I guess so," I replied. Rick grunted again. "I know what you're thinking and I agree. They were up to no good and good riddance to them. I can't help but think Janet was behind it all. What a psycho bitch!"

"You got that right, brother," Rick said. I heard him taking slow sips from his bottle. He was going to finish it off before he would be able to sleep without the nightmares. "Zach, I'm glad we're friends," he said quietly.

"Me too, buddy. You may not realize it, but you saved my life. I don't think I've thanked you properly. By the way, Merry Christmas."

Rick chuckled. "Hell, I'd forgotten what day it was. Merry Christmas to you too, kid. Oh, wait, I've got your Christmas present," Rick said and delivered a long, noxious fart. It sounded like a hippopotamus dying. Moe took offense and snorted.

In spite of the fetid odor, I laughed. We talked some more before I eventually drifted off to sleep. There was no way of knowing, no indication, and no omen of what was going to happen next. Sometime during the night, Righteous Rick died.

Chapter 15 - A Proper Burial

I shot Rick in the head before breakfast.

It was a no-brainer, no pun intended. When I finally accepted the fact he had died in his sleep, I carried him to the barn and laid him on a tarp. I sat on the cold ground looking at him for at least an hour. I thought of all of the good times I had had with the old man and how much he had taught me.

I did not wonder so much about how he died. Bad heart? Too much whiskey? Lack of pussy? I did not know, and it did not really matter at this point. He was the father figure I never had, a good man. I was going to miss him terribly. He was the last person on Earth who cared about me, and now, he too was gone.

He did not turn. His body did not reanimate, nor was there any hint of him becoming a zombie. Nevertheless, I stood, took careful aim, and fired. Rick understood.

I buried him on a small hill overlooking the brook bordering the east side of the farm. Rick had once told me it was an old Indian mound. I had to use the backhoe to break the frozen ground. I buried him deep. The boys watched quietly. Only once did a forlorn whimper come from Moe. I was going to put up a tombstone when I had the chance. After covering him up, I did something I never did. I prayed. I prayed to God that Righteous Rick was finally at peace.

The rest of the day went by in a blur. I went through the motions of the never ending chores. At the end of the day, I started the generator and took a long hot shower.

Yeah, I cried a little.

I could not tell you specifically what I did for the next month. I performed chores. I ran for miles at a time. I worked out with an old rusty set of weights. There was an old punching bag hanging in the barn. I would punch it until my fists pulsated in pain and my arms were so fatigued that I could not hold them up. I knew I was burning calories, but Rick had stored enough food to keep me fed for years.

Occasionally, I turned on the Ham radio. I'd capture bits and pieces of someone talking or Morse code, but nothing of consequence. There was one man I spoke to when the atmospheric conditions made for good skip, or radio waves bouncing off of the ionosphere. He lived somewhere on the Cumberland Plateau. He really did not have much to say, just the usual. Zombies everywhere, lots of dead, etc. I never answered anyone else. I did not have it in me to talk to anyone. I just went through the motions. At night, I'd sit by the fire and brood. The dogs were my ever present companions. They would try to play with me, but after a while, they would give up when I did not respond.

Depression had returned with a passion. I really missed the old man. My grandmother, Felix, Macey, I missed them all. Now, with Rick gone, I found myself asking daily why I should go on.

I had nobody.

One particularly cold evening, I had wrapped myself in a dirty blanket and sat in Rick's chair. His bottle of whiskey, still half full sat beside it. I opened the top, wiped it off, and then drank until I passed out. I felt like I dreamt of many things, but the only part I remember was a nudge on my shoulder. I dreamt I opened my eyes and Rick was standing there, grinning at me.

"Wake up, kid," he said. As I roused from my sleep and everything came into focus. Rick was gone, but the boys were sitting there staring at the spot where I dreamt Rick was standing. Strange.

Yes, it was strange. I got up quickly and went through the house, searching every room and closet, even the root cellar.

Nope, nobody here but yours truly and three stinky dogs. I hustled outside and retrieved some eggs. I checked the barn while I was at it. Empty, except for the calves and their mommas. They had steadily been putting on weight. I had turned them out to pasture a couple of weeks ago, but they'd keep seeking shelter in the barn. I shooed them out again and closed the double door.

The sun probably would not make an appearance today. It was cold and windy. I made a decision as I ate breakfast. It was time to start clearing houses and scrounging for supplies. Rick and I had talked about it, back when he was still alive, and we speculated a zombie's motor skills would be severely hampered by cold weather. I even made it a rule, even though it was untested. Well, today would be a good day to test the theory out. Rick had one of those large thermometers, the kind with a tin frame painted with an advertisement for a soda, nailed to one of the columns on the front porch. It read twenty degrees. Perfect. The decision was made. I'd clear a few houses, scrounge for supplies, maybe I would even find some fellow survivors.

I rushed through the morning chores, loaded the truck with equipment, gassed it up, checked the fluid levels, and the tires. When I was satisfied I had thought of everything, I headed out. I took Moe with me. He was some kind of shepherd mix and was a decent watch dog. He only barked when a stranger came near. He would have to be my security monitor while I went through houses and buildings. I put Moe in the truck and got in behind him. "You're going to have to watch my back, Moe, okay?" Moe looked at me then licked me on the face. I interpreted it as a yes.

Rick and I had many discussions about clearing buildings and scavenging. It was going to be an essential element of long term survival. Here is the plan we devised.

First: One should always assume a structure is occupied. Second: If a house appeared to have an alarm system, leave it. Most alarm systems had a battery backup, so in theory, they could still be activated, even after several months. Noise was bad. Third, if it was obvious the house may be occupied, determine if the occupants were real or infected. If it had real people and they weren't sociable, back off. Go to another house, or even better, move on to another neighborhood. Rick surprised me with a tidbit of logic. He said any house occupied by zombies was going to be goldmines of needful things. It made sense, I guess. Zombies weren't going to eat up all of the food, nor would they use toothpaste and toilet paper. Well, I don't believe infected people bothered with those things, but I couldn't swear to it.

Since I was going to be doing this solo, I was going to restrict my work to smaller homes or small businesses. Imagine trying to clear out a large office building by yourself. You round a corner only to run into a dozen or so infected secretaries who were fresh out of donuts. Nope, not me. I'd stick to small stuff. Even then, I almost screwed the pooch on the very first home I went to.

I started with a quaint community in the southern area of Nashville known as Lennox Village. I turned in and drove up to the front door of the closest one. I sat in my truck for a couple of minutes to see if there was any type of reaction, living or otherwise. There was nothing. Only the ticking sound that a hot car engine makes when you first shut it off, and a couple of noisy birds fighting over a worm or something. I got out and knocked on the first door while giving an innocent salutation.

I'd say, "Hello? I'm friendly, not looking for trouble, anybody home?" I was just about to make entry when the door suddenly burst open. An older woman, wearing nothing but an untied bathrobe and her hair in those big round curlers, ran out. She was screaming like a banshee. The suddenness of it startled me. Even more unsettling was the visual image of her open robe. I stumbled backward while pointing my handgun at her. She continued screaming while running to God knows where. I watched in rapt befuddlement as she rounded the corner of a townhouse and disappeared.

No. I did not go after her. She had obviously lost her mind, and all of the screaming was going to attract zombies. Or whatever you wanted to call them. I moved on to another subdivision a couple of miles away. As one may expect, I was extra cautious with the first house. There was another old woman in this one as well. She did not run out screaming though. She sat there at her kitchen table looking at me. She was obviously infected, but made no effort to stand or chase me. She merely snarled at me when I entered the kitchen. I dispatched her with a quick headshot and carefully cleared the rest of the house.

I cleared almost twenty houses before noon. I did not run into any other live people, but did encounter eight more zombies of various types. Quite a few homes had stinking, rotting corpses. One house had a family of four that were all infected. I gave the front door a little knock and was shortly rewarded with moaning and scratching on the door. Nice, I thought. I kicked open the door and put three of them down with head shots. I was feeling smug with my skills, until the family's little girl crawled out from under a bed and tried to bite my ankle. It was a good thing I was wearing heavy boots. If I had my running shoes on, I would have been bitten. I stomped on her head until it made squishing noises and she stopped moving.

After the first hour, and constantly repeating my congenial greeting, I became bored. My salutation soon went from friendly verbiage to, "Any zombie cocksuckers in there?" I guess it was fortunate I did not have any human contact. They would have thought I was the one who was crazy.

Breaking into a residential house was actually quite easy. I had a set of skeleton keys that were used in most residential door locks and used a technique called lock bumping. Rick showed me a video tutorial on the Internet. It only took a couple of minutes and was relatively quiet. If it did not work, I had one of those long pry bars firemen used. It could usually snap the door right open. No wonder there were so many burglaries back in the day. On those occasions where I encountered security doors, I broke out a window. If the windows were barred, I hooked up the winch from the truck and pulled the bars down, or moved on to another home. If I activated an alarm, I moved on to another neighborhood.

After encountering several zombies, I came to realize they were quite predictable. They heard a noise, smelled something, saw movement, and they responded to it. They did not sneak up on you or lay in wait to ambush you. They did not have the mental faculties for it. Along the same line of thought, they were incapable of planning or coordinating a mass attack. They merely responded to stimuli and the rest was instinctive. Consequently, they did not seem to need sleep, nor did they feel pain, anguish, or fear. They moaned, wandered aimlessly, bumped into stuff, or sat there and stunk to high heaven until something caused them to act. A zombie form of Weber's law, if you will.

What did it mean in common terms? Zombies were easy to spot and easy to kill. But, one had to be vigilant, or else you would become zombie food. There was a zombie law in here somewhere. I would have to think on it. Nah, zombies weren't a problem unless you happened upon a group of them and did not have an escape route or enough ammunition.

Humans, live humans, they were the potential problem. I had no illusions about all humans being good hearted people. Someone might see me and kill me for what I had. Someone might believe I was a threat and shoot me in a perceived act of self-defense. I was hoping my act of announcing my presence before entering someone's house might negate any hostile act, but hell, you just never knew. They might be just like the woman in Lennox Village, crazier than an outhouse rat. Those were the ones that will hide in a closet just waiting to blow your head off. I had to be careful or I'd end up dead.

I took a break and looked over my newly acquired property. The pickings were slim, but not altogether bereft of goodies. I took an inventory with my notepad:

Some gently used clothes that fit me. Fresh bed linens. A set of Ruffoni brand copper cooking pots. Very nice. They would replace the Goodwill rejects that I currently had. Over a dozen Tupperware bowls. They were one of those items in which you could find a thousand and one uses for. Containers were essential for hunter-gatherer societies. They were like weapons and tools and you could never have enough. A couple of boxes of Kleenex, several half used rolls of toilet paper, several used tubes of toothpaste, and a box of nine millimeter bullets. I had no nine millimeter guns. Rick hated that size, only women shot nines, he would say. I took them for trade purposes.

I continued jotting: some assorted food items, including an unopened bag of coffee beans, four boxes of rice, a dozen boxes of Jell-O, two boxes of powdered milk, and an unopened box of Mexicana Cal, which was good for nixtamalization. Several used boxes of laundry detergent. Almost every house had either powdered or liquid in various levels. I guess when people decided to bug out to wherever they were going to, a used container of detergent was useless in their minds. Along that line, I also found a few half empty bottles of bleach. Two five gallon gas cans. These I suspect were also going to be a rare find. And finally, I scored a major coup in the last house I checked. Three cases of an expensive brand of dog food! The boys would be happy.

I found many other small items and dutifully jotted them down on my inventory list. Yeah, I know, I'm the only one around, no need to write out a list that was already in my head, but old habits die hard. I finished the list and reviewed it twice. It was definitely turning out to be a successful day.

I also noted some houses that were closer to Old Hickory Boulevard had already been searched. Several had windows broken out, along with other assorted acts of vandalism. This particular subdivision stopped at a dead end street. Three of the houses at the end had burned. Upon closer inspection, I determined a car had crashed into the front door of one of the houses. I surmised the wreck caused the fire, and it spread to the other houses. I wondered what had happened. Was the driver trying to escape from somebody? Had they been attacked?

I pointed this out to my companion. "We got some survivors out here that aren't so nice. We've got to be careful." Moe wagged his tail appreciatively. He was a good listener. He never once interrupted me or flipped me the bird. Oh, he occasionally farted, but Rick farted a lot as well, so I was used to it.

I stood and stretched. It was good getting out and moving around. Only now did I realize being cooped up at the farm all by myself was causing me to sink into a deep depression. I needed to get out more often.

The last house I cleared before lunch had a bedroom that had obviously been once occupied by a couple of teenage girls. There were pictures of them in a cheerleading outfit and pom-poms fastened to each corner of the dresser mirror. They were two very cute twins. I went through their dresser drawers. It looked like most of their clothing was left behind. I wondered what had happened to them. Were they twin cheerleading zombies now? I opened one drawer and found a bunch of bras and panties. They were all very sexy looking. French cut or thongs, lacy, silky, various colors. I looked at the sizes. Very petite, but the bras were c-cups. Nice. I held up a pair of panties and felt the silky smoothness. I realized I was becoming aroused and had the sudden urge to masturbate with them. I looked at the picture again. They were blondes with pretty hazel eyes, cute little butts and nice muscular legs. They were wearing sweaters, which prevented me from assessing any opinion about their breasts. They reminded me of Macie. I thought about her too much. I muttered a curse and threw the panties back in the drawer.

I had almost gotten myself in a good mood, now I was getting depressed again over a woman, a woman who had hurt me deeply. It seemed like I've met a couple of those lately. I should have bent Julie over and diddled her brains out when I had the chance. Or Janet. No, scratch that idea, not Janet. If I had made a pass at her, Rick would have been hurt. The thought reminded me of something I needed to do. Anyway, I squashed any teenage urges and walked out in front of the house. It was a fairly large two story with white vinyl siding. I spray painted the standard FEMA symbol on the front door, and then affixed rule number three on the white siding in large block letters for everyone to see: RULE #3 THERE ARE NO RIGHTEOUS ZOMBIES! Z.

"That one's for you, Rick," I said sadly. I admired my work for a minute, and then headed on to the next street.

Moe and I worked through a few more houses. The results were limited. Several of the houses had decomposing bodies. Those were the houses that had no food, but they still had their most prize possessions hidden. You know what I mean, expensive jewelry hidden in the freezer, guns stored in the attic with insulation piled on top of them. Sounds good, right? All I found were a couple of diamond necklaces and a twenty-two caliber revolver with a suppressor attached to the barrel. I thought the necklaces were basically worthless, but took them on the chance I could use them for barter. The revolver could come in handy for quiet work, but I had no ammo for it.

About midday, I had to take a break. I sat on the tailgate of my truck deeply inhaling the icy, but fresh air. The houses that were occupied with corpses and/or zombies reeked of putrescence. I tried clearing a house while wearing a mask, but it made me feel claustrophobic and restricted my peripheral vision, so I left it in the truck and suffered the stench. It was getting a bit nauseating.

In spite of the foul odor, I was hungry. I cleaned my hands and then got a couple of sandwiches out of the cooler. Moe whined and began giving me his poor pitiful starving dog expression. It worked, I gave him one, and the two of us ate in silence. Suddenly, Moe started growling. I praised him and then quickly shushed him. The zombie was down Old Hickory Boulevard a little over two hundred yards away. I was certain it had not seen me. It was shambling down the road with no particular destination in mind. I watched in halfhearted amusement, wondering how close he needed to be before he finally spotted us. Suddenly, the zombie made a beeline over to a car parked on the side of the road. He never stopped his shambling gate and literally bounced off the car. Regaining his balance, he then started slapping and clawing at the windows. It was almost comical to watch if you ignored the fact that any physical contact with him could be potentially lethal.

I retrieved my binoculars and looked him over. This one, a man, could have been in his twenties or his fifties. It was hard to tell. He had apparently sustained a harsh act of violence. It looked like one of his arms had been torn off. His stump consisted of torn flesh and jagged pieces of bone sticking out. There was no blood flowing out of his stump. Was it due to no circulation system? Or does zombie blood coagulate quickly? I did not know. His lips had rotted off, or maybe another zombie had chewed them off. The rest of him looked awful, advanced decomposition, tattered blood stained clothes, eyes almost rotted out. I wondered how it could still see, but apparently, it could. It definitely saw something in the car.

I contemplated my options. Kill the zombie or drive on to another neighborhood? I needed more gas. The truck was down to a quarter of a tank. I did not want to take a chance of driving too far, not finding any, and running out before I got back home. There were plenty of cars around here I could siphon from. I had been experimenting with different siphoning methods. Most of them were laboriously slow. I ended up with a battery operated drill I rigged up to a small mechanical pump. I attached a three foot piece of garden hose connected to each end. Voila, I could stick one end into the gas tank, the other end into the truck's tank. It was quiet and efficient. So, the decision was made. I would kill him and continue with the scavenging in this neighborhood.

I did not want to make a bunch of noise. After all, attracting more zombies would defeat the purpose. I still had not found a compound bow or crossbow, nor did I have any bullets for the newly acquired silenced revolver. It then occurred to me, I had brought a machete. It was in the bed of the truck. Hmm. I quietly opened the door and put Moe inside. He would probably attack the zombie, and I did not know if he would become infected. Getting the machete, I started walking and approached as quietly as I could.

I got to within ten feet before he heard me. He turned and looked at me as if I were some type of apparition. Imagine a zombie with a decomposed face and rotting eyes looking frightened. It was so odd, I laughed. I then lunged forward with a sweeping arc of the machete.

A skilled martial artist could have easily ducked or moved out of the way. But zombies aren't martial artists. His head came off somewhat cleanly, fell to the ground, and was still rolling when the rest of the body collapsed.

I checked myself quickly for any harmful fluids that might have gotten on me, and retrieved my ever present bottle of waterless antibacterial soap. I cleaned the machete first and wiped it down in the snow before cleaning my hands and face. It reminded me back to when I killed Jasper. I had been splattered with blood from head to toe. If a police officer had stopped me, I would still be sitting in a jail cell. Whether or not I would have been alive, dead, or zombified was anybody's guess. I guess I was lucky. I was still smiling at the thought when I peered in the car to see what had captivated this thing's attention.

There was somebody lying down in the back seat.

Chapter 16 - A Reunion of Sorts

I recognized Julie immediately. Skinny, petulant Julie. Even though she had her oversized coat zipped up and the collar pulled up to her face, there was no mistaking those blue eyes with the green speckles, the splash of freckles across her cheeks, and her tousled chestnut brown hair. She was looking up at me in sheer terror.

Shit, this was not good. I dropped the machete and drew my Glock as I backed up and looked around. I scanned every nook and cranny but did not see anyone else. If Julie was here, Don and Janet had to be nearby. I walked back to the car and watched her hands as I tried to open the back door, but it was locked. I motioned for her to come out. She shook her head. "Come on out, it's okay." She shook her head again. I was not going to break out the window, nor was I going to beg. I shrugged. "Have it your way." I had too much to do and she was not on the agenda. I retrieved my machete and got about halfway back to my truck when I heard the car door open. She ran toward me until she saw the gun. She stopped suddenly. "Where's Don and Janet?" I demanded.

"Don's dead," she said. How many teenagers do you know call their grandfather by their first name? I suddenly recalled Janet calling him by his first name as well. I did not find it odd until now. I filed that tidbit away.

"Where is your mom?"

Julie's lower lip quivered. "She's not here. She…we met some people. Mom said we should join in with them," she looked at me. "They're not very nice."

I walked closer to her and suddenly reached out to frisk her. "You got a gun on you?" I demanded. She shook her head quickly. I squeezed the pockets of her jacket, felt around her waist band, and wasn't shy about grabbing her crotch for any indication of a weapon. She flinched, but did not protest. Satisfied, I stepped back. "Tell me about Don. What happened?"

She had a familiar expression on her face, as if she was about to say something smart about me grabbing her crotch, but then thought better of it. "Zach, it was so weird. After we left you guys, Don started acting really strange. We drove around in circles for half the night before Mom finally convinced him to stop until daylight. He'd mumble stuff to himself and was just kind of zoning out. He kept insisting we go back to downtown Nashville. He said he saw real people and there had to be a FEMA camp around there somewhere. When the sun came up, Don somehow figured out how to get to Nashville. We got to somewhere around Vanderbilt. Don got out of the car with the shotgun and started looking around. A zombie came out of nowhere. He actually ran up to Don and jumped on his back. He started biting him and clawing at his face before any of us could do anything."

I held up a hand. "Wait. The zombie was actually running, are you sure?" I asked. She nodded. Wow. I had heard of this during the initial stages of the outbreak, but did not realize a zombie still had the capability of running. "Did you note the amount of decomposition?"

Julie gave a halfhearted shrug. "There wasn't much at all. That may have been why Don didn't react right away. His eyes were crazy looking and his face was reddish, like he had a fever or something, but otherwise, he almost looked normal."

So, a freshly turned zombie can run. Interesting. Even more interesting, if what she was saying was accurate, this person had turned at a much later time than everyone else had. Did I say it was interesting? A more appropriate word would be alarming. "Okay, what happened next?"

"Don was fighting with it, trying to keep it from biting him. And Mom..." I could tell she did not want to tell me, but I needed to know. I held my hand up and made a swishing motion - tell me. "So Mom got into the driver's seat and drove away. She left Don. He didn't deserve that." She brushed some hair out of her eyes. It had gotten longer since I last saw her. I had to admit, it enhanced her femininity. Mine had grown out as well. I started keeping it tied back in a ponytail. I really hoped it did not enhance my femininity.

Julie continued. "After that, we just drove around aimlessly. We'd park in obscure areas and sleep in the van at night. Sometimes, we'd find something to eat and Tommy got pretty good at getting gas. He'd crawl under the car and knock a hole in the bottom of the gas tank. Then he'd fill up empty milk jugs," she said, smiling proudly at Tommy's ingenuity. I had thought of this technique as well, but once you've done it, the automobile was inoperable unless you fixed the tank. I did not feel it was prudent thinking and did not do it.

She continued talking. "Mom even talked about coming back to you and Rick. She seemed to think she could smooth things over. You know, blame everything on Don. That's my mom. Nothing is ever her fault, always somebody else's." She paused a moment, I guess she was thinking of the character that her mother was. I was pretty sure I knew how she felt. Everyone wants their parents to be perfect. When you figure out they're not, or worse, when you figure out that they are majorly flawed, it hurts. Deeply.

She then flipped her hair back and continued. "We had been just kind of driving around avoiding zombies, no real destination planned. Then the van broke down. We didn't know what was wrong with it and we couldn't fix it. I made a comment about how Don could have probably fixed it and mom threatened to lock me out of the van. It was getting late in the day when we saw them. They were in one of those Hummer limos. There were six of them. They were riding around and they were standing out of the sun roof like stoned idiots taking pot shots at zombies, or anything that looked like zombies. Or windows, Darius seemed to be fascinated with shooting out windows. They were smoking weed, drinking, and just having a good old time. Mom stepped out of the van, smiled real big, stuck her chest out, and waved at them. Long story short, they invited us to join them."

"Where are they now?" I asked.

She pointed back over her shoulder. "They're staying in someone's house back that way about ten miles."

It seemed like she was being truthful, but I was still suspicious. "What are you doing out here by yourself?"

She shook her head, as if she was trying to shake away a distasteful memory. "Yesterday, two of us decided to go out looking for food and stuff. I thought Darius was a good guy, but he pulled over on the side of the road and tried to, well, you know. I convinced him I had to pee first. I got out of the car and made a big deal out of finding a good place to squat. I took off running and managed to hide from him. He drove around for about an hour looking for me. Then I guess he gave up and left. I've been walking ever since. I was doing a pretty good job of hiding from the zombies. They don't move so good in this cold weather, but then that one found me sleeping in the car."

She gestured at Mr. Headless. His mouth was opening and closing slowly. It still was not quite dead, even without anything below the neck. "That was pretty cool, what you did with the machete."

She reminded me of the zombie. I walked over and looked at his neck where the head used to be. There was some kind of black goo slowly oozing out of the neck. It may have been blood, but it did not look like any blood I had ever seen. Okay, so if there is no blood, or I guess I should say no red, oxygenated blood, the circulation system must be compromised. I thought maybe that also applied to the respiratory system. It answered some questions, but seemed to create more questions as well. I then tore open the shirt and looked at the armpits. There was distinct swelling of the lymph nodes. So much so, it looked like cantaloupes were stuffed under each arm. I straightened, used my waterless soap again, and focused my attention back on Julie.

"Alright, so this guy tries to rape you and you escape. Where did you think you were going to go?"

She shrugged and stuck out her lower lip. I was not sure if it was a natural mannerism or if she were putting on an act, like her mother had. "I was hoping you and Rick would let me stay with you."

I scoffed and started to shake my head. "Please? I'll be good, I promise! I'll cook, clean, feed the chickens. You name it, I'll do it," She proclaimed. I had several responses on the tip of my tongue, but we were interrupted by Moe barking. I looked down the road. There were three figures. They were kind of standing there. Well, that was being a bit subjective. They were hunched over, definitely not standing erect.

"Wave at them," I said. Julie looked at me as if I was crazy. "You said you'd do anything, was that a lie?"

Much to her credit, she immediately started waving vigorously. No response other than the distinctive shambling walk. "Zombies don't seem to wave back. So that one you saw running, he wasn't doing that?" I pointed at the trio.

She shook her head. "The one that attacked Don, he definitely ran. And he was pretty fast too."

I thought about what she said. I wondered if one of them would still be able to run in cold weather.

They were still a good distance away, but getting closer. "Are you going to shoot them?" she asked.

I shook my head as I holstered my weapon and retrieved my machete. "This is a scavenger mission, not a go out and kill zombies mission. I've got to get at least twenty more gallons of gas and anything else I can find. Time to leave. Are you coming?" I trotted back to my truck without waiting for an answer. She followed.

"Did you bring any clothes with you? Food, toothbrush, female stuff, anything?"

She shook her head. "I didn't think that I'd be running away. Well, let me change that. I had planned on running away when the opportunity was right, just not right then. So, it was either get raped or take off empty handed, and that's exactly what I did. I think I could eat a horse right now I'm so hungry."

I nodded my head in understanding as I retrieved the spray paint can. I still had time to paint some rules.

RULE NUMBER 4: FRESH ZOMBIES CAN RUN, OLD ZOMBIES CAN'T. Big block letters so everyone could see it. I added two more.

RULE NUMBER 5: THE COLD SLOWS THEM DOWN.

RULE NUMBER 6: DON'T LET THEIR BLOOD GET ON YOU!

RULE NUMBER 7: HIGHER BRAIN FUNCTIONS ARE DIMINISHED, BUT THEY'RE STILL DANGEROUS.

I finished it off by signing a Z underneath.

Julie looked at it and smiled. "Nice. Are you putting these everywhere?" she asked.

I nodded. "Everywhere I can. Maybe it will help other survivors."

When we got to the truck, Moe instantly attacked Julie with devastating licks to the face. He barked, jumped, and spun around in the truck the way excited dogs will do. I had no idea that the two of them had bonded in the short time that she had been with us. He apparently missed female company too. Julie hugged him and shortly spotted the cooler sitting in the back seat. I had no doubt she was as hungry as she claimed. I cocked my thumb at it.

"I got some food and a jug of water in there. Help yourself. Now, let's see if we can get you some clothes."

She quickly turned in the seat and dove into the cooler. "Whoa, whoa, hang on," I reached into my jacket pocket and retrieved the waterless hand sanitizer. "Always use this or some equivalent. We don't exactly have ready access to antibiotics and doctors."

She looked at me funny. "I never thought of it like that," she said and squirted her hands liberally and rubbed them together before looking in the cooler. I made a U-turn and headed back to the cheerleaders' house. I ignored all of the stop signs and we arrived in short time. I parked and pointed. Julie had already finished the sandwich, and was wolfing down a Twinkie as I parked. I cleared my throat. She looked at me with a dirty mouth. "I've already cleared this house. There's a bedroom upstairs that looks like two sisters lived in. There are some clothes that I think will fit you. Go up and grab what you want. Don't waste your time on the frivolous crap like high-heeled shoes, focus on the practical," I handed her some of my newly acquired trash bags for her to put her clothes in.

She nodded, and I watched as she tore into a Three Musketeers candy bar. Damn, I was saving that for desert. "Aren't you coming with me?" she asked between bites.

I remained seated. "I'm going to watch for zombies."

She stared at me with those bright baby blue eyes. The chocolate smeared lower lip stuck out for a moment. "Are you going to leave me?"

She had me on that. I must admit I had considered it. I considered it strongly. Something about the way she looked at me though caused me to make a decision.

"No. but we might have to have a little talk in a minute. Now, go get some clothes and don't forget feminine hygiene stuff," I directed. She smiled tentatively and jogged to the front door.

While I waited, I let Moe out so he could do his business on the snow covered lawn. He sniffed a bit, dug at the snow, and then dropped a big steaming turd. He sniffed his creation and then looked at me for approval. I gave him a thumbs up. One less pile I would have to shovel out of the yard back home. A couple of minutes later, Julie came running out of the front door with two overstuffed black plastic bags and put them in the back of the extended cab.

"Just one or two more loads!" she said breathlessly. I handed her some more trash bags. She nodded gratefully and ran back inside. She came back out two more times. The last time, she showed me a bag full of bras and panties and then put them in back with the rest. "I found some shoes and socks too."

I hoped she chose something like running shoes or hiking boots. Her brow was glistening with perspiration. "All of that running got me hot," she laughed as she unzipped her jacket. She was wearing a plain tee shirt that offered me an occasional glimpse of her breasts pushing out. They were not as large as Macie's, but they were still nice. You know, it was a stupid thought. I'd not seen any breasts from a living woman since the fateful night with Macie. Almost any breasts would look nice right about now.

I waited for her to get settled in the truck. She was still breathing hard and her cheeks were a rosy red. The way she looked, and the way she looked at me, caused my loins to start aching. I focused out the window, like I was watching for zombies and not imagining her all sweaty and naked. "So, did you find any hygiene products?"

She nodded. "I found a travel bag with a lot of stuff in it," she pointed it all out. Good, she found a few boxes of tampons, something I definitely did not have back at the farm. Maybe that was what Rick was thinking about when he tried to get me to buy them back in November.

I pointed at the pile of clothes. "So what's with the bras? Seems like they're a little too big for you," Yeah, I know, I couldn't resist.

She reached over and punched me in the arm. "You are so mean sometimes. I'll have you know my boobs are a decent size for my age. I've lost a lot of weight recently, as if you didn't know. Don't think you won't be staring at them when I gain my weight back," she finished with a scoff. She was probably right about that, but I was not going to admit it. Moe snorted and licked a spot of chocolate off of her face.

I stifled a sigh. "Well, about that. I think it would probably be better for me if I put you up in a house on your own. Maybe this house, or one like it."

"But, why?" she asked.

"Because I am convinced you and your family were being untruthful when we first met, and therefore I'm not so sure that I trust you now. What do you have to say to that?"

She caught her breath, held her hands in front of her and spread her fingers. "All of that wasn't my idea, it was Mom's, and she told us to go along."

I made another 'continue please' motion with my hand. "Don is not really my grandfather, he was Mom's boyfriend. She was screwing around on Dad, who apparently had his own girlfriend. Don owned a car dealership in Fayetteville and she worked for him. He is, or was, pretty rich, and he spent a lot of money on mom. She was always driving a new car. He even bought her a boob job," she sighed, held her hands up, and then dropped them limply in her lap.

"It was just a fucked up situation. The part about the gym and dad getting killed by zombies is true. When that happened, the rumors started. They were saying that somehow Mom set dad up to be killed," she shook her head in disgust. "He's the one that volunteered to go out. They didn't set him up. He was just trying to impress the women. My dad was like that. He wanted to be a hero, but there were too many zombies to shoot and his group was overwhelmed. People are fucking crazy."

"So, why the subterfuge?" I asked.

"The what?"

"Why in the hell did your mom and Don create such an elaborate crazy story? Why not simply tell the truth?"

"Oh," she fidgeted a moment before answering. "Mom thought you two would be all about having a single woman around. We saw Rick and were about to drive up when Mom told Don to stop the car. That's when she came up with the story. She said if Rick thought he was helping out a family who just happened to have a single woman, he'd be more than eager to help. I was so hungry I would have done anything."

She sighed. "Well, anyway, it seemed harmless enough. Strange, but harmless. And then you pop up out from that boat. Why were you hiding in there? To shoot us?"

I shrugged. "We did not know if you guys were hostile or not."

"Oh. I guess that makes sense. Well, anyway, Rick looked like some kind of wild man, and then you popped up holding a rifle. I was scared at first, but you two turned out to be really nice. Later, Mom said since you and I were the same age, you two would be even more willing to help us out. She told me to flirt with you at every opportunity and she was going to do the same with Rick. She kept saying when the time was right she and Don would tell you two the truth. But, instead of doing that, they came up with some kind of crazy plan to get rid of Rick," she said and scoffed. "Getting rid of him is how mom described it. I guess it was a kind way of saying they were going to murder him."

I started. "So Rick was right, your mother was planning on driving off and leaving him for the zombies."

She squirmed uncomfortably and glanced back at the cooler. "I didn't know she had planned it to happen exactly the way you said, but she told me about it after they got back when you and Rick were in the barn. I asked her why. She said Rick was leering at me and she thought he was going to try to rape me. Then she had me hide the gun. She and Don didn't think you two would find it if I were the one hiding it." She shook her head at the logic. "I think she was planning on using it against you two when she had a chance." Her voice lowered. "Y'all found it anyway and still gave us food and gas. I guess she was lying about Rick."

I clenched my teeth. "You're damn right she was lying!" I barked. "Rick was the consummate gentleman. He would have never raped anyone. His nickname was Righteous Rick for a reason!"

She did not respond. I took a deep breath. To think that bitch was talking about Rick like that after all we did for them. It pissed me off. I took a moment to calm down. "Okay, is there anything you left out?"

She slowly nodded her head. "The group of people we hooked up with. They know you. A few of them went to school with you, and one of them, a guy named Chad, he said you and Rick murdered his friend in cold blood."

Chapter 17 – Friends and Foes

"Who are they?" I asked.

She held up her fingers. "Jason and Macie. Tay, Darius, Chad, and Trina."

So Macie and Jason were still alive! There were a million things that I wanted to know about them. "How are they doing? Are any of them sick? Do they have plenty of food and water?"

She held up a hand. "Whoa, slow down. Okay, so the answer to your first question is they're just getting by. Nothing special."

"How are they doing with food and water?"

She made a flippant gesture with her hand. "They just go out breaking into houses and stores looking for anything to eat. Canned sodas are usually what we've been drinking, when we can find them. We went a couple of days without finding anything to drink, so one of them got the bright idea of boiling creek water. It didn't work out so well. Everyone got a bad case of diarrhea. Oh, and they have some guns."

I needed to know more. "Tell me what they're doing to insure their future. Are they distilling water, growing gardens? Anything like that?"

She shook her head. "They don't have anything stored, or a garden, or any semblance of planning. So, when everyone got sick off of the water, Mom told them about all of the food you two had and the clean well water."

Wonderful. It was now a matter of time before they worked up the courage to come and visit. When the hunger pangs got strong enough, they would find the courage. It deserved careful consideration. I would need to think it over more when I got home and got a hot meal in me. If I were to guess, they could be considered foes. Enemies. Even Macie.

I was not sure what to think of Julie, or if I could even trust her. It had been so long since I had actually talked to a live person though. I was just not going to kick her out of the truck. At least, not yet.

I started the truck and soon came upon a business park just off of Old Hickory Boulevard. There were quite a few cars in the parking lot. It was full of cars, which was amazing. There were people still going to work in the middle of a global crisis. I scanned the area with my binoculars, but did not see anything. The office building was dark and quiet. When I stopped, Julie grabbed the binoculars out of my hand for a look. It irked me slightly, at first. She made slow methodical scans back and forth. Impressive.

"You see any zombies?" I asked.

"Nope."

"You see any indicators that there are live people around?"

She looked at me and then back into the binoculars. "I don't think so."

"Look at the parked cars carefully and tell me what is significant about them," I said. She looked them over.

"I don't see anything that jumps out at me. They're just all covered in snow," then it hit her. "That's it, isn't it? The cars are covered in snow. If they were being used, they wouldn't have snow on them, right?"

"Right you are. Also, there are no tire tracks in the snow. Or footprints. Alright, here's where you start earning your keep. We need fuel. Regular gas. We have plenty of diesel fuel at the moment, but we need gas. Most of the tanks at gas stations and convenience stores were emptied out when people started panicking. Also, cars abandoned on the road are probably going to be empty. So, instead of wasting time, we apply some logic. Here are a bunch of cars parked in a parking lot. When people fled for their lives, did they drive all over, run out of gas, and then park their cars in an orderly fashion in a parking lot? No, of course not. So, the odds are, they still have gas in them."

Julie nodded in understanding. "Yeah, it makes sense. Do you want me to crawl under them and drain the tanks while you keep guard?"

I shook my head. "We're going to do it differently. C'mon I'll show you." I parked near some cars and retrieved my pump. "This way, we're not ruining any gas tanks. It may or may not matter, but you never know. Now, when we're done, just leave the gas cap cover open."

"So we know we've already drained the gas," she said.

"Exactly. And don't forget to look inside every car you can. We might find a present or two. Just be careful there isn't a bad surprise waiting to sink their teeth into you."

She smiled with nice, white, straight teeth. She'd been brushing regularly. "Does this mean I get to live with you and Rick?" she frowned suddenly. "Where is Rick?"

I kept a poker face and tried to sound nonchalant. "He's out on a recon mission. He's going to be gone for a while. And yes, you can stay with us. I certainly hope you're not the same impetuous brat who I met a month ago," I proclaimed. To my surprise, she squealed and grabbed me in a hug.

"You won't regret it, Zach. I promise I'll be good and I'll do anything you say."

I allowed myself to smile. I hoped I was not making a mistake, again. I checked my watch. "Let's get some gas and then we'll head back."

We started at the back of the parking lot and worked our way up. We had the truck's tank filled in under an hour and now only needed to fill the five-gallon cans I had. Julie pointed at a utility van. "I bet that one has a big tank."

I nodded. "Absolutely. Let's do it."

We trotted over to it. Julie tried the door handle. It was unlocked. She started to jump in. "Careful," I chided. She stopped and peered in carefully. Satisfied nobody was inside, she checked it out. I looked around for any company. Paranoia kept you alive, Rick would say.

"Whoa, hey look!" she said.

I instinctively reached for my Glock. "What is it?"

She stuck her arm out the door and held up a set of keys. "They were above the visor. You want me to see if it will start?"

"Sure. This thing will be a gas guzzler, but we may be able to use it." To our surprise, it started right up. "How much gas does it have?"

She looked at the gauge. "Almost a full tank."

"Awesome. Can you drive it?"

She grinned. It was a grin I was quickly beginning to like. "One way to find out. What do you have in mind?"

"Let's take it home with us," I said.

Julie followed me closely. I bet she thought I might try to speed off and lose her. The truth of it was, I was lonely. Very lonely. Achingly lonely. I could have done without a woman I suppose, if Rick were still alive. He and I were a good team. We worked well together and I enjoyed his company. I was no hermit. I needed a friend and a partner. Being an incredibly cute female the same age as me might work out very nicely. I hoped.

We neared the intersection where the road to the farm intersected with the state highway. I pulled over and stopped about a hundred yards away.

"What are we doing?" Julie asked when she got out.

"Let's park this van off the side of the road right here. It'll be a backup vehicle," I said.

She gave me a confused look. "I don't understand."

"We have plenty of vehicles at the farm, three automobiles, two tractors, and two ATVs. We need to spread it out. We're going to start parking backup vehicles at various locations."

She nodded in understanding. "Ah, smart," she then gave a small frown. "We should disable it somehow, so nobody else can take them, but it needs to be something that we can fix quickly."

I nodded in surprise. I had not thought of it. "That's a good idea," I pondered it over for a minute and then opened the fuse panel located on the side of the instrument panel. Sure enough, there was one fuse I could take out and the van would not start. "Okay, you see which one I've loosened?"

Julie pressed up against me and looked closer. Macie was the last girl who had pressed up against me. Even though both of us were wearing heavy coats, the close contact was making me nervous.

I cleared my thoughts and explained. "This way we don't have to do something outside of the van to get it going, and it's a quick fix. Just open the panel and push it back in." I took the key out of the ignition, put it under the visor, and straightened. Julie straightened as well, but remained standing next to me in the doorway of the van.

"See, we're making a pretty good team already," she looked at me expectantly. "Have I done a good job today?"

"I must admit, you have." More than you think, I thought silently. You've made me smile. I've not even felt like smiling since Christmas.

"Good enough to deserve a hot shower?" She smiled hopefully.

I laughed now. Something else I'd not done in a while. "I don't see why not, I could use one as well."

I stopped at the head of the bridge and used the binoculars on the house, which was about two hundred yards away. It was on a small rise about thirty feet above the level of the creek. Nothing appeared out of order. I got the backhoe out of the way and motioned for Julie to drive the truck through. I'd been leaving the concertina wire out of the way because it was such a pain in the ass to move into place, but now, I painstakingly strung it across the bridge and tied it down. Larry and Curly ran out of the barn to greet us, and after we petted them, they ran over and sniffed Moe's ass.

"You get your clothes inside. Oh, and I found some fresh sets of bed linens. How about changing out the beds? I'm going to get the rest of the stuff and get the gas stored. Then, we'll get the generator going and start supper."

Julie smiled again. "Okay," she replied and grabbed an armful of stuff.

I have to admit, I got everything unloaded, the gas stored, and the generator going quicker than I ever had before. I was a little winded because of it, and took a moment to catch my breath before I went inside. "Hey, it's me," I said as I walked in the door.

"In here!" she replied. I walked in my bedroom. She had taken her jacket off and hung it up in the closet. The tee shirt advertised the Fayetteville High School. She had lost even more weight since I had last seen her. Still, my loins were awakened. "Oh, I guess I should have asked first. Can I share drawer space with you? I don't have anywhere to put these clothes. They won't take up much room."

"Oh, I didn't think of it either. Sure, no problem. You'll be using Rick's bed while he's gone. On our next scavenging trip, we'll see if we can find a suitable bed for you. We have an extra bedroom that's full of stuff at the moment. We've just been using it for storage. I can clean it out and fix it up."

There was a moment of awkward silence while we stared at each other's feet.

"I got the generator on. It usually takes about fifteen minutes for the water heater to warm up. I was planning on fixing up a casserole dish. I kind of just mix different stuff together and cook it up. Does it sound okay?"

"It sounds wonderful! Let me wash my hands and I'll help," she said eagerly. I nodded appreciatively. I did not want to be constantly chiding her about hygiene. I washed up in the kitchen and went to work with the newly acquired copper cookware. Julie joined me a few minutes later. "Those are nice. They look like they were expensive."

"I imagine they were. Did you know copper is an incredible metal? When it is heated, it can actually kill bacteria. It has a very high thermal conductivity as well. Copper was used in cookware before the birth of Christ. Did ancient people somehow know that it killed the bacteria in the food they were preparing?"

I don't think she was impressed. She shrugged and pointed. "So, what are you going to dump in there?"

Note to self: not everyone is impressed with your factoids of information. "I thought I'd boil some rice. We've got some ground burger I put out to thaw this morning. I'll cook it and then throw them into a pot together. Add some chopped onions, some salt and pepper, tomato sauce, throw it all together, stir it up, put it all in a casserole dish and then put it in the oven for about twenty minutes. The recipe book calls for cheese, but we're out at the moment," I remembered the last time I cooked up this particular dish it was pretty bland. I got some salt out of the cabinet and put a decent amount into the heating water.

"What do we have to drink?"

"Right now, just grape Kool-Aid and coffee," I said. "I'm out of sodas and juice. Sorry."

Julie shook her head. "No, don't be. It all sounds delicious." She grabbed the box of rice and began to open it, but stopped. "Zach, I have this speech prepared and I was going to do it over dinner, but I've got to get it out of me."

She turned and looked at me. "I was a real bitch before, and I want to say that I deeply regret my behavior. And, it was really stupid of me to go along with mom's bullshit. For some unknown reason, she has to create drama wherever she goes. I went along with it, although I've no idea why, so I guess I'm just as guilty.

When you guys made us leave, I was missing you before we even made it halfway down the road. When that asshole thought he was going to rape me, I kept thinking if you and Rick were around, he'd be too afraid ever to try something like that. And, I kept watching all those so-called men. It was like the difference between night and day. You two plan, organize, and take action. You've got your shit together. Those idiots don't do much but sit around smoking weed and talking in one syllable words about their glory days in high school. You would have thought Jason was the next Peyton Manning or something, the way they talked."

Yeah, he was going to be a superstar, but it did not matter anymore. I really did not want to talk about them at the moment. Maybe later I'd fully debrief her about them.

She continued. "Anyway, what I'm saying is, none of us appreciated you two, me especially, and I am truly sorry. I'm so glad you found me when you did. I feel like I've been given a second chance and I'll try my hardest to make good on it."

I must admit, it really did sound sincere, but just in case, I was still going to sleep with my gun. I responded with a small grin. "Apology accepted. I think the water is hot enough for you to take a shower. I'll get dinner finished up. It should be ready by the time you get out."

"Would it use too much hot water if I shaved? I haven't done that since the last time I was here. My armpits feel like two miniature jungles."

I said it would be fine, but I honestly wondered how long it'd take to shave a month's worth of growth. "Thanks, Zach, you really are a good guy," she said quietly. She began to walk back to the bathroom. I turned toward the stove. She suddenly kissed me on the cheek and then hurried to the bathroom before I could react. The boys were sitting there on the kitchen floor, raptly watching the whole encounter. I guess it was more entertaining than sniffing each other's ass.

119

Chapter 18 – Training

I did not sleep well. It must have been something to do with the way she smelled after she got out of the shower, her scrubbed face with no smudges of dirt. Oh, and the shiny damp hair she had carefully combed out. Maybe it was what she was wearing when she joined me for dinner, which was one of my flannel shirts, some socks, and nothing else. At least, nothing else I could see. I imagined she was wearing a pair of those sexy panties I was tempted with earlier. I stole a few looks at her legs. They had a wonderful silky smooth, freshly shaven look.

We conversed as we ate.

"Were you involved in any sports when you were in high school?" she asked between bites.

I nodded. "Cross country track. I was a long distance runner." Being tall and skinny were positive attributes for long distance running. "How about you?" I asked.

"I was on the swim team, but I kept getting ear infections so I quit. After school, I had a part time job at a grocery store. Were you planning on going to college?"

I nodded. "Sort of, I was going to need a scholarship, or become hopelessly in debt with student loans. I had considered joining the military after graduation, but my Grandmother and Rick both were against the idea."

"Rick was against it? Isn't he a veteran or something?" She asked.

"Yeah, he was a highly decorated Vietnam vet. He said the military isn't so bad as long as nobody was shooting at you."

We both laughed at his logic. There was a pause in conversation as we ate. I decided I needed to make sure Julie was on the same page as me.

"Okay, let's talk about some slightly serious stuff," I said.

Julie stopped with a fork halfway to her mouth. "Okay," she replied quietly.

"Well, where to start." I scratched my chin, much as Rick would scratch his beard. "Lately, I've been a little bit depressed," which was an understatement. Little hell, I was so far down in the doldrums I was ready to eat a gun. I squashed the thought and continued. "I've said it before, but I'll say it again, the world as we know it has irrevocably changed and it will not recover anytime soon. You seemed to have been in a bit of denial the last time we spoke about it."

Julie nodded. "Yeah, I guess I was. It was really hard for me to get it, you know?"

"I agree. It's a real kick in the ass when you get over the denial stage and realize it. I let it get the better of me, and I had become quite depressed."

"What about Rick?" Julie asked. I suddenly realized I was speaking as though Rick were not around. I had to be more attentive.

"We never discussed it directly, but I think he knew. I had been doing a lot of moping around. But, I got up this morning and made a decision, enough moping. I am going to survive no matter what happens. I'm going to make it work. It's not going to be easy. In fact, it'll probably be tough as hell. There are going to be a lot of obstacles along the way and a lot of long days with very little sleep. If you want to be a part of our team, I need to know if Rick and I can count on you."

Julie started to answer and I held up a hand. "Before you respond, let me give you your options. Stay with us and you can expect a lot of long days, hard labor, and orders being barked at you constantly, which you will be expected to follow without argument. If you want no part of it, it's no problem. We can set you up in a vacant house, or we can even rig up that van for you to travel and live out of until you find other people to join up with," I took a breath and was about to continue when Julie stopped me by tapping her glass of water with a fork.

She fixed me with those beautiful blue eyes. "Treat me good, Zach Gunderson, and I'll be with you until the end," she said quietly. I did not know how to interpret her statement correctly. Instead, I nodded, uttered something unintelligible, and finished my meal quickly. Later, I lay awake for a long time after lights out. I imagined I could smell her, even from the other bedroom. I drifted off to sleep wondering what it would feel like to have her in my arms.

I tossed and turned most of the night. When I realized I was not going to get any sleep, I rolled out of bed and stretched the kinks out. It was still dark out. I dressed quietly, grabbed some night vision gear, an AR-15, and some other stuff. I closed the door quietly and made a roundabout route to the bridge. I was probably just being paranoid, but I was certain Jason and his group would be paying us a visit sometime soon. I checked the concertina wire for any evidence of tampering, but it appeared secure. I then rigged up some chlorine bombs with some soda bottles. They would not kill anyone, but when triggered, they would explode, and anyone within close proximity would receive painful burns on any exposed skin. I rigged them to sections of the concertina. As long as nobody jiggled them around, they would not activate. But, the first time someone tried to move the concertina wire, boom! They'd get a fiery surprise.

I jogged down the drive toward the state highway. When I neared the intersection, I left the road, hid behind a large tree, and had a look around. The intersection was T-shaped, an unremarkable joining of two rural roadways. I did not see any kind of movement, no people, nor any zombies. The green glow from the night vision equipment made the trees seem surreal. I was going to have to get used to the effect.

I went back into the woods for twenty-five yards and walked back and forth until I found a spot with a good view of the intersection. Satisfied, I went to work preparing a sniper position. I chose a position behind a fallen tree and drug some additional limbs around and over it for added concealment. I got as many leaves as I could and spread them on the ground where I foresaw myself lying in wait at some point in the near future. I was going to stock it with rations and ammo later during the day. I lay down behind the tree and sighted my AR-15 toward the intersection. It was a decent field of fire.

It was getting daylight now and I wanted to get back to the house before Julie woke up. I took off the night vision apparatus and placed it on the log. I walked back to the intersection and turned around. You could only see it if you knew where to look and looked really hard. Good enough.

Julie was standing beside the bridge when I got back.

"What are you doing here?" I asked suspiciously.

"I woke up and you were gone. I was worried," she said with a little bit of apprehension in her voice. She was dressed in Jeans, the flannel shirt she'd worn to bed the night before, boots, and a waist length jacket. I did not search her for a gun. Maybe later.

After a few seconds, I caught my breath. "Alright, let me show you something." I showed her the booby traps and explained what they did when they were moved. "So anyway, I'm glad you didn't decide to fool with this or else you might have gotten hurt."

Her face lit up. "Does this mean you actually like me?"

I smiled. "I suppose I do. Let's go eat. I'll race you!" I took off running. Julie squealed and hurried after me. She kept up pretty well, in spite of my head start.

I finished first and waited on her. "You cheated!" she lamented as she ran up. I laughed, and soon she was laughing as well. "I'll get you back, you just wait."

I was still chuckling as the two of us prepared a meal of eggs along with a batch of biscuits. I had several jars of jam and butter, but the flour would only last us a couple of more months. I ground up some of the coffee I had recently acquired and it was surprisingly good. Julie was savoring each bite. "I've not eaten any eggs since before Christmas."

"I'm glad you like it. Eat up, because we have a lot of chores to do today. Now, while you eat, why don't you tell me all about the crew your mother is currently with?"

"And Tommy, don't forget Tommy," she said.

I nodded. "Of course."

"Let's see," she counted off with her fingers the same way she did yesterday. "There is Darius, Jason, Macie, Chad, Trina, and Trina's uncle. I never heard his real name but they called him Tay. I guess it's a nickname or a shortened version of his real name, like Tayvon or something," she stopped long enough to finish eating a biscuit. I fixed another one for her. She definitely needed to gain some weight. "Thank you," she smiled appreciatively, but then she became serious.

"So, they told me all about you and Macie. Trina went into joyful detail about how she dumped you for Jason," she paused a moment. "They showed me the video Trina made."

So, Trina was the person who made the video. She's probably the one who posted it on the Internet as well. Obviously, she was not very nice.

I drank some coffee and refilled both of our mugs. "Did they talk about their other friend, the other one who kicked and stomped on me after I was down?"

"Yeah, somebody killed him. He was found stabbed to death. The cops never had a chance to figure out who did it." She started to bite into the biscuit, but stopped midway. "Wait, did you kill him?"

"Yes," I replied nonchalantly.

Her jaw dropped. "Holy shit, Zach! They said he'd been stabbed over thirty times!" she stared at me incredulously. I did not respond. Didn't need to.

Julie stared at me for a moment longer before realizing I was not going to elaborate. "Okay, well continuing, they are currently living in a house previously occupied by some rich people Chad knew. Apparently, Tay is some gang banging drug dealer. He had just gotten in over a hundred pounds of weed and never had a chance to sell it. They've been spending their days smoking it all up."

"Even Jason and Macie?" I asked.

"Jason, yes. Macie, no," she paused a moment and grabbed my hand. "She's pregnant with Jason's child, so she doesn't smoke or drink."

Pregnant. Wow. That was quick. I nodded and redirected the conversation.

"What kind of guns do they have?"

"They have two rifles and two handguns. One of the handguns, the larger one, they're out of ammunition. The smaller one is a twenty-two caliber, and they have plenty of ammo for it. I don't know about the rifles."

"Do you know what caliber they are? What type?"

"They're just like the one you were carrying this morning," she answered.

"Ah. AR-15 assault rifles," I said.

"Are those dangerous guns?" Julie asked.

"They're dependable and accurate, if they're kept clean. Three hundred meters is about the best you can hope for, but an expert marksman can hit a target up to around four hundred meters under good circumstances. If they're not automatics, they have a sustained rate of fire of twelve to fifteen rounds a minute. Any faster and they'll overheat. But, they've got to be fastidiously maintained. Otherwise, they're prone to jamming. Did you notice if they cleaned them?"

Julie snorted. Well, it may have been a laugh but it came out as a snort. "Not at all. Well, let me rephrase. Tay cleaned his one day, but it didn't seem like he did a very good job. He just rubbed an oily rag over it," she covered her mouth and burped. "Excuse me. I've eaten more in the last twelve hours than I've eaten in a week. I feel like I'm going to bust."

"I hope you don't stop up the toilet," I quipped. She stuck her tongue out at me. "Okay, you've been avoiding some things. Tell me what they said about Rick and me when our names came up."

"Darius doesn't think very highly you. He's made more than a few snide remarks." She wrinkled her nose when she spoke about him. "He would act nice, but when he looked at me it was always a dirty leer. I should have known better than ever be alone with him. Trina is basically stupid. I'm talking like she's borderline retarded or something. She goes along with whatever anyone else says and laughs at things that aren't even funny. Tay's mostly high all of his waking moments. He sits around, smokes his weed, and talks about what a big time gangster he is. Chad seemed to both like and fear you at first, now he says he's going to kill you and Rick. Whenever they retell the big fight, Jason grins and looks all smug. Macie doesn't say much of anything," she paused a really long time before talking again.

"My mother. Good old Mom. She told them they ought to come out here and take over," she scoffed. "Don't worry though. She doesn't remember how to get out here. One night, they sat around a map half the night, smoking weed and trying to get directions out of her. It would have been funny if what they were planning wasn't so terrible."

"But, you remembered where we live," I replied.

Julie shook her head. "I was so turned around I only remembered the Interstate and the road where we first met. I was totally lost. It was a pure stroke of luck we bumped into each other again."

I suddenly remembered my dream of Rick. You old fart, were you taking care of me, buddy?

Julie did not notice my change in expression and continued talking. "Don't worry, my mom has been smoking weed like there's no tomorrow. There's no way she'll remember." She finished the last biscuit and began cleaning the table.

I sat there in silence. There was one small problem. Macie had been here. She may be a lot of things, but she was not stupid. She would remember. And I could not rely on the late great Righteous Rick to protect me from everything. "When they talked about it, what did Macie have to say?" I asked.

Julie shook her head. "Not much of anything. She's very quiet. Was she like that in school?"

I smiled halfheartedly. Macie was very gregarious and popular in school. It seemed like everyone liked her.

"If they do show up, it sounds like your mother is going to be one of the primary agitators," I opined.

Julie snorted again. "You got that right. She's got Tay wrapped around her finger. I don't get my mom. She calls him a nigger behind his back, but still sleeps with him." She sat back down and frowned.

"Once, about a year ago, they were having a birthday party for Don at the car dealership he owned. I overheard some of the salesmen talking about her. One of them said she's had more cock in her than a used pair of Hanes underwear. They all laughed. I was furious at them at the time, but the more I get to know my mother, well, you know. Anyway, Darius says Tay has killed some people, so if it's true, he might be dangerous."

Was it true or was it just a punk trying to improve his street rep? I did not know, but it was still good information to know. "Hey, Julie, I forgot to ask, but did you guys ever see anyone else, or did they talk about seeing any people who weren't infected?"

"I haven't. Macie said she saw a plane in the distance one day. Everyone laughed at her, so she shut up. They claimed they shot at some people, but there is no way of knowing if it is the truth or they were full of shit." She got up and stretched. "I'm stuffed."

It was a lot of information to take in. I must have sat there lost in my thoughts for several minutes because Julie had come up behind me without my noticing. She started rubbing my shoulders.

It felt really nice. I think it was the first time anyone had ever rubbed my shoulders.

"Are you okay, Zach?" she asked. "I'm sorry about telling you all of those things. It must have been really hard to hear."

I reached up and patted one of her hands. "Not at all. Thank you for being truthful with me."

She leaned down and rested her chin on the top of my head. "We're a team, right?"

I squeezed her hand now. I did not want to let go. "Yes we are," I sighed. "I think you should know that Macie knows where the farm is located. She's been here before. When they get hungry enough, they'll show up."

She gasped and stood. "What are you going to do?" she asked.

"If it's just Macie and Jason, I'll try to help them out," I replied.

She gasped again. "Really? After what they did to you?"

I shrugged one shoulder. "Macie can't help it that she fell in love with someone else. It hurt, sure. It hurt like hell, but I'm over it."

"But what about Jason? He beat you up," she said.

I laughed without pleasure. "I swung at him first, remember? I lost fair and square. It's the other one I have an issue with. If Darius shows up, I don't know. I doubt it will be pleasant."

Julie moved from behind me and refilled our mugs before sitting back down. "Are you going to kill him too?"

"I don't know. I don't like him, but I don't know."

"Why would you help any of them?" she asked. She was looking at me somberly.

"My logic for helping them is a little complicated," I said.

She grinned. "So try me."

I grinned back. "Okay, I'll try. Think of it from this perspective. It all centers on the collapse of our society. It is up to the survivors to rebuild. Old grudges and differences of opinion should be set aside. It is essential for people to work together. If everyone pitches in, we can slowly rebuild our civilization. Or, if we don't, we'll quickly revert back to how we lived a few thousand years ago. It's up to people like you and me, Julie. Everyone we come into contact with, we have to try. Otherwise, mankind is more than likely doomed." I took a few sips.

"Here I go rambling on again. The first thing we need to do is maintain a suitable life for ourselves. We've got a lot of work to do, and I've got some training for you. Come on, you're helping out. No Xbox for you today."

Her mouth fell open. "Oh, you smart ass."

I got up and Julie smacked me on the butt as I walked away. I jumped and she giggled. I couldn't help but grin. I'd been doing a lot of grinning lately. It felt good.

We finished up the day in the barn. I had cleared off one of the work benches and had all of our weapons lain out. "I think I remember you saying you've shot a gun before."

"Yeah, I had a boyfriend who liked to skeet shoot with his father. I tried it out a few times."

"Boyfriend huh, did he survive?" I asked.

She shrugged. "We had broken up about a month before the outbreak. I never saw him at the school gym, so I honestly don't know. It wasn't anything serious," she picked up a pistol and aimed at an imaginary target. "How many people do you think survived?"

"It's difficult to make an accurate estimate. There are a lot of variables to consider. If it is a one in six survival ratio, that's a little over one billion worldwide. One in ten ratio, about six hundred million. You get the idea."

"And then there are the zombies," she added.

"Yeah, the zombies are a major variable. A lot of people are going to be killed because of this plague and the ensuing chaos. I've got a working theory about the zombies, but right now, I'm going to teach you about firearms. Let's get started."

I spent the next two hours going over the various firearms in our inventory. We started with the shotguns, which she already knew the basics of.

"The twelve-gauge is a natural man killer. There are larger bores like the ten gauge, eight gauge, and I believe there is even a four gauge, but those are meant to be used on large game. We don't have any of those, so don't worry about them. This one here," I picked up a shotgun, "is a Remington, model 870 twelve gauge shotgun," I pointed to another shotgun. "His brother here is a Remington model 1100. The 870 has a pump action, see?" I demonstrated and worked the action. "The 1100 is a semiautomatic. That's the only real difference. Both of them are twelve-gauge," I continued with each weapon, going over the advantages and limitations of each.

Julie bit her lip. "I hope I can remember all of this," she said.

"Don't worry. I'm going to be repeating all of this info over and over until I'm blue in the face and you're sick of hearing it, but you'll have it all memorized before I'm done. Now, I'm going to show you how to break each one of them down and how to properly clean them."

I spent the next two hours going over three weapons, the 870 shotgun, the AR-15, and the Glock model 23. I only worked with her on those three because I wanted her to be proficient in as short a time as possible.

"Where did you learn all of this from?" She asked.

I smiled. "From Rick. He taught me the exact same way I'm teaching you. The man is amazing."

"When he gets back, is he going to be okay with me being here?" Julie asked. "I mean, he seemed ready to kill all of us the last time I saw him. He was really mad."

I missed the man. I had to be careful or I was going to tear up. "I'm betting he already knows you're here. It'll be fine."

"I hope so. I'm starting to like it here."

I looked over at her. She just smiled and continued scrubbing the AR-15's bolt. We eventually finished cleaning all of them. It had taken the rest of the afternoon and the sun was setting. I finished with showing her how to load and fire the AR-15.

"This one is sighted in at one hundred yards. Let's take a walk outside."

We walked in front of the house. It was on a hill overlooking the creek, bridge, and roadway.

"How far is the bridge from here?" I asked.

"Um, one hundred yards?" she scrunched her eyes up as she guessed.

I grunted. "Two hundred. So if you aim at someone on the bridge, when you look through the scope you aim one mil higher. Try it out. Do you see the little dot?"

She held the rifle up and squinted into the ACOG scope. "Yeah."

"Okay, good. Now, look at the bridge and the area immediately around the bridge. What do you see?"

"You've got some fence poles and barb wire strung up on the far side of the creek, and you have the backhoe blocking it on the other side. Can't people just wade through the creek?"

"It runs about six to eight feet deep. Plus, right now, the water is really cold and the banks are slick. It would be very difficult. Rick has also rigged up some booby traps in the creek bed. Anyone walking through there will get his or her foot impaled on a sharpened spike. What else do you see?"

She squinted, but came up with nothing. "Look at the tree limbs. See the various white strips of cloth tied to the limbs?" I asked. She nodded. "They give you an indication of your wind currents."

"You guys put them there on purpose for adjusting your aim, right?"

I nodded. "I know what that's called, Kentucky-windage, right?" she asked.

"Exactly," I replied.

"You guys have really thought this all out."

"When we go inside, I'm going to teach you the purpose of the range cards we have beside each window as well," I said.

"After dinner, I hope. Can we take showers tonight?"

I thought about it and shrugged. "We have laundry to do as well, so we'll have the generator going anyway."

At this, Julie put her arm through mine and hugged herself against me. And yes, I felt her breasts press against my arm. At least, I believed I did. We both lapsed into a comfortable silence and stood there admiring the sunset the way romantic couples do.

Our reverie was broken when I heard the sound of crunching gravel. A car was approaching. I was pretty sure I knew who was coming. "Here, take the rifle and crouch down behind the truck. If it's who I think it is, I don't want them to see you."

I reached into the cab of the truck and retrieved the binoculars. It was a black sedan and there were two people in it. It approached very slowly, as if the driver was uncertain what awaited them. "Do they have a black four-door? Maybe a Dodge Stratus, or something like it?"

"Yeah, Jason has one," she said.

I nodded knowingly. I knew they would show up eventually, especially after everything Julie told me about their living situation.

My estimation was off though. I thought it would be at least two more days before they got up the nerve. The car stopped in front of the concertina. A short time later, Macie exited from the passenger side. I did not recognize her at first. Her facial features were drawn and stringy hair peeked out of a soiled stocking knit cap. She looked around and approached the wire. There was no way I could stop her in time if she tried to climb over it. Thankfully, she stopped a few feet away and started waving a white rag.

How quaint.

I set the binoculars down and spoke to Julie. "I'm going to go down there. Watch my back. If there's trouble, start shooting."

She was looking up at me now. "You remember how to lock and load, and take the safety off?"

She performed the actions in front of me. "Like that?"

I nodded in satisfaction. "Yeah. Now here's another quick training lesson. There are hand signals Rick and I use. There are only two I need you to know right now. If I raise my hands like I'm surrendering, it means my life is in danger. If I have my hands down and cross my hands behind my back like this," I demonstrated with my palms out and crossing my hands behind my back a couple of times like I was trying to wave away a smelly fart. It was a signal from some old warrior poetry, Keats or Kipling I believe. One thing was for certain, none of them read poetry, not even Macie. "Okay, if I make this signal, it means all is well and to hold your fire. Got it?"

"Yeah, okay. Zach?" She looked concerned. "Be careful, and come back to me, please," she said earnestly.

"You got it," I replied. On a sudden impulse, I bent down and kissed her on the top of the head. Why did I kiss her on the top of her head? I knew damn good and well I was dying to kiss her on the lips. I sighed as I walked away. It was a lot easier when it was just Rick and me. With Rick, there was no kissing under any circumstances.

I did a quick press check of my Glock and put it in my jacket pocket. I was going to keep my hand on it and shoot them through my jacket if I had to. Rick had some cases of Army rations called MREs, or Meal, Ready to Eat. I hated them, and swore I would only eat them if I were on the brink of starvation. I retrieved two cases and put them on the back of the ATV. Macie waved the white rag again as I approached.

I parked the ATV on the opposite side of the concertina wire, and sat there a minute looking them over. They were certainly a sorry looking pair. Their clothes were looking rough and stained. It was hard to see their physiques because they were both wearing loose fitting heavy clothing, but their faces were thin and drawn. Their car did not look much better. The windshield was cracked in a starburst pattern and there appeared to be hair and small pieces of flesh embedded in the cracks. The hood was dented also, along with a broken headlight.

"Hello, Macie," I said lightly. She was wearing a black turtleneck sweater, which, like the jeans she was wearing, had gone a few days without being washed. I noticed a small bulge to her tummy, but otherwise, she looked emaciated. Like one of those anorexic runway models. Or maybe one of those starving African kids with distended bellies they show on late night TV commercials. She was still beautiful though.

Jason was standing beside the car when I drove up.

As I spoke to her, he walked over beside her and put an arm around her possessively. He still had his height and broad shoulders, but his neck was now ultrathin and his once handsome face was pockmarked with blackheads. I could not see his ribs, but I bet they were poking through. He had bloodshot eyes also. I could not tell if he was sick or had been smoking marijuana. Dirty jeans and roughly scuffed boots completed his ensemble. He may have been armed, but if he was, it was in the car or hidden under his clothing.

Macie started the conversation. "Hello, Zach. I know we're probably the last people that you want to see."

"And yet, this knowledge did not stop the two of you from showing up anyway. What happened to your car?" I asked.

Jason spoke up. "One of those zombie creatures ran out in the roadway. I ran his ass over." He smirked, like it was some kind of amazing feat. I remembered that smirk.

I nodded, but said nothing. An awkward silence ensued for several seconds. Well, it wasn't awkward for me. I guess they thought I would be interested in hearing the story of the mighty Jason Argos smiting an evil zombie. Not.

Macie broke the silence. "Well, I'm glad you're alive, Zach."

I scoffed. "If you say so," I said, to which there was more awkward silence before I spoke again. "Anyway, I guess I am glad the two of you have survived as well. I mean it. But you two did not drive all the way out here just to convey your heartfelt love. What's going on here?"

She looked down a moment and then inhaled before answering. "We were hoping you would provide us with some food," she said.

"Now, why in the world did you think Rick and I, of all people, would have enough food to go around?" I was met by downcast stares. "I guess what I'm asking is, is there some kind of information you two possess which makes you think that we have loads of spare food? Spit it out."

There was no pun intended in that last remark. I swear.

Jason looked up then. He had a hint of a scowl. He did not like the way I was talking to them. "We've met some people that said you guys have plenty, more than enough in fact," he said.

I thought about his statement and how he said it. "What exactly do you mean by more than enough?" I got more silent stares. "Who told you that load of crap?" I tried to sound casual. I knew who they were referring to. I just wanted to see if they would give me an honest answer.

"Janet, Julie, and Tommy Frierson." Macie answered. Jason cut his eyes at her, but said nothing.

I slowly nodded. "They were here a while back along with a man named Don, but they're exaggerating a great deal. We have some stuff Rick and I canned back this fall, but quite a bit of it is gone, thanks to the Friersons. All they ever did was sit around and eat."

I acted as though I were thinking it over. I kicked a pebble with my boot. "I suppose we can spare a small amount. What do you have to trade?"

This earned me a stupefied look from both of them. I frowned. "Wait, am I to understand the two of you rode up here expecting a free handout?"

Jason could not hide his scowl any longer. "Look, Zach, we aren't looking to bother you or anything."

It was a lie. He suddenly squinted up toward the house. I bet he was wondering where Rick was, and if he was about to be shot. Good. "As you can see, Macie is pregnant. She needs food."

"Not just food, she needs sustenance. Nutrition. Have you two even bothered to determine the daily nutritional needs of an average person? Calorie intake? How about the daily amount of water the average human needs?"

I did not get a verbal response, only silent stares. I sighed and shook my head. Yeah, I was being a smartass, but so what. "So, you two didn't answer me. Do you or do you not have anything to trade?"

Macie actually hung her head now, like a puppy dog being scolded for crapping on the carpet. A part of me hoped I had punched some buttons with her self-esteem. Much like she did to me not so long ago. Jason, on the other hand, narrowed his eyes and rubbed his hands together, as if he wanted to hit me again.

He took a slow breath and spoke. "No, Zach, we didn't think to bring anything. I have no idea what you would want anyway."

I clenched my teeth together and forced myself to be silent for a moment. My emotions and my aforementioned logic of putting aside old grudges were contradicting each other. I got my thoughts in order before responding. "Okay, fair enough. Think of it from this perspective. There are many products out there that would be sought after commodities. Food, fresh water, medical supplies, fuel, you get the idea. One thing I really want from you two is honesty, and I believe you are being at least somewhat honest with me, Jason."

I walked over to the ATV and retrieved the MREs. "Here," I said, handing the cases over the wire to him. I then did a quick signal behind my back. It was good for now, but it could change. I watched their hands and kept an eye back down the road. I mean, it was entirely possible the two of them had dropped their friends off before driving up here and they were now sneaking up through the woods to take a few shots at me.

"It's not much, but if you ration it out, it'll keep you two going for a couple of weeks. How many are in your group?"

Jason looked over at Macie. She answered. "There are eight of us altogether."

I whistled and shook my head. "There is no conceivable way we can feed all eight of you. I might be persuaded to butcher a cow, but cows are hard to come by these days. What you have in your hand now will be the only freebies you'll get. We're not a welfare agency. You come back with stuff to trade, or don't bother coming back at all. And only you two, I'm not interested in meeting your friends. In fact, if any of your friends show up, it will tell me you told them where Rick and I live. Then it'll be open season on all of you, you included, Macie," I said pointedly. Her eyes widened at this threat.

"Oh..." I acted as if I was in deep thought. "Speaking of friends, Jason what was the name of your center on the football team?"

His eyes narrowed. "Jasper Goad, why?"

"He was one of the punks who put the boots to me. The other one, your friend, Darius, did he survive?"

They both nodded. I looked at Macie. "Have you seen Felix?"

"I haven't seen him," she answered. "I've not seen anyone else from High School."

Jason interrupted. "Wait, wait. Why did you want to know Jasper's name?" he demanded. His eyes were still narrowed at me.

I fixed him with a stare of my own. "We bumped into each other one night in a parking lot. He never bothered telling me his name, but he attacked me again and tried to rob me. He bit off more than he could chew, metaphorically speaking."

Both of them paled in realization. My voice went down an octave. "Jason, keep your boy Darius away from me. As far as I'm concerned, he's a kill on sight target."

Jason nodded his head slowly, but there was no friendliness in his eyes. "I wouldn't go around making offhanded threats like that if I were you, Zach. Darius is pretty tough."

"I'm sure people said the same of Jasper. If Darius is truly your friend, you'd best warn him."

I was through with the chit chat. Jason was starting to irritate me and I really wanted this to be a civil meeting.

He stared at me for a moment. I was not sure what he was thinking. Any thoughts he may have had about how he was going to handle me seemed to have fizzled. He did not like me, but hunger was the stronger feeling. He looked over the boxes. Macie pointed at them. "What are those?"

"Military rations. They're stored in individually sealed packages. Each package is supposed to have the correct amount of nutrition." I did not tell her they tasted awful. She looked at me appreciatively and silently said thank you.

"When can we come back?" Jason asked.

"I'm thinking Sunday afternoons will be good for Rick and me. Make it two weeks from today."

"Where is Rick?" Macie suddenly asked. I bet they were wondering the whole time where he may be.

"Oh, he's nearby. Guys, I guess I should have said this earlier, just don't do anything sudden or anything which could be perceived as hostile. He's probably got his crosshairs on one of you. I don't know which of you he dislikes the most." I looked around nervously and lowered my voice to just above a whisper. "Listen, steer clear of him. Just between us, he's gone off the deep end. He thinks he's back in Vietnam and wanders around the farm dressed like Rambo. It's got me a bit worried."

Jason scoffed and kicked at a rock. Macie looked around worriedly before she continued. "Uh, okay. What kind of items are you willing to trade for? I mean, like Jason said, we have no idea what you want."

I sighed deeply. I couldn't help it. "I'm getting the distinct impression that the two of you and your group have done no planning whatsoever."

Jason scoffed again. He did not like being on the defensive. "Here is why I say that. If you think it through, you will know exactly what commodities are valuable items. Those same items would make them good for barter as well," I tried to keep it simple. "Food for example, if you find four boxes of Corn Flakes, bring two of them back here and we'll work out some kind of trade. And of course, there are many other items that would be considered valued commodities like gasoline, hygiene products, toilet paper, toothpaste, dental floss, weapons, ammo, and any type of medical supplies. C'mon, you two, think it through. Put together a plan with your friends on how you can most efficiently gather supplies. You get the idea, right?"

They looked at each other and nodded grudgingly.

"Good, because we only have a limited supply. Rick and I will be lucky if we can last until summer, but I'll try to work with you two." I looked at them. They seemed to be accepting the advice that I was offering them, but you never know.

I glanced at my watch. "We need to wrap this up. I've got stuff to do now, so we can talk again in two weeks. Meet me at this spot at... let's say four p.m. By the way, congratulations on the pregnancy. I truly hope you two are happy and you have a healthy baby." I turned to go, but stopped.

"If you don't mind me saying so, get away from those so-called friends. Find an out of the way place and make yourselves a home. We'll try to help if we can. We'll give you some cattle. We'll help you get a garden going in the spring. I mean it."

Jason motioned with the boxes of rations. "Thanks, man."

I nodded in acknowledgement. Macie did not respond. She just stared at me sadly. I could see her eyes watering up. They drove away soon after.

Chapter 19 - Learning to Share

It all started with sharing the shower. One evening after a hard day of work, Julie pointed out we'd save water and generator fuel if we shared a shower. I immediately concurred with her astute logic. Sharing was always good, right? She was even kind enough to help soap me up. I returned the favor of course. After helping dry each other off, we agreed, by extension of her logic, sharing the same bed would keep us both warmer at night rather than the illogical practice of using separate beds.

You get the idea. We were attracted to each other. I think we both knew it from the start, but we were still awkward teenagers. Nevertheless, the more time we spent together, the stronger our mutual attraction became. It was inevitable I suppose. I missed Rick. I missed him a lot. But, Julie was turning into a pretty damn good friend.

Once we became intimate, it was as if the dam had burst. We went through a couple of boxes of condoms in no time. After one particularly invigorating lovemaking session, we were entwined in each other's arms talking about an unplanned pregnancy.

"I think I'd like having your child," Julie commented. It was muffled because her head was buried in the crook of my neck. Even so, I heard it clearly. "What do you think?"

"There is the potential for a lot of problems in pregnancy and childbirth. Back before the outbreak, the maternal death rate was approximately 200,000 to 800,000 a year. A lack of access to health care in the third world countries accounted for the largest percentage of those numbers. That's essentially what we are now, a third world country. It'd be risky, nothing at all like that old Brooke Shields movie."

"Which one?" She asked.

"Blue Lagoon," I answered.

"I've never seen it."

"It's one of those mushy romantic movies made in 1980. Two kids played by Brook Shields and Christopher Atkins are stranded on an island together. They grow up. They figure out how to have sex. She gets pregnant and has a beautiful healthy baby. All is perfect. They never even get a mosquito bite."

"Sounds cheesy," she said. I grunted in agreement. "So what will we do?"

I shrugged. "Out of all of these survivors, one would hope there are a few doctors and nurses out there. I need to get on the Ham radio more often and reach out to these people," I said and chuckled. "Maybe you should be the one on the radio. If it's your voice, some old lonely, horny doctor will surely come out of the woodwork."

Julie giggled. "I guess in the meantime, I should learn how to give a blowjob. Maybe I should start right now." She moved her head off my shoulder. I soon let out a long involuntary moan.

Afterward, I got up and checked on the laundry. We had clotheslines strung up inside the house due to the freezing temperatures outside. I retrieved the clean clothes from the washer and handed them to Julie. She started hanging them to dry. "I need to turn the generator off before bed. I'll be right back."

"Okay, handsome," she smiled warmly at me. She was wearing nothing but a pair of silky, white, lacey panties. When she raised her arms to hang the clothes, it caused some kind of change to her physique that was just…erotic. It reminded me of a lithe ballerina. She had gained weight in all of the right places. I think I could have watched her all night. She caught me looking.

"What?" She asked.

"You're beautiful," I said simply.

She smiled warmly. "The sooner you get the generator turned off, the sooner we can go back to bed." She smiled again and went back to hanging up clothes.

I started to don some clothes, but figured why bother. I put my heavy parka on and sneakers. Nothing else. Hell, I was only going to be outside for a second. I turned the light off before opening the door. It was a habit instilled upon me by Rick. You never wanted to be silhouetted in a lit doorway, an easy target for your enemy.

It was cold out and there was a full moon hanging in a crystal clear sky. The icy air felt invigorating, but I definitely did not want to be outside for more than a minute or two. I trotted to the back of the house. We had a lean-to built around the generator that was closed in on three sides and insulated in order to keep the sound down, but it wasn't completely soundproof. The generator needed air circulating around it. Otherwise, it'd overheat, and it needed somewhere for the exhaust to go.

As I walked in the open portion of the lean-to, I quickly realized I was no longer alone. The reeking stench was my first warning. Standing in front of the lean-to was a massive rotting hulk, clad in gore encrusted bib overalls. He was well over six feet tall, maybe closer to seven feet, and had to weigh at least three hundred pounds. Either he was attracted to the sound of the generator, or perhaps he was admiring Rick's handiwork. Hell, maybe he was planning on stealing it and taking it back to his zombie house. He was certainly big enough to carry it over one shoulder. I stood there confused. Where the hell had he come from? How did he get past the fences and the creek?

Somehow, he heard or sensed me and turned around. I stumbled back. A portion of his face was completely rotted off. He had a long beard on his good side that had pieces of putrid flesh stuck in it. Whether it was his flesh or someone else's, I had no idea. He emitted a raspy, phlegmy howl, and lunged toward me. I tried to back up but stumbled over something in the yard, probably a big frozen pile of dog shit. I managed to catch myself from falling, but it allowed the hulk to close the distance between us. He grabbed my arm, pulled it to his mouth, and chomped down. He was amazingly strong for someone who was decomposing. I felt the crushing pressure of his jaws clamping down on my forearm. I thought he was going to snap it in half. Fortunately for me, I had my parka on. It was thickly insulated. The padding allowed me just enough slack to wiggle my arm out of danger.

So now, I was totally naked, except for a pair of shit covered sneakers, in a life or death struggle with an abnormally large zombie. I ran backwards and bumped up against the wood pile. I suddenly remembered, I had a nice pile of kindling split up and lying at one end. They were a mixture of seasoned hickory and oak, nice and hard. They were about two feet long and just small enough in diameter for me to get a good grip. I grabbed one in each hand. Big boy had realized there was now nothing edible in my parka and dropped it. He stretched out his arms and made his way toward me.

It was time for a little bit of Mohammed Ali. I danced around him, slipped in and hit him in the head with one of my pieces of kindling, and then would dance back just out of his reach. Mr. Ali would have been proud. I kept this up for what seemed like several minutes, the big behemoth had a head as hard as an anvil. I was knocking pieces of flesh off each time I hit him, but it did not seem to matter. He would stagger with each blow and then start shuffling toward me again. I finally knocked his arms away with one swing and got in one terrific blow to the top of the head. Big boy went down to his knees. I moved in, dropped one of the pieces of wood and used both hands to launch a grand slam home run against his head.

Mr. Ruth would have been just as proud as Mr. Ali. The zombie's head cracked open like a ripe watermelon and putrid brain tissue flew out.

It was about this time Julie ran up. I had no idea how long she had been standing there. She pointed a shotgun from about six inches away, and put some double-ought buckshot into his head for an elegant, but needless, coup de' grace. He was finished. I must confess though, I did not even see him fall, because at the moment, I was staring at Julie's jiggling breasts and very erect nipples. She had not bothered with clothes either, not even sneakers. She was only clad in a pair of those incredibly sexy panties.

She looked over at me wide-eyed, breathing heavily. "I forgot about the safety!" I smiled nervously and slowly pushed the barrel away from me, as it was currently pointed at my nether regions. We made sure big boy was truly dead, and then made a quick walk around the yard looking for any other possible threats. It was quite cold, so we made it a quick search, hurried, and went inside.

We were both shivering quite a bit now. The cold, combined with the adrenalin dump, was having an effect. I motioned outside as I looked over at Julie. "We'll drag him to the sinkhole and burn him, but not tonight, first thing in the morning."

Julie nodded. She then leaned the shotgun up against the wall and jumped on me, wrapping both her arms and legs around me.

"Oh, my God, that was a rush! I mean, I was watching you fighting that thing and all I could watch was your dick flopping around, and when I shot him, I think I had an orgasm!"

We fell to the floor then. We didn't even make it to the bedroom.

We had slept later than usual. It was already past six when I opened my eyes. The three stooges were all lined up with their muzzles on the bed, staring at us expectantly. I nudged Julie. She moaned and pulled the covers over her face. She was definitely not a morning person.

"C'mon, we need to get the body disposed of. Afterward, we'll have some breakfast. We've got a hell of a lot of things to do and I've got a lot to talk to you about," I said with another nudge. Larry gave a small whimper. I suspected he needed to visit the yard badly.

I got no response until I pulled the covers down. Julie groaned. "You always have this sense of urgency thing going on. Can't we just have one lazy day?"

"Maybe one day, but not now. We have so much to do and a limited amount of time, so you've got to work with me. You must trust me. I've got our best interests in mind."

Julie groaned again, but threw the blankets off and shuffled to the bathroom. She stopped, yawned, and rubbed her eyes.

"I do trust you. You know that, right?" she looked at me sleepily. Her face was puffy and her hair was disheveled, but she looked beautiful. I smiled with the realization I was falling for this girl.

We dragged the remains of the zombie to the sinkhole with the ATV. It was about eight feet deep and ten feet long and shaped like a poorly drawn oval. It was used because it was in a remote location and several feet below the elevation of our well. Julie rode on the back with her face close to mine. We used some precious diesel to get a good fire going, and then we sat and watched the body burn. "You know, I have no idea where it came from. We should check the fence line. Can you hold off from breakfast for a few?" I asked. She nodded agreeably. "Good. I want you to see the property too."

We rode the fence line until I found a portion of the fence with a post tilted at an odd angle. It looked as though one or more of the cows had pushed against it and the soft soil gave just a bit. The result was part of the fence line had sagged close to the ground. I looked at the fencing closer and found some scraps of denim caught in the barbed wire, presumably from the zombie's bib overalls. I had tools and a tamping bar on the back of the ATV. Julie and I had the section of fence repaired in no time. We did not come across any other zombies, which further convinced me big boy was a farmer who had lived nearby. Somehow, he heard the sound of the generator and was drawn to the house. It is a quandary I needed to figure out a solution for. "We'll have to inspect the fence like this frequently, but I think that we're good for now."

"Yeah, whatever. Is it time for breakfast now?" she asked indifferently. I think my jaw dropped, and then she burst out giggling. "Got you!" she was right, she got me.

Not to be outdone, I grabbed a handful of semi-frozen cow manure and started walking toward her. Her laughter turned into a shriek and she ran. Like a girl. I told her so.

Chapter 20 – Betrayal at the Bridge

I finished butchering the cow with the band saw. It was the first one I had ever done. I had watched Rick and Mr. Parson do it once, which was about the extent of my knowledge in this particular expertise. I started by killing it three days ago and left it hanging so all of the blood would drain out. It was not a clean operation, but I got it done. I had a chart of all of the different cuts of meat and sort of got it figured out. I would cut a slab with the saw and hand it over to Julie. She'd rinse it off and put it in a cooler, which had some ice lining the bottom. I had set several ice trays filled with water outside the previous evening. It was yet another tedious chore, but, like all of the other chores, very necessary. I hoped we could better preserve the meat this way, rather than smoke curing it or freezing all of it outright. We worked it out and cleaned up the residual products. As I finished cleaning, I began questioning Julie.

"Okay, go over it again."

It had been two weeks. We were expecting visitors this afternoon.

She made an exaggerated sigh. I looked over at her. I'm sure I irritated the crap out of her at times, but this was important, so I stared at her pointedly. She relented.

"I'm going to hide in the sniper hole behind the tree and watch for Jason and Macie to drive up. I'm to call you on the walkie-talkie and let you know if it's just the two of them or if there is anyone else with them. If everything goes well, you're going to radio me when they leave. If I don't hear from you, or I hear gunshots, when they drive back down the road, kill them both. If I can't get a good shot on them, disable the car."

"What about your escape?" I asked.

"Bug out if I'm able, if not, hide in place," she replied.

"For how long, and what is your bug out route?" I continued pressing.

"Wait until well after dark. Recon the bridge for at least an hour for enemy movement with the night vision gear. If there are any enemy and if I have an opportunity, shoot them and then sneak back to my hole. If there's nobody there, go through the concertina the way you showed me. Recon the house and make sure there are no enemy. Oh, if I'm inside before you come home, you're going to throw a couple of rocks at the door before coming in. That way, I'll know it's you and you're alone."

"And if you're inside alone and someone walks through the door without first throwing a few rocks at it?" I pressed.

"I'm to keep all of the lights off and use the night vision gear. If someone comes through the door and it isn't you, shoot them."

I stopped what I was doing and made eye contact with her. "Do you think you can do it? Kill a real person?" I asked. She nodded her head.

"Okay. I believe you can too. According to Rick though, when you're at that critical moment, your moral consciousness will sometimes…"

She cut me off. "I can do it, okay? As far as I'm concerned, we should have killed them the first time they showed up."

I nodded. She was a feisty one. I walked up and kissed her. We held each other for several silent seconds.

"Alright, let's get cleaned up and we'll have a bite to eat. I want to get you in place at least a few hours before they're scheduled to arrive."

We ate the rest of our lunch in relative silence, with the exception of the dogs emitting pitiful whines in hopes of food scraps.

*****

Julie was in place. Zach had placed her there with instructions only to sip her water when absolutely necessary. Otherwise, she would have the urge to urinate every ten minutes. He had fashioned a pseudo camouflage outfit made out of strips of burlap bags. Hopefully, it provided adequate camouflage. Underneath, she had on some oversize long johns, three pairs of socks, jeans, and boots. It was quite cold out. She got in the hole he had dug out behind a fallen tree, and then put branches and leaves over her. She checked her watch that Zach had given her. It was a Tactical 5.11, just like the one Rick and Zach were wearing when she first met them. It was just before four p.m. She'd already been sitting there for two hours. There had been no sign of life, and she had drunk more water than she had intended to. She did not fully understand why Zach had wanted her in place so early, but did not question him. She had realized early on that he was smarter than most people were. And he was her boyfriend. She liked thinking in those terms. Just as she thought of him, his voice softly came out of the walkie-talkie.

"It's getting close to four now. How are you doing?" He asked.

"I'm fine," she whispered. "Nothing here but the trees so far."

He acknowledged and the radio became quiet. Her thoughts soon wandered. She liked Zach. No, it was much more. She was in love with Zach. The first time she met him, he seemed a bit…arrogant. Arrogant and bossy. She was attracted to him, but at the same time, she was put off by his attitude.

He acted as if his opinion was the wisest in the group. It was a turn-off. And Rick, who was old enough to be his grandfather, always seemed to defer to him. But Rick knew how smart Zach was. Julie realized it now. She also knew Rick must have died or something. She did not say anything, but one day, she would ask what happened. Zach would tell her the truth, but she knew it was not the right time.

She checked her watch again. It was right at four. They would be coming soon. If Jason and Macie betrayed Zach, she was going to kill them. She was especially going to Jason. She didn't like him from the first moment the two of them met. Macie was not much better. When they first met, she had barely said hello. She had whispered to Jason, but it was loud enough for Julie to hear. Macie did not want them there. If it were not for the fact Tay was practically eye-fucking her mom from the get go, she was sure they would have been turned away, maybe even shot. After their first encounter, Macie was always aloof. The only nice gesture she ever extended to her was to hand her some napkins when she was on the toilet with diarrhea and had run out of toilet paper.

Julie had watched the video. Her mother had cackled in laughter. Julie did not, and in fact, she immediately became angry. Her feelings confused her. Why was she angry over somebody getting beaten whom she did not like? It was then she realized that maybe she was attracted to Zach more than she wanted to admit. The video made little Tommy cry. He liked Zach as well. God how she missed her pesky little brother!

Zach did not look the same in the video. In the video, he looked like a helpless little boy. Now, he was bigger, more muscular. His expression was harder, no longer a skinny little boy, but a grown man. Watching him beat the big zombie down the night before was both frightening and exhilarating. His muscles literally rippled in the moonlight, and even the frigid air did not cause much shrinkage of certain appendages. She smiled at the visual image. It had greatly aroused her then, and even now, she felt a stirring. She involuntarily gasped in wonderment of the feelings she had for him.

She had kept waiting for him to make a pass at her. When he didn't, well, she did. Zach was not her first. Hell, he wasn't her second. Her first happened after school one day on the family sofa. She thought she was in love then. What did she know about love? The relationship lasted less than a month. Her second lover, the memory of him brought a grimace. He was nothing more than a big dumb country boy. Their relationship mostly consisted of sitting around, smoking weed, having sex, and playing video games. She actually convinced herself for a while that she loved him, but one day, she watched as he misspelled his own mother's name. In an instant, it went from love to disgust, and then later to pity. Zach was different. She was glad he took her back.

Her reverie was interrupted by an approaching car. They still had the broken windshield, and it looked like someone had made a half-assed attempt to hold it together with several strips of silver duct tape. "Black Stratus approaching." She whispered into the radio. There was a click of acknowledgement. "Two figures inside." Another click. The car stopped. It took her a moment to adjust the binoculars, but she soon recognized the occupants. "Correction, it looks like there're three people. It's Jason, Tay, and Darius." She nervously reported. Zach's response was a slow click of the microphone. He heard and he knew that he had been betrayed. If she were still a petulant brat, she would have used the opportunity to say she told him so. Instead, she stayed dead still and watched with the binoculars. She felt her heart racing and took a deep, slow breath. "Okay, Tay and Darius are getting out of the car. They have AR-15s. They're going into the woods and it looks like they're going to make their way toward you. I need to be quiet now." There was a quick click of acknowledgement. She listened as they noisily made their way through the woods. City boys. She would have laughed at them under any other circumstances.

Jason remained in the car. She wondered what he was doing, but did not want to run the risk of exposing herself. After ten minutes, she heard him put the car in gear and drive down the side road toward the farm. Julie fervently hoped Zach knew what he was doing. She slowly moved her head down and checked her weapon, which she had done at least a dozen times already. She also realized she needed to pee.

*****

I had a plan. It went something like this. I had made a dummy. That's right, a dummy. A scarecrow, whatever the hell you want to call it. I got some of Rick's old clothes, he wouldn't mind, and filled them with straw. I complemented the get up with boots, gloves, jacket, and a cowboy hat. I had put the dummy in the cab of my little Ford Ranger truck, which I had parked on the bridge, and positioned it to appear as though Rick had fallen asleep waiting on them. I put the cooler on the hood of the truck, which would partially obscure anyone's view of the scarecrow. Hopefully, nobody would recognize it for what it really was, at least until they got close.

I armed Julie with an AR-15. I had a Winchester model 94. It was an excellent bolt-action, long range rifle. I made a slow jog over to Rick's hill, which was five hundred yards south of the bridge along the creek line. I had several burlap bags that I had cut into long strips loosely tied around me to help break up my outline. Five hundred yards was well within range of a 30-06 bullet, especially when fired from a nice rifle. I was counting on the premise that these thugs had limited training and were only going to be armed with the .223 caliber assault weapons. The range on those weapons were limited, the little field manual that Rick made me memorize said they only had a maximum effective range of 460 meters. That converted to roughly 503 yards. I felt confident none of them could hit the side of a barn at that distance.

I positioned the rifle on a sandbag, got myself as comfortable as possible in a prone position, and started thinking all of it over again for at least the hundredth time. Was I being overly paranoid? Should I have even allowed them to come back in the first place? I had decided to err on the side of caution, hence, the scarecrow in the truck, and the two of us set up as if expecting a war. However, if Julie called me on the radio and says it's just Jason and Macie, I was going to hustle back to the truck and meet them when they drove up.

Alas, it was not to be. Julie radioed and gave me the bad news. Surprisingly, it saddened me. I really wanted to help out Macie. Jason, like him or not, was part of the package. After all, I still loved her. I was no longer *in* love with her, but I knew I would always care about her. I actually wanted to believe I could trust her, even after everything she had said and done to me.

Deep down though, my gut feeling told me this was exactly what would happen. A minute or two passed, and then I heard at least one of them in the woods. Even from five hundred yards away. It sounded like he fell down or walked into something. They were so noisy and clumsy it was pathetic.

Was it Macie's idea? No. I was convinced she had nothing to do with it. It was Jason. Jason and his buddies. Starvation will make a person do things they normally would not do I guess. Instead of working out an amicable relationship, they believed it would be far easier to kill everyone and take what they wanted. It was not going to happen if I had anything to say about it.

I turned the volume on the walkie-talkie down. Rick had purchased headsets for the radios, but had not gotten the correct models. We made do without them. But, if you were not careful, you would have your volume loud enough for everyone within near proximity to hear. I did not want any possible noise giving away my position, so I turned the volume down to its lowest level. I wiggled the rifle a bit to get snugged down in the sandbag, and put my eye to the rifle's scope. Slowly and carefully, I scanned out the wood line and undergrowth. It took me a moment, but I was able to pick out the one who I believed was Tay easily. He was just barely in the wood line. Incredibly, he was wearing a bright red bandana around his head. He stood out like a turd in a punch bowl. He was also leaning up against a tree breathing heavily. He was probably certain he was hidden from view of anyone in the truck. Soon, Darius joined him. I recognized him immediately. They did not even spread out. They were standing there, side by side, like buddies sneaking a peek on big breasted women skinny dipping in the creek. Idiots. I was tempted to put a round in the tree they were standing beside and scare the shit out of them, but I held off. I was curious. I wanted to see what they had planned.

The black Stratus appeared around the curve in the road and moved slowly. When it got to within ten feet of the bridge, the driver parked and got out slowly. It was Jason. He looked around nervously. He should be nervous. His actions were going to dictate what happened to him in the next few minutes. My anger had grown into a cold block of ice.

I was once again thankful for inheriting Rick's paranoia, which made me plan for this contingency. I refused to let anyone take anything from me anymore. I focused the crosshairs on Jason. He walked closer to the truck and I could see his mouth move, as if he was calling out to me, or Rick. He walked a couple of steps closer when he was suddenly dumbstruck with realization. His mouth fell open and he started to yell. Whether he was yelling at them to open fire or yelling a warning, I did not know.

Whatever he was shouting was drowned out by sudden gunfire. Darius and Tay shot the living shit out of my truck, my scarecrow, and my cooler. They had thirty round magazines, but it did not take long for them to fire all of their ammunition. Jason, the only one with half a brain, dropped to the ground as soon as they started shooting, lest he became a casualty of friendly fire.

Darius and Tay must have believed they had killed me, Rick, or whoever. I don't think they were very concerned if they hit Jason or not. They emerged out of the wood line, pointing their weapons toward their targets, entirely unaware that those thirty rounds mags were now empty. I took aim. I had a sudden recall of the video. Darius was the one who had kicked a field goal with my testicles. Well, now, how does the old saying go? Paybacks are a bitch. Something like that.

I had my range dialed in. The wind was negligible. The sun was just over my left shoulder. I caressed the trigger with my finger and gently squeezed. The bullet exited the barrel of the rifle, soared magnificently for the length of five football fields, and went through his groin. I'd guess the point of entry was about half a centimeter above where his cock was previously attached. It exited right about the top of his butt crack. I watched the impact. It looked excruciatingly painful. Darius fell to the ground and howled in agony. Tay stood there astonished. He then tried to shoot at the scarecrow, realized his weapon was empty, and fought to put in a fresh magazine. I waited patiently. Tay finally managed to seat a fresh magazine and get the bolt shoved forward. I was tired of lying prone, so I sat up and waved. Tay saw me then. His razor sharp intellect deduced that I was not in the truck after all, but sitting on top of a hill some distance away. He started firing. Just as I thought, he had no idea what he was doing. His rounds were falling short by over a hundred yards. I certainly gave him a chance, a chance to surrender. I took careful aim and shot him through the heart. I gazed through the scope for a couple of seconds.

Satisfied with my accuracy, I stood up and walked toward the surviving betrayer.

Chapter 21 - There Is No Redemption

In full tactical gear, I believe I could have run the five hundred yards in just under two minutes. However, I did not see any need to hurry at this point. Far better to walk and conserve energy.

Jason had slowly lifted his head when the two idiots had stopped firing. He watched in dumbfounded befuddlement as I shot his two friends. Tay was quite dead. Darius was lying on the ground in a fetal position, clutching what was left of his genitalia. Jason finally looked around and spotted me. He stood slowly as I approached. I could see the animosity in his eyes as I got close. I looked over at Darius a moment. He was whimpering pathetically. I felt no guilt or pity. I might have once, but those days were over. I retrieved my radio from my cargo pocket. "What's your status?"

"Good to go," she answered.

"Same here. Stand by," I responded. Julie answered my transmission with a click of her talk button. Good girl. I propped my foot on the front bumper of the Stratus and pointedly stared at Jason while pointing my rifle at his midsection.

"Zach, I didn't have a choice! They've got Macie. They're holding her hostage," Jason whined. Darius groaned feebly. He was dying. Jason nervously looked over at him. "Zach, I'm begging you. Just tell me what to do, and I'll do it, man."

His face was oily with a mixture of sweat and grime. I motioned with the rifle. "Slowly take the gun out that you're hiding and toss it."

He paused for a moment, and then reached into his back waistband, pulled out a black revolver and threw it to the ground.

I nodded, picked it up, and inspected it. It was a 22 caliber Ruger. Loaded, but very dirty. It looked familiar. I tossed it in the weeds. I then looked at him and sighed.

"Why didn't the two of you get away from that group, huh? Isn't that what I suggested? Leave and start a new life, just the two of you and your unborn child."

Jason's mouth dropped open and he held up his hands as if to say, I don't know why the hell I didn't listen to you, but I see the wisdom in your logic now.

I sighed. "Ah, Jason, what a history the two of us have in such a short time. You know, we've never really talked on a one-to-one level. Let's do that. So, let's see, where do we start. Let's recap our history together. I had never done anything to you. I was just a lowly sophomore, head over heels in love with a pretty girl, and you were the hotshot senior athlete. You had a lot of teenage girls who were dying to drop their panties for you, but instead, you steal my girl. And then you punch me out, although, I guess I can understand your reaction a little bit. After all, I did take a swing at you. But you had size on me back then. You could have just grabbed me in a bear hug and wrestled me to the ground. Did you know, on that day, I had just come from the hospital? My grandmother, the only family I had, just died? Did you know that?" I asked. Jason started to protest.

I held up my hand. "Hush, I'm talking. So, where was I? Oh yeah, I took a swing at you. You knocked me down and then you let your boys kick the shit out of me. Now granted, you pulled them off me, but you let them put the boots to me for just a few seconds before you intervened. I watched the video. How could I not, it was sent to me the next day. I saw you stand there motionless with that damn smirk on your face for just a little bit longer than necessary before stopping them. So, who put the video on You Tube?"

"Trina," he answered, "I had nothing to do with it."

I shook my head. "I may have believed you once, but I'm not so sure anymore. I'm thinking you pulled the usual Jason Argos pattern of behavior. You condemn the action, but only after the fact." I shrugged. "Oh hell, it's a moot point I guess. So, where was I? Oh yeah. I do ramble on sometimes, so I'll skip everything else and fast forward to the present. You and Macie decide to come begging for food. What did I do, Jason?"

He stared at me in silence. "Answer me, please."

"You gave us food," his response was emotionless.

I nodded somberly. "In spite of our past, I gave the two of you food so you could survive and have your kid. I wanted to help you two, you stupid shit." I had lowered my voice a bit. "Go over there and look in the damn cooler."

He reluctantly did as I directed. "Look at all of those beautiful fresh steaks. I told you guys to bring stuff for trading. I'm betting you did not even bother, am I right?" I asked. He looked at the steaks. He was so hungry I thought for a second he'd grab one and start eating it raw. Even with all of the fresh bullet wounds.

"I knew you'd show up empty handed, but I was going to give those steaks to you anyway. But, a little nagging voice kept telling me you'd bring your boys with you. Hell, if all of you came in peace, even Darius, I was still going to give those steaks to you," I said quietly. "I just wanted you to know it. You betrayed me, Jason."

He held his hands out and he looked around as if he was looking for his ever present homeboys to come to his defense, and eventually spotted Darius. I guess he had forgotten all about him. "Man, why did you shoot my boy like that? Can't you do something for him?"

I shrugged my shoulders. "Of course," I set my rifle down against the front bumper of his car and walked over to Darius. He was bleeding profusely and had lost consciousness by now. I retrieved my lock-blade knife, bent down, and slit his throat. He gurgled once and then became still. He was going to die anyway. I merely hastened the process by a few seconds. I avoided the spurting blood from the neck wound, wiped the knife blade on his jacket, stood up, and turned.

Jason had my rifle. He had his finger on the trigger and the barrel pointed at me. "You should put the weapon down," I said. He ignored my suggestion and brought the rifle up to his shoulder. "I would prefer you not do that."

His mouth dropped open and he arched his eyebrows in mock surprise. "Oh, you would prefer it? You would prefer it? Fuck you and your preferences! You had your chance. Instead, you just had to go running your punk mouth. Now shut the fuck up, because now, it's my turn to talk. You are a fucking loser, Zach Gunderson, you always have been. You think that since the world went to hell, now you're something special 'cause you got a supply of food and we don't? Fuck you, Zach! Fuck you!" I think he was trying to tell me something. "You ain't nothing!"

I nodded my head and tried to act as if I was duly chastened. "I'm sure your friends would agree with you. Well, if I hadn't killed them, but if they were alive, they would certainly agree with you. Oh well, fuck them. More steaks for you, right?"

He continued glaring at me. I think my facetious logic confused him. "Jason, I'm asking you to put the rifle down. I can help you get Macie."

"I don't want your fucking help, Zach. I'm going to kill you and that old man, wherever he is, and then I'm going to get Macie. We're going to move in your fucking house, we're going to eat your fucking food, and I'm going to fuck her in your own fucking bed!"

"You sure do say fuck a lot," I lamented. "A limited vocabulary is an overt indicator of stupidity, did you know that, or are you too stupid to comprehend how utterly stupid you really are?"

In case you're wondering, yes. I was goading him.

It worked. Spittle flew out of his mouth as he screamed. "Shut the fuck up!" he took aim and fired. No, not really. He took aim and pulled the trigger. The rifle was empty. I had unloaded it during the casual stroll from Rick's hill to the bridge.

I shook my head and sighed. "You are one dumb fucker."

He tried to work the action of the rifle, but apparently was unfamiliar with it. So, out of frustration, he yelled and charged me with the rifle held high over his head. I'm sure he had seen this move in one of those old World War Two movies. I guess he thought he was going to bash my head in with the butt stock. I had my Glock, but did not bother using it. When he got close enough to touch me, I deftly side stepped him and thrust my knife with a backhand stab into the side of his neck. He grunted in sudden pain, reached for it, but I pulled it out before he could grab it. I had hit an artery. He was going to bleed out in a matter of seconds. He grabbed at his neck where the knife had entered. Blood spurted between his fingers. I changed my grip on the knife, took a lunging step, and stabbed him again. This one entered just below his sternum. It was merely for good measure. He dropped the rifle and fell to the ground. The stab in the neck was probably adequate, without an ambulance to come save him, he would have bled out, but I wanted to make sure. This man was, and had been, an albatross around my neck.

I sat down beside Mr. Jason Argos and waited for the shakes to stop, as I watched him exhale his last breath in a bloody gurgle. I squeezed my eyes shut for a long minute after his final death rattle.

When I opened them again, my breathing had slowed and the shakes had abated. I was surprised at how much rage I had for him, but I worked it out, I think. Good riddance. I gave him every chance I could to make amends with him.

I looked around and surveyed all of the damage. In addition to the shot up truck, ruined cooler, bullet infested steaks, he had dropped Rick's beautiful rifle. I picked it up and inspected it for damage. There was a small scratch on the stock, but more importantly, the scope was broken. Damn. I checked myself for any injuries and then retrieved some hand sanitizer out of the glove box.

While I was lost in thought, the Dodge Stratus started up and backed out quickly. Who the hell was in the car? The driver did a 180 degree fishtail, threw it in drive, and floored it before I could even react. The sunlight was glaring off of the windshield, preventing me from seeing who was driving. I retrieved my Glock and managed to shoot once before it rounded the curve. I retrieved my radio. "The car is coming out. Take care of it!" I got a click in reply. I guess it was time to see what kind of mettle she had. I started running toward Julie.

*****

Julie gasped when she heard the gunshots. It was a frenzied staccato of fire from at least two rifles. She became worried until she heard the booming report of Zach's hi-powered rifle. It had a quite distinctive sound. There was a minute of silence and then she heard more gunfire. It was followed by another report of Zach's rifle.

She knew, well she hoped, that all was good. Zach was a really good shot. He confirmed it a moment later on the radio. She breathed a sigh of relief until she remembered that there were three of them and she only heard Zach shoot twice. She looked around for any threats, but the immediate area, or what Zach called her AO – area of operation, was deathly quiet. She sat in silence. It seemed like an eternity had passed since Zach had spoken to her. She was getting worried again. She thought she heard yelling and the faint sounds of a struggle, but could not be sure. A few more minutes passed, and then she heard tires squealing.

"The car is coming out, take care of it!" Zach shouted into the radio. Julie keyed the microphone once in acknowledgement. It must be Jason. He's escaped. She checked her weapon once more, making sure this time she had the selector lever set to fire. She was ready. The car appeared. She had a brief moment of anxiety as she wondered where to aim first. The radiator, the tires, or through the window? She chose the latter. Julie fired three quick rounds where the driver should be sitting, fired three rounds into the front grill, and then shot continuously as the car drove by and approached the intersection.

The car continued through the intersection and crashed into the ditch on the far side of the roadway. Julie stared at it stupefied for a moment. Then she realized she had the rifle in a death grip and could not feel anything from the waist down. She wondered if she might have been shot. She pried one of her hands loose, and started feeling around her face and torso. Satisfying herself that there were no unnatural holes in her body, she climbed out of the sniper position and slowly started walking toward the wrecked car. She held the AR-15 stiffly in front of her, and got to the middle of the road before stopping suddenly. The car's engine was revving at a high rate of speed, as if the driver had the accelerator mashed to the floor.

She felt the sudden need to reload the weapon. She took a hard look at the car and tried to spot any movement through the windows. Nothing. She fumbled with the release button and got the empty magazine to drop, fumbled with the tactical vest, finally got a firm grip of a loaded magazine, and was able to get it seated in the rifle in one try. Tugging on it to make sure it was seated properly, it suddenly dawned on her that standing in the middle of the road with no cover was a very stupid place to reload one's weapon. She was glad Zach did not see the faux pas. She inched her way forward to the car, finally made it to the driver's side, and peered in. It was Chad. His head was tilted forward, and it looked a bit like he was sleeping.

The driver's window was either busted out or rolled down. She shouted to him over the noise of the engine. "Chad, turn the damn car off!"

He ignored her. "I said turn the car off!" This time, she nudged his shoulder with the barrel of the rifle to emphasize her demand. His head rolled. That was when she saw the right side of his head. Somehow, the .223 caliber bullet did not penetrate all the way through. Its shape was probably deformed when it passed through the passenger side window. The window must have slowed the velocity of the bullet enough so that once it entered the skull, it stayed there.

Somewhere, she heard a small voice telling her she had missed all of the front shots and did not hit Chad until he was driving past. She hoped Zach would not notice. She continued staring at Chad. He was quite dead. She was still staring at him when she heard Zach's voice.

*****

I ran as fast as I could. It was about a hundred yard jaunt around a blind curve. I had no visual whatsoever of Julie and what may have happened. I had heard the gunshots, but could not be sure they all came from her weapon. As I came around the curve, I first spotted the black Dodge Stratus, wrecked on the far side of the two lane roadway. I then spotted Julie standing beside the driver's side. I slowed, held my handgun at the ready position, and approached slowly.

I took slow deep breaths. "Julie!" I yelled.

She didn't seem to hear me or was ignoring me. "Julie, it's me! I'm walking up!" I definitely did not want her to shoot me accidentally. I stared hard at the car, wondering who or what she was looking at. I finally got beside her and gently touched her on the shoulder to let her know I was there. She finally turned her head toward me as I was peering inside the car.

It was Chad and he was quite dead. Walking over, I carefully looked in the floorboards to make sure there was nobody else. Satisfied, I reached into the car and turned the ignition off. The engine died painfully, whereas, Chad probably never felt a thing.

Just as I suspected, they never brought anything to trade. The only things in there were a lighter and a bong. They had no other plan in mind other than killing Rick and me, and then taking what they wanted. If they had succeeded and had found Julie, well, I'm sure it would not have been pleasant. The interior reeked of marijuana. I had no doubt they had gotten high on their drive over here. I guess they needed it for courage.

I straightened. Julie still had the assault rifle pointed at Chad, so I put my hand gently on the barrel and got her to lower it. "Was there anyone else?" I asked. She blankly looked at me and shook her head. I looked again at Chad, back at Julie, and gave her a kiss on the forehead.

"Good job, girlfriend," I said with pride.

I'm not sure what I was expecting, a proud grin? A high-five? What I got was Julie suddenly bursting into tears and sobbing uncontrollably. I reached out, took the rifle from her hands, and held her as gently as I could. I mean, I had two weapons in my hands at the moment. She cried quite hard for a few minutes. Hard enough where the tears were like waterfalls and snot drooled out of her nose like a freshly turned zombie. I let her cry. I stood there quietly and held her. I guess it was the overwhelming realization that she had just killed a real live human being. She did not know it yet, but she did well.

I was not going to tell her the circumstances. Specifically, I was not going to tell her Chad had never fired a shot. It appeared he was not even armed. In a civilized society, her act could be called murder. But I knew it was necessary. He knew where we lived. I could not allow it. However, I did not want Julie to think of herself as a murderer. If she ever asked, I did not know if I was going to fabricate a story or tell her the truth. I'd cross that bridge when I got to it.

After a minute or two, she seemed to gather her senses just a bit and I thought it was over. "Zach, there's something I have to do," her words came out in between sobs.

I let go of her and stood back. "Okay, sweetheart, you name it," I responded. She fumbled with her pants, succeeded in pulling them down and then squatted right where she stood. It sounded like a Jersey cow pissing on a flat rock. I stared at her in amazement. She must have been holding it in for hours. She continued, and continued, and continued. And the whole time, she was sobbing like a baby.

Chapter 22 - A New Friend

After Julie finished emptying her milk jug sized bladder. She stood up, zipped up, and gave me a harsh stare. "Enough of this bullshit, I want to get my little brother."

I tried to keep a straight face. I mean, the swollen red eyes, the tear streaked cheeks, I was fine with. It actually was endearing. But, she had these two really long snot trails streaming out of both nostrils. They were like, hanging down, but they defied gravity just enough to prevent them from breaking free of her nose. I turned quickly before she saw me smiling and renewed my inspection of the remains of Chad Smith.

"I think we can do that," I stood there with my hand over my face as if in deep thought, which I sort of was, but I was mostly hiding my stupid grin. I resisted the urge to call her snot face, or something equally juvenile. "What about your mother?" I asked through my fingers.

"The hell with my mother! I want my little brother. He'll be safer and better off with the two of us."

I think she realized what I was trying hard not to stare at. She untied one of the burlap bags that was around her head and shoulders, and used it to wipe her face before throwing it on the ground. I was about to tell her to stop wasting stuff, but stopped myself. Now was not the time.

I shrugged with agreement. "Alright, let's do it. I'm thinking we should get the service van we have parked up the road. We've got to get rid of these bodies first. If we don't, they'll attract vermin and zombies. So, we load up the bodies, dump them in the sinkhole, and go get your little brother."

Julie nodded. "I knew you'd think of a good plan. Let's get going."

She did not even wait for me to respond. She started purposely walking down the highway. I hurried to catch up and started trying at least to formulate a worthwhile plan. Her mother, Trina, and even Macie might not care much for us to show up and claim Tommy. If we agreed to take them into the fold, it would probably make it easier, but to be quite honest, there was no way in hell I was ever going to accept Trina with open arms. If the two women were really holding Macie hostage, we might actually have to harm them. I had no problem with it, but I knew Julie would not hurt her mother, even if she was presently resenting the hell out of her. It could be a problem, and I wasn't sure how it would end.

I was still thinking it through when we drove the van back to the bridge. I got out and guided Julie as she backed up to the bodies. I got the rear doors opened and we were about to start loading when I heard a horse whinny. I peered around the van. A cowboy was riding up on a beautiful Appaloosa horse. When I say cowboy, I'm saying he had a cowboy hat, pointy toed boots with stirrups, and a weathered duster. He was an older guy, I'd say around fifty, tall, rawboned and lanky, with a deeply weathered face. He reminded me a bit of Rick. He held a rifle casually across the saddle. It looked like a stainless model of a varmint rifle with a scope attached. I let my hand drift close to my holster and stood close to the rear of the van. I whispered at Julie. "Grab the AR, but don't point it at him." As he approached, I waved. He responded with a wave, but kept his rifle handy. Even so, it looked promising so far.

He stopped about twenty feet away from the van and casually looked around.

"Howdy," he said evenly. He gazed at the bodies with no change of his expression.

"Good afternoon," I replied.

"I seem to have come at a bad time," he said. I shrugged a shoulder. "I heard all the shooting and thought I'd come see if I could help out. Looks like you two took care of it though," he peered closer. "Were they those infected things?"

"No sir. I'm afraid these were real people," I said plainly.

He nodded, but offered no comment. "My name's Fred. Fred McCoy. I live down the highway about a mile or so. I'm looking for my baby brother."

I walked up and offered my hand. "Zach. Zach Gunderson," I nodded over my shoulder. "This is Julie Frierson. We're very pleased to meet you."

He shook with a calloused hand and tipped his hat at Julie. Julie waved, but was warily keeping the rifle handy. "I'm sorry, Fred, but we've not seen any real people in quite a while. Well, except for these," I made a sweeping gesture. I tried to explain. "I knew these people previously and I tried to be hospitable. Unfortunately, they had other things in mind."

He looked up the hill and gestured toward the house. "This is the Parson's farm. They had a tenant living in the house. Fella by the name of Sam Hughes, I believe. Is he around?"

He was testing me. I knew it. I hoped Julie knew it and did not say anything to get this man's hackles up. We needed friends, not enemies. "Well, sir, you are right about the Parsons, but I never heard of a Sam Hughes. My co-worker, Rick Sanders lives here. He's the foreman for the Parsons. I work for him. When my grandmother died over Thanksgiving, I moved in here with him."

I pointed a thumb at Julie. "Now, my girlfriend lives with us. The Parsons were in their winter home in Florida when all of this zombie stuff started happening. I haven't seen them since."

Ironically, the Parsons' winter home was in Winterhaven. Honest.

He took in what I said, chewed on it, and slowly nodded. "Is Rick around?"

"Yes sir, he is, but he's not available at the moment." I did not explain further and he did not ask.

He gestured toward the bodies. "They'll need burying. I'll be glad to give you a hand. We can use that backhoe there."

"I'd be glad for the help, but we have a bit of a pressing matter at hand." I motioned at Julie again. "She has a baby brother as well. He's ten. He is currently in the custody of some people that are tied up with them."

I pointed at the bodies. "These three were a part of that group. Julie believes, and I must agree, that her brother will be better off living with us. We are going to dump these bodies down the road for now. Julie would like to get her brother immediately. Once we have him home safe and sound, I'll dispose of the bodies properly."

He digested what I said for a moment and then motioned with the brim of his hat toward the setting sun. "It's going to be dark soon. Very risky to travel at night nowadays. Lots of black ice still on the roads and that van could slide off in a ditch before you know it. If you can hold off a bit, I'll help you get everything tended to here. Then, if you'd like, tomorrow, I'll go along with you two," he looked over at Julie. "Ma'am, I'd be happy to help you get your baby brother back. I'd hate to have him suffer the same fate as my baby brother."

Julie was perplexed. "What happened? I thought he was alive. Isn't that why you're looking for him?"

I must admit his statement perplexed me as well, and then it came to me.

I snapped my fingers in realization. "Your baby brother, would he happen to be a rather large baby brother?"

Fred stared at me quietly, somberly. "You've seen him then."

I explained the encounter that Julie and I had with the huge behemoth Fred referred to as his baby brother. I omitted the nakedness part and immediately afterward, Julie and I engaged in perhaps the most intense act of fornication known to what was left of mankind. Fred listened quietly. When I was finished, he slowly put the rifle in a saddle holster and dismounted. "Let's get these bodies taken care of, and then I'd like you to take me to my brother."

We loaded them up in the van and hauled them to the sinkhole, while Fred followed on his horse. I drove slowly on purpose. I needed to think of the proper words to say about the late baby brother McCoy. The sinkhole came into view too quickly. We stopped and got out. "Mr. McCoy I..."

"Call me Fred, please," he said.

I nodded and cleared my throat. "Ah, Fred, about this sinkhole. Rick and I have been using it to burn trash. And, um, we came to the conclusion the best way to dispose of infected dead was to burn them."

I was not sure how he was going to react, so I paused a moment.

"Zach, are you saying my brother is in the sinkhole?" he asked. I nodded reluctantly. He got off his horse and walked over to the edge. The corpse was burned beyond recognition. He stared a long couple of minutes in silence.

"We have no idea if people that are infected will infect other people after they are dead. And, some of those news stories said the dead could reanimate into these zombie things. This method seemed a prudent means of containment."

I could have related a few historical anecdotes to give my logic some weight, but Fred did not seem the type of person who liked big talkers. I chose silence.

He slowly nodded in understanding and looked at me somberly. "You did what you thought was the proper thing, Zach," he pointed. "Is that another body?" he asked. I nodded. "Another zombie, or was it like one of them?"

"It was Susan Riggins. She wandered up one day. She had turned," I said.

Fred sighed. "I knew her. I imagine Henry is dead too, or walking around somewhere, infected."

He took his hat off and wiped his forehead with his shirt sleeve. "I am going to carry my brother home and give him a Christian burial. I would appreciate the loan of your van."

He was quiet a moment. "I knew he had turned. He killed my wife and mother-in-law. I wanted to put him out of his misery."

I looked up at the sky. It was starting to get dark. "Do you want to do it tonight?" he nodded. I withheld any derogatory reply. "Alright, sir, I'll be glad to help. If we use the backhoe on the tractor, we should be able to lift him out a lot easier."

Fred agreed and we went to work. We used some ropes and a tarp. Most of him stayed in one piece. It was not fun.

When we got Fred's brother secured, we drug the recently deceased idiots out of the van and dumped them into the sinkhole. I poured a liberal amount of kerosene on them, added a couple of old tires, and lit them up. It would be a slow burn, and I would have to repeat the process a few more times to get the job completed. Fred watched in silence.

Julie stayed behind and cleaned up the mess around the bridge. I drove the van and Fred followed on his horse. Turns out, he lived fairly close. It was an older, but nice two-story home. I had driven past it dozens of times but never knew who lived there. He had about a hundred acres he said. We dug the hole with the aid of the headlights on Fred's John Deere. He buried his baby brother, also known as Franklin McCoy, next to their mother, and quietly recited the Lord's Prayer.

It was very late when I got back. I was exhausted and filthy. I stood on the front porch and stripped off my grime infested clothing. I would decide what to do with them in the morning. "It's me," I said as I opened the door. Julie was sitting on the couch, wrapped in a blanket. Her assault rifle was right next to her. She smiled tiredly at me.

"Well, hello sailor," she said, "do you always walk around naked?"

I chuckled. "My clothes are pretty much beyond hope. Let me get cleaned up and I'll join you in bed."

She readily agreed. I went to the bathroom and washed off with a bath rag and soap before crawling into bed next to her. She was wearing one of my tee shirts and socks. Good. Her feet were always ice cold. I snuggled up beside her and kissed her on the forehead. I was dead tired. No extracurricular activities for me tonight. I filled her in about the burial of the late Franklin McCoy.

"What do you think about Fred?" she asked in between a yawn. She sounded as tired as I was. Her yawn instinctively caused me to yawn as well.

"He's quiet natured. Stoic would be a good word to describe him. When things started getting bad, he hunkered down in his house with his wife, mother-in-law, and brother. Somehow, his brother had turned. He doesn't know how. They had been isolated from the rest of the world for at least a month and he had gotten sick somehow. Fred was out tending to his cattle when Frank attacked the women. When Fred returned, Frank had already wandered off. We compared timelines. He said it happened three days before Frank had wandered over here. There is no telling what baby brother had gotten into before our encounter with him. He has a daughter who lives somewhere on the west coast. He had a business, building prefabricated greenhouses. Not the big commercial sized ones, but smaller ones for yuppies to put in their back yard. Their farm was mostly a hobby."

"Do you think he can he be trusted?" she asked.

"He seems alright. He has plenty of food and a well for water, just like us. He's got a couple of his greenhouses set up and although it was dark, I think I saw some solar panels on his roof. He seems to have a decent set up. We don't have anything he wants. Maybe the pleasure of our company, but that's it. He seems like a bit of a lone wolf, so the solitary life won't be a major annoyance to him I'm thinking. You know the actor Josh Brolin? Fred looks like him," I stopped talking long enough to realize Julie had fallen asleep. I smiled as I stroked her hair. It had been a long day for her. Hell, it had been a long day for all of us.

Chapter 23 - A Rescue Attempt

I felt like I slept like a rock, but was still up before sunrise. When I opened the door to let the boys out, Fred was sitting in one of the rocking chairs on our front porch. He nodded at me and continued drinking some coffee out of a thermos. His Appaloosa was grazing in the field and the saddle was sitting on the porch. The horse, a mare, was freshly brushed and looked magnificent.

"Good morning," I greeted.

"Good morning," he replied. He was wearing the same hat and duster, but it looked like he had on a clean pair of jeans, and had exchanged his cowboy boots for some Skecher brand hiking boots. He had the same rifle leaned up against the porch railing. He nodded toward the horse. "Her name's Prancer. She's a darn good horse."

I nodded quietly, as Fred frequently did. Julie and I must have been very exhausted, we never heard him ride up. Funny, none of the dogs had barked at him, they scampered over and sniffed him up and down. He gave each of them a pat, and then they ran off to empty their bladders.

"So, young Zach, do you have a specific plan in mind for rescuing Julie's little brother?"

"I believe I do. Julie is positive she can lead us back to the house where they are staying, and then..."

"Okay, but before we talk about it, I'd like to hear about what led up to you killing those men yesterday," Fred said it plainly, matter-of-factly. I could not read what he was thinking. Was he being judgmental?

I inhaled. "Well, it all started a few months ago, back in High School..." I started with my brief romance with Macie and went from there. I tried to provide all of the pertinent details. I told him how Rick had perceived that the apocalypse was actually going to happen, and had done a good job of planning for it. I recounted how we met the Friersons. I summarized our falling out and how we had evicted them. I then described the circumstances of finding Julie and how we reunited. I shyly admitted we were now more than just friends. I caught him smiling a bit when I spoke of it, but he remained silent. I then recapped the first meeting with Jason and Macie.

"I imagine it was pretty tough seeing those two together after everything that had happened," Fred opined.

I shrugged. "When they drove up, the first emotion I had was contempt. After I started talking with them, I actually started feeling pity. I was happy Macie was alive, but I had no feelings one way or another about Jason. I wasn't jealous. Any personal feelings I once had for Macie have faded. I imagine the feelings I now have for Julie had a lot to do with it. Does it make sense?" I asked. Fred slowly nodded.

I went into how the Friersons had joined up with Jason and his group. Fred interrupted at that point. "And one of those boys at the bridge is the one who tried to rape Julie?" Fred asked. I nodded. He looked down at his empty cup a moment. "You knew they were going to set you up."

I nodded again. "Rick taught me to have a contingency plan, always. I planned for it, but had hoped I was being overly paranoid and it would work out for the better."

"Your suspicions were on the money it seems," Fred said.

"I was hoping for a more peaceful outcome," I replied.

"You took a knife to one of those boys."

I sat silently for a moment. Fred glanced over at me. "To be honest, Fred, I used a knife on two of them. I shot one and finished him with a knife to the jugular. The other one was Jason. He was ultimately the one who betrayed me. As to why, well, I'm not sure I can explain where it makes sense. I could have shot him, but I was very angry."

It probably sounded bad, but it was the truth. I was not going to apologize for it.

Fred grunted and refilled his plastic cup. "Alright, so on to this rescue plan. Are you planning on killing everyone or what?"

"The house is in a gated neighborhood in Brentwood. If you're serious about helping us…" Fred confirmed his willingness with a small nod. "Good. I was thinking we could keep it simple. I'm thinking of having Julie go up and knock on the door. I'll stay back a little bit, just in case. Since none of them knows you, I'd like you to stay out of sight and provide security with your rifle, just in case it goes bad. I'm assuming you are a decent shot." Fred nodded slightly. I guess I'd have to take his word for it.

"Okay, as far as we know, the only ones who are still there are Julie's mother, little Tommy, Macie, and a girl named Trina." I paused a moment before continuing. "Fred, I'll be honest with you, I don't want the rest of them to join us. Just Tommy. But, I've no desire or reason to hurt any of them. I guess I'd do whatever it takes though. It will just have to be up to how they respond. If I have to invite Macie and Janet to come live with us, so be it. Not Trina though."

"What if they say yes? Would it work out? Especially after what Janet tried?" Fred asked quietly.

I threw my hands up and shook my head. "I've no idea. Julie wants her little brother back. I don't blame her. I figure, get Tommy back and deal with the rest of it later."

Fred rocked back in his chair and sipped his coffee for a moment before speaking. "Sounds agreeable enough. We don't shoot anyone unless we have to. I'm good with that."

We were on the road thirty minutes later. I returned to the location on Old Hickory Boulevard where I found Julie. She had no problem with tracking her route back to the neighborhood. The house was two blocks down from the gated entrance. I stopped at the entrance and let Fred out. The gate appeared as though somebody had smashed through it with their vehicle. It made me think of Rick and I smiled. "Are you ready to do this?" I asked Julie.

"You're damn right I'm ready. The house is down the street, first left, and third house on the left."

I repeated the information to Fred. He nodded and took off at a trot. I slowly drove toward the house.

I stopped just before turning onto the street. We got out and started walking. Since we knew they were unaware Julie was now living with me, it was agreed she'd walk up by herself and knock on the door while I hid. She'd try to coax Tommy outside and we would snatch him. If she were unsuccessful, we were going to storm the house at gunpoint. Whatever it took to get Tommy.

On the ride over, I came to a decision. I was willing to let Macie and Janet come with us, if it was going to be the only way we'd get Tommy, but Trina was going to be on her own. She was not my friend and never had been. I voiced this to the two of them and they agreed. If anything went wrong, or if we encountered violence, Fred assured us he would shoot anyone who appeared to be a threat.

As it turned out, none of it mattered. Trina was sitting on the front steps. She made eye contact with us, but did not move. I was a bit confused, I expected her to give a shout of alarm, shoot at us, or something. Instead, she sat there smoking a cigarette. I stopped beside a car with flattened tires. "Just use the hand signals," I said to Julie. "We'll start shooting if anything goes wrong." Julie nodded. I pressed the mike on the walkie. "Fred, do you copy?"

"Roger. I'm in position," he replied tersely. I acknowledged and turned to Julie.

"If anything happens, get out of the line of fire. Fred and I will be shooting. If any zombies pop up, run like hell for the van," I grabbed her hand. "If Tommy is still here, we're not leaving without him. You have my word." She nodded gratefully and approached Trina.

Trina watched Julie approach silently. She continued smoking, but otherwise, did not move. I had not intended for her, or anyone else, even to see me. Rookie mistake. Next time we got into this type of situation, I was definitely going to plan it out better. Rick probably would have pointed out that we did not even conduct a recon mission first. I did not want anyone shooting at me out of the windows, so I took a knee beside the car. It suddenly occurred to me, if they were smart, they'd have someone set up in a second floor window of one of the houses across the street. I quickly started scanning the windows. It didn't matter. After a moment, Julie crossed her hands behind her back and then motioned me to come to her. "Fred, I'm going to join Julie and see what's up," I said quietly. He clicked the mike.

"Everyone is gone except Trina," Julie said as I walked up. I frowned and gave a questioning look. "Trina said when she woke up this morning, all of them were gone. They must have left sometime during the night."

Now that I was closer, I scrutinized her closely. She was not the same Trina that I remembered. The old Trina was rather thick, large breasts, large waist, and bulbous buttocks. This Trina was saggy, droopy, and practically anorexic. And she smelled like diarrhea. I cleared my throat. "Jason said you and Janet were holding Macie at gunpoint."

Trina scoffed. "It was all Jason's idea," She looked at me. "He's a devil in disguise, but you know that already."

"Do you know where they went?" I asked.

"Fuck that, I'm checking the house," Julie interrupted before Trina could answer, and walked off before I could say or do anything. So, I did what any manly man would do. I hurried after her.

It was a large house. There were six bedrooms and each room had its own full bathroom. It was very nice, except for all of the filth. The latest occupants were not clean people. The whole house smelled like a locker room. There was debris everywhere and the toilets were filled with trash and excrement. Very nasty.

But there was no Tommy. There was nobody at all, just like Trina said. Finished with our search, we walked back outside. Trina had not moved. "Okay, Trina, where did they go?" I asked. Trina shrugged her shoulders. Julie grabbed her by her chin.

"Listen, bitch! I want to know where my little brother is!"

I gently grabbed Julie and eased her away from Trina. Julie glared at me. I raised my palms out.

"Just wait," I whispered and turned back to Trina. "Trina, we don't want any trouble. We just want to check on Tommy and make sure he's okay. Could you help us out here?"

Trina continued staring at a vacant point in space. She was defeated, she had given up. I could see it in her face. I squatted down to where my face was level with hers. Only then did she look at me. "Where is my Uncle Tay? Where're Darius and Jason?"

"They're dead, Trina. They came at us with the intent of killing us. They lost."

Trina did not move. "I figured as much when they didn't come home last night," she said and looked over at Julie. "I didn't know you hooked up with Zach."

Julie did not bother answering. Trina drew on her cigarette before continuing. "I don't know where they went. Your momma said something about Nashville, but I don't know why they'd go there. Nothing but zombies in Nashville. Thousands of them." She seemed to lose focus, but then turned her head back to me. "We're all gonna die."

I almost felt sorry for her at that moment. Hell, I was very close to hauling her butt back to the van, and then the radio crackled to life. "Zach," Fred was whispering, "we got zombies, about two dozen of them. They're all in one group. One block over."

They were close. Too close. I motioned to Julie. She heard Fred loud and clear. We began running toward the van. I tried talking on the radio between hurried breaths. It was a lot harder than the movies portrayed it. "Fred, can you make it back to the van, or do I need to drive to you?"

He responded calmly. "Drive straight ahead and make a right at the next street, be watching for me."

I clicked the talk button in acknowledgement as Julie and I got into the van. Fred emerged out of the front door of a house just as I turned, and jumped in the passenger side. "There's a whole passel of them," He pointed down the street. "I never seen them group together like that before."

I looked, and sure enough, there were twenty to thirty of them shambling along, slowly and steadily. They were in various states of dress and decomposition.

I used an empty driveway to turn in, back up, and turn around. The sound and movement of the van apparently attracted them. A couple of them actually reached out as if to grab us, even though they were still half a block away. I began backtracking our way out of the neighborhood.

"Fred, I got some theories about them, which means I'm doing a lot of guessing, but I think the cold weather slows them down. They're moving like old, ugly people."

Fred looked in the passenger mirror at the retreating forms. He nodded in agreement. My earlier assessment of Fred's demeanor had not changed. He was very quiet natured. Taciturn, would be a good word to describe him.

"Did you find the kid?" I looked in my rearview mirror at Julie. She was quiet as well, just sitting there staring at nothing in particular.

"Everyone is gone except Trina. She believed Julie's mom and Tommy may be headed toward Nashville. Macie might be with them as well," I said, and waited for an emotional outburst from him. Okay, I'm joking. Fred nodded, and then looked out the window as if we were out on a Sunday drive. "We have plenty of daylight left. I'd like to leave this neighborhood, cover a route toward Nashville, and see if we happen upon them. If, along the way, we see anything which we might be able to use, we'll grab it."

He nodded. "What kind of car do you think they're in?"

Fred did not bother asking if I thought they were on foot. That'd be stupid with all of these zombies around. I answered his question. "One of the men, Chad, had a baby blue BMW four-door. It wasn't in the garage and I didn't see it parked on the street. That's what I'm guessing."

"I'll keep an eye out," he said with heated emotion. Well, okay, not really.

We drove a route in which I assumed Janet might have driven in order to go to Nashville. The truth be told, there were multiple routes from Brentwood to Nashville. I just picked one and went with it. Julie did not know any better, Fred kept any opinion he had to himself.

We encountered zombies here and there, aimlessly wandering the roadways. I drove around them while they moaned and reached for us.

"Why do they walk along the roads?" Julie asked.

"I'm guessing they're merely following a path of least resistance, at least until they sense something edible," I just discovered another zombie rule and made a mental note. "I don't think they are communicating. More likely, they are randomly encountering each other and then stick together. A pack mentality type of behavior so to speak."

Either we drove around them, or, if we could not, we would turn down side streets. Fred agreed the best course of action for now would be to avoid them, if possible.

There were a few houses on fire when we drove down Franklin Pike, multiple wrecked or burned cars, and a few corpses. Occasionally, we saw a pack of dogs roaming.

"Those dogs could be dangerous when they get hungry enough, as if we don't have enough to worry about," I said, mostly to myself. Julie and Fred seemed to be in their own respective worlds. I knew what Julie was thinking about. I could only assume Fred was thinking about his daughter and the recent loss of his family.

We did not see a single blue BMW anywhere. At one point, we passed a tow truck going the opposite direction. "Hey, look! Live people." I stopped the van and waved out of the window. I was kind of hoping they would stop too, and maybe we could make some new friends. There were two of them in it, an older man and woman. They did not even slow down and passed us by without even a wave. I grunted. Fred was so devastated that he could not even speak.

I eventually worked our way over to Harding Place. There were no less than three pharmacies at the intersection of Trousdale and Harding. Two of them had been burnt to the ground. The third one, a CVS store, was still mostly intact. The windows were broken out, and it was obvious it had been looted. I avoided some large potholes and stopped in the street.

"There might be something left that we could use. What do you think, Fred?" I asked.

"Sure, let's give it a look."

Julie stood guard outside while we cleared the interior. We slowly rounded each aisle one by one. Suddenly, Fred gave a small hiss. I glanced over and he nodded at the next aisle over. I peeked through a crack in between the store fixtures. Then I saw it. It used to be a middle-aged man. He was wearing a white lab coat. I wondered if he was the store's pharmacist. I held up one finger to Fred and pointed where the zombie was. I started edging closer when Fred gave another hiss. I looked back at him, wondering what was going on.

He held up a finger and then gave a small grin. He stepped out into the main aisle and pulled his duster back with his left hand. He stood facing the aisle where the zombie was. He started whistling some unknown tune. I stifled a chuckle as the zombie started moaning. He slowly shambled out into the main aisle. Fred was standing with his feet spread apart.

"Draw," he said in that raspy voice of his, and then did something quite amazing. He drew his pistol with his right hand, shot the zombie pharmacist between the eyes, and then holstered the pistol before I even realized he had fired a shot. If I had blinked, I would have missed it.

"Holy shit!" I exclaimed under my breath as the zombie fell to the ground. "That was incredible!"

Fred winked. I edged around the zombie and we finished clearing the store. I trotted back to the front entrance. "All clear," I said to Julie. "You want to look around and I'll take watch?"

She shook her head. She had not said more than one or two words since our encounter with Trina. I nodded and went back inside.

The store had been severely looted, but it was not totally bare. I grabbed a shopping cart, found some plastic bags behind the counter and started in. The first place I headed was the birth control section. Sure enough, there were a dozen boxes of condoms left. Whoever had looted this place had emptied the store of all of the food products, beer, and pain medication, but there was still inventory on the shelves a competent survivalist could make use. I loaded the condoms into a plastic bag and looked up to see Fred watching me.

"Ah, to be young again. So, is there anything special you want, besides those I mean?" he asked.

I smiled sheepishly and nodded. "Antibiotics. Are you familiar with any of them?"

"A little bit, my mother-in-law was a nurse." His voice caught a bit at her memory, but he recovered quickly. "I'll head back into the pharmacy and concentrate my search there. Any particular brand name I should look for?"

"Anything that ends in i-l-l-i-n, anything that starts with c-e-f or c-e-p-h, anything that ends in c-i-n…"

He interrupted me. "Okay, okay, I got it," He snapped his fingers. "I just thought of something. Without the government around, nobody is going to spray for mosquitos anymore. It'll be like a jungle this summer. Find any and all bug repellent you can. I can't think of anything else at the moment, but I'm sure you will. By the way, good idea about the birth control."

He grabbed a plastic bag and walked off without waiting for a response.

Our looting ended with just one half-full shopping cart. There was nothing left. He was right about the mosquitos. They were responsible for more human deaths than any other animal, combined. I located several plastic spray bottles of repellent and took them all. When we finished, we left the pharmacy and continued on Harding. I was about to suggest heading back when suddenly, Fred sat up.

"There is a National Guard headquarters on Powell Avenue and Sidco Drive, not too far from here. A couple of gun stores are also nearby, and lots of businesses. We might find some good supplies," Fred said. I nodded and proceeded ahead. There was indeed a plethora of businesses.

We came upon the National Guard location first, or Houston Barracks as it was known. We had to stop about one hundred yards away. There were several bodies lying about. I stopped the van and we stared. "Lots of decomposition. They're zombies, no doubt about it. I don't see any that are normal looking ones."

"It looks like they've all been shot all to hell," Julie opined. She was right. Each zombie had multiple gunshot wounds.

"A lot of wasted ammo," Fred mused. He retrieved the binoculars and began scanning the various buildings. He handed the binoculars to Julie. "Your eyes are younger than mine. Look up at the roof of the largest building. I think I see little puffs of steam."

Julie looked. "You're right. I see it too," she looked at me. "What does it mean?"

"It means the building is probably occupied," I said. "The steam is coming from a vent stack for the heating units," I pointed toward the scattered corpses. "They're the ones who killed the zombies. It must be soldiers."

Julie handed the binoculars back to Fred. He did another scan. "I believe you're right, Zach. In fact, we have someone checking us out right now."

Chapter 24 - Houston Barracks

After a moment, he lowered the binoculars and turned to us. "It looked like he called somebody. He's got a walkie-talkie radio and he spoke into it for a spell."

"Let's see if we can talk to them," I tried CB channel nine and nineteen several times, but received no response. I grunted and retrieved a can of spray paint out of the van.

"What are you doing, Zach?" Julie asked me.

"It's a good time to introduce the rules," I walked in front of the van about ten feet where there was a spot in the road not covered by zombies or gore. "Poor shooting discipline, wasted ammunition, a lack of knowledge of Zach's Rules of Zombies. Time to help them out."

I gave the can a good shake and sprayed out all of my previous rules. Then I added a few more:

RULE NUMBER 8: BURN THE CORPSES!

RULE NUMBER 9: THEY HAVE A HERD MENTALITY.

RULE NUMBER 10: THEY FOLLOW THE PATH OF LEAST RESISTANCE.

"Don't forget to sign it," Julie said. I smiled and added my trademark signature, a capital Z in block form.

Julie watched me, and then turned to Fred. "Well, Fred, did he watch Zach painting?"

Fred lowered the binoculars. "Every word I believe. It looked like he read it out to his friends on the radio as well," He looked over at me. "We can sit here and wait on them I suppose. Or we can try something else."

I looked at him questioningly. "I believe if we just get in the van and drive off, curiosity will get the better of them."

Julie frowned. "We're not going to leave, are we? They might know something about Tommy and Mom."

I knew she would be even more upset if we left without trying to talk to these people.

"Alright, I think Fred may be on to something. We have a dozen steaks sitting in the cooler, plus a grill." We had been keeping the meat on ice, but they were going to turn rancid soon and we either needed to cook them or throw them out. "Let's find somewhere nearby, but away from all of these corpses and fire up the grill. I'm willing to bet somebody will come check us out."

"Do we just sit here? Can't we signal them somehow?" I gave her a shrug. She was getting impatient. I understood, but there was nothing any of us could do to alleviate that.

Fred grunted. "Baby girl, they know we're here. They might be a bit worried. They might believe we're up to no good." Fred took his hat off and scratched his head while looking at the buildings. "Of course, they could have a sniper in one of the windows about to shoot us," he put his hat back on. "I wouldn't try to go through their entry gate uninvited."

Fred made a good point.

We were hungry, and we all agreed we did not want to eat while in close proximity to a bunch of stinking corpses. "There's got to be somewhere close where we can set up," I said as I carefully drove over the bodies. Every few seconds, there would be audible crunching noises. Occasionally, I'd run over a head and there was a distinctive popping noise, like a watermelon exploding. Rick would have laughed in glee. I would have too if it was just him and me, but today, I kept quiet and continued down Sidco Drive.

In many places, the bodies were stacked two and three deep. We travelled about a hundred feet before the roadway finally cleared. Fred suddenly straightened. "Let's stop here. The parking lot is clear and the business might have some stuff we can use." I looked at the business he was pointing at. It was a manufacturer for swimming pool heaters.

"Okay, fine with me." I looked in the backseat to see if Julie would object. She looked at me wistfully, but didn't say anything. I drove in and circled the parking lot. The back gate was open, so I stopped in front of the building. "Uh, Fred, is there anything in particular we're looking for?"

Fred gave a slight nod. "Copper and copper fittings. I told you I was an engineer. I got a few ideas," He was animated now. No, not really. He just kind of dipped his head when he was talking about something he felt passionate about. "We're going to build a greenhouse for you two, and I'm going to work on some modifications. We'll need plumbing for irrigation."

"Oh," I said, but I was a bit perplexed. There was a Home Depot approximately four blocks from us. Plenty of plumbing fittings there.

Fred must have read my mind. He pointed back toward Houston Barracks. "We stop here in sight of them, they'll come. You wait and see. Besides, I got a few more ideas as well. C'mon, let's go inside and I'll show you," He turned back at Julie. "Baby girl, why don't you set the grill up and get a fire going. I expect we'll have company very soon." He gave her a wink. "We'll fill their bellies up and they'll answer anything we ask them."

Julie understood the logic and smiled hopefully.

We had no trouble prying open one of the bay doors. We waited a minute to see if the noise we made attracted anything. There was no response, so we went inside and spent the next ten minutes clearing the building of any possible zombies. We were fortunate. Not a single one.

The business had various types of heavy machinery. There was no way we could haul any of it back in the van, we'd need to use a tractor trailer rig. But, there was a lot of material, consisting of tubing, fittings, thermostats, and plain sheets of copper in various gauges. Fred motioned me over and pointed.

"We've got everything we need right here to make solar water heaters. The only power you'll need is for the water pump, but we can incorporate solar panels, or even fashion a windmill for power." Then Fred did something quite odd. He smiled. "We can make some really good stills too."

"You mean moonshine?" Fred nodded. "Do you drink a lot, Fred?"

"Seldom, if ever." Now he gave me a wink. He was very emotional today. "I'm betting there are a lot of survivors who do though. Alcohol will be an excellent trading commodity."

I nodded and smiled in understanding. I had to hand it to him, this man was smart.

"Besides, a still doesn't have to be used only for alcohol. They make great water distillers as well."

He was right. A still could be used for a lot of things. I was about to enumerate a few dozen, and then thought better of it. Fred looked around and shrugged. "Are you getting hungry?" he asked. I nodded. "Me too, we can load up this stuff after lunch."

I agreed, and we went back to the parking lot and joined Julie. She had the grill going and had even found some chairs for us to sit in. She looked up at me as I approached, "Do you think this will work?" she asked.

I kissed her on the forehead and sat down. "I think so. Look," I pointed. "You can see a couple of the upper floors of the tallest building. You can bet the soldier with the binoculars is watching us. I don't think they'll ignore us. They probably have to talk about it first, but eventually, somebody will come to check us out. Probably a squad of four or five men. We'll talk to them, offer them some food, and most importantly, we'll ask about Tommy." I gave an encouraging smile. I hoped I was right.

The steaks were just about cooked when Fred gave us a heads up. A Humvee loaded with five soldiers drove up. We waved. They stopped near the entrance about fifty feet away and got out casually. They were in military uniforms and all were armed with M-4 automatic assault rifles. I stood and waved again. Two of them tentatively waved back.

I looked at my partners, shrugged, and walked over to our new guests. "Are you men hungry? We've got steaks and boiled corn. We only have water to drink, but it's clean." The smoke was carrying the aroma toward them and it could even be smelled over the lingering stench.

The passenger looked to be in his mid-thirties. I could see the rank insignia affixed to his headgear, a silver rectangular bar, indicating he was a First Lieutenant. As I looked him over, he removed his hat and wiped his brow. His ebony black head was clean shaven. His features were sharp, chiseled. He reminded me of a track athlete. He was obviously the one in charge, but before he could speak, the driver interrupted.

"What's your name, boy?" he demanded.

Did he just call me boy? I looked him over. The nametag said Hart and his rank indicated he was a corporal. He was maybe twenty or twenty-one. He was a couple of inches shorter than me, maybe five-eleven. The loose fitting uniform made it difficult to tell how much he weighed, but nothing disguised his butt-ugly face. He had thick lips that were severely chapped, heavy lidded eyes, and a greasy face dotted with acne.

"Knock it off, Hart," the lieutenant responded. He directed his attention to me. "I'm Lieutenant Ward. I'm in charge here." He pointed at the other two. "These two are Privates Dawson and True." They waved half-heartedly. "And this one is the never ending pain in my ass, also known as Corporal Leon Hart."

"It's a pleasure to meet you. I'm Zach," I pointed to Julie and Fred, "these are my friends Julie, and Mister McCoy," I leaned forward a little bit toward Leon. "If you see a boy anywhere around here, you just go ahead and knock him down." I punctuated it with a challenging wink. He responded with a humorless smile, showing yellow teeth. They reminded me of kernels of corn.

"Are you serious about those steaks?" Private Dawson piped up. "I haven't had a steak in a coon's age."

Dawson was obviously from a more rural area. He had a distinct southern twang. He was also one of those people who could go without eating for a week and still be fat. His double chin jiggled when he spoke. It was hard to tell his age, but he appeared to be the same age as Hart. He smiled at me hopefully.

I glanced at True. He was a light-skinned biracial man. Clean shaven with just a hint of a moustache. He reminded me of a smaller version of Jason. I hoped it was only a similarity in looks and not the personality. He cradled his M-4 in a safe manner, but could bring it on target quickly. He never said a word, just kept scanning the area. I presumed he was watching for zombies. Or perhaps he was on the alert for an ambush. Pretty smart.

"Of course," I said. "We were hoping to meet survivors, so we brought extras. Come join us by the grill."

The lieutenant nodded a tacit approval, and the men walked with me over to where Julie and Fred were now standing. Fred nodded at them but made no effort to shake hands.

Leon leered at Julie and offered his hand. "Wow, you're the most beautiful woman I've seen in quite a while. It is a pleasure to make your acquaintance," he said. Julie reluctantly extended her hand. Leon pulled close and kissed it sloppily. Julie yanked her hand back, which just caused Leon to chuckle. "Relax, babe, you'll grow to like me. All the women do."

His crass remark got a chuckle from Dawson. Leon glared at him. Dawson shut up immediately.

"Corporal Hart, could you mind your manners just for a few hours?" Lieutenant Ward said tiredly. It looked like there was an ongoing battle of wills between the two men. I also noticed the Lieutenant visibly grimaced when he sat in one of the chairs. Fred glanced at me. He noticed as well. Ward looked over at Private Dawson. "Dawson, get some of those bottles of Gatorade out of the back. The least we can do is share." Dawson grinned and trotted back to the Humvee.

Ward looked around and pointed at the building. "What were you two doing in there?"

"Waiting on you gentlemen, of course," I said. He looked at me questioningly. "We were not sure what kind of reception we'd get if we walked in the front gate, so we went for plan B." I gestured toward the freshly cooked steaks. "C'mon guys, let's eat."

I did not have to say it twice. Julie played hostess and filled each plate with a large steak and two ears of corn on the cob. I watched as the men savored every bite. Leon ogled Julie continuously, but she acted as though she did not notice. Fred caught my eye again. I knew what he was thinking. This Hart was potential trouble and would bear watching.

Corporal Hart finally turned his attention to me and smiled without humor. "So, Zach is it? Where are you guys from?"

"Well, Leon, we live not too far from here." I pointed out to some nondescript area over his shoulder. "Out in the country. We thought we'd come into town and see if there were any other survivors, scrounge around for stuff we could use, you know."

He grunted. "Just so you know, this building and all of these buildings in this area are under military jurisdiction. Nothing leaves without our approval."

Fred had remained quiet until now. "That's awfully pretentious of you, young man. Perhaps you would be good enough to show us the paperwork giving you this so-called authority. Maybe those steaks are under your jurisdiction as well. Hell's bells, maybe we should ask for your forgiveness for butchering the poor cow." He was leaning casually against the van, and he looked very nonthreatening; at least he did to everyone else. Julie and I knew better.

Lieutenant Wardwas working his mouth trying to phrase a response. Leon reacted by hurling a bottle of Gatorade at Fred. Fred deftly caught it and looked at it.

"I prefer the purple flavor, but orange will do. Thank you, *boy*," he emphasized the last word. I liked it. Leon didn't.

Butt ugly boy had his M-4 slung across his shoulder. He scowled and started to reach for it. I held up my hand and pointed. "Lieutenant, is this the way you normally treat people? Is this how the military is supposed to act?"

Lieutenant Ward pointed at Leon. "At ease, Corporal. You're out of line. And get your hand off of your weapon," the Lieutenant warned. Leon glared at the Lieutenant for a lingering moment, but acquiesced.

Lieutenant Ward stared at Hart a moment longer and then looked over at Fred. "My apologies to all of you. Yesterday, we thought we were going to be overrun by those damn things. The firefight lasted for over an hour. We're all still a little keyed up, right Hart?"

Hart was still glaring, but then looked down. "Yeah, we've been through hell. Killed a ton of those sons of bitches."

I knew then he was the one to watch. He would be the one to cause trouble. If shots were going to be fired, Fred would kill Leon first. I really doubted Dawson would do anything. I kept my attention on True. For some reason, he seemed like the most deadly. Leon was definitely a bully, and therefore dangerous, but True was different. I suddenly realized that he acted a lot like Fred. His body position never moved during Leon's antics. He just kept eating while watching the road.

I needed to get the tension down. "Hey, I understand. We've all been through a lot. There is absolutely no need for us to be hostile to each other," I looked over. "Hey, Julie, Private True there looks like he could use another steak and a couple ears of corn," True never turned his head. Instead, his hand shot up and he extended a thumb.

"How about you, Corporal? How about it, Dawson?" Hart's stomach outvoted his hostility. He quickly agreed along with Dawson. Julie refilled all of their plates with the efficiency of a waitress at a greasy spoon. Dawson thanked her profusely. True nodded. Leon tried to make leering eye contact with her, which she pointedly ignored. He didn't get it.

Everything settled down then, and for several minutes, there were only the sounds of contented eating.

Finally, Lieutenant Wardpaused long enough to speak. "I would really like to debrief you three. I need to know what you guys have been seeing out there."

I chuckled. "We'll answer most any questions you have, Lieutenant." I looked at Fred, and he nodded. "Fred and I live out in the country. When the world started going to hell, we bugged in and hunkered down," I sliced a piece of my steak, which was surprisingly tasty, and chewed on it for a moment.

"We met Julie and her family later. Say, Leon, how's the corn?" Leon looked up at me with a mixture of kernels and juice escaping down his chin. He nodded appreciatively. I think we had him calmed down, at least until the food was gone. I continued. "Julie's become separated from her mother and little brother. Her mother's name is Janet Frierson. Tommy, her little brother, is ten. They might be with a pregnant girl. Have you guys seen anyone who matches that description?"

Dawson acted as if he wanted to say something but was worried about the repercussions, so he stared at the ground.

Julie saw it also and spoke up. "Private Dawson, your jaw dropped when Zach spoke of my family. Have you seen them?"

He worked his mouth nervously and looked at the Lieutenant for direction. "Uh, I'm pretty sure that your mother and brother are here, with us."

We all stared at him. "Well, not with us right here in the parking lot, but in the barracks with the rest of the civilians," he said.

Chapter 25 - A Reunion on Sidco Drive

Lieutenant Ward directed Corporal Hart and Private Dawson to drive back to the barracks and fetch them. While we waited, we recounted what we had seen and tried to answer the Lieutenant's questions. He listened patiently, absorbing everything we said. When we were finished, he nodded and spoke.

"If you guys want, we can take you in. We don't have a lot, but it is a good secure area. We can offer protection against the zombies."

Fred scoffed. I shrugged. "We're good, thanks. But we appreciate the offer." I stood and began gathering up the trash, piled it up, and lit it on fire. "You guys need to burn those bodies."

Lieutenant Ward chuckled. "Oh yes, rule number eight. I watched you paint those. What does the Z mean?"

"Zach," Julie said quickly, with a little bit of pride. She was antsy now and could not sit still.

The Lieutenant laughed, but caught himself short. A flash of pain went across his face. "I've been sitting too long." He stood slowly, painfully.

"I got in a car wreck when all of this stuff first started. I messed up my back pretty badly. I probably need surgery, but," he shrugged awkwardly, "no doctors anywhere." He fished a pill bottle out of his pocket and took a couple. True glanced over briefly. I don't think he liked what he saw, but he said nothing.

"How bad is it?" Fred asked quietly.

"It's not getting any better." He wiped his hands on his pants. I offered him a squirt of hand sanitizer, which he gratefully accepted. "I suppose it's no use trying to talk you guys into staying. We can always use some more people who know how to use firearms. We got a bunch of civilians who are mostly in the way. All they do is complain and try to shirk work details."

"How many?" I asked. I wanted a count to get an idea of how many survivors there potentially were out in the world.

"There are twelve soldiers and fifteen civilians. We've lost a lot. I used to send out patrols on regular intervals, but too many of them never came back. They either met with trouble or deserted. Now, we confine our activities to within a one mile boundary around the barracks."

"Do you know if there was a FEMA facility set up in Nashville?" I asked.

The Lieutenant frowned and nodded. "Oh yeah, it was thrown together rather quickly. They used the Titan's stadium as a staging center. The problem with it was infected people were mixed in. It became total chaos within a day or so." He stared out at the roadway. "They all either died or turned. The infection must have spread like…"

"Wildfire," I finished the sentence for him.

He nodded. "That's as good a description as any. We were successful in evacuating a small amount of people and brought them here. It worked out pretty good, at first. The infected seemed to stay in or around the stadium. All we've had were stragglers, one or two here and there. Yesterday, they came in a big horde. It was the strangest thing. They all seemed to be acting in concert."

"Rule number eight, they have a herding mentality," Julie said. "How long are they going to take, Lieutenant? Can you go get them?"

Lieutenant Ward ignored her. He was in his own world at the moment. "I've not had any radio contact with command in over two weeks. The last communication I had was from Cheyenne Mountain through a satellite link, but now they're silent. I'm afraid our government may be lost."

He continued rubbing his back. "You know, I was a human resources manager at a tire factory when this shit started. I'm no real soldier, just a weekend warrior. Houston Barracks is not a combat arms unit. We mostly handled staffing and logistics," he slowly shook his head. "True is the only one who has any actual combat experience. The rest, including me, are just paper pushers. Hart and Dawson are mechanics."

"How are you fixed for food and water?" I asked.

He scoffed. "We don't have steaks or any other fresh meat, but we've enough MREs for the next ten years. We got a distiller, so the water is good. We'll be out of fuel soon though," he looked at us. "How are you guys faring? Do you need any MREs?"

"We're doing okay. And no, we're not desperate enough for those things yet. Maybe later," I said. "Do you have any dog food?" He looked over at Private True. True shook his head.

I thought for a minute and pointed at the building. "I don't want to sound pretentious here, but we are in need of some materials in there. We need to make our own water distillation equipment. We're not looking to get into some kind of pissing contest about who has jurisdiction over what."

He held up his hand. "Don't worry about it. Take what you need."

We heard the sound of the Humvee approaching. "Miss Julie, I think your family is here."

Tommy spotted us first. "Julie!" he yelled and jumped out of the vehicle before it was parked and ran over to us. Julie dropped down and gave him a hug. She didn't cry, but she had trouble speaking for a minute. The kid looked okay. A little thin, maybe not very clean, but otherwise he looked okay.

He turned and saw me. His jaw dropped. "Zach!" he ran over and hugged me as well. I was surprised, to say the least.

I knelt down and hugged him back. "Hey, big guy, I sure am glad to see you."

"Hello, Zach," Janet said icily. She had walked up while I was hugging Tommy. Like Tommy, she had lost weight. Her once curvy figure was now slim, which only accentuated her large breasts. In spite of the hard times, she had managed to take care of herself and was still very attractive. I could see where Julie got her looks. I had no doubt she was receiving a lot of male attention.

"What the hell are you doing here?" she practically snarled it. The beauty was obviously only skin deep. She turned to Julie without bothering to wait for an answer.

"Hello, Mother," Julie said quietly.

"Where have you been? I've been worried sick wondering about you."

It almost sounded heartfelt.

"Obviously, not worried enough to come looking for me though," Julie retorted.

"Don't take that tone with me, young lady." Her tone changed back to a snarl. In fact, her whole demeanor changed at the blink of an eye. Concerned mother to hateful bitch in under a second. I hoped like hell Julie had not inherited this character trait.

Julie held up her hand. "It's okay, Mom, I get it. You always thought of yourself first, then us kids. I understand now." She looked at me with warmth in her eyes. "You don't have to worry about me anymore. I've got a new home."

She pointed at me incredulously. "With him and that old drunk? What are you, their whore?"

Before I could blink, Julie took a quick step toward Janet and slapped her. Hard. I think all of us, even Fred, were shocked. She did have a bit of her mother in her after all.

"No, mother, I'm not their whore. I'm not like you. Don't disrespect me again," she responded with a threatening tone to her voice. I'm betting Janet had never had her daughter speak to her in such a manner.

Janet's mouth opened in shock and surprise. She held her face where she had been slapped and stared at Julie incredulously. Julie returned her glare with a clearly conveyed look of contempt.

Janet then looked around at the soldiers. "This girl is a minor. She's a runaway. She belongs with me, her mother." She pointed at me angrily. "You need to arrest him or something."

Corporal Hart stared at me hard. He was the first one to speak up. "Well, little buddy, she makes a good point. Julie needs to come with us."

Before I could say anything, Julie retorted. "The hell I will." She quickly walked to the front bumper of the van where we had leaned our rifles and grabbed one. "Don't even think about it, boys," she said gruffly as she flipped the safety off. I have to admit, she looked intimidating. Fred, who was standing nearby with his right hand hovering beside his pistol, looked very intimidating. I had my hand on my Glock, which was in my jacket pocket and ready for action, although, I doubted I looked the least bit intimidating.

Once again, we had a tense moment. It could go downhill very quickly. I needed to do something.

"Listen up, guys, Corporal Hart. This is a different world than what it once was. There are no longer any laws dealing with juvenile custody issues or any shit like that. It's all a matter of survival now." I pointed with my free hand at Julie. "As for Julie, she's free to stay here or go with us. I think you all would agree. It's her choice and nobody else's. Anyone who thinks differently and tries to interfere, well, I'd say Julie will more than likely shoot you in the ass."

Dawson chuckled, even Private True smiled, which was what I was hoping for.

Lieutenant Ward spoke up. "Point taken. We're solders, not truant officers. Julie is old enough to decide for herself."

I turned my attention to Julie's mother. "Janet, we'd like Tommy to come with us. He'll be safe with us and he'll be with his sister."

"Like hell. You and that drunk are the ones who kicked us out, or don't you remember?" Janet's tone indicated she thought she was somehow the victim of a terrible sin committed by Rick and me.

I nodded. Oh sure, Zach, you just say we want Tommy to go with us and his mother will drop to her knees thanking the heavens for our generosity. Yeah, right. I raised my empty hand in a placating gesture and walked over to her. When I was close enough, I spoke in a low voice.

"I thought that would be your response. I know you don't like me, and quite frankly, I don't like you." I looked around. Corporal Hart walked closer and was listening intently. I spoke loudly for everyone to hear. "We met recently; her, her family and her lover. They were lost and starving. We took them in and they plotted to kill us in our own home. We made them leave. Julie and I have since reconciled. Janet has chosen to be vindictive. She plotted with some people to kill us."

I looked at her pointedly. "It didn't go so well for them."

Leon arched both his eyebrows in surprise and looked over at Janet for some type of denial or confirmation. He got neither.

I gave a placating shrug. "So, here is my offer to you, Janet. Tommy comes and lives with us. That'll free you up. Without a kid to care for constantly, you'll be free to be, well, you."

The implications of the statement, I hoped, were clear. "Whenever we come into town, it'll be our priority for him to visit with you. In addition, I'll make it worth your while."

I was now close enough to lean forward and whisper so Corporal Hart would not hear me. "I think you know what I mean. We can give you extra food and supplies. You can keep it, trade it, hell, you can throw it all in the garbage if you want. With extra food, you'll have bargaining power, much more than you do now." I straightened.

Janet glared at me, and then she glared at Julie. She had no idea who Fred was, but she glared at him too. She waved a dirty finger at all of us. "You would really like that, wouldn't you. You've stolen Julie from me, you got Don killed, and now you want to take Tommy from me. Are you fucking crazy?"

I stopped myself from shrugging again. There was somebody here who was crazy alright. I did not want to do this, but felt I had no choice. "Alright, fair enough. You are welcome to come back with us too, you and Tommy. We'll all be together. We'll get you set up in your own house near where we live. Oh, and by the way, don't try to blame us for Don's death. I know what really happened."

She answered quickly, but it wasn't quite the answer that I expected.

"All of you can go straight to hell!" She grabbed her child by the hand and dragged him along as she walked back to the Humvee.

Little Tommy kept looking back at his sister as he was being dragged along. Tears were falling on his cheeks. It was hard to watch. Tears started flowing down Julie's cheeks as well. After a moment, she walked back to the van and shut the door quietly. I sincerely doubted Janet was crying.

Corporal Hart snorted and grinned in amusement. "Hoo boy, she doesn't like you at all!"

He seemed to take great pleasure in it. Janet shouted at him and ordered him to take them back. He grinned at me again with those yellow teeth, ogled Julie one last time, and hurried back to the Humvee without bothering to get permission from the Lieutenant.

We spoke a few moments more with Lieutenant Ward and made tentative arrangements to visit again and hopefully work out a beneficial trading arrangement.

"I'm going to get back to the barracks. The walk may work the kinks out of my back. I wish you all well," he said. We shook hands with Lieutenant Ward and Private Dawson and watched as they walked away. Private True was already walking ahead of them. He did not bother saying goodbye.

When they got out of earshot, I sighed. "Our first encounter with live human survivors. Seems like it could have gone a little better."

Fred snorted. "It's not your fault. The Lieutenant is a decent sort, but he's injured. Corporal Hart senses weakness in him. He has no respect for him. Probably the others as well. He's not going to be able to hold them together as a cohesive group for much longer I'm thinking."

I agreed with Fred's assessment. I could not see Julie. She was in the van out of eyesight. I knew she was upset. It was time to leave. "Hart is definitely a loose cannon. Let's load up the van with whatever we can and get out of here before he gets some ideas and does something stupid."

Chapter 26 – Adoption

The thunder awakened me with a start. At first, I thought someone was trying to break in, but once I realized what it was, I lay there and listened to the patter of rainfall on the old fashioned metal roof. It reminded me of past thunderstorms. Back then, it was relaxing, soothing. I tried to let it relax me now, but I couldn't. I kept thinking about the day's work awaiting me.

Among all of the other chores, I would need to check the farm to insure no damage had been caused as a result of the storm. I'd also need to check on the livestock. I'd need to do a lot. I did not think I had anything to worry about, but at some point during the night, the storm was intense enough for the mutts to jump into bed with Julie and me. I was thankful we had given them all a bath just yesterday.

I glanced at my wristwatch. It was just after four in the morning, which coincidentally was the number of rear ends, three ugly dogs and one beautiful woman, currently snuggled up against me. I was glad we had found a queen sized bed to replace the old twin size.

It took some finagling to work my way out of bed without waking Julie. I debated on an early morning shower, but realized I was going to be spending a few hours outside in the rain and mud, so settled for washing my face, brushing, flossing, and coffee.

I stoked the fire, got the tea kettle going and walked out on the porch. The boys were awake now and followed me. They needed to do their business, but were reluctant to step off of the covered porch and into the heavy downpour. I helped Larry by nudging him, not so gently, off the porch with my boot. The other two followed grudgingly. They ran out, quickly sniffed out a suitable spot, did their thing, and were back on the porch before I had gotten seated.

The three of them looked at me expectantly. "I know. I know. You bastards want to go inside and jump your wet asses back on the bed, but it's not going to happen."

They gaped at me with those big puppy dog eyes and acted like they didn't understand, but I knew better.

The dawn sky was a dark shade of gray, almost black, but not completely. The sun, even though it could not be seen, still had its omnipotent presence.

I rocked contentedly while looking over the front yard. It was a muddy mess. I wondered if it would be worth the time and effort to seed and fertilize it when the weather warmed, or should I leave it looking worn and bare. A well-kept lawn would shout out to anyone that the house was occupied. I made a note to ask Fred's opinion and wondered if he was going to join us this morning. He loved to take Prancer out on morning rides, but I didn't see it happening today. The rain was really coming down. I heard the door open and Julie joined me a few minutes later with two mugs of coffee. She was wearing sweatpants, sneakers, and a jacket. One morning, she came outside with nothing more than a blanket casually wrapped around her, only to find Fred sitting in one of the rocking chairs. Since then, she got dressed first.

"Thank you, beautiful," I said as she handed me the mug.

"You're welcome, handsome," she replied. "Is Fred going to join us today?"

"I don't think so. I don't believe he'll get Prancer out in this rain. He dotes on her like a teenage boy and his first love."

We chuckled, but my statement had inadvertently made me wonder about Macie. Lieutenant Ward had said she did not arrive with Janet and Tommy. She would be in her second trimester by now. I hoped she was okay.

I stood up and stretched. "Why don't we grab some eggs and stuff, and just drive over to his house? I want to check out the creek anyway, and I can feed the livestock afterward."

Julie agreed and it was decided. We drove in Rick's truck, or I should say Julie drove, which allowed me to run out in the rain, disarm the booby traps, move the backhoe and wire, and then move them all back again before we left. One day, I was going to need to build a sturdy gate. Fred was sitting on his own porch when we drove up. "I tried to raise you two on the CB," he said to us as we walked up. None of us had extensive knowledge of the Ham radio system, and the repeaters had gone down several weeks ago. Channel one on the CB radio was 26.965 Megacycles. We opted to use that channel for talking and scanned the other channels for any radio chatter. It was much simpler.

"I didn't have the radio on. Sorry about that. I unhooked the antenna cable last night to prevent a lightning strike from frying it. We brought some breakfast, are you hungry?" Fred nodded hungrily. Or, more accurately, he gave his typical curt nod and led us inside. His furnishings were of the pseudo rustic farm style, a product of his wife's decorating tastes, Fred had told us. It gave the house a homely ambience. We all migrated into the kitchen and then worked as a team preparing a nice country breakfast. Julie cooked up the eggs, Fred worked on the country ham, and I made biscuits. Fred had a milk cow and a pasteurizer, which was a nice luxury nowadays.

We got everything ready and sat down at the table. Fred insisted on prayer before we started. He told the Lord we were grateful and thanked him for his kindness. We had a good meal in front of us. I supposed, all things considered, I was indeed grateful. I had lost a lot, but I had survived, I was healthy, I had a home, and I had Julie. "I was not a religious man before I met my wife," he said a moment after he had finished.

"Oh, yeah?" I sort of asked, but I did not think we'd get any more of a response. Fred did not talk much, and he definitely did not talk much about his family.

He proved me wrong on this occasion. "I was a bit of a hellion in my younger days. After graduating High School, I got on with the rodeo circuit and was a trick shot artist."

It certainly explained why he was so quick and accurate with those pistols. "My father had taught me how to ride and shoot. He was a former Texas Ranger. I was pretty good at it, if I do say so myself. One day, I was in a rodeo at the agriculture center here in the county. I had gotten myself thrown off of a bronco and was cussing up a storm about it when I saw her in the stands. I was dumbfounded. She was the most beautiful woman I had ever seen. I was in love right then and there. Then the damn horse kicked me."

We laughed, and even Fred smiled. "Yeah, he caught me on the side of the head, just enough to knock me silly."

We continued chuckling.

"What happened then?" Julie asked.

"That's when I met Connie Sue. They had carried me to the back area where they had an ambulance and paramedics standing by. I had a knot on my head the size of a softball. She left the stands and came to see me." Fred smiled again at the memory. "I said hi, and she told the paramedics they needed to wash my mouth out with soap."

We laughed harder now. "She was the daughter of a preacher and cussing was taboo with her."

His smile faltered and he looked out of the kitchen window at the rain. "We would have been married twenty-three years this spring," he looked down at his plate of scrambled eggs and then at us. "We only had one kid, a daughter. There were complications and Connie Sue couldn't have any more kids afterward. So, needless to say, we spoiled Betsy rotten."

Julie reached over and put her hand on Fred's. "Fred, where's Betsy now?"

Fred's demeanor changed, the muscles around his mouth tightened just slightly. If you blinked, you would have missed it. As I said, Fred was not a man of emotion.

"She wanted to be an actress. She moved to Los Angeles. It was hard on us having our little girl grow up and move out. She's a good girl though. She called her mother and me on Skype every morning. She had actually landed a small role in some kind of romantic comedy type of movie, but that was just before, just before all of this started."

He was looking at a blank spot on the wall, but now focused on Julie. "You remind me of her," he commented. I smiled, but inwardly, I was concerned about the location. Los Angeles was one of the first U.S. cities Rick and I put a red thumbtack on. He squeezed Julie's hand before letting go. "I have to place my faith in the good Lord that she's doing okay. Maybe one day, she'll come back home."

"Have you ever thought of going out to Los Angeles and finding her?" she asked.

"Sure I have, at least a million times. But even if I made it across the country in one piece, I would have no idea where to look for her."

He pointed to a small laptop with a solar panel hooked up to it. "I know the Internet is not working, but I have it opened to Skype, just in case."

"Tell us about your brother," I asked.

Fred smiled a bit. "He was a big one wasn't he?"

I readily agreed.

"He was big even as a kid. He weighed eleven pounds when he was born. He had great potential in sports, wrestling, football, you name it, but he just didn't have the competitive drive for it. He was a big overgrown kid with a heart of gold. A gentle giant was a good way to describe him. He was the kind of person that you always wanted to have around. He ended up being an elementary school teacher. The kids loved him. Hell, everyone loved him. He helped me with the greenhouse business when he wasn't playing with the kids. Somehow, he got the bug and turned. When everything started going bad, we all hunkered down here. We had plenty of food, water, the usual stuff. Everything was going pretty good. No confrontations with any zombies or hostile strangers. We were just keeping to ourselves. We figured one day it would all blow over, the TV stations would come back to life and the news people would tell us order had been restored. Well, you all know how it went."

Fred paused a moment before continuing. "Frank got up one morning and he said he didn't feel well. I told him to stay in bed and rest," he paused again and sighed. "I should have known better. He had been a picture of health his entire adult life, hadn't been sick since he was a little kid. When I got back after tending the cattle, he had already turned. He killed my wife and mother-in-law," he pointed into the den. "He got ahold of my mother-in-law in there. Connie Sue must have been outside and didn't hear anything. I found her in the yard. After killing them, he took off. I buried them, spent a little time mourning, and then went hunting him. That's when I met you two. Aside from Betsy, they were the last of my family."

Fred finished the last of the breakfast quietly. He wiped his mouth with his napkin and surprisingly, grinned at us.

"You two kids are my family now. I hope it's not something you find disagreeable."

I was stunned, and looked over at Julie. There were sudden tears in her eyes, but she was smiling. "I think I speak for Julie when I say that we're honored that you have such a high of an opinion of us."

Julie nodded, jumped up, and gave Fred a hug.

Fred nodded awkwardly and grabbed his napkin. "You keep that up and I might start crying myself."

We all laughed and hugged. The only thing missing were the three stooges sniffing our asses.

We spent the morning helping Fred around his farm. At noon, we broke for lunch. After, we talked him into showing us his shooting skills. The rain had stopped, temporarily. The sky was still overcast, and we could hear an occasional rumble of thunder in the distance. We went out behind the barn and set up some targets.

"Alright, kids, you two seem to know the fundamentals of gun safety, but I want to go over them again and make sure," he said. Julie and I nodded. "First, always assume the gun is loaded, so that means you don't play around with it and point it at each other, right? Which leads to the second basic rule, always be mindful of where the barrel of the gun is pointed. Imagine there is a deadly laser beam coming out of the end of the barrel and wherever it is pointed, that beam will burn right through it. Number three, keep your finger off the trigger until you're on target and ready to fire. And finally, rule number four. Always be mindful of what's behind your target. You don't want to kill someone you care for accidentally. Okay, are you two ready?"

I smiled and nodded. I had basically given Julie those exact same instructions a couple of weeks ago. Which, coincidentally, were the same instructions Rick had given me about a year ago. Julie nodded attentively and said nothing. Good for her.

He nodded curtly. "Good. Now, I am going to show you two the fine art of the fast draw, a technique called instinctive aiming and the thousand repetition rule."

Fred was amazing with his shooting skills. He would draw his pistol, shoot a round, and then holster his pistol in the blink of an eye. Then he'd do it again and put the second bullet into the hole from the first bullet. It was amazing. After showing off his skills for a minute, he spent a while instructing us the proper techniques for the quick draw. We then practiced with paper pie plates. It was fun. I thought I knew how to shoot, but Fred proved I was still an amateur. We had each gone through a hundred rounds in no time. I questioned Fred about this, but he told me not to worry, he had plenty. Afterward, we went back to Fred's barn and cleaned the six-shooters.

"Fred," Julie asked, he looked over, "you never said what the thousand year rule was."

Fred shook his head slightly and corrected her. "Sure I did, but it's not the thousand year rule, it's the thousand *repetition* rule. In order to gain proficiency of any act, you need to do it at least a thousand times."

He holstered one of his pistols and drew it out slowly, exactly like he had shown us earlier. "Practice drawing the weapon out of its holster slowly and with perfect form. Do it a thousand times in order to develop proper muscle memory. Once you've done that, you can draw the pistol out and put it on target like this without even thinking about it."

Fred drew the gun out deftly and quickly. "Then, once you've got to this point in your training, practice it one million more times. Only then, will you be able to draw it like this." He drew the pistol out with lightning speed. He repeated it a couple of more times for emphasis. Julie and I were properly impressed.

Fred gave the pistol a fancy reverse spin, holstered it deftly, and glanced over at me. "Okay, enough of the pistol lessons for today. It's my turn. Zach, I've heard you mention a time or two you have some sort of theory about these zombies. I'd like to hear it."

I shrugged as I worked the cleaning brush through the barrel. All the way through, all the way back out. "I'm not sure any of my theories have any type of scientific foundation to back them, Fred. Heck, I didn't even graduate from High School."

Fred pressed. "Even so, I'd like to hear it."

I removed the brass cleaning brush and replaced it with some clean gauze before I answered. I took a deep breath. The smell of gun cleaning solvent was heady.

"Okay, well, how to start. Somehow, a person becomes infected. There was a lot of speculation about the cause and origin, but I don't think I ever heard a definitive reason given. Something takes over the body. I don't know if it is a parasite, a virus, or perhaps something altogether different. There were some news reports and computer blogs saying the infected person actually dies and then is somehow reanimated. I'm not so sure about that, but again, I don't have the knowledge or enough data to determine if it's true or not. What I do know, is an infected zombie is decomposing. They're rotting. The fact they are decomposing almost begs the question, do they need to eat live meat in order to regenerate? It's possible I suppose, but we're not seeing any regeneration. I believe the desire for living meat is just a consequence of the infected person's brain reverting back to its primal state. Again, I don't have anything to back up my hypothesis, only some deductive reasoning based on very limited information. For instance, they don't seem to attack each other, at least not after the infection has set in. Why? Is it because they instinctively know when a person is infected? It's odd behavior for which I have no explanation, but it's not really relevant to my hypothesis."

"Okay, I'll bite. What is your hypothesis?" Fred asked.

"So, here it is, they are going to die out in a relatively short time."

They both looked at me in surprise. "Are you kidding? How is it going to happen?" Julie asked.

"A decomposing organism is going to have a limited life. A living human is comprised of a lot of stuff, mostly liquid, and as you know, liquid evaporates. The body is dependent upon many things, air, water, sustenance. All of those items are essential for life and regeneration. The cellular structure of a zombie is presumably dead and rotting. It doesn't appear there is any type of functioning circulatory or respiratory system. At least, not in a normal manner. I'm betting the digestive system doesn't work either. I bet they don't drink water anymore. Therefore, I don't think a body in such a state is capable of cellular regeneration, which means they can't keep going. Eventually, they're going to drop and not get back up." I looked at them pointedly.

"They're all going to be dead, really dead, by this time next year, especially if we have a good hot Tennessee summer. Hot weather will speed up the decomposition process exponentially. We just have to survive until then." I paused for a moment. "If we really want to know the answers, it will require capturing a few of them and performing experiments." I looked at them and grinned. "I don't know about you two, but I have no desire to be up close and personal with any of those stinky things."

They laughed and readily agreed.

"But, I'm sorry to say, other real problems will be manifesting themselves. There are more things than zombies we have to worry about."

Fred grunted. "You know, Zach, I believe your logic is sound. But you're right, the problems are just starting."

Julie was obviously confused. "What are you two talking about?"

"The infrastructure of the country, for that matter, most of the civilized world, is entirely dependent on human upkeep and maintenance. Without it, everything will be going to shit," I said.

Julie rolled her eyes. "So, we'll have more potholes in the roads and the street lights won't work, big deal."

I chuckled. "What?" She asked.

"More than that, much more," I replied and counted with my fingers. "Nuclear plants melting down, dams busting, factories with dangerous machinery which weren't properly shut down will be exploding." I thought for a minute. "There are going to be numerous fires and explosions. There will also be natural disasters. All of these have the potential to cause massive damage, and none of it will be repaired."

I listened to the rain. Fred spoke up. "Remember the big flood here in 2010? It caused a lot of damage. Let's see, we had a big tornado in '98, and a huge ice storm in '94." Fred thought a moment and then snorted, "I guess the ice storm happened before the two of you were born. The point I'm getting at, Julie, is that they all caused a lot of damage. Those particular disasters were confined to the Nashville area. Now imagine the same stuff happening worldwide. You know, hurricanes, massive snowstorms, forest fires, and there was a big Tsunami in Indonesia in 2004. Those are just some examples. All of those natural disasters won't stop occurring. They'll keep happening, but the collective recovery efforts will cease."

I nodded and spoke up. "There are going to be a lot of hazardous material issues as well. I suspect the ground water is going to become a lot more toxic for the next year or so. Also, a toxic nuclear cloud could come through and kill us all as well."

Julie frowned. "How can something like that happen?" She obviously had not thought of all of these issues.

"If a nuclear power plant is not properly shut down, it'll melt down. The byproduct will be a toxic nuclear cloud," I said.

"Is there a plant close by?" Julie asked.

I nodded. "Watt's Bar in east Tennessee is the nearest. It's a little over one hundred miles from here. I think we're mostly safe. Prevailing weather patterns should keep any toxic cloud away from us. Unless of course, there is a major storm off the east coast around the Carolinas at about the same time a plant melts down. Then it'd push it all this way."

I pulled my miniature notepad out of my shirt pocket and wrote down the need for a weather station with some type of radioactive monitor. I also added water testing kits for the well water. When I was finished, I continued talking.

"You know, Fred, it'll be the responsibility of the survivors to recreate a semblance of modern society. If it does not occur, then what is left of civilization will regress back to pseudo Iron Age hunter-gatherers. All of the tremendous strides mankind has achieved over the past four thousand years will be lost. It will only take about a hundred years to revert, give or take."

Fred grunted. "And we haven't even discussed what the survivors are going to do. We can most likely see a lot of lawless gangs. We're definitely going to need to expand our group if we want to survive."

After a minute, he tilted his head toward the barn door as if someone were going to walk in. "What does Rick think about your theories?"

Julie inhaled sharply and inadvertently dropped her pistol. I looked at her. She knew. Yeah, she had figured it out, but never said anything.

I gently set the pistol down and placed both of my hands on the bench. After a moment, I came to a decision. I guess it was time to tell them the truth. I took a deep breath.

"I woke up one morning, the day after Christmas to be exact, and Rick was dead. He had died in his sleep. I don't know the cause, maybe a heart attack," I choked up a little bit. I had suppressed the pain of losing him and now it was threatening to break through like a dam had burst. "There is an old Indian mound down by the creek. I buried him there."

"I know that mound," Fred said quietly. "It's got history."

I coughed and cleared my throat. "I made sure he would not turn into a zombie, so you two need not trouble yourself asking me about the details."

They were silent then and made a point of not noticing my tears. Good. I went back to cleaning the pistol.

Chapter 27 - April Showers

The creek was starting to run over the bridge when we got home. Fred had followed us with the intention of helping me with the cattle. I got out and looked at the sky. It was still a dirty dark gray with lots of low hanging clouds. "I think we've got more rain coming."

"Mm-hm. There's going to be some serious flooding," he said.

Now that Fred had adopted us, he was more talkative. Not much more, mind you, but it was a nice change. "I'll handle the cattle. This bridge is going to be flooded over in a short time I think. It'll be a couple of days before the water recedes. I'd hate for you to get trapped on the wrong side. Prancer would die of loneliness."

Fred frowned. He actually thought my quip was a valid concern.

"I believe you may be right. I'll monitor the CB. Give me a shout if there's any trouble. After the weather clears, I believe it'll be time to start plowing the fields."

I nodded. Spring was on the way. The three of us agreed we were going to raise as many crops as possible and hopefully use them for bartering. Which meant a lot of work. He stuck out his hand. I shook it. He looked over at the distant mound where Rick was buried.

"I liked Rick. He was a good man. I believe he'll watch over you two, so don't fret over it too much." He waved at Julie in the truck and then left. I moved the John Deere out of the way. I did not want the possibility of it sustaining flood damage, so I drove it up to the barn. Almost immediately after getting it parked in the barn another torrent broke loose.

I had no intention of running around outside in the middle of a thunderstorm. A bolt of lightning shortly followed by a crack of thunder, confirmed my feelings. The cattle would be fine without a fresh supply of hay for one day. I just needed to feed the chickens and check on their water. Then, I believe I was going to play around with Julie. Maybe she and I could share a candlelit bath together.

*****

Fred got into his truck and instead of going home, continued driving. Talking about his family had made him a bit melancholy. He was not in the mood to sit around in an empty house, so he decided to check out the roads. He eventually found himself on Interstate 840. He and Zach had discussed the possibility of clearing the roadways in the immediate area. He could readily see it was going to take a lot of work. There were abandoned cars everywhere.

The rain was coming down hard now. He figured that the zombies might actually be more active, but the sound of the rain would mask any noise he made. Just as he thought that, he spotted three zombies walking down the middle of the Interstate, occasionally bumping against an automobile. Their shambling walk made it obvious. They had their back to him, so he stopped and watched them for a minute. To Fred, it seemed as though they were following the line markings on the roadway. He grunted. Zach would like to know about this so he could dutifully write it down in his zombie notebook. Maybe even make it a rule. He smiled at the thought. The young man was something else.

The three were a man in his thirties or forties, a woman about the same age, and an older woman. They were dressed nicely, at least before they had turned. The women were in torn dresses, the man in a dark gray suit and the remnants of a tie. No overcoats though. They'd turned before it had gotten cold maybe? The clothing was tattered, but otherwise, they looked like a family on their way to church. The rain had probably washed most of the gore off them. Fred eased closer and then slowly drove around them. They finally noticed him when he started driving around them. In unison, the three of them opened their mouths wide and tried to grab for him. The younger woman somehow managed to grab the edge of the mirror. Fred continued driving forward. The momentum of the truck pulled the woman forward. Since she refused to let go, the truck pulled her down. Fred felt a bump as his left rear tire ran over the body.

The number of abandoned vehicles was minimal at first. That is, until he got to the I-65 junction. There were five semis on one side and two more on the other side. Their sheer size had blocked the entire roadway, causing total gridlock. Fred put his cowboy hat on and got out to inspect closer. There were multiple wrecked and abandoned automobiles. On the other side, most of the vehicles were burned out. Amazingly, the fire was contained to the east side. The westbound lanes were untouched, but still jammed tight with cars and trucks. He realized with no small concern many of the vehicles were occupied. There were dead people in a few, and some not-so-dead in others.

Fred retrieved a rifle from his truck, a Ruger mini-fourteen this time, and cautiously approached one of the occupied cars. Two women had tried to wedge their Chevy Cobalt in between a jackknifed semi and the guardrail. They got stuck. Even the doors were jammed shut. What happened next was subject to speculation. It appeared their windows were broken and they were attacked. The women did not even think to unbuckle their seatbelts. It must have happened too quickly for them to understand and react.

Fred shook his head slowly. These two women appeared to be in their early twenties. They had probably never experienced a stressful situation any tougher than a rude comment on their Facebook page. They were obviously escaping to somewhere. Where they had planned to go that was safe for them was unknown. Now, the two of them had their respective sides that were closest to the windows chewed off. Their flesh was now slowly decomposing. Even so, the two women were, alive? Fred could not think of a proper term that would adequately describe them. They were definitely animated. As he stood there, they were trying in vain to get at him. However, they could not fathom the act of unbuckling the seatbelts, so they were effectively trapped.

Fred stood perpendicular to the driver's side, crouched a little so that he was even with them and waited. The two young women stopped thrashing for just a moment and stared at him. It's what Fred was waiting for. Their heads aligned in his sights and he fired one shot. The bullet went through the driver's left eye, exited out of the back of her head, and entered the passengers head at the left cheek. Their heads flopped forward. Now they were really dead.

He looked around quickly for any possible threats and then fished the keys out of the ignition. Just as he suspected, there were suitcases in the trunk. He was certain they were filled with clothes and other items Julie could use. He retrieved the suitcases without bothering to look in them and tossed them into the back of his truck.

He almost forgot, but Zach's nagging voice found its way into his consciousness. He grabbed the hand siphon and one of his gas cans.

Fred managed to siphon five gallons from the women's car, poured it into his truck, and got another few gallons out of another abandoned car. He then focused his attention on the trailers of the wrecked trucks. He was wondering what goodies they might contain, when he was startled by a man's voice.

Chapter 28 – Interlopers

I rounded the corner of the chicken coop and stopped suddenly. The chickens were scattered throughout the enclosure.

Dead.

All of them.

I saw movement and drew the pistol. Two coyotes scrambled under the fencing on the far side of the coop and took off running. I tried shooting them, but I did not have the skills Fred possessed. I missed and they were soon out of sight in the pouring rain. I swore under my breath. Looking around, I found where the sons-of-bitches had dug through the mud and got under the fencing. It must have taken them hours, but they were successful. I cussed some more. They had chewed up the chickens pretty good. It made them worthless for dressing and eating. Julie soon came running out with her own pistol. She saw me and started to ask me what was wrong. Then she saw the dead chickens. She looked at me again.

"Fucking coyotes," I said disgustingly, "they killed all of them."

She let out a few expletives of her own. I looked around some more. Some of the eggs were still intact. "I've no idea if these are brooding eggs. We can try to keep them warm and see if they hatch."

There were tears in her eyes. "Nothing ever seems to go quite right, does it? I mean, it's never going to get better, is it, Zach?"

It was more of a statement than a question. It was hard to stay positive, but I had to. Julie did not stop though.

"It's like you said earlier, if it's not bad enough we have these zombies walking around killing people, we're going to have all kinds of other problems with natural disasters and stuff. It's just not going to end."

Julie was crying freely now. I holstered my handgun and held her tightly. All it seemed to do was make her cry harder. She pulled away and wiped her eyes. "I'm sorry, Zach, it's just my time of the month. My hormones are going crazy."

Ah, yes, it explained everything. At least she wasn't pregnant.

I held her close and kissed her. "Do you know how much I love you?"

"I love you too, Zach," she said. We embraced, kissed again, and held each other for several minutes in the rain before we came to our senses and began cleaning up the mess.

I was not done with them. As much as I wanted to play around with Julie, I needed to do something about these coyotes. With no chickens left, they would start killing the cows. The next morning, just before dawn, I took the remains of the chickens and put them out in the middle of the field. Julie and I had set up sniping positions. Then we waited. We armed ourselves with our AR-15s. If they came in a pack, they'd scatter after the first shot, but they would be in the open for several seconds before they could run far enough to be out of range. Julie was going to open fire as soon as I shot. Hopefully, we'd kill all of them.

Sniper work requires patience. Julie and I sat motionless in the rain for at least three hours before they came back. But first, the buzzards came. I was worried they'd eat all of the remains, but we were lucky for a change. There were three of them. They started working their way toward the chicken coop and then they caught the scent of the dead chickens, which I must admit, I added some fresh cow fat to for effect. They were wary, like all coyotes are. They looked around and sniffed the air. Then they trotted over to the remains and gnashed at the buzzards. There was one of them distinctly larger than the rest. I was sure he was the alpha male and lined my sights up on him. He moved around quite a bit, until he decided it was safe enough to approach the bait.

I fired. He died. The other two took off at a run. Julie fired and one of them yelped. He was wounded and limping. I took aim and fired. Julie fired almost simultaneously. Coyote number two was down. Coyote number three escaped.

Two out of three, not bad. The buzzards had perched in some trees and waited patiently. If they could shoot a rifle, they would be excellent snipers.

"We're not going to eat them are we?" Julie had joined me as I walked toward the dead coyotes.

"Oh no. We're not desperate for food, at least, not yet. I once read somewhere if you hung a coyote's carcass from a tree, it'll scare away any other coyotes from the area. But I'm afraid it'd also attract zombies, so we'll burn them instead."

We carried them to the sinkhole. I watched the carcasses burn and felt reasonably certain our coyote problem was taken care of, at least for now. "Now, we need to find some more chickens to raise. If we're successful, we'll need to reinforce the coop so they can't dig under the wire."

After taking care of the coyotes, we checked the bridge. It was about two feet under water. It wasn't washed out, but we would not be travelling across it for a day or two. "Wow, that is a lot of water," Julie said. I nodded. I'd never seen it this high. "How long do you think before we can cross the bridge?"

"At least another day. We should get on the radio and see if we can contact Fred."

"I hope he's okay," she quietly stated. I looked at her. Her lower lip was sticking out. For some reason, it was getting me aroused.

"Don't worry about him. He's hell on wheels with those guns. Let's go inside and try the radio." I had other things in mind as well, but suddenly remembered what she had told me yesterday. Mother Nature was paying her a visit.

"Maybe, after lunch, we can share a nice hot bath," I suggested.

She looked at me mischievously. "That would be really nice."

Chapter 29 - Honey & Panties

"You sir, have caused me pernicious consternation."

Fred looked around slowly. There was an old man standing in the pouring rain beside the jackknifed semi. He was aiming a double barrel shotgun at Fred.

"The hell you say," Fred replied as he sized up his current adversary. The man was much older than Fred was. Maybe in his late sixties or even late seventies, it was hard to tell. He was wiry, stoop shouldered, wearing thick glasses, bib overalls, long johns, and a hound's tooth fedora, just like Bear Bryant used to wear. His beard was snow white and unkempt. His GQish ensemble was complemented by a pair of bright orange Keds hi-tops. Fred knew he could draw and shoot him before the old man could pull the trigger on the old shotgun, but he waited.

The old man chuckled. "You have indeed, you have indeed. You killed my women," he motioned with his shotgun toward the car.

"Do you mean those two girls who had turned into zombies?"

"Those are the ones. They were my women. I came here every day and fed them. They were not related to me, mind you, I was courting them. Courting them like a proper gentleman. You killed them. A dastardly deed, sir, a dastardly deed."

Fred looked him over and realized he was serious, as in seriously crazy. Crazier than an outhouse rat type of crazy. Fred had an uncle much like him, and so was no stranger in dealing with old crazy men. "Did they ever thank you?"

The old man scrunched up his face. "Are you mocking me, sir? I'll kill ya' if you're mocking me."

"Not at all. If the ladies were ungrateful toward your generosity, the way I see it, I did you a tremendous favor," Fred held up his left hand passively and casually let his right hand drift closer to his pistol. "An ungrateful woman is the most horrendous indignity any man should suffer."

The old man was now downright confused. He jutted his head forward, as if moving his eyes two inches closer would reveal a heretofore unobserved detail. "You are perplexing me, sir. Perplexing me. May I have the wisdom of knowing your name?"

"It's Fred, Fred McCoy. I live just a short stretch from here," Fred's concern was increasing. This old man was very odd, perhaps even insane, but he decided to play along. "May I too have the wisdom of knowing your name?"

The old man suddenly lowered the shotgun and walked toward Fred with an outstretched hand. "The name is Bernie Best. Everyone calls me Bernie the Beekeeper. I'm an apiarist. Do you know what that is?"

Fred's stare was nondescript. "Would it have something to do with beekeeping?"

Bernie cackled. "You are of deep conjugation, sir, deep conjugation. I can see now that you are worthy of continued life."

"Does this mean that you're not going to shoot me?" Fred asked wryly.

Bernie shook his head vigorously. So hard that his glasses were tossed askew. He carefully readjusted them and focused on Fred.

"You want some honey? I got some good honey. The best in the world."

Before Fred could answer, Bernie fast stepped back to the front of the truck and disappeared for a moment. Fred held his hand at the ready, just above his pistol. Bernie reappeared and walked back toward Fred. He moved quickly for an old man. He was carrying an old canvas knapsack and retrieved a mason jar from it.

"This is superior clover honey, Fred McCoy. Very healthy. If you digest a couple of tablespoons a day, you will never suffer from hemorrhoids, dropsy, or constipation." He tapped his chest vigorously. "I'm living proof," he cackled again.

"That is very generous of you, Bernie." Fred reached for the jar of honey. Bernie jerked back.

"Sir, you have not opened the vestibule of barter."

Fred looked at him. Now, he was thoroughly confused. Bernie helped him out. "A trade, sir, we must trade. A trade is the epitome of good business!"

Fred stood there and stared at crazy Bernie. He was very tempted to get in his truck and leave him, but in the back of his mind, he kept hearing what Zach had talked about. We needed to meet other survivors and connect with them, he'd say. Besides, the honey did look delicious.

Fred cleared his throat. "Please accept my apologies for the oversight. As you pointed out, an open vestibule is the proper course of action, and I have been remiss. Bernie, I must confess, I've not come prepared for barter. I don't have much." Fred stopped when Bernie suddenly turned and walked stoop shouldered over to Fred's truck.

Bernie pointed into the bed of the truck. "You, sir, are not beguiling me, no sir, not at all. You have items of barter here before my very eyes!"

Fred walked over somewhat tentatively. He looked in the bed of his truck at what Bernie was pointing at. "You want those girls' suitcases?"

Bernie looked at his Keds and responded abashedly. "You are wise and sagacious, Fred McCoy. I am being overly greedy. Avarice, a sin that will surely kill if one is not duly chaste." Bernie removed his hat and appeared to say a silent prayer. He put his hat back onto his head before continuing.

"If I may inspect the inventory of said suitcases, perhaps we can come to an equitable agreement."

Fred grunted, reached over and opened one of the suitcases. Bernie fumbled around with the contents and made various oohs and ahhs. He came up with a pair of women's underwear. Fred had not noticed until Bernie held up the panties, but at least one of those girls was a large woman, at least a size fourteen. Bernie held up the panties in front of him and suddenly began sniffing the crotch. There was a look of pure bliss on his face.

"Bernie, if that pair of, uh, scented panties is not worth a jar of honey, I am at a loss as to what would be."

Bernie readily nodded. "Divine words, Fred McCoy, divine words. I agree to your terms, a jar of honey for a delicious scent of heaven."

In another life, Fred would have emitted a rip roaring laugh. On this occasion, he stared at Bernie without emotion. "Bernie, let's sweeten the pot." Fred hoped Bernie missed the pun. "How about all of the panties in both suitcases for your knapsack of honey?" he said as he eyed Bernie. "I just bet there are more undergarments hiding in there for your olfactory pleasure."

Bernie gasped and looked at Fred in wonder. Once he had gathered his senses, he stepped toward Fred. "A commitment of this magnitude should be consummated in a formal handshake, Fred McCoy, a formal handshake."

Chapter 30 – Setting Traps

"So, you're saying he's loco," I asked.

"Oh yeah. But the honey is good." Fred had regaled us with the story of his encounter of Bernie the Beekeeper over breakfast. "Amazingly, he's connected with other people in the area and trades his honey for food and other things."

"Like women's soiled panties," Julie chimed in. We all laughed. Well, Fred smiled. Barely.

"You know, my mother-in-law worked with a young nurse. Pretty thing. She had a website where she would advertise used panties for sale. She had pictures of her wearing them and the customer would choose which pair to buy. Apparently, she made a lot of money doing it."

Julie chimed in. "Bernie was probably her best customer."

I laughed some more. She was full of herself this morning.

"Even so, we can benefit from his beekeeping skills. An apiary in the fields will be very good for the crops," I looked at them mischievously. "The art of beekeeping goes back to ancient Egypt. There are hieroglyphs depicting bees and beekeepers dating back to 2400 B.C. The main center of beekeeping was in southern Egypt. Many of their methods are still in use…"

Julie cut me off with a punch in the arm.

Fred continued as if he did not notice. "I agree, but I'd worry about him coming into contact with Julie."

"I agree as well. We'll make sure he's not alone with her," I said.

"Hey, I can take care of myself."

"Of course you can, but you'd shoot him if he tried anything. I'd rather you didn't."

Julie frowned, but reluctantly agreed.

After breakfast, Fred and I went out on the farm where we believed the coyotes were living and set traps. It was agreed the coyote problem needed to be eliminated as quickly as possible. "Bernie swears he knows a man who'll take any coyote pelts we have. He knows of another man who is an auto mechanic. He's set up in a Goodyear tire shop on Nolensville Pike. They all have a bartering system going."

I chuckled as I helped Fred place some raw meat on the trip lever and set the trap. "Isn't it ironic that a crazy old man has managed to establish a trade network? I talked endlessly about doing something like that and never even got off to a good start. It just goes to show you," Fred looked at me, "well, it's obvious. You can attract more flies with honey."

Fred snorted at my pun, which was his equivalent to laughing hysterically. "Or soiled panties," he muttered. I laughed. Fred was hilarious.

We were in Rick's truck. Fred had an older cow that had not fared well over the winter. We talked it over and a couple of days ago, we killed and butchered her. We now had several choice cuts of meat sorted out in five different coolers. Our first stop was the auto mechanic at the Goodyear store. Unfortunately, the place was locked down tight and nobody seemed to be home. The man had welded various pieces of scrap steel and made security bars across the windows and doors.

"What do we do now?" Julie asked.

"Not much," Fred responded. "We can leave a note I suppose."

I agreed. I wrote out a brief but detailed note. I mentioned Bernie, hoping they would not equate us with Bernie's craziness, and summed up who we were. I stuck it through a gap in the steel bars and then we were on our way to the National Guard on Sidco Drive. We had plenty of steaks. Hopefully, they had some good stuff to trade. Julie had been antsy all morning and was looking forward to seeing her brother.

We never got there.

Chapter 31 – Hello Leon

We had driven along Nolensville Pike toward downtown Nashville. There were only a scattering of abandoned or wrecked cars. "It looks like someone has been busy," I commented.

Julie was looking out and pointed. "Yeah, look at the street, there are drag marks in the asphalt. Someone moved a car out of the way." I pointed out the open gas cap. It appeared someone had also been siphoning gas. As we approached the Thompson Lane intersection, we saw more evidence of activity. They had the intersection completely blocked with wrecked automobiles. It was not a small intersection. Each roadway was five-lanes wide. The wrecked and abandoned autos had been pushed together and some were even stacked on top of each other. The result was a complete roadblock with the exception of one narrow opening just wide enough for a vehicle to drive through.

We stopped about two hundred yards away. Fred retrieved the binoculars and scanned it out. "I believe I see the corporal we met a few weeks ago and a few of his fellow soldiers."

"Well, that's who we came to see. May as well drive up and say hello."

"I don't like it," Fred opined.

"Me either," Julie said. "Something's fishy. It looks like a trap."

"Okay, I agree. You two get out of the truck and find cover. I'll drive on up and check it out. I'll have the walkie handy, but don't forget the hand signals. If anything goes wrong, bug out to the Goodyear store. I'll make it back there eventually."

They started to get out. "Fred," he glanced back, "just in case, better take the bug-out bag," I suggested. He nodded in agreement.

After waiting a minute, I drove up to the roadblock. I heard Fred on the radio as I approached. "They've been watching with binoculars, they most likely know we've gotten out of the truck. Two of them have taken up flanking positions." I acknowledged with a click. Corporal Hart was standing there in front of the roadblock when I drove up. He was holding an M-4 assault rifle casually. So were the other men. I counted three including Hart. Dawson and True were not among them. The count did not include the two Fred warned me about. So, there were five we knew about and now two of them were unaccounted for.

"Well, hello, Leon, how are you?" I asked.

He smiled without warmth. "Why, it is none other than Zach." He looked at his friends. "Men, it is our lucky day!"

They laughed, and I don't think it was a friendly laugh. "How have you been, Zach? Where're Julie and the old man?"

I motioned behind me. I also gave a hand signal. As Julie said, something was fishy. "They jumped out of the truck back there somewhere."

"Now, why did they do something like that? That's downright unfriendly."

I feigned indifference. "Oh, they'll be along shortly. They wanted to have a look around. What's with the roadblock?"

"We have roadblocks strategically placed at intersections surrounding Houston Barracks."

I nodded. "That's smart thinking. I've got the feeling you're the brains behind it."

"You got that right, little buddy. We're taking over this place, doing it the right way this time. Say, buddy, did you bring any steaks with you?"

I nodded. "I did. You got a grill out here? You guys can cook some up for dinner."

"That sounds wonderful, buddy. How many did you bring?"

I chuckled. "Well, it depends on what you have to trade for," I replied. A moment of anger flashed across his face, then it was gone and he chuckled halfheartedly. I casually scratched my head and gave another hand signal. "Relax, buddy, I'll give you guys a few just for having to man this roadblock. Is the Lieutenant back at headquarters? I'd like to talk to him."

This time his smile was genuine. I knew this because he was showing all of his yellow teeth. "Ain't got no Lieutenant anymore, buddy. I'm in charge now."

There was something wrong here, and I'm not referring to Leon's teeth or his butchering of the English language. "Oh? What happened to him?" I asked.

"Let's just say he expired of lead poisoning," he responded. This got a laugh from one of the other soldiers.

"Ah, well. Some people are prone to that I suppose," I was treading on thin ice. It was a good bet Leon was deciding on whether or not to shoot me. I gave a casual shrug. "Oh well, shit happens I guess. Let me get those steaks for you guys, and then you can tell me all about it."

"Why sure, buddy, and while you're at it, why don't you get on your little radio there and invite Julie to come on down and join us," he leered when he said it. Yeah, right.

"Okay, sure, buddy," I retrieved my walkie-talkie from my tactical vest. "Hello, Julie?"

"Go ahead," she replied after a moment's hesitation.

"Why don't you come on down and join me with Corporal Hart and his pals. You're going to be surprised, he's in charge now."

There was a long moment of silence before Julie responded. "That's wonderful! I knew he'd get promoted. Tell him we're doing a little scavenging and then we'll be right there. Oh, hey, tell him to get my mother and brother. We've found some good stuff. We'll have a surprise for everyone."

The word 'surprise' was our code word for danger. Julie acknowledged what I was telling her when she used the word as well. They both had rifles. Julie had an assault rifle, and Fred had his bolt-action, which was a good sniper rifle. They were now probably waiting for me to either raise my hands in the air or go for my guns. Then the fireworks would begin.

"Well, you heard the woman, Leon, she wants to see her mom and little brother. Do you think you could get on your little radio and call for them?"

He did not like it when I used the same condescending verbiage. His smile left his face. I kept my smile and turned to walk toward my truck. He followed me. "Where do you think you're going?" he demanded.

I stopped at the back of my truck and lowered the tailgate. "I'm getting your boys some steaks."

There was a little bit of distance between us and the other soldiers now. I lowered my voice. "Leon, I'm sensing some underlying animosity here." I realized by the look on his face that I was using words he did not understand. "Is there something wrong? Have we done something to piss you off?"

Corporal Leon Hart stared at me with flat eyes. Then he smiled again. "Only if you brought some bad steaks, buddy. Let's have a look."

I shrugged and opened one of the coolers. Leon whistled. "Hoo-boy, those look good." I grabbed the cooler and carried it back to their makeshift command post. "Well, don't stop there, buddy, get the rest of those coolers unloaded."

I nodded and started walking back to my truck. Leon didn't follow me this time. He was telling something to his men and they started laughing. I got the impression it was at my expense. I stopped and turned. "Oh, hey, buddy?" Leon looked at me. "What do you have to trade for the rest of these steaks?"

Leon looked surprised. "Did you hear that guys? Young Zach here is wanting something in trade."

They laughed again. What a bunch of ass kissers. "You don't understand. You're giving us those steaks. All of them. Consider it a road tax." He was about to say more, but was stopped by a radio transmission.

"We got her Corporal," the soldier's voice said. Leon grinned sadistically. The blood drained from my face.

"Did you hear that, little buddy? My soldiers found pretty little Julie." He retrieved his radio. "Where's the old man? Did you get him?" Leon asked.

"That's a negative. She said he got scared and ran off," the soldier responded.

Leon gripped the radio tightly as he spoke into it. "Bullshit, he's still around. Bring her here, and tell Smitty to find the old man and kill him if he resists."

Leon looked at me and smiled again. He smiled too much. I didn't like it. He pointed behind me. "Look, there they come."

I looked back. A soldier had Julie by the arm and was escorting her to us. I watched as Julie kept moving toward the center of the street. I casually side stepped a couple of feet away from Leon. That kept me out of Fred's line of fire. I had full confidence in him. "So here's how it is, Zach. You're going to get on your little radio and tell your friend to come join us. Oh, and if he has any weapons, he's going to give them up. Which reminds me," he walked up and reached over to take my handgun out of the holster. I responded by knocking him on his ass. His face registered a pained expression of surprise. I think he was even more surprised when I was able to draw my gun out and point it at him before his buddies could react.

"Don't even think about it, fuckers! If any of you move, Leon here gets it between the eyes."

It sounded good, but it did not exactly go as planned. It seems as though they did not like Leon any more than they liked me.

Chapter 32 – Shot

One of those damn soldiers shot me. He was not in the least bit swayed by the fact that I was aiming a weapon at his fellow soldier. It sure didn't work like the movies. The soldier who shot me, perhaps he did not think I would really shoot, or maybe he believed he would be able to kill me before I fired. Or maybe he did not care one way or another if I shot Leon.

Whatever his thought processes, he sealed the fate of Corporal Leon Hart.

I shot Leon twice before I fell to the ground. I think that I blacked out then. Maybe just a few seconds, maybe a minute, I was not sure. My next conscious thought was of a close up of asphalt and hearing the sound of frantic screaming along with multiple gunshots. I can't say how, but I intuitively knew that they were no longer shooting at me.

I could hardly see, and my head was pounding. In addition, there was something warm running down my face. I reached up and tried to wipe my eyes. My hand came away warm and sticky. It definitely was not a good sign. I felt around. When it felt like I was digging a red hot iron rod into the side of my head, I realized that I found the gunshot wound. So, I've been shot in the head. No wonder I hurt so badly.

I forced myself to think. I had no idea why I was not dead. Maybe I was. Or maybe I was in the process of dying. I would have to figure it out later. I looked around and tried to determine what the hell all of the shooting was about. The problem, anything beyond a few feet was nothing more than a fuzzy blur. The only thing I could readily make out was Rick's big red truck. It was right in front of me, I think.

Slowly, painfully, I worked myself onto all fours. It seemed to take forever. I reached out and made contact. A little voice told me it was the front bumper. The gunshots continued at an intense fury, along with a lot of panicked yelling, but I did not feel anything hitting me. Maybe I was bullet proof.

No matter, my inner voice was telling me to get the hell out of there. I worked my way down the side of the truck. Somehow, I got the door open, crawled inside, and shut the door behind me. I searched with my hands until I found something made of cloth. I grabbed it and gingerly held it to my head. The gunshots were growing fainter. At some point, everything went black.

*****

"I'm going to find a way to get up on the roof," Fred whispered. He set the bug out bag on the ground. "You stay here and keep watch, baby girl. I'll cover Zach."

Julie nodded and watched as Fred disappeared behind a building. She was crouched down beside a car and watched with a small pair of binoculars. She could see Zach and Corporal Hart. Although she could not hear what was being said, the hand signal for caution was very clear. After a minute, she watched as Zach retrieved his radio and was startled when she heard Zach's voice. Oh shit, she thought, I've got the volume up way too high. She fumbled with the volume knob and turned it down as she listened to Zach.

"Hello, Julie? Why don't you come on down and join me with Corporal Hart and his soldiers. You're going to be surprised, he's in charge now."

Surprise? Surprise meant danger. She took a deep breath. Don't panic, she thought. She pushed the talk button and responded good-naturedly, repeating the code word to indicate she understood. She was anxious now. Julie stood and turned to go find Fred. Instead, she was stunned to see a soldier standing behind her. He had his assault rifle pointed at her and an unfriendly smirk on his face.

Fred listened in silence to the radio conversations. He heard Zach use the code word. It was his idea. Fred realized that he probably never would have thought of setting up code words and hand signals. He was sitting in the middle of the roof, and had started to sight in on the Corporal when he heard the second radio conversation. He froze in position, silently cussing at himself. He should have anticipated something like this, he thought. So, they had Julie. Fred figured one of them was going to keep guard on Julie and the other soldier was going to keep hunting for him.

Fred left his rifle lying on the roof. He was going to come back for it, but he had some close up work to do first. He quietly worked his way to the back of the building, crouched down, and waited. He knew the other soldier was looking for him, he only hoped he could take dispatch him quickly. His fatherly instincts were causing him to worry about Julie. In spite of the chill in the air, he was breaking out in a sweat.

He did not have to wait long. The soldier led with the barrel of his rifle as he made his way around the back corner of the business. Fred saw it poke around the corner first, a rookie mistake. He readied his pistol. He was just about to shoot when he heard gunshots. They were coming from the direction of the roadblock.

The soldier took off at a dead run back toward the road block. Fred ran over to the rifle and used the scope to get a look. The first thing that he saw was Zach lying on the ground. Make that Zach and the Corporal. Julie apparently saw it too. She had wrenched herself free from her captor and was running toward Zach. The soldier was running after her. Dang it all! He took aim and fired.

Fred shot him between the ears. He was dead before he hit the ground. The other soldier stopped as he heard the gunshot. He spotted Fred on the roof and began wildly firing. Fred had no choice but to take cover. He cursed at himself. The gunfire ceased momentarily. Fred took a quick peek and spotted the soldier. Actually, he only saw one boot. It was sticking out in front of the tire of a car he had taken cover behind. Fred aimed the rifle and waited. The soldier got a fresh magazine inserted and then stuck his head over the hood of the car. He was just about to shoot at Fred, but Fred was a touch quicker. The bullet struck the soldier between the eyes. The two threats had been efficiently and quickly eliminated.

He stood and shouted at Julie. She had run approximately fifty yards, but stopped when she heard Fred.

"Grab the rifle, I'll cover!" he yelled. Julie ran back to the first dead soldier and retrieved the M-4 from his death grip. She was just about to start back toward Zach when there was an intense fusillade of gunfire. She instinctively hit the ground. Fred quickly brought the scope up and looked at the roadblock. He saw that the soldiers were yelling and firing, but not at them. They were shooting at somebody, or something, on the other side of the roadblock.

Julie could barely feel her legs. She was scared. The soldier, one she had never seen before, leered at her unabashedly. He was unshaven and did not look like he had bathed in a while. Another one appeared on the other side of the car. She did not recognize this one either. He was not much cleaner than his friend was.

"Drop the gun, bitch, now!" he yelled. She reluctantly obeyed and her AR-15 clattered onto the sidewalk. He used a walkie-talkie to inform Corporal Hart that Julie was now their prisoner. He was leering at her the whole time. He had not shaved in several days. He probably thought it made him look ruggedly handsome. Julie could see blackheads on his face so large they looked like freckles. Where the hell was Fred?

"Where's the old man we seen you with?" the leering soldier must have been reading her mind. She certainly knew what he was thinking.

She hoped Fred was on the roof and waiting for the right moment to shoot them. "He said something about looting some of the buildings. I think he was just scared and took off."

The soldier scoffed and relayed the information to Hart. Once receiving their orders, the two soldiers conferred a moment. One agreed to stay behind and the other was going to escort Julie to the roadblock and the waiting hands of Corporal Hart. As they walked, the only thing she could think of, was to work her way toward the middle of Nolensville Road so Fred would have a good shot. Then she heard the gunshots coming from the roadblock. She just caught the sight of Zach falling to the ground. She could not see everything because Rick's truck partially obstructed her view. Only a part of him was visible and it did not look good.

"No!" she screamed. She struggled out of the soldiers grip and started running toward Zach.

All she could think about was she needed to get to him. She heard a gunshot behind her and thought for a moment the soldier had just taken a shot at her. She looked back just as she saw him fall. She watched as the second soldier took cover behind a car and started shooting at Fred. It did not take long for Fred to kill him as well.

She started running again when Fred yelled at her and directed her to get a weapon. She ran back to the fallen soldier, grabbed the M-4, and started running toward Zach again. But, she quickly realized something was not right. The remaining soldiers started shooting, but not at her. They were shooting in the opposite direction, the other side of the roadblock. As she got closer, she saw Zach get on all fours and then make his way down the driver's side of the truck. She smiled, but only briefly. His face was covered with blood.

Then she heard the other two soldiers scream as they were being attacked by zombies. No matter how much they fired, it was not enough. The men were grabbed and pulled to the ground, whereupon, they became zombie sandwiches.

There were too many to count. They were swarming around the roadblock in a massive horde and had surrounded Zach's truck before Julie could take another step.

Chapter 33 – Trapped

Julie watched in horror. The invading legion engulfed the roadblock and truck in mere seconds. The horde crammed against the cars and their sheer volume actually pushed them out of their way. The front ranks fell. Zombies began stacking up, which allowed the rear ranks to walk over them and continue their relentless juggernaut.

She began shooting then. There were multiple targets, and in her panic, she forgot rule number one. She ran out of ammunition quickly. When the noise of the gunfire ended, it was replaced with a deafening din of moans and wailing.

They started working their way toward her. Their inertia propelled them forward. Julie tried desperately to espy Zach, but she only saw zombies. There were so many now she could barely see the truck.

Several of them jumped on Leon's now lifeless body, and several more spotted Julie. She knew she had no choice but to turn around and seek safety. She saw Fred waving frantically, and then he started shooting as well.

Fred saw the zombies closing in on Julie. He started methodically shooting them, but the sheer numbers were threatening to overtake Julie before he could shoot them all. He shot as quickly as he could. He desperately wished for a high capacity weapon like an M4. He shot and reloaded his bolt action rifle as quickly as he could, and still the zombies were closing in on Julie. They were now within ten feet. He continued firing. "Run around to the back of the building, I've got a ladder!" he yelled. She did not need to be told twice.

When Julie made it halfway to the top of the ladder, Fred leaned over, grabbed her arm, and yanked her to the top. Julie grunted in pain. "I'm sorry, baby girl, no time to be delicate." Fred yanked the ladder up just as a large man/zombie reached for it. There was a brief moment of a tug-of-war with the ladder, and then other zombies joined in. Fred was overpowered. He had no choice

225

but to let go, or else be pulled off the roof. He got his pistols out of their holsters and prepared to shoot.

He did not have to.

He watched in surprise as the zombies tore at the ladder for a minute, dropped it, and then stood there stupidly reaching upward toward him.

Julie tentatively walked over and looked down. She was breathing heavily from both running and the adrenalin pumping through her veins. "Why aren't they trying to use the ladder?" she asked.

"I don't think they know how to anymore." he grunted. "Let's move away from the edge so they don't see us, maybe they'll forget about us and move on."

Unfortunately, they did not.

Chapter 34 – Rooftop Purgatory

"Don't they ever stop moaning?" Julie and Fred were sitting against an HVAC unit on the roof. They talked in whispers so the zombies did not hear them. They were still hoping the zombies would wander off. Some did. Quite a few did not. They continued to either aimlessly wander in circle, or stand in one spot awaiting some unknown stimuli.

"It doesn't seem so. I don't think they sleep either." Fred looked at his watch. They'd been trapped on the roof for twelve hours now, and their bug out bag was still sitting on the sidewalk where he had left it. He silently cursed himself for his *faux pas*. "You feel up to telling me about Zach now? I'm afraid I had my hands full and didn't get a good look at what happened."

Fred had asked Julie about Zach earlier, but she just could not talk about it then. She felt the tears and quickly wiped them away. "One of the soldiers shot him."

"Was it Corporal Hart? I'm going to kill…"

Julie interrupted him. "No, it was one of the soldiers standing on top of the cars. When he shot Zach, it looked like Zach shot Corporal Hart. And then Zach went down. It seemed like the zombies showed up immediately after. The soldiers started shooting at them, but there were way too many." Julie shuddered at the thought. "If Hart was still alive, the zombies got him too."

She took a slow, deep breath. "Fred, I saw Zach get up and make it back to the truck. I think he got in." She could see Fred nod his head in the dark. "Do you think he's still alive, Fred? Please tell me what you think."

Fred was quiet for several long seconds before he answered. "Baby girl, it's hard to say. It depends on what kind of wound he has…"

"His face was covered in blood. That's all I saw, his face covered in blood." An involuntary sob escaped before she could stifle it.

"And if he is in good enough shape to administer first aid to himself," Fred continued. "He's smart enough to know he has to get the bleeding stopped, and don't forget there is food and water in the truck. So, he may be okay, for now." Fred sighed. "We're not so lucky."

He felt her shudder again and put his arm around her. "We can't last up here for very long without water. We can go several days without eating, but we need water. Three days, we can't go longer than three days without liquid." Fred silently cursed himself for getting all of them in this predicament.

"So what are we going to do?" Julie asked.

"Eventually, we're going to have to jump off this roof and make a run for it," he said. Julie gasped. "We've got no choice. If we stay on this roof, we'll get weaker and weaker."

Fred thought about the bug-out bag Zach had carefully packed with, among other things, food and water. It was currently lying on the sidewalk, unmolested by the zombies walking around it. "We'll either die of thirst, or we'll be too weak to make a run for it," he gave her a squeeze around the shoulder. "We can try to wait them out for a little while longer, see if they move on, but eventually, we're going to have to make a break for it."

Julie stifled a sob. "We're stuck on this damn roof and Zach is all alone, and we can't help him," she started crying freely now. "I'm sorry, Fred, I always get overly emotional when it's that time of the month."

Fred grunted. "I know, TMI. I'm sorry," she lamented.

"What does TMI mean?" Fred asked.

"Too much information," Julie said. It was getting colder. "You're an old soul, Fred, but I like you. In the short time I've known you, you've been more of a father to me than my real father ever was. My mother and father had a strange relationship, and he wasn't around much. Don, my mother's boyfriend, he was actually a nice guy, but it wasn't the same."

Fred squeezed her shoulder. "I'm glad you think so, because I have a bit of an idea. It might give us a chance to make a run for it, but it's going to be a little bit embarrassing for you," he began telling her what he had in mind.

Chapter 35 – Escape

I had no sense of time. My first thought upon waking was that my head hurt like hell, I was seeing double of everything, and my mouth was as dry as an old woman's cooter.

Now, understand, I did not just wake up immediately. It was a long, drawn out process. I think I dreamed or hallucinated, I'm not real sure. Then my eyes sensed some type of brightness. It was daylight I guessed. The bright sunlight was a subtle clue. Apparently, it was some sort of primordial cue for my brain to give a command to my bladder, which led to the next conscious thought I had, which was, I was pissing myself.

Very embarrassing. Even though I was alone. Anyway, it was quite a while, I think, before my brain rebooted itself and I became aware of what had happened to me. Without thinking of the consequences, I reached up and touched my head. Oh yeah, I was rewarded with a stab of pain.

Better idea, use the rearview mirror. I could see how bad it was without touching it. Good idea, Zach. Using the mirror was much less painful, and although I was still seeing double, I could make out a little. It did not appear I had an extra hole in my head *per se*. More like a long crease from the top of my right ear, going in a downward trajectory. The bleeding had stopped, and now the side of my head was a coagulated mass of dried blood.

Remembering my thirst, I found one of our plastic military surplus canteens and took a deep gulp. It tasted like manna from heaven. There was a small part of my brain telling me to slow down and take small sips, which I readily complied to. As I drank, the memories of how I got shot slowly worked its way back into my conscious thought. Looking out of the window of the truck, I saw quite a few zombies aimlessly standing around. Any thoughts I had that they were not aware of my presence were stymied when one of them slapped the passenger side of the truck and tried to claw his way in. It caused me to jerk, which sent spasms of agony through my head. The pain was reminiscent of the beat down I had suffered not very long ago.

The door locks! I suddenly remembered them, reached over, and hit the automatic lock button. How in the hell those zombies had not figured out how to open one of the doors was truly amazing, but I was thankful. If they had been successful, I would have been a goner for sure. The protective hardware cloth that Rick and I had mounted on the windows had sufficed, along with their limited brain functions.

Another spark in the gray matter occurred and I remembered the granola bars stored in the console. I grabbed one and tore open the package hungrily. But, chewing was painful and difficult. Somewhere between the second and third bite, another neuron spark alerted me to the fact that I had not come to this location by myself.

Julie and Fred. Where were they?

Shit. I had no idea.

I slowly, arduously, twisted my body and made a 360 degree scan. No Fred. No Julie. Just a bunch of stinking zombies.

How long had I been out? Were my friends dead? Did the zombies get them? Or maybe the soldiers rescued them? If it were the soldiers, were they safe inside Houston Barracks? Or were they prisoners?

I spotted Leon lying on the ground. Or, should I say, I spotted what was left of Leon. It was not pretty. His face had been chewed almost completely off. He still had his nametag on his uniform in case you're wondering how the hell I knew it was Leon, and it looked like his gastrointestinal tract was the *repas du jour*. I was not saddened by this. In fact, it kind of made me warm and fuzzy all over. Or maybe it was the urine soaking my pants. Whatever caused the feeling, Leon wasn't going to be answering any of my questions. I silently scoffed. No military funeral for you - *buddy*.

Anyway, I knew I had to get out of there. That was not the difficult part. The difficult part was going to be attempting to drive, and more importantly, what was my destination? Should I try to make it to Houston Barracks, or try to drive home? I could not answer myself. I think my brain was going to be riding the short bus for a little while. So, I did what anyone would do in my situation. I worked my way into the driver's seat, started the truck, put it in gear, and let fate decide.

*****

Julie removed her tampon, replaced it with a fresh one, and quickly pulled her cargo pants back up. Fred had kept his back turned during this activity. "Okay, I've got it."

Fred turned now and grimaced. Julie scoffed. "You were married for over twenty years and have a daughter. Quit acting like it's the first one you've ever touched." She held it out for him.

"I hate to break it to you under these circumstances, but in fact, I've never seen a used one, I've never touched one, and I don't believe I'll touch that one either." He looked at Julie with a smirk, "TMI?"

"Smart ass," Julie scoffed and peeked over the side of the building. The number of zombies had lessened considerably since yesterday, but there were still at least twenty of them around the building they were currently on top of.

"Are you sure this is going to work?" she asked with more than a touch of concern in her voice.

"I honestly do not know," Fred replied. During the night, he had worked loose a piece of steel rail from the HVAC unit. It was approximately six inches long, one inch wide, and had a few holes in it. Fred estimated its weight at about a quarter pound, heavy enough for him to be able to throw it several feet.

He held it out while Julie gingerly fed the string of the tampon through one of the holes and tied a knot to secure it.

"I see about twenty of them. Can't we just shoot them?" Julie asked.

Fred shook his head. "There are still plenty of them in the area and we're low on ammo. Gunfire will attract them I'm thinking. Then we'll be back in the same predicament," he crooked his thumb toward the meandering zombies. "We've got to distract these somehow. I'm hoping they'll hear the sound of the metal when it hits the concrete and walk over to inspect it. If they get a whiff of the blood, I'm betting they'll start moaning and carrying on long enough to attract all of the others in the nearby area. If it works, they'll forget about us for a minute or two, and it may buy enough time to get off the building. If we're successful, then I think we can make a run for it. The plan is, we'll run from building to building. If we get some distance between us and the zombies, we'll look for a car we might be able to use."

"How will we start it?" Julie asked.

"Back in my younger years, I was known to hotwire a car or two. All we'll need is a car with a good battery," he winked at her. In truth, he was not very optimistic, but there did not seem to be any other alternative.

Julie started to nod in agreement. She suddenly cocked her head. "Do you hear that?"

Fred cocked his head as well. It was the sound of rumbling exhaust pipes. "That's the truck. I'd recognize that sound anywhere."

Julie climbed up on the HVAC unit and squinted toward the roadblock where the truck was parked. Fred decided it'd be easier to use the scope of his rifle. "Is it Zach?" she asked him.

"It could be, but it's hard to tell. Somebody is definitely in the truck, and they're driving in our direction," Fred whispered. He continued watching for several seconds. He looked up at Julie. "Get down from there. This might be the chance we need and we've got to be ready to act quickly."

The truck moved slowly, less than ten miles-per-hour. When it was within fifty yards, Fred tossed the piece of steel with its bloody attachment, over the back of the building. It hit the ground with a distinct metallic clank. There was no response for a moment, and then the moaning intensified. He peeked over the roof and nodded at Julie.

"Alright, most of them have taken the bait. Let's go," he directed. They quickly ran to the front of the building. Fred held Julie by the hands and lowered her as far as he could and then let go. She dropped the remaining few feet and landed deftly. He then dropped the rifles to her. Here's the hard part, he thought. He draped his torso over the side, hung from his hands, and dropped. The problem was, the drop was still several feet down. Fred landed hard.

Julie helped him to his feet. "Are you okay?" she asked anxiously. Fred could only nod. He, in fact, felt like he'd just been thrown off a horse. "Here comes Zach, c'mon!"

Fred looked up as the truck slowly approached. The problem was, there were zombies closely following.

Their first act was to run in front of the oncoming truck and wave their arms. When they were almost run over, they realized Zach probably was not thinking straight.

"Zach! What the fuck!" Julie shouted.

"Jump in the back!" Fred yelled as the truck passed by. Julie did so with ease. Fred was a bit more awkward, but managed to get in without any additional damage. Julie tried yelling at Zach again, to no avail. Fred peered in. "He looks like he has a head injury. He's probably punch drunk. Keep yelling his name," he said. Julie nodded and the two of them banged on the roof while shouting Zach's name.

*****

As I drove, I kept thinking the engine was going bad. I had not driven very far when I started hearing loud banging noises. And the damn radio was blasting. I reached over and turned it off, or at least I tried to. Try as I might, I could not get the noise to stop.

Then it dawned on me. Those noises were not coming from the radio. Someone was shouting my name. I stared hard out of the wire covered windows, but all I saw were zombies. It was a good thing I had locked my doors, because one of them was trying to open my driver's door. Damn. I was going to have to write it down in my list of zombie rules when I got home.

I alternated between watching where I was going and peering through the rearview mirror at two zombies who had somehow gotten in the bed of my truck, which was also strange. I was certain zombies were no longer capable of higher functions. And furthermore, they were the ones who were yelling my name. One of them, a girl, was actually cussing at me.

I stopped the truck suddenly at the sudden realization. Zombies couldn't talk! It was all so weird. I watched as the male zombie suddenly turned around. He raised his rifle and began shooting other zombies. The female was telling me to unlock the doors. She sure did look familiar. Then it hit me. It was Fred and Julie. Just to make sure, I waved.

"Goddammit, Zach, open the fucking doors before we get killed!" she bellowed. Well, she didn't have to be so mean. I pushed the unlock button. The two of them jumped in and shut the doors. Or tried to. A zombie had wedged himself in the open door and was trying to attack Fred.

"Zach, hit the gas!" Fred yelled. I did as he ordered. Fred kicked at the zombie and he fell. There was a thump as I ran over him. I cackled. Fred shut the door and looked over at me.

"Should I lock the doors or will that cause you two to cuss at me again?"

Julie looked at my blood encrusted head and her mouth fell open.

"Oh, my God, Zach," she gingerly touched the side of my head. "You've been shot!"

"You know, I think that's why I don't feel so good." It was about all I could think of as a clever response.

Fred took charge. "C'mon, Zach, let's get you moved over. I'll drive and Julie will fix you up," Fred said. I went along, but I'm not sure what they did next, because I think I passed out again.

Chapter 36 – Reunited and it Feels so Good?

I woke up lying in my bed. Curly was lying beside me. When he saw my eyes open, his tail began thumping the bed happily. I rewarded him with a scratch behind his ears. With some effort, I was able to sit up and get a good look at myself in the dresser mirror. I looked awful. There was enough gauze wrapped around my head to make me look like a mummy. I touched the right side of my head gingerly. I was just about to apply pressure when my thoughts were interrupted.

"How is that hard head of yours?"

I looked in the open doorway and saw Julie. She was smiling nervously, but otherwise, looked great.

It took a moment before I could formulate an answer. "I think I'd describe it as a dull ache, and there is a constant ringing in my right ear. How long have I been out?"

"About eight hours," she said. I nodded gently, but gratefully. If I had been out any longer, and without professional medical care, my chances of living would have been very slim. It's not like those cheesy action movies where someone is comatose for days at a time and then miraculously recovers.

Julie sat on the bed beside me and carefully kissed me on the cheek. "So, be honest with me, do I have a bullet in my brain?" I asked.

Julie shook her head and held my hand. "It looked like just a graze," she said. It sure did not feel like a graze. It felt like someone had hit me with a sledge hammer. "Do you remember what happened?" she asked.

I recounted the events as accurately as I could. As I spoke, I realized my speech was clear and my memory seemed to be intact. The telltale signs of brain damage did not seem to be present, which was good.

"The last thing I remembered was getting inside the truck and suddenly there were a lot of zombies everywhere. I must have blacked out then, because my next conscious thought was seeing you and Fred."

Julie nodded. "There was a large amount of blood in the truck. It's only a miracle you did not bleed out and die. We got your wound cleaned up pretty good. Fred said there was no penetration of the gunshot and he thinks if there is a fracture, it is very minor. Still, you're not out of the woods yet," she moved closer and stuck a thermometer in my mouth. "I read that I need to check your pupils for proper dilation."

I nodded and followed her instructions as she flashed a penlight into each eye. She then checked my grip strength and tapped my knees. I was impressed.

After a minute, she checked the thermometer. "You're right at a hundred degrees." She looked at me with concern. "Everything seems okay, Zach, but I'm not a doctor. Is there anything else I should check?"

I gave her a crooked smile. "I think you've done fine, Nurse Good-Body."

She looked like she was about to give a sassy retort, stopped, and smiled patiently at me.

"You must be hungry. How about some soup?" she asked. I nodded. I was hungry. Thirsty too. "I'm afraid I have some more news. Some of it is not very good."

My bladder was begging in protest, but I held off for a minute. I had to hear what was wrong. "What is it? Is Fred alright?"

She squeezed my hand. I think she was telling me to shut up and let her talk. "Fred is fine. After we got you fixed up, he went around taking care of the chores. That included checking the traps."

I realized Moe and Larry were missing and had a sinking feeling.

"We got one coyote, and Larry got caught in another one. Fred had to put him down. We don't know where Moe is," she finished with a sad smile at Curly. Curly must have sensed what we were talking about. He let out a small whimper and nudged his head under my hand. "There's more. When we were driving home, we encountered somebody."

"Who?" I asked. I did not have to wait long for an answer. Macie heard her cue and appeared in the doorway.

"Hello, Zach," she said quietly.

I eyed her warily as Julie filled me in. It was obvious that she had not had it easy. She was practically emaciated, but freshly bathed. Her blonde hair was a darker shade now, but was still pretty, especially with it glistening in the light. She was wearing a plain tee shirt. Her pregnancy bulge was more pronounced than the last time I saw her. "She was walking along the road toting an oversize suitcase." Julie leaned closer. "Zach, we couldn't just leave her. There were zombies everywhere."

I looked at Macie and cocked an eyebrow. "Well, one thing is for sure. We now have extra dog food on hand, so she'll have plenty to eat."

"Zach!" Julie was aghast. There were many emotions swirling in my head, but aghast was not one of them. I pushed the covers aside, ignoring the fact that I was naked. Standing was not as hard as I thought it would be, but it still intensified the headache. The two women watched me with their mouths open as I walked somewhat stiffly to the bathroom.

Julie attempted to follow me and knocked on the door as soon as I shut it. "May I have some privacy please?" I asked plaintively.

"Are you okay?" she asked. I stifled a smart assed retort.

"I'm fine. I'll be out shortly." I guess she understood. After emptying my bladder, which seemed to take an hour, I decided on a bath. There was some hot water left, so I filled the tub with roughly two inches of water and enjoyed a nice lukewarm bath while I tried to calm down and clear my thoughts.

So Macie was here now. I had occasionally; well, more like often wondered if I would ever see her again. I tried to think it all out, but my head was just not cooperating. I knew I could not, and would not, order her to leave. She could stay with Fred, I supposed, but apparently, Julie had already made the decision she was going to stay with us. When I realized I was doing nothing but confusing myself trying to think it all through, I got out of the bath.

I managed to brush my teeth and get some fresh clothes on without too much discomfort. As long as I went slowly, my head did not throb very much. I watched myself in the mirror as I stuck my tongue out and moved it from side to side, and then up and down. My analysis was that my tongue was in working order, which was somewhat of an indicator I had not suffered any kind of stroke or seizure after being shot. The headache may be an indicator otherwise, but I was optimistic. I wolfed down several ibuprofen tablets before joining everyone in the kitchen. The dinner table conversation was quiet, maybe even a bit tense.

Fred broke the silence by recapping me on the events that transpired when I got shot. He pointed at Julie with his spoon. "Two of those soldiers caught Julie. I was on the roof about the time you got shot. Then the zombies came a-calling." He filled me in on what they did next. Everyone chuckled when he stammered through the tampon idea. "Anyway," he said in an effort to stop talking about girl stuff, "we spotted you and got back into the safety of the truck. Zombies were everywhere, Zach."

"Did you get a good count?" I asked. "How about their level of decomposition?"

Fred shook his head as he finished up his soup. "There were at least a thousand of them, maybe more." He waved with the spoon. "I know you're going to ask me a dozen questions about them. Let's see if I can answer. They moaned a lot. It seemed like if one moaned it would cause all of them to moan. They were loud, so at least if there is a big pack of them wandering around, we should be able to hear them coming well in advance. And the smell, they smell really bad." He set his spoon down and drummed the tabletop with his fingers. "I was unable to get a good visual examination of them, but I'd say most, if not all of them, were in an advanced state of decomposition. I didn't see anyone that looked fresh. Did you, Julie?"

Julie shook her head. "All I know is they stank and all of the moaning was very irritating."

Fred nodded. "A thousand rotting zombies definitely emit a foul odor. If we're down wind of them we'll know," Fred snapped his fingers. "Oh, here's something rather interesting. They couldn't figure out how to use the ladder to get to us, but at least some of them still had enough of their brain working to realize we were on that roof, even though they had not actually seen us in several hours. The trick with the tampon confirms they're attracted to sound and smell," Fred was silent for a moment while I jotted down everything on my note pad. He ate his soup and watched until I got caught up before continuing.

"It appeared as though they didn't merely crawl over the roadblock. The sheer inertia of all of them pushing each other forward propelled them over and through it," he frowned a little. "So, I think a big question has to be: what made a thousand zombies decide to leave the downtown Nashville area and walk en masse down Fourth Avenue. They continued down Fourth, across the railroad tracks which is where Fourth changes into Nolensville Pike, past the old fairgrounds, across I-440, and on down Nolensville to the roadblock. I've no idea what caused it, but they came out in droves."

He continued frowning. "You know, we're making a rather asinine assumption here. We're thinking all of them came down Nolensville Pike. It's entirely conceivable a couple of thousand went east, a couple of thousand went west, and a couple of thousand took a detour onto I-440. Hell, for all we know, there are hundreds of thousands of them. We just came into contact with one group."

I nodded and tried not to grimace. "Did they follow us in the truck?"

Fred nodded. "They attempted to. While Julie was tending to you, I was trying to make a zigzag route back here. I went down Haywood Lane real slow so they would follow us, and then sped off through back roads until we lost sight of them."

Fred drummed his fingers on the table. "I almost forgot something important. When we got out of sight of them, I doubled back and went to Southern Hills Hospital. It was just as you had predicted. The hospital was full of zombies and rotting corpses. There was smoke coming from part of the building. It may be burned out. It's a shame, there has to be some good medical equipment in there."

I nodded thoughtfully. It made sense, where do people go when they get sick? The hospital, of course. Rick and I had figured all hospitals would be danger zones, at least until all of the zombies died off.

"So, we decided to get back to the house as quickly as possible. We got just over the county line when we spotted Macie. She was by herself. Now, I know you two have a, shall we say, a storied history, but we couldn't leave her," he left the rest unsaid and took his dishes over to the sink.

I started getting sleepy, but forced myself to concentrate. "Okay, Macie, your turn. Where had you been and where were you going?"

She looked directly at me. "After Jason cooked up his plan, I waited until they left, packed up what I could and snuck out."

"Why?" I asked. The question seemed to have caused some emotional pain. She wiped away some tears with a trembling hand. I did not care. I wanted answers. I stared pointedly at her.

"He was not the person I fell in love with. He had changed, or maybe it took the end of the world to occur before I saw his true character. Believe me, it wasn't an easy decision. I was scared to death. I was scared of the zombies and scared what would happen if any of them caught me, but I had to leave."

"How did you get away?" I asked.

"I had previously found a car in the neighborhood with the keys still in it. So, when I heard them hatching their plan, I made up my mind."

I continued with the questioning. "Where did you go? Why did you not go back to your parents' house?"

She shook her head. "They were both dead." She looked at everyone and then down at the table. "I guess I should explain. I came home from school one day and they were in the house. It looked like they had attacked each other. There was blood everywhere. I ran outside and called 911, but nobody ever answered. I called Jason. He came over and picked me up. We stayed in his house with Darius and Trina. We met up with Tay a couple of days later. Chad spotted us a couple of weeks ago and invited us to live with him," she moved some hair out of her face with a trembling hand.

"So, I did not go back home. I went to my Aunt and Uncle's house. They live in the Crieve Hall neighborhood. I found them in the garage. They had shut the garage door and started their car. I guess they decided it wasn't worth living anymore. I didn't have the strength to drag them out, so I left them there and spent the night in the house. I couldn't stay. It smelled too bad in there. I left the next morning. I drove around to the houses of various friends, but they were either gone or dead. Then the car ran out of gas. I didn't know what to do. I slept in it for a few nights and then started walking. I was hoping to make it here without getting killed by anybody. I didn't know about Julie or Fred. I was hoping you and Rick would forgive me and take me in."

She took a big gulp of water before continuing. "Julie told me what happened with Jason, Darius, and Tay. All I can say is that I'm so very sorry. Jason should have listened to you. I should have listened to you," she took a deep breath. "I'm sorry for everything, Zach."

Julie piped in. "Have you seen any other live people recently?"

She nodded. "After I left my aunt and uncle's house, I saw a group in a couple of cars and a school bus, but I was too afraid to approach them. They all had guns and looked pretty rough. There were a couple of women with them and they looked pretty rough as well, so I hid from them," she sucked on her lower lip. The mannerism reminded me of Julie. "I'm pretty sure I saw a plane not too long ago, but everyone else said I was just imagining and made fun of me."

I suppressed a contemptuous snort and pretended to take notes for a few minutes while I thought of something to say. Finally, I looked over at Julie and Fred. "You two already know about our ugly break up. I was beaten, it was posted on the Internet, my house was vandalized, and I was degraded on my Facebook page. What you two do not know is, after all of it had happened, this person felt it necessary to call me and point out all manner of deficiencies she saw in me. It was very cruel and humiliating," I pointed at her. "She is a person who only thinks of herself. I tried to put personal feelings aside, help her, and help her friends. But we all know how it turned out."

"I had nothing to do with that, Zach, I swear. But you're right. I was a very shallow person. You did not deserve to be treated how I treated you."

She stared at her soup, not daring to make eye contact with me. Was she telling the truth or was she a co-conspirator in the failed ambush? I wanted to believe her because I loved her once. "You are judged by the company you keep, Macie. There is the stink of Jason on you," I said. Her hair was hiding her face. I saw a tear drop into her soup, but she said nothing.

I turned my attention to my real friends. "I have serious doubts she will ever be a person I will look upon as a welcome member of our group," I said quietly. I had gotten my blood pressure up and it was not helping that dull throb in my head. I kept my hands under the table. I had been clenching them but did not want anyone to see it. Julie stared at me quietly. Fred gave me a nod as if to say, it's your call, Zach. I nodded back and sighed. It was a little melodramatic I'm sure.

"However, I agree with you two. If she had been left out there on her own, her chances of survival would have been very slim. She's incapable of taking care of herself in her present condition."

Julie reached under the table and squeezed my leg.

"Alright, Macie, you can stay with us. After your child is born, we'll see how it goes. Maybe," I had put my hand on the table and found myself drumming my fingers. I was having a difficult time thinking logically. "Maybe by the time you've given birth, we will have met other people. Maybe we'll find a group you can live with."

"Thank you," she replied, almost in a whisper. I looked at the three of them. Fred nodded and gave me a wink. Julie smiled. Macie wiped away some more tears. I was tired. I was having a hard time being pleased with any of our successes without reminding myself of all of our setbacks.

I nodded quietly. The rest of the conversation was short and quiet. Macie had very little to say.

"I found some decaf coffee hidden behind some cans in the cabinet, would anyone like some?" Julie asked. We nodded. Julie picked up the plates and put the teakettle on. A short time later, we were enjoying a steaming mug of stale coffee.

"I have a suggestion," Julie said, "Macie needs to stay close to the house and she can't be doing any heavy lifting. She could earn her keep by doing light housework and monitoring the radio."

Julie was smiling hopefully. I shrugged. "It sounds agreeable enough. Macie?" I asked. She readily agreed and there was no more commentary. I finished my coffee, excused myself, and went back to bed. The tense dinner conversation must have worn me down. I never felt Julie crawl in beside me. Or Curly.

Chapter 37 – A Man to Man Talk

I awakened at maybe three in the morning. Early, even for me. Armed with flashlight and gun, I ventured outside on a moonless night and searched the farm for Moe. If he were alive, he would have come home by now. I was looking for his carcass, or perhaps he had become infected somehow. If I found him, I was going to bury him next to Rick. Rick would have enjoyed the company. After the sun came up, Fred rode up on Prancer and walked with me in silence. Julie must have called him on the radio. I knew Fred had already made a painstaking search, but I had to be sure. After a while, I gave up and accepted Fred's offer to ride back to the house on Prancer in silence.

"You know, I've been thinking. We need to acquire some live traps. Or we make our own. It shouldn't be too difficult."

"Sure," Fred sure could get a conversation going. We were sitting at the kitchen table. I had more soup for breakfast and Julie had changed my bandages. It was the first time I had gotten a good look at my wound. It was going to be an ugly scar, but I was alive. It was more than Leon could say. Or Jason. Or Darius, Tay, and Jasper. Damn, I did not realize until now how many people I had killed. It did not make me feel good.

I lightly rubbed my fresh bandaging. I no longer had the mummy turban, now only a patch on the side of the head. It required shaving off the hair on the injured side, which looked stupid, so I had Julie shave my entire head. It felt funny and looked funny. Julie said I looked handsome, all the while trying hard not to laugh. Even Macie was hiding a smile. Fred declined Julie's offer of a haircut, preferring to stick with cutting his own hair.

"We need to capture some rabbits and chickens, live ones. We can breed them for food and trade," I finished up my bland soup and vowed to grow some spices in our newly built greenhouse. "I should have thought about it sooner, but we had plenty of chickens not too long ago."

Fred grinned, sort of. It consisted of a slight upturn of the corner of his upper lip. Hell, it might have been a symptom of gas for all I know. "I believe for the first time I am one up on you. I've already set up six traps. If you feel up to it, we'll go check on them."

I readily agreed. Our high hopes were quickly dashed at our findings. We had netted precisely one rabbit and one skunk. Fred managed to get the skunk released without being sprayed. "I've already got a rabbit pen built. We'll put this little girl in there and maybe find her a boyfriend soon. We should build at least a dozen more traps though."

I nodded absent-mindedly. Fred saw it. "What's wrong, Hoss?"

I shook my head and sighed. I've been doing a lot of sighing since Macie moved in. Or maybe getting shot caused some sort of brain damage. "I'm in no hurry to get back to the house. You want to get out for a while? Ride around?"

Now Fred actually chuckled. "I think I understand. I loved my wife, daughter, and mother-in-law, but I have to admit, I spent a lot of time in the barn. Get Julie on the radio and tell her what we're doing so she won't get worried. Let's get a few jars of those stewed tomatoes and go see Bernie. You'll get a kick out of the old coot," he said. I readily agreed.

"Zachariah Gunderson, Zombie killer." Bernie the Beekeeper was inspecting me closely. His glasses reminded me of Snotgrass and her dirty bifocals. He lived in an old house deep in a wooded hollow surrounded by dilapidated sheds full of junk. His house was also overflowing with various types of junk that appeared to have been accumulated over several years. A true hoarder.

"I have perused your rules with great fascination. Great fascination. Tell me, young Mr. Gunderson, how many rules are there? During my travels I have counted six."

"There are currently ten."

Bernie gasped. I enumerated each of them. Bernie had me repeat them, twice. I finally tore a sheet of paper out of my notebook and wrote them down for him. I used large, block script for his convenience.

When I was finished, Bernie looked over at Fred. "Deep conjuration, these rules are of deep conjuration to me," he refocused his attention to me. "Tell me, Zach, are there more rules forthcoming?"

"Yes, absolutely." I said. Bernie nodded in grateful admiration. He then turned his attention to the jars of tomatoes. He inspected them closely through his dirty glasses and clucked his tongue. Maybe it was my recent brain injury that caused a limited amount of patience, but I could not stand it any longer. "Uh, Bernie, may I see your glasses?"

He looked at me questioningly, but acquiesced. I used some water out of my canteen and spent a good two minutes rubbing the grime off with the tail of my shirt. Bernie watched in silence and carefully put them back on, as if I might have applied poison to them. Then he gave me a big smile with his bright white dentures.

"Why, Mr. Gunderson, you have helped me significantly already. I had no idea that my specs were so dirty."

I shrugged. "Some things you get used to and not even realize it."

"Deep words, sir. Deep words," Bernie replied with seriousness. Fred was behind Bernie and was giving me a half-cocked grin.

"Bernie, I was wondering." Bernie looked up at me expectantly. His now clean glasses magnified his eyes, making him look like an old version of Felix. "We have started sowing crops, corn and wheat mostly, and we have some spices and such planted in our greenhouses. Fred and I were wondering, what would your thoughts be about putting some beehives in our fields?"

Bernie clapped with glee. "An excellent idea, gentlemen! Excellent idea! Bees are magical you know. They'll pollinate your crops and make them grow splendidly," he clapped again and smiled with his bright white dentures.

"Of course," Fred added, "the vestibule of trade will be wide open for this endeavor. Wide open." I looked at Fred. He kind of shrugged, which I interpreted as meaning he would fill me in later.

Our conversation was interrupted by a Hummer coming up Bernie's gravel drive. I instinctively reached for my Glock, but Bernie put his hand on my shoulder. "No need for that, Mr. Gunderson. Those are friends."

We were soon introduced to Howard Allen, his wife LaShonda, and their two preteen kids. We made a round of shaking hands.

"I'm a mechanic. Any work you men need on your vehicles, just come on down to the old Goodyear store on Nolensville Pike. If it has an engine, I can fix it," his wife added an Amen for emphasis. He looked over our truck. "That's some pretty fancy window dressing you have there. How effective is it?"

"It's great for keeping zombies out, but you have to unscrew the frame work to clean the windows. When I have the chance, I've thought about modifying it with removable mounts or maybe hinges. It's on the list of things to do."

He nodded his head in understanding. "I've got a truck that was shot up pretty badly. I'm not sure it can be fixed. Would you be willing to look it over? We've got cattle. I can butcher up meat that we can trade, and we should have some good crops in a few months, would that be suitable barter material?"

"Absolutely, honey," LaShonda replied before Howard could speak. She was a tall woman, about five-ten, with very wide hips. "These kids are always hungry," Howard nodded and absently rubbed his belly at the thought of a juicy steak.

We talked a while. Howard was in his mid-forties. He was probably fat before the shit hit the fan. He was much thinner now, but he still had the torso of a wine barrel.

"We had plenty of food at the bakery and the stoves ran on natural gas," he said. He told us he was a mechanic at the Goodyear Store, and LaShonda owned a food catering business. "You see, it was located in a basement. When LaShonda would start cooking, the food aromas seemed to come out from up top of the building, so anybody who happened to be sniffing around couldn't locate us. It worked, for a while. Then one day, there was a grease fire and we couldn't get it out. The whole building went down."

"What happened to your home?" I asked. LaShonda made a sorrowful sigh.

Howard shook his head. "Them zombie things were all over the place. We couldn't make it back to our house. We barely got out with our lives," he grimaced and shook his head again. "Anyway, we had some supplies and ended up at the Goodyear store where I worked. I found a construction site nearby. It was going to be fancy condominiums. I found a lot of stuff, including a couple of generators. We've remodeled the store into a home. I also found a whole bunch of rebar. I'm a pretty good welder, so I fortified the whole place with the stuff. Now, we scavenge for food and make do. By the way, I can rig you up a frame on the front of your truck that'll push them zombies out of the way. Kind of like a cattle catcher on old trains," he said.

He was quiet for a minute and looked at his wife. She nodded. They had been together long enough to know what the other one was thinking. "Let me ask you three a question, have any of you seen any other African-Americans? You know, black folks? We've not seen any. We were wondering if there were any left alive, or if the disease targeted minorities."

"You see, we're worried about exposing our kids to anyone if they're more susceptible to being infected," LaShonda added.

I cleared my throat. "We have. We met some soldiers with the National Guard unit, and then there were some others I came into contact with. I don't believe any of them were infected. The soldiers seemed to be good guys, but we've not seen them lately. Unfortunately, the other ones I encountered meant to kill me and I was forced to defend myself," I briefly explained the circumstances and the untimely demise of Jason, Darius, and Tay. I left a lot of information out, to which Fred gave me a brief nod in agreement.

I saw Howard looking at LaShonda again. She nodded somberly. He frowned a moment before speaking. "Yeah, there are some people out there who are downright mean. We need to warn you about a few we've met. We encountered a group of people just a few days ago. They were in a school bus."

I sat up straighter. It had to be the group Macie had seen. I kept quiet and listened. "Man, you should see this thing. They cut holes in the top and got some M60 machine guns mounted. There were ten of them in that bus. They were all armed and rough looking."

"Were they military people?" Fred asked.

Howard shook his head quickly and then seemed to have changed his mind. "Well, I say they wasn't military. They didn't have no military uniforms on or nothing like that," Howard paused and wagged a finger. "Except for one of them. He's a big man, full of muscle. Now, he's ex-military, at least that's what he claims. He said he's Special Forces. He wears a camouflage uniform and a green beret."

I had pulled my little notepad out of my shirt pocket and began taking notes. Howard saw this and provided more detail. "He's around forty or so, shaved head, Wears one them moustaches that make you look like a walrus. He's got lots of tattoos, and a big thick neck. Hell, he's all muscle, looks like one of them pro wrestlers. You'll know exactly who he is if you ever run into him."

I looked at Fred. He actually frowned. I knew what he was thinking. These people sounded like bad news. "How did you guys meet them?" I asked.

Howard began wringing his hands. "One day, not too long ago, I was fighting with a rototiller, trying to get a garden plot tilled up. I must not have been paying attention. Before I knew it, I was surrounded by a couple of those rough looking men with guns pointed at me, and they weren't there to help me plant my garden, no sir. They took me to the Captain, that's what they called him. He was standing outside his bus looking at a flat tire and slapping the tar out of a teenage boy who had run over a pothole or something. So, they walk me up to him and tell him where they found me. He gave me a look, like he was looking at a pile of garbage and said, 'you're the first nigger I've seen in quite a while.' Well, I was mad, but I held it in. I knew I was on thin ice."

He grimaced at the memory. "I tell you, I've been scared a time or two in my life and this was surely one of them." Bernie had fixed a pot of tea and came in with several cups of various shapes and sizes. We each gratefully accepted a cup but quite frankly, I was wary of drinking it. Howard nodded in thanks and took several small sips before continuing. "But he let me live, and you guys want to know why. Well, after he had called me a nigger, I just looked at him, pointed at the bus, and told him I had some brand new tires back at the shop and they'd fit perfectly on his bus. I spent the rest of the day working on that damn bus while LaShonda waited on them hand and foot. They ate most of our food. If that weren't bad enough, he openly talked with his men about killing us."

Lashonda put her hand on her husband's and squeezed. "Well, just before they left, the Captain told me in no uncertain words he was going to allow us to live, at least for a while. And then he told me, no that's not right, he *ordered* me to report to him if I ever met any other people. He also said we were not to tell anyone about his group," trembling hands spilled some of his tea.

"He's an evil man," Lashonda added before testing Bernie's tea. She decided that she liked it and took a few more sips. Fred and

I glanced at each other in silent agreement and took a drink. It was amazingly good and obviously had some honey added to it. I looked up at Bernie and he was beaming with satisfaction.

Lashonda continued. "If it wasn't for Mister Bernie here, we would be starving. He came along and fixed us up," she laughed suddenly. "You should have seen him the first time we laid eyes on him. He was riding along on his bicycle without a care in the world, and he had one of them wooden beehive boxes strapped on the back." She laughed again. "Well, I tell you, them bees were all circling around him and he didn't seem to mind a bit. There must have been a hundred of them," Lashonda laughed at the memory.

Bernie cackled. "Bees are my friends. They'd never hurt me."

We all chuckled. LaShonda continued. "He spotted us at the Goodyear store, hungry and looking all pitiful. He stopped and brought us some honey. That was what, about two weeks ago I believe. He's been helping us ever since. We're very indebted to him."

Fred spoke up. "Bernie is indeed a very interesting man. I believe I can speak for both Zach and myself, we'd like to be included in this group. We'd like to help as well."

Everyone readily nodded in agreement. We made arrangements to deliver the damaged truck and plenty of steaks to the Allen family the next day. On our drive back, we reconnoitered some of the countryside in the southeast portion of Williamson County near the Rutherford County line. The area was mostly suburban neighborhoods. Everything appeared abandoned. We saw a lot of decaying corpses and maybe a dozen zombies aimlessly roaming. I shot one, but even with earplugs, my head started throbbing.

Fred cleared his throat. "If we do any scavenging, we may have to shoot a few, so maybe we better hold off on that for now." I had to agree. Instead, I made notes as Fred drove through the neighborhoods. I saw an old pole barn with faded white paint and pointed it out. "It might have something inside."

Fred grunted and stopped the truck. We cleared the barn quickly and found a five hundred gallon tanker, although, it was empty. After we got it hitched up, I leaned against the truck and looked around.

"How's the head?" he asked. I shrugged noncommittally. I had a headache, but on a scale of one to ten, it was only about a five. "Is

something   else   on   your   mind,   Zach?"
I shrugged wearily. "It's a lot of things, Fred. I seem to keep
screwing up, and just the other day I almost got myself killed. I
mean, look how arrogant I was, thinking that I could just charm the
pants off anyone," I glanced over at him. "We were extremely
lucky. You know that, right?"

Fred nodded. "What else?"

I frowned. "Then there's Macie. The mere sight of her pisses
me off now. I mean, I was so damned whipped on the girl and she
caused me so much pain," I sighed and tried massaging my neck
muscles.

"And seeing her pregnant. I mean, I'm not jealous that she's
pregnant by another man. I would have been at one time, but Julie is
the only person I think of in that way now. When I see her and her
tummy bulge, all I can think of is that I want to have kids with Julie.
I remember you telling me about your wife and how she had
complications in her pregnancy. But back then, there were hospitals
filled with doctors and nurses. We don't have that luxury anymore.
It'd kill me if Julie got pregnant and then something happened to
her or the baby," I started to sigh again but held it, lest Fred decided
I had contracted some kind of sighing disorder.

"Fred, I feel like I'm not very competent at this survival stuff.
It's only a matter of time before I screw up and get someone I care
about killed."

Fred continued driving. I continued scouting. "You know," I
continued, "Leon almost had me, but he's nothing compared to this
Captain dude. I've got a bad feeling about him. It never seems to
end."

Fred was silent for at least five minutes. I had decided he was
going to offer no commentary and was about to suggest we head
home when he cleared his throat. "We're going to make mistakes,
Zach. You're not the only one who screwed up. I was supposed to
have your back and look what happened. I wasn't on the ball. Those
two soldiers were able to sneak up on us and capture Julie. You're
right, we were lucky, but in the words of the infamous Gunnery
Sergeant Highway, we adapted, we improvised, and we overcame.
Hopefully, we won't make any more mistakes, but it could happen."

Fred continued. "Don't think that a day doesn't go by when I
second guess and blame myself for the death of my wife and her

mother. You though, you are selling yourself short. You have done some remarkable stuff and have made a nice home for Julie and yourself," he cleared his throat, "and of course, Macie," he continued quickly before I could respond.

"You defended your home from enemies who had you outnumbered, yet, you prevailed. When the horse throws you, you get up, dust yourself off, and jump right back on that SOB to show them who's the boss. That's what you've been doing, Zach, you just don't realize it," he gave me a slap on the back. "Now, as far as those women go, my advice is to spend a lot of time in the barn, especially when that baby comes. Maybe you should get yourself a horse."

I could not help but laugh. We had totally forgotten about the Captain and talked of a few more inconsequential things. "Most of the stores were depleted of regular gas, but maybe one of them still has diesel," Fred agreed. We found one at the next intersection, cleared the immediate area, and only located one zombie. I distracted him while Fred snuck up behind him and dispatched him with the trusty machete. I managed to get the top off of the underground tank fairly easily and peered in with a flashlight.

"Is it the diesel tank?" Fred asked. I confirmed that it was with a quick whiff of the fumes. He found the measuring stick and dropped it in. "Oh yeah, there's plenty in here. That's surprising. I hope it's not too contaminated."

I nodded in agreement. We got our pump set up and spent the next two hours filling the tanker.

While Fred monitored the pump, I made my way into the store and looked around for anything that could be used. The store had been completely cleaned out of all food, beer, and dry goods. The only things left were the store fixtures and a used mouse trap. Even the postcards and maps were gone. Whoever had looted this store had been thorough. There was not any vandalism or random destruction, just a thorough job of scavenging. I was impressed. I also wondered why they did not take any fuel. Were they using the tanks as storage and using only what they needed? If so, they may take offense at our actions. I voiced my concerns to Fred.

Fred took his cowboy hat off and scratched his head. "You want to put it all back?"

I scoffed. "Oh, hell no. I was kind of wondering if we should leave a note or something. You know, hello this is us. Yeah, we took the diesel but don't be mad, yada yada."

Fred put his hat back on. "Up to you, but make it quick." He pointed to the western sky. The sun had set. With no street lights, it was going to get dark quick. We still limited our night travel. It seemed to be prudent to do so. I realized there was no time for any note, or for that matter, no time to paint the rules. I opted instead to spray paint CB channel 19 on the side of the wall.

Fred drove while I took in the scenery. There were multiple side roads that we had not yet explored. I notated the names of the roads dutifully in my notebook as we drove by them. Fred glanced at me from time to time. "Have you given any thought to Nashville?" I looked at him questioningly. "You know, scavenging missions. There are numerous businesses and residences. Plenty of potential. On the river not far from the Titan's stadium is a large fuel reservoir. You know, those huge holding tanks you never think of until you see them on the news when they've caught fire and exploded? There is a site right on Main Street. Those tanks must hold several thousands of gallons."

Fred was right. It was a lot of fuel. "There is a similar location out in the west side of Davidson County near Cockril Bend. I think BP owns it," he said. I jotted it down. "If we can ever get up a decent sized group of people, an operation of that size would be very doable. Having a tanker truck would be a plus. I suppose the three of us could do it, but it could get hairy."

We passed a street before I could catch the name. I instinctively turned in my seat in hopes that the taillights would light up the street sign, momentarily forgetting Rick and I had disabled them several months ago. I did not see the street name. I saw something else. "Fred, I think we're being followed."

Chapter 38 – The Scouts

"There's a car back there. About a quarter of a mile. Their lights are off but I caught a reflection from the moonlight."

"Is it following us?" he asked.

"I don't think they're out for a moonlight ride and forgot to turn their headlights on." I thought my response was rather witty.

"We can't outrun them while hauling the tanker," Fred said. I thought a moment and then remembered the night vision gear stowed in the back seat. "I'm going to pull over. If they're following us, we need to stop them," Fred stopped the truck, turned it off, and then took up a position in front of the truck with his trusty six-shooters. I got out of the truck as well and tried to listen.

Fred must have read my mind. "I don't hear any sound. They've stopped and turned their car off. Probably waiting to see what we're doing."

I agreed and donned the gear. I was instantly rewarded with the green hue. When I switched to infrared, I immediately picked up the heat signature of the car's engine block and the two occupants.

"I see them. They've stopped." I whispered.

"How many?" Fred asked.

"It looks like two of them. Judging from their size, I'd guess they're both adult men. They're not moving, just sitting in the car," it suddenly dawned on me. "Fred, I think they have night vision gear as well."

Fred grunted. "Makes sense," he said and spat. "Wonder how long they'll take before they make a move."

We stood there in a silent standoff. It was a testament to their discipline. They did not open a car door, light a cigarette, or anything else, which would have given away their position. I must admit I was concerned. These two were out at night and were not afraid to follow us. It took me a bit to figure out what they were up to. "Fred, I'm not really sure when they spotted us. I would guess they saw our headlights purely by coincidence."

"I got a pretty good idea why they decided to follow us," Fred said. "What's your opinion?"

"I think they're following us in order to find out where we live. That's why they did not try to make contact, or otherwise engage us. They're thinking of the big payoff," I opined.

"I believe you're right, young Zach. Those two are a scouting team. They drive around at night looking for lit up homes and such. Once they find targets, they report back to their boss and come back with the rest of their buddies. It kind of makes me believe we're dealing with somebody with military training. Somebody who has a tricked out school bus with machine guns."

"We could be overestimating them, but I doubt it," I said. "Look at them. They're too careful to charge us and they haven't tried to take us out with a sniper rifle. They're with the Captain's group alright, and they want to find out where our honey-hole is."

Fred was kneeling beside the truck. He spit again. He seemed to do that a lot when he was conflicted or worried. "We need to either engage or get away from them. We can't lead them back to where we live."

I agreed. "We've got to lose them. The only way we can do it is by driving without headlights. I'm not so sure I can drive the truck with the night vision gear. At least, not with the little gremlin inside my head pounding on it with a hammer. What about you?"

"I suppose that I can try. Either way, we'll have to unhook the trailer or we'll never lose them. Another option is we can meet them head on."

I definitely did not want to get into another possible gunfight before I had even healed up from the last one. I voiced this opinion to Fred. He grunted in reply. "Okay, how about this. We unhook the tanker. I'll leave a note on it trying to establish the infamous vestibule of barter and invite them to join us tomorrow morning for some merry conversation on the CB. It's the only way we're going to be able to shake them. They can conceivably follow us all night with night vision. I think they'll get greedy and go for the tanker. We'll have lost them by the time they get going again."

"Alright, sounds like a plan, but I sure do hate we're going to leave this diesel for them."

I grinned in the dark. "We may be leaving the diesel and a nice tanker for them, but how far do you think they're going to get without lug nuts on the wheels?"

Fred worked quickly with the lug wrench while I kept watch on the scouts. Afterward, we got a good chuckle out of our cleverness with the lug nuts. Fred made good time and we were home within twenty minutes.

Fred stopped at the bridge, took the night vision gear off, and looked at me quietly. "Zach, there is something I want to talk to you about."

In retrospect, I should have begged Fred not to go through with his idea, and we should have killed those two scouts when we had the chance.

Chapter 39 - Starry Starry Night

"Okay, I see the Big Dipper, but where do I look now?"

I took her hand and pointed with her finger. "Go up the outer edge of the dipper, now do you see the Cassiopeia group?"

Julie was lying beside me. She shook her head. "It's five stars shaped in a W. The middle of the W and the outer edge of the dipper line up. Right in the middle is the North Star, in between the two constellations. It is part of the little dipper, which is known as Ursa Minor. It's the star at the end of the tail."

It was an unusually warm night for the first of May. After dinner, we found ourselves outside, lying on the ground, looking up at the stars.

"The sky is so clear out. There must be a billion stars in the sky," she said in amazement. I grunted in agreement, although her estimate was very low. "Who is Cassiopeia?"

"She was a queen in Greek mythology. Let's see, she was the mother of Andromeda. She was a vain woman and once bragged Andromeda was more beautiful than the Nereids, which are sea nymphs. Apparently, it was the wrong thing to say. So, as punishment, the two of them were banished to the stars, or something like that."

"You are really smart, Zach, have you always been that way?" Julie asked.

"He has."

I looked over. Macie had joined us. The constant ringing in my right ear had kept me from hearing her walk up. "He was always correcting our teachers. It didn't win him any awards, but the teachers soon learned not to challenge him academically. May I join you two?"

I was about to tell her to go wash the dishes, but Julie spoke up quickly. "Sure, we were just lying here looking at the stars. It's so clear out tonight. Zach said it's because there is not as much pollution and no city lights reflecting off the atmosphere."

Macie awkwardly worked her way to a supine position and lay beside us. It wasn't long before Curly trotted up and worked his way in between Julie and me. "You're right, it's really clear out. It reminds me of that old Don McLean song, Starry-Starry Night. Oh look!" Macie pointed. A bright meteor streaked across the sky, leaving a greenish tail in its wake.

Julie gasped delightedly. "You know what it means? We get to make a wish."

I chuckled. She reached over Curly and goosed me. "You go first, Macie, what do you wish for?"

"Easy, a healthy baby," she said.

"That's a great wish! You next, Zach," Julie said.

I shrugged. "I've got so many popping up in my head I don't know which would be the best one. What about you?"

She grabbed my hand and squeezed. "Oh no, you're not getting off so easily. Name three."

I chuckled. "Okay, let's see. A good crop, the death of all zombies, and a live rock concert."

I got a small laugh out of both of them.

"I want us all to be a happy family, I want my little brother, and I want to give you a son," Julie said. The last one shocked me. I looked over at her. "Macie and I have been reading up on childbirth. Fred found some of his mother-in-law's nursing books." She had rolled over on her side to look at me, now she rolled back and looked at the night sky. "It'll work, Zach, just you wait and see."

I smiled in the dark. It was a beautiful night. I did not have the heart to tell them Fred was leaving.

Chapter 40 – Back to the Present

After dispatching the two scumbags, I was inclined to get in my truck and leave the boy. But I was concerned. I got to within ten feet from him when I stopped suddenly. I was dumbfounded for a long five seconds.

"Tommy," it was all I could say. He was crying and trying clumsily to pull his pants up. He stopped when he heard his name and turned to look at me. His mind was not the quickest. It took at least twice as long for him to recognize me.

"Zach, is that you?" He had forgotten about his pants and just stood there staring at me. He suddenly remembered his two assailants and looked them over. The fear on his face was apparent. "Did you kill them?"

I nodded. "Did you know them?"

He sniffled and wiped his nose. "Yeah, they were mom's friends. I didn't like them."

So, his mother had found yet another group to hook up with, and her son has to suffer for it. Figures.

"Get your pants fixed, Tommy," I said. I could inspect him for injuries at a later time. "So you and your mom found another group of people to live with?" I asked, and he nodded. "Are there more than these two?" he nodded again. "How many of them are there?"

Tommy looked at the sky a moment and then started slowly counting on his fingers. "There are seventeen."

He said it slowly, but with resolve.

"Does that include these two men and your mom?" Tommy nodded slowly. He did not understand why an accurate count was important.

At my direction, Tommy showed me the car they had been using, which was a beat up Chevy Yukon. It had an odd assortment of stuff in it. They had been on a scavenging mission as well. With Tommy's help, I transferred anything I thought was of value into my truck. We managed to get the two inside the SUV. I then shoved a rag in the opening of the gas tank and set it on fire. It was an easy way to conceal evidence. Their friends would find them eventually, and maybe even figure out what happened, but no reason to make it easy for them.

"Zach?" Tommy asked. We had been silently watching the SUV burn. I looked at him. "Can I come live with you? I don't like those people. They're mean to me and make fun of me."

I patted him on the shoulder. I had a flashback of Felix always patting me on the shoulder. "Sure, buddy," I looked somberly at him. So much had happened since I last saw him. Good, bad, and downright ugly. I had a lot of questions about this new group and questions about what his evil mother had been up to, but first, we needed to get out of there. The gunshots and the fire would no doubt bring unwanted attention.

We got in my truck and headed out.

The End

CPSIA information can be obtained
at www.ICGtesting.com
Printed in the USA
LVOW04s1918201215
467322LV00022B/1972/P